THE WAITING ROOM

"Every child deserves a hero; some just need one more than others."
~ Jasper Wolf

ISBN: 978-0-9944968-3-6

Cover design and formatting by Tugboat Design

Dedicated to Clint Anderson
A True Friend and the Real Jake Miller

Go to www.jasperwolfauthor.com
for more information on Jasper's latest releases

Become a subscriber and receive
chapter excerpts—pre-release special

Contents

PART ONE

The Missing

Chapter 1

Shevd had watched the cop run from the tunnel, carrying one of the girls, all hero-like.

Soon he would want to return to the thick of the action. Soon he would want to go back in. Soon he would hear the sound of the gun, and before he could react he would be dead.

Shevd hadn't taken his eye from his scope in minutes. He wanted to see the cop's face when he killed him. All he had to do was wait for him to reappear.

His breathing was steady, his eye focused on the target, his finger relaxed and ready. Even in the heavy rain, he found him. The cop's shoe was sticking out from the base of the tree. He had placed the girl out of danger. Now, Shevd just needed to wait for him to run.

It reminded him of when he was shooting deer as a kid in the Ukraine. "Be quiet and patient," his father would say, "the deer will hear the slightest noise." The deer never knew it was about to be killed. It would be at a stream drinking and then the shot would echo through the forest, but before the deer could react to the sound, it would fall to the ground.

The cop was as helpless as the deer.

I'll get you, Shevd thought.

* * *

The storm had ramped up and it was raining so hard, it felt like hail. I was struggling to see more than a few metres in front of me. The girl bounced in my arms as I ran. We made it to the forest edge and I was hit by the smell of forest freshness and rain. The air was fragrant with the smell of pine trees. Christmas would be here soon, I thought.

The large pine provided Chloe with plenty of cover from the storm. I untied her and covered her with my jacket. "You will be safe here," I said.

She sat silently, curled up into a ball.

In the distance I could hear not only gunfire, but voices, loud voices, yelling. There were more children here somewhere, but how many perpetrators were left? The only thing we knew for sure was that we had found the spider's web I looked at the base of the tree. They were hell-bent on getting out of here. They were not planning on giving up. There was no jail for them. They knew it was death for them if they couldn't escape.

"Mikayla, you need to go back for Mikayla," Chloe said, quivering with the cold.

I knew there were more kids and I had to go back. I couldn't leave Jake. I had to go back. I had to do my job. I had to help. I would never forgive myself if something happened to Mikayla or Jake.

The thought of the tunnels terrified me, the smell of death; it was the cabin all over again, the fear of the unknown and the darkness, the fear of death. I pushed the fear aside and took a deep breath to steady myself. The smell of the pines once again made its presence felt. It was a beautiful smell and I took in as much oxygen as possible ready for the sprint to the tunnels.

I darted out from the tree. I had taken three steps before an ear-piercing crack echoed through the night.

Chapter 2

Two Weeks Earlier

Stevie Bradley was sound asleep and dreaming about Ellie Davis. She had thanked him for picking up the books she had dropped on the way home. He stood close as he handed them to her. Her hair smelt like peaches and her skin smelt of perfume, one he didn't know but that he would recognise again in an instant. Her hand touched his, her skin soft and delicate. She leaned forward into him. His heart skipped a beat, her lips pressed against his and they were soft and a little wet. It was an amazing kiss. Until he was woken by his father. "Get up and get ready for school. You're going to have to walk, your mum has a migraine. I can give you a lift but I'm leaving in 15 minutes." Stevie, who still had Ellie Davis on his mind, didn't really want to be rushed this morning so he decided it would be best if he walked.

The sun was streaming in through his bedroom window so he figured it was a nice day outside. By the time he headed out the door for school it was 8.15. It usually only took him 15 minutes if he cut through the reserve at the end of the cul-de-sac. If he walked around it took an extra 10 minutes.

Stevie was right, it was a beautiful day. The sun was strong and his shadow was long as it walked beside him. He trudged along without a care in the world, hoping his dream would become a reality. His backpack, full of books and his lunch, was slung over his shoulders, and his drink bottle was sitting snug in the side mesh pocket of his bag. He bounced his basketball between his hands, occasionally crossing it over between his legs and then behind his back; he was good at it, he had not missed a step.

Stevie was so busy playing with the ball that he didn't notice the van pass him as he entered the reserve. He continued his dribble on the path up through the park, now doing figure-eights as he walked. He had begun to sweat a little. Walking up the hill dribbling was tougher than he expected. As he reached the top of the park, he placed the ball down and removed his backpack to reach his drink. He placed his bag on the path beside him and the ball rolled to rest against his bag.

Stevie bent down to place his bottle back in his bag when the white van mounted the kerb in front of him. Before Stevie realised what was happening, a man in a joker's mask was upon him. His large arms wrapped around him, pulling him into the van.

Stevie screamed.

His scream was quickly silenced by one of the man's hands smothering his mouth. With one arm free, he felt above for the man's head, trying to locate one of his eyes. All he could find was the loose plastic of the mask. He felt higher. He could hear the van door opening; he was being dragged in. He had little time left before he would be inside it. He pushed his thumb hard on what he thought were his eyes. The man made no noise even though Stevie thought he must be in pain. He heard the man step inside the van. He could see the inside of the van now, only his legs remained on the outside.

Stevie reached for the side of the door with his free hand but it slid straight off. The man was too strong. Less than a second later, he was inside the van and the door was being closed. Before he could say anything, tape went across his mouth and a bag was over his head. Something tightened around his neck.

"If you make a sound I'll fucking kill you, do you understand?"

Stevie nodded. He heard a door at the rear open and close again and then seconds later another door at the front opened.

It had only been a few moments and then they began moving. Stevie sat in the darkness swaying with the movement of the van.

He lost track of how long they had been in traffic but guessed about an hour, he couldn't be sure. The van had stopped many times during his trip, Stevie assumed for sets of traffic lights. The radio was switched off soon after the van started up.

He felt the van make another turn, this one slower, then the van came to a stop. The door at the front opened but he could still hear the motor running. Again the door shut and the van moved forward slowly.

As the van stopped and the motor cut, Stevie could hear loud metal banging, followed by what sounded like locks.

"Out!" the voice called. Stevie felt the bag tighten around his neck and he was pulled to the left.

He felt a hand pinch the back of his neck. He was pushed forward six or seven paces. "Stop," the voice said as the rope pulled him back slightly. "Sit down." Stevie did as he was told. The ground was full of loose stones. "Move forward on your butt until you feel the edge," the voice commanded. Again he did as he was told, moving forward by dragging his butt along the ground. His feet fell into emptiness. "Stop," the voice called.

"Now, you'll need to drop down off the edge, it's not far, you'll be ok."

Stevie sat for a moment. Was he dropping into his own grave? he wondered.

Where the hell was he?

Tears began to flow.

Before he could muster the courage to drop, he felt a hard push in the middle of his back.

For a brief moment he was falling, then he stopped suddenly. His ankle rolled and his shoulder hit the ground. He heard a girl scream, then what sounded like someone walking down metal steps.

His hood was removed. His eyes took some time to adjust but when they did he saw the worst thing he had ever seen. Several cells with a path between them leading to a red door. He could see two other children, both of them with their heads down, crouched in the back of their cells.

A hand spun him around. "You scream, you die right here."

Stevie nodded and his tape was ripped off without warning.

Despite the fact that the man was wearing a joker's mask, Stevie could tell he was balding, and big, over six foot. He was podgy. What little Stevie could see of his mouth revealed yellow teeth. The sides of his face and hands were very grubby and it looked as if he hadn't showered recently. It definitely smelt that way.

He was wearing stained tracksuit pants and an old torn flannelette shirt.

The fat, dirty, balding man threw him into a cell on the same side as the girl but there was an empty cell between them. The other boy was on the other side.

The man removed the rope from his neck, and closed the door to the cell behind him.

He stood on the other side of the bars looking him up and down. "They're going to love you," he said as he headed towards the ladder. "Remember, no talking. If you talk, there will be punishments."

He left, climbing the ladder, closing the lid behind him. Stevie's cell went into complete darkness. He could hear movement above and then music. Suddenly the lights went on and he could see again.

Chapter 3

"What's your name?" Stevie asked the girl who was two cells down from him. She looked about a year younger than he was.

"Chloe," she answered from her dusty, dark cell.

"Where are we?" Stevie asked. Chloe shrugged her shoulders as if to say, I have no idea.

The boy opposite them put his finger to his lips. "Shhh, he will hear you," he whispered.

Stevie looked around: there had to be a way out. He counted six cells the same as his.

The bars went from the concrete floor to the concrete celling. Each cell had a light attached to a beam that ran above the middle of every cell. In between the two rows of cells was a simple gravel path. It led from the trapdoor to a bright red door that stood like a beacon at the end of the cells.

On the floor of his cell lay a dirty old mattress and a blanket. There was a bowl of water but no food. In the opposite corner was a bucket. He hoped this wasn't his toilet.

The other boy was in the cell at the end of the path on the opposite side.

Stevie could see him but the lack of light made it hard to see all his features. From what he could make out, Stevie was at least a couple of years older than the boy, maybe a little more. The boy had sandy blonde hair and looked fairly athletic for his age. Probably a football player, he thought.

The girl looked young and thin. She was still in her school uniform.

The boy looked familiar; maybe they went to the same school, although he couldn't quite place him. He was in normal clothes but they were worn and dirty.

"What's your name? How long have you been here?" he asked the boy.

"Shhh," he said again. "He will hear you. You don't want him mad." The boy did not answer either of Stevie's questions.

"His name is Scott," Chloe whispered, ignoring the plea for silence.

"Please stop talking, he will come if we make noise," Scott said as quietly as he could.

That was when Stevie recognised him. It wasn't school. It was on the news. He had been missing for over six weeks. Scott Western was sitting opposite him and he was still alive.

Then he looked at Chloe and remembered her too but he couldn't think of her surname. They had both been on the news. Scott had been taken on his way to school.

Chloe had been taken on her way to school. Just like he had.

Before he could tell Chloe and Scott that their families were still looking for them, music blasted from above them and all the lights glowed.

Scott instantly shuffled to the back of his cell and curled up. Stevie turned towards Chloe; she had shuffled back as well.

The trapdoor remained shut.

False alarm, Stevie thought.

Chapter 4

What had the world become?

It was a question that I found harder to answer since the Slayer case. Even though it had been over 10 years since Mason Belic had been placed into the ground, my mind often returned to the events within that dark cabin.

I wondered what reason he would have given for doing what he did. Was there ever a reason or had it just been a sick and twisted fantasy? It was something I would never really know.

Was there more violence in today's world? Maybe crims just received more media exposure these days. Either way, there didn't seem to be any shortage of evil amongst us.

Currently, I had three case files under my review and the days of my private practice were long gone. I was now a fulltime detective. I was given the cases no one could solve.

The first kidnapping was a 10-year-old boy in Sunbury, Scott Western. On his way to school he had vanished and only his bike and bag were found in the gutter. Missing now six weeks. No leads. Nothing to go on.

The second one was a 12-year-old missing girl, Chloe Henderson. She had been walking to school in Boronia and had simply vanished. Missing now two weeks. No leads. Nothing to go on.

Even though these cases were miles apart geographically, they were eerily similar in detail. Both children vanished out of thin air, no witnesses.

Then just two days ago, it happened again. An 11-year-old boy, Stevie Bradley, same MO, was walking to school, never made it. The only item recovered was a basketball lying in the gutter. He had simply vanished.

I was to provide a report on the possibility of the same offender.

Considering it was a different geographical location, two boys, one girl, it was highly unlikely to be the same person. Usually killers prefer a gender, and once they choose one, they stick to it.

Unlikely but not impossible.

My final case I considered cold. It was 16 years old now and bordering on the impossible. Three street workers had disappeared off the streets and all had been found murdered. All three had been posed provocatively, their wrists tied and their legs spread, on the banks of the Maribyrnong River.

All three had worked the streets of St Kilda. I was sure these cases were related, I just wasn't sure why they had stopped. Serial killers usually didn't stop of their own accord. In the late 1990s, the tabloids had been in a frenzy of fear, labelling him the 'Night Stalker'.

Maybe he was dead? Maybe he had moved?

My thoughts wandered back to the children.

Nothing was worse than a missing child. Except three missing children.

After the Mason Belic case, Jake had been physically ok. However, mentally he had been a mess. I suppose being buried alive in box with a snake will do that to you. He had been required to undergo counselling, as had I. Jake wasn't the type of person who would easily open up. He was very reserved at the best of times.

His girlfriend Hayley was given permission by the department to receive counselling from the same psychologist. The joint sessions were of benefit to them both. After six months of therapy, they stopped the sessions and everything seemed normal.

Until a few weeks ago anyway, then Jake started seeing Salma again.

Something was haunting Jake, I just didn't know what.

My sessions always helped me. I had no problem discussing the events from that day. It was the flashbacks and the smells that still haunted me. Usually they came to me in my sleep. Some nights, I would wake up and I could smell the death in that cellar as if I was there again.

Salma George was the psychologist of choice for Victoria Police and all its employees. She was a great psychologist, full of empathy and insightfulness, which only the good ones had. I had known Salma reasonably well before my own sessions began. She and I had taken some of the same classes and had sought each other's counsel on matters from time to time.

Her career had gone from strength to strength and she now also held the position of head of psychiatry at North View treatment centre for the mentally ill. Salma was the type of woman who interested me. Not only on a physical level, as she was very attractive, but also as a woman who surpassed me intellectually. She had seen what evil had done to both sides of the law, the victims and the police. It was a rare perspective and one I admired more every time I saw her. Or was it Salma I was admiring more and more?

Chapter 5

Major General Austin Campbell had been in the SAS Second Commando Unit for over eight years, the last five being spent in high-end intelligence operations in Afghanistan. For the last two years, he had been in charge of the Second Commando regiment. Their creed was 'Foras Admonitio', 'without warning'.

He had done everything in his career, from rooftop sniper, to search and clear scout and finally regiment commander. His tour was over and he was ready to live his life. He had a wife, Sarah, and a daughter, Mikayla, who were at home waiting for him.

He had not seen them in six months and he missed them terribly. Soon, he would be back in Australia and able to hold them both tight. The plane was due to land in Melbourne in just over two hours. The RAAF plane had landed earlier in the Western Australian Army Barracks and the debrief and final sign-off on his latest tour, complete with the Medal of Gallantry, had taken just over four hours. The prime minister had formally presented the medal as part of the Anzac commemorations.

He sat patiently waiting for the plane to reach its destination.

He was in his civilian clothes and his new life had started. He doubted he would ever go back, although his motto had always been 'never say never'. He sat amused by the goings-on of the civilian passengers. In the aisle opposite, a businessman was requesting to be moved from the two children seated next to him. The hostess politely told the gentleman, for at least the second time that Austin had heard, that the plane was full and there were no spare seats.

"Beverage sir?" the hostess asked. The drinks trolley bumped his elbow on the way through. "Just a water, thanks," Austin replied. She passed him a chilled plastic bottle of Mount Franklin water and held out her hand, "That's $4," she said, smiling. Austin would have to get used to this again, paying for food and drinks that were normally provided to him free of charge. He reached in his pocket and clasped a note. It was a fiver, more than enough to cover the charge.

Despite his thirst, Austin sipped his water. It had become a habit not to guzzle it down. After all, he had been trained to survive on very little.

Less than on a 600-ml bottle of water, that was for sure.

The plane bumped and jostled around as it hit a pocket of turbulence and the fasten seatbelt sign flashed on, followed by the accompanying announcement.

Austin tried to relax. He would love nothing more than to close his eyes and have sleep take him. But sleep was hard for him. It had become increasingly harder as his time in Afghanistan had lengthened.

When he did sleep, the nightmares tagged along. They often involved an accident in war, usually resulting in his own death. Then he would startle awake, usually finding himself drenched in sweat. Lately, the dream had involved him clearing a house in the small town of Musa Qala. Every time he entered the third home, he forgot to check the corner. He would turn around just in time to see the AK-47 begin firing at him.

There was nothing he could do.

He died every time.

Well, he assumed he had, but he always awoke before he knew for sure.

With the muttered chatter of the passengers, Austin did sleep and for the first time in a very long time, there were no dreams at all.

He woke when he heard the pilot announce, "We are beginning our descent into Melbourne, local time is 9.25 pm. It's a balmy 22 degrees outside. On behalf of Virgin we would like to thank you for flying with us today."

The plane began its slow descent. The cabin crew checked the overhead compartments and made sure the passengers were buckled in correctly. A few minutes later, the announcement came for the cabin crew to be seated for landing.

The landing was smooth and almost bump free. The plane taxied to the terminal and came to a halt. The seatbelt sign flashed off with a 'ping'. People scrambled for their overhead luggage and almost fought for the door.

Austin had no reason to rush. Sure, he wanted to meet his family who were awaiting his arrival in the airport, but he had waited six months and a few minutes more wouldn't kill him. The aisle cleared and Austin stood up, removing his backpack from the overhead. As he stood, he had to stoop to get his large frame out of the seat.

The air was fresh and the sun was shining brightly, if not strongly, and the Melbourne sky was clear of cloud. Spring was in the air.

* * *

Inside the terminal, Sarah sat with Mikayla on her lap. Mikayla was busy playing on her mum's phone. Subway Surfers was all the rage; nothing kept an 11-year-old occupied like an iPhone. Her pink dress was new and free of food stains; this was a personal best achievement considering she had been wearing it for over four hours. Her blonde hair was tied back in a ponytail with a pink ribbon.

Sarah was not the type to do herself up, but this morning she had taken a little extra care in her presentation. Shaved a few areas that had become unkempt, added a little extra makeup, put on her good jewellery and her special perfume, the one she saved for special occasions.

Chapter 6

ook at you, you're a disgrace. You really disgust me."

Beau Delacroix made no response to his mother's outburst. It was just another episode of her nagging at him. At 33, he was well and truly used to it.

"Is that what you're going to do all day, sit on your fat arse watching TV eating leftovers?" Again, Beau ignored her ranting, but inside he was starting to hurt. He tried to fix his attention on the cartoons on the TV in front of him.

"You've been out for almost eight months and what do you have to show for it? You don't even have a proper job."

"I have two jobs," Beau replied, not looking away from the Tom and Jerry cartoon.

"You can't count them as proper jobs. One is a part-time handyman and the other is a shit-kicker for a signwriting place."

Annabelle stood leaning against the wall waiting for her son to reply. She removed a cigarette from its packet, even though the one in her mouth still had a couple of drags left in it.

"It's hard to get a job when you've been inside, Mum. I-I-I a-a-am d-do-do…" His stutter started up as it always did when he was nervous or worried.

"Don't you start that stuttering with me. Maybe you should have thought of that when you were robbing those houses. Maybe if you did something with yourself and made yourself look respectable, you would have a girlfriend. You wouldn't be getting your jollies trying to abduct kids from a playground." She lit the cigarette with the butt of her old one and then discarded the old butt in the fire. Her face was wrinkled, not from age but from smoking. Her fingers were yellow, her teeth discoloured, her hair grey and in need of a colour.

Beau stood up out of the recliner and faced his mother.

"What? You stand up to your mother, do you want to hit me?" Annabelle said as she blew smoke into his face.

Even though Beau was six foot and solid, Annabelle knew she was in control.

"You wouldn't want to have a go at me, I'd knock your block off."

Beau took a step back. "I'm going to the shed," he said.

His mother stepped in front of the doorway that separated the lounge from the kitchen. "What you do you do in there all the time?"

"Fix the vans, practise my painting and play with my trains," he replied, hoping she would let him pass.

She didn't; she had more to say.

"You not doing any drugs in there? Not doing anything you shouldn't be?"

"No, just trying to keep busy."

"Make sure it stays that way, you go back inside you ain't coming back here!" It was the only sentence she spoke without a smoke in her mouth. "When you're done in there, be a good boy and go up and get our Thursday night fish and chips for dinner," she said. "Get me the usual."

Annabelle's usual consisted of two potato cakes, chips, flake, and two steamed dim sims.

Beau nodded in agreement. Annabelle let him pass.

Beau hitched up his tracksuit pants and grabbed the hoodie hanging on the back of a kitchen chair as he passed. He put the hoodie on and raised the hood to cover his head that was now balding. His wispy hair not only knocked his confidence, it made him look way older than he was. Beau's family wasn't rich; in fact, they were downright poor. His dad had died in a car accident when he was young. He had no memories of him at all. His mother had raised him on her own. The only thing his mum owned was an old weatherboard house.

The house stood on an acre of land and had originally been a farmhouse. Now it was on the edge of suburbia. High-voltage power-lines ran across the rear of the property, which was in need of repair.

His mum lived on disability benefits from the back injury sustained in the car accident that had claimed his father's life. Any spare money usually went on ciggies and alcohol and medicine for her back. If money was tight, it was usually the medicine that missed out.

The shed sat directly under the powerlines, and Beau liked it that way. It was away from everyone including his mum. It was big enough to work on six cars, still with room to use the work bench. Even though he had two vans, neither of them were being repaired. It just gave him a reason to get away from his mum. He had other hobbies that he preferred to work on.

The train set was laid out on a two-metre by one-metre piece of chipboard. It was complete with mountains, bridges and stations, trees and little people. The landscape had several settings, one a country town with a coal mine and sawmill. The other end of the set was a more suburban setting that included Walthers Cornerstone Merchant's Row opposite the station. Next was an ice-cream stand. His most prized locomotive was a rare Pennsylvanian Mantua steam engine. It made his coal mine complete.

The train set ran the length of the garage and took up the far right wall. Although it didn't look like it, it could be moved. The vans were on the far left. Against the far back wall sat a long tool bench. On it his computer was especially set up for WOW. It was the only online game he liked.

Under the bench was a set of drawers with the usual workshop tools, spare batteries for his mouse and everyday junk.

Beau loved his trains, but what was underneath them was his real interest.

* * *

Tyler Parsons had only done three break-ins before he had been caught. His stint in the big house was the first, and it was a real eye-opener. He had gone in a petty thief and come out ready for real crime, with the connections and knowledge about how to profit from his ventures.

He had been out exactly four days, and tonight he would put his new skills to the test. No longer was he going to steal TVs and DVD players to sell at Cash Converters.

Tonight was his first big job; well, scouting for it at least.

He was going in to the high end of town. He was after the expensive jewellery, not costume jewellery.

He had been given the name. His instructions were simple. He was to call a number, ask for a Mr Lee, then a private number would call him back with an address. He was to take any jewellery to the address for exchange.

No other instructions were given. The rest he would have to find out for himself.

While in jail, he had also been given what they called 'the word'. It was a simple code that reset all ADS security systems. He was told the code was legit. Unfortunately, there was only one way to find out.

Home owners thought they were enhancing their crime prevention when they stuck the ADS stickers on their windows. In fact, it was the exact opposite. Now that he had the code, the stickers told him which homes he could target.

He knew he had to double-check everything in daylight, before committing himself to the job. On the inside, he had been given an address that was supposedly an easy target. Apparently they were well off and the husband was away overseas. He was an army officer. Only a mum and a daughter were at home. Word in the joint was the safe in the house held valuable jewellery and cash. They even gave him the location of the safe – in the walk-in robe of the master bedroom.

Tyler parked his Mitsubishi Lancer five houses down from the target. His dog sat panting on the back seat. Tyler thought he had bought a Staffy; however, it turned out he had got something completely different, more likely a boxer. While it wasn't what he had wanted, he loved it anyway.

He had named him Rocky after the movie.

Tyler took Rocky from the back seat and hooked the leash to his choker collar. His plan was to walk him up and down the street a few times. No one ever took notice of a person walking a dog; it was the least suspicious thing someone could do.

He reached his target and even though he was on the opposite side of the street, he could see enough. The home was set back on a large block protected by a brick and wrought-iron fence, and electric gates. The home was large, two-storey, brick, with an upstairs balcony and a tiled roof. It was nice. The right side had a three-car garage, while the left had a gate that led to the back yard and perhaps a pool. The view to the back yard was hidden by two large trees each side of the gate. Rocky was sniffing around the opposite owner's front nature strip, doing his business as he pleased.

Tyler walked on. He would walk up the street for at least 10 houses and then cross the road and come back to have a closer look the second time round.

Rocky was enjoying the walk as usual. To him it was just another fence, just another bush. Just a different scent.

On the second run, Tyler got a better look at the property. He noticed a camera on the gate and one on each corner of the roof, another at the front door. He assumed there were also cameras out the back of the property. He noticed that there was no camera on the balcony.

He had seen enough; he knew his way in. His plan was coming together.

His pay day would soon be here.

Chapter 7

Beau had finished his fish and chips, yet his mother was still nagging at him. Lighting her third cigarette since finishing her meal.

"Louise called for you while you were up the shop, she wanted to know why you hadn't paid her the money this month?"

"Why do you still talk to her? She has nothing to do with us anymore. She divorced me, remember."

"She was too good for you, that was the problem. I knew you would never keep a girl like her." Ignoring his mother, Beau stood up from the table, washed his plate and placed it in the dish rack beside the sink.

"She cheated on me, Mum, and she divorced me. Now I'm stuck somehow, paying for her car."

"I know she cheated on you. Had you done a better job of satisfying her, she wouldn't have gone looking for sausage somewhere else. If you didn't turn into a stuttering mess every time you went out together, she might have been more inclined to stick around."

"I can't help my stutter, it didn't help me that you teased me when I was at school," Beau replied, standing in the doorway ready to end the conversation with his mother simply by heading back to his shed.

"I was only joking around with your friends, trying to make them feel comfortable."

"Is that like walking around the house in next to nothing when I had friends over?"

"Oh, you're being dramatic, Beau. Is it hard for you to believe I was just being friendly and if the occasional friend of yours found me attractive, who was I to argue with a teenage boy?"

Beau simply ignored this comment and headed outside, as he should have done a minute earlier.

He entered the shed and bolted the door behind him. He pulled on the handle to double-check it was locked. All secure, he thought.

Beau removed the red ladder from the wall and leaned it against the bench. He went over to his train set and walked around to the inside corner. He pulled the lever and the train table moved sideways. To the naked eye, moving the train set looked impossible and that was exactly how Beau had wanted it. The set was designed in a box shape, just over a metre high from the floor.

Below the train set was a mat, just a typical indoor thin carpet mat. When the train set was lengthwise, the mat was hidden.

Beau lifted the mat, folding it over itself. He unlocked the four padlocks that held the sunken wooden hatch. The concrete floor had been cut to allow for a door to be installed.

He placed the ladder down the hole and began his descent.

Beau unlocked Chloe's cell and walked in. Chloe was sitting as far away as she possibly could. As the man came towards her, she tried to shuffle back, but there was nowhere to go. He grabbed her by the hair. She began to scream and cry, "Let me go, please, let me go!"

"Q-q-q-q-quiet," he responded.

Chloe tried to keep as quiet as she could. She was aware of Scott's warning. She wasn't the smartest girl in her grade but she was close. She had noticed three things since the man had come down the ladder.

1. The door which he came down was still open.

2. The keys were still in her cell lock.

3. He had a stutter.

The man smelt worse than before. He held her by the throat. His hand felt greasy and his breath stank of onion and garlic.

He grabbed her by the hair with his other hand, leaving the keys in the door and the trapdoor open. He shuffled her towards the red door at the end of the corridor.

He turned the handle. There was no lock on this door. He released her hair momentarily and flicked a switch on the inside wall.

Chloe looked at the room and immediately her heart sank. She could see a bed with cuffs coming from the two rails that ran horizontally between the two end posts. On the concrete wall above the bed was a cross. It wasn't just a plain cross. It was one with 'Jesus' on it.

The balding, mask-wearing man with sweat patches under his arms and stinky breath threw her onto the bed. Chloe thought she knew what was going to happen to her, but at 12 she could not understand the gravity of the situation.

The bald masked man spoke, but not to her. He was speaking to the wall or the Jesus that hung on it.

"Forgive me," he said. He touched his forehead and then his crotch and crossed his chest. Chloe had not seen that before but she knew it was some sort of prayer.

He closed the door, bolting it behind him. He moved towards her. She thought about moving, but where would she go? Before she knew it, her hands were cuffed. He sat on top of her and removed her top and pants. Chloe couldn't move, he was so heavy.

His plump face came closer to hers, the breath was stronger, it was disgusting.

Panic set in. She lay there looking at the Jesus through her tears and wondered where was God now. What sort of God created monsters like this?

Her fears were worse than what she was actually going to endure. Just as he had removed her clothes, he pulled a phone from his pocket. He dialled a number. He waited only a short time before he spoke. "Father, I have what you asked for. Do you want me to send you a pic as per normal?"

He paused as he listened to the person on the other end. "Yes, she is undamaged." Pause again. "It's too soon." Another pause. "Yes, I understand. Ok, I'll see what I can find. Has delivery been arranged for M10?" Beau questioned. "I can't keep him much longer, he's been here too long already." Pause. "Ok, but by next weekend I will need to deliver him," he agreed. "I also found an M11 two days ago. Do you want him?" Pause. "Yes, I can send it tonight." Pause. "Yes, I can find another, why does he want two of them?" he answered the person on the phone. "No, don't tell him I w-w-w-won't. I-I-I-I will get the other one soon, week and a half tops." Pause. "Maybe I could deliver one of the goods on Saturday night and part two next Saturday when I deliver you your outstanding order? That might keep him happy? At least he'll have something to play with for the week." Pause. "Well, I'll deliver part two directly to him on the same night," Beau said, getting frustrated at the sudden extra demands.

He now had four deliveries in two weeks. Two to the 'Priest' and two to the 'Ukrainian Monster'.

Chloe had no idea who he was speaking with, maybe his dad? But before she could continue her thought, his phone flashed. Her photo had been taken; she was just in her undies and nothing else. Who was he sending the photo to? she wondered. Who would want to see her in her undies?

"Why did you take my photo?" she asked.

"For your ransom. Once your parents pay, you will go home."

Chloe didn't know why, but for some reason she didn't entirely believe his answer.

Chapter 8

Father Peter O'Riley had run the Saint Alexius home for children for over 40 years. It was set on 12 acres, just outside the town of Learmonth, 40 minutes north-west of Ballarat. The home consisted of 60 squares of residence. The St Therese wing housed the girls, while the boys stayed in the St Sabinus wing.

There were also an additional two wings that were specially equipped for the Wards of the State. These were troubled children, often abused, raised amongst drugs, prostitution and crime. They were what Father Peter O'Riley referred to as 'damaged'.

Capacity was set at 20 children per wing. There were another 10 per wing for the Wards of the State children.

In the grounds were two grass tennis courts and a separate indoor pool and of course the church itself. Attached to the church was his sacristy and three confessional booths.

As well as running the home for children, Father O'Riley offered Sunday services and confessional for the community. His parish consisted of many of the townspeople and local residents, including a magistrate of the county court, a police senior superintendent, teachers and general members of the community.

He had been preparing for his final rounds for the evening to ensure all the children were in their rooms, ready for lights out, when his mobile rang. It wasn't his normal mobile either, it was what he referred to as his personal phone. It was one that he had bought off the Internet. It had a sim card that was assigned to no one and the phone IMEI could be changed at a whim. In other words, the number could change and in effect, become a ghost phone.

He knew what the call was, even before he answered. His latest order had been fulfilled. He had several clients who had requested specific requirements. These requirements came with a premium price tag of $50,000. Money was cash only, hand delivered at the drop.

"Yes," the Priest answered.

"I'm going to have to send the buyer for the M10 a reminder, a nudge shall we say," the caller said.

The Priest paused.

"Holding him one more week won't kill you. Next weekend, I'll take delivery. I'll have it sorted by then," the Priest said. "Is the product still undamaged?" he asked. "Good, my son," he said when the caller replied.

"Yes, my son," he answered the caller's question. "I never pass up a free M11. Can you send him tonight?" Pause. "Send the conformation pic of F11. And I need you to fill another order. I need another F10-11 white." This was code for female aged 10-11 Caucasian.

"You should never ask why when it comes to the Monster. Do you want me to tell him you can't deliver?" the Priest asked. "Deliver the one you have this weekend. I will tell him the second one will be delivered next weekend. Once you have the second part of the order, text me conformation immediately. I don't want to go getting the Monster angry. He'll be anxious for his delivery." He added, "Meet the Batman at the normal delivery spot." In answer to his question, the Priest said, "No, my son, you will need to deliver both the F11s directly to the Monster himself, you know where to go," he said, and then reminded him, "be there this Saturday night. I'll let M know to expect you."

Moments later, a pic arrived on his phone. It was exactly what the Monster had ordered. However, it was the wrong gender to excite him.

The Priest's ghost phone had only two numbers: one was his supplier's and the other was titled UM.

He selected the picture on the phone and sent it via message to the only other number in his phone.

He then unlocked the glass doors located in the middle of his bookshelf. The bookshelf sat directly behind his desk. He removed a box from the middle of the shelf. To the left of the box was his Bible. To the right was his red stole, folded neatly so the tassels at each end met.

He opened the box. It was a black carrying case made of hardwood with blue velvet interior and black Rexene exterior.

Inside, the communion set included:

The gold cross he wore on Sundays and in the confessional.

The gold chalice he used at Sunday services.

Two candle holders.

Two glass cruets.

One paten.

One pix.

One purificator.

Except for the glass cruets, all the items were gold, and both the cross and the chalice featured ruby stones. The cross had one large stone in the middle, while the chalice had several stones around the lip.

Under the velvet interior was another ghost phone.

He had several more hidden within his office and around his sacristy.

He removed the phone from the box, and sent the photo in a message to the number for 'UM': *F11 x 2 50ea*. He used code to record all his clients, and then also recorded their details in a journal hidden under his mattress. In the subject line he stated, *first part ready for delivery.*

He never named them via text even though he knew them all. Anonymity was best for everyone concerned. Everybody except for himself. He recorded as much detail of the deliveries as he could in his journal. If his empire ever came crashing down, he would bring everyone down with him. The journal was his insurance.

Along with the two letters at the beginning, he sometimes used numbers, e.g. 'J8' meant John 8 to identify the person. In this case, 'UM' stood for the man who was known as the Ukrainian Monster, a man the Priest had never met and never wanted to meet.

The Ukrainian Monster was the only client who made his own rules and while he didn't consider him his boss, he knew he would always do as the Monster asked.

According to the underworld, the Ukrainian Monster was not called by that alias because of what he did to his collectables. It was because of what he did to those who threatened his control, his way of life or his seat at the head of the table.

F11 was the order, yet in this case, it meant two of them. Fifty was the cost: $50,000 each had been agreed to be paid upon delivery.

The phone vibrated. *That's only half of what I ordered. You have 14 days. New price 40 each.*

Agreed, the Priest replied, *delivery direct Saturday night.*

Last chance, was the response from UM.

Beau would have to take a cut in his share. Father O'Riley knew this might cause an issue but he also knew how to best control any such problem.

Anytime Beau wanted to renegotiate or argue with him, he only needed to say, "I will have to ask the Monster and see what he says." That comment always ended the negotiation, always with the same response from Beau. "No, it's ok, I'll let it slide this time," as if trying to convince himself and others that he was in control.

Father O'Riley removed another phone from his bottom drawer. This had several numbers in it, all clients who had placed orders for children. He scrolled down and pressed enter. When he came to C9, he wrote the following message.

Payment overdue. Final date set for next Saturday night.

Confirm payment

His phone vibrated.

Can't make payment will need to cancel, the client replied.

Father O'Riley replied, *Unacceptable*

Father O'Riley deleted both messages from both phones and placed them back in their hiding spots.

A threat was necessary. No one backed out of a deal, but that would have to wait for now. It was time to prepare for evening service and then the evening rounds.

It was his favourite time of day. In just a few hours, it would be a great day.

Chapter 9

Sarah Campbell was still sitting in the arrivals terminal waiting for her husband to arrive. Although it had only been six months, it felt like years. Her daughter Mikayla sat next to her, having switched from Subway Surfers to Candy Crush.

Sarah had sat patiently for almost an hour. She was now hoping the time would pass faster than normal. With nothing else to do, she couldn't help but notice the different types of people who visited the airport.

Across from her sat a pretty young businesswoman, dressed in a dark blue pants suit, busy checking her emails on her phone. Probably sent to pick up an interstate business colleague of some sort, Sarah thought.

A few seats down sat an odd looking man, who looked like he was stuck in the 80s. He was dressed in denim, head to toe, his jeans so tight they looked as if they would need to be cut off. His hair was long at the sides and back and spiky on top. He was a cross between Elvis and Mick Jagger. Every time Sarah glanced over, he would smile and give her a wink. She thought, sleaze-ball, and shuddered inside.

She looked away from Denim Elvis and noticed a younger woman sitting to her right. She was naturally beautiful. She looked all of 22 and was done up to the hilt. Sarah thought maybe she was meeting a mystery man from interstate, most likely from one of those Internet dating sites.

Sarah noticed she was missing one of her hoop earrings. She leaned over towards her. "Excuse me, I think you've lost an earring." She pointed to the girl's left ear. The young girl reached for the right ear, and corrected herself when she saw Sarah pointing to the other side.

She reached at her ear with her other hand and felt around for a hoop that wasn't there. She then stood up, looking at her seat and the floor, hoping it had dropped somewhere nearby. There was no luck. It was gone, and she could have lost it anywhere in the airport.

Sarah noticed she spent the next 10 or 15 minutes looking for it, before finally giving up the search.

"You waiting for someone special?" the young woman asked Sarah.

"My husband, he's been away on business," Sarah replied. She had stopped saying he was in the army three tours ago. One time a lady had asked her the same question and when she said he was coming home from Afghanistan, the lady said, "Oh, I see." She might as well have said, "Oh, waiting for a baby killer, are you?"

Now she always replied he was away on business. She was proud of what her husband did and always would be, but answering that way was likely to cause a lot less confrontation.

She looked at her watch: 9.25 pm. Then she looked at her daughter, who was starting to get tired. It was late for her to be up. The arrivals screen to her right flickered and the status of VA116 from Darwin changed to 'landed'. Sarah's view of the screen was interrupted by Denim Elvis. "Excuse me, Mam, I couldn't help but notice you kept looking in my direction. Thought maybe I could buy you a drink, how does that sound?"

A little taken aback by Denim Elvis' forwardness, Sarah responded, "I am sorry, I didn't mean to look at you, I was deep in thought and wasn't really looking at anything."

But Denim Elvis was a persistent one. "Sometimes the eyes see what the mind wants." He winked again. "Now how about that drink?"

"I am sorry, I am waiting for my husband, he is in the Special Forces just coming back from Afghanistan. I see his plane has landed so he should be coming out any minute," Sarah said, looking at the gate and the adjoining bridge.

"I beg your pardon, Mam, I didn't realise." Denim Elvis turned and returned to his seat.

Maybe telling people her husband was in the Special Forces had its benefits after all.

The first two passengers made their way out of the gate. Both were plump older ladies who looked very similar, possibly sisters. They were greeted by a younger woman with three small children. The children were introduced as if they hadn't met the ladies before.

A few businessmen followed the ladies, most busy switching on their phones.

Still no sign of her man.

Then there he was, towering over the other passengers, with a big smile on his face stretching from ear to ear. He looked more muscular than the last time she had seen him. Maybe it was her memory or maybe he had become bigger. Either way, she liked it.

It was an emotional reunion; she cried almost the instant he picked her up and hugged her. His smell was amazing. They kissed lingeringly but not passionately.

Mikayla hugged her dad around the leg. He placed his wife down and picked up his girl, the one he called his princess. She was beautiful. He had noticed she had lost a front tooth, but she was gorgeous nonetheless.

Mikayla fell asleep in the car on the way home.

While she slept, they caught up on what had been happening around the house. What had been happening at Mikayla's school. All the gossip that normal mums have. The one topic they never touched on was the war. She knew he wouldn't tell her and she didn't really want to know.

They arrived home and waited for the electric gate to open and allow them through. The gate shut automatically behind them. They parked in the garage and headed inside.

The one thing Austin loved to do was carry Mikayla to bed. It was one of the best memories he had as a child. Nothing beat being carried to bed by your parents.

He placed her in her bed, switched the lamp on and just sat there staring at her. He wondered if she had done what they had promised each other before he had left for his tour. They had agreed they would both stare at the stars whenever they missed each other.

He had spent many a night looking up at the stars and thinking of his princess. How he loved her!

Tonight, he wouldn't have to look at the stars. She was right here in front of him asleep, with not a worry in the world.

He had been there 15 minutes when Sarah came in. "You ok, babe?" she asked, standing there in her nightgown.

"Fine," he replied.

"You want to come to bed?" she asked as she took his hand.

He could see her nipples through her nightie. He took her hand and followed her to the bedroom. As was often the case, absence had made the heart grow fonder.

Not only had he missed her, he had missed being with her. She took off her clothes and began kissing him. She unbuttoned his shirt as she sat on his lap. There was a new scar; she touched it, and kissed him again. She thought about asking about it, and then thought better of it.

Her hair smelt beautiful; it was a smell he had tried to hold onto while he was in the desert. The memory of her only lasted a week, maybe two, and by the second month, he could no longer visualise her naked.

Her skin was soft and smelt of musk. He wanted this moment to last forever. They reacquainted themselves with each other several times that night. Each time was longer and more enjoyable than the preceding one.

Chapter 10

Since I'd joined the detectives' team, I'd been promoted from a cubicle to an office. Jake sat on the edge of my desk, fresh coffee in one hand, chocolate doughnut in the other.

He had brought me a hot chocolate and a chocolate doughnut. I sipped the hot chocolate. It burnt my tongue and a little of my bottom lip. "Ow," I moaned.

"Careful, Brucey, it might be hot," he said sarcastically.

I smiled.

"So what did you want to discuss?" Jake mumbled with a mouthful of doughnut.

"I have concerns about these cases. Something doesn't seem right, something isn't adding up."

"Run it by me, mate. What are the issues you're having?"

"Ok, Scott Western, aged 10, riding his bike to school, never made it there. Local residents found his bag and bike lying on the footpath. Gone. Vanished."

"Yeah, kidnapping," Jake added, as if to say, what's unusual about that.

"Then a few weeks later, other side of the city nearly 60 kilometres away, 12-year-old Chloe Henderson also never made it to school. No items were left, just never made it, vanished, gone."

"Ok, so another kidnapping," Jake said, "what's your point?"

"We have them listed as two separate cases and most think it's two separate offenders."

"You're not sure?" Jake sipped his coffee.

"The MO is very similar but what bugs me is I've never heard of a paedophile who likes both genders. It's normally one or the other." I continued. "Just two days ago, another boy, Stevie Bradley, 11 years old, totally different location, disappeared going to school. All they found was his basketball lying in the gutter. Something tells me they're all related."

"Maybe one was watching the news report about the boy and adopted the same method because it worked," Jake said. "I think you're reading too much into it. Just relax, not every crime is a serial killer. Quite frankly, the Slayer case was enough to last me a lifetime."

"That makes two of us," I replied. "Maybe you're right, maybe it's just coincidence." Although I said this to Jake, something in my gut told me it wasn't. Problem was, I trusted both.

"Any progress on the "Night Stalker?" Jake asked.

"No, I'm still sorting through potential suspects who have jail sentences that coincide with the cooling-off period. I'm assuming he's alive and in jail, then I'll look into sexual offenders who died after the last killing. Unless we get a new lead, we're going to struggle."

The kidnappings had been grinding in my head all morning. I had to try and settle some of the queries I had.

"Jake, do you think it would be ok if I got involved in these kidnappings?" I asked, unsure of the protocol.

"Aren't you supposed to just review them and make recommendations?" Jake asked me.

"Yeah…but I think they're related and I recommend we set up a task force," I answered.

Jake closed his eyes and sighed loudly. "Well, if that's what you think needs to happen, then recommend it, but I doubt the chief will give it to you, you're in Homicide, remember? Not Missing Persons."

I nodded. "I'll make the recommendation that they be considered linked and send it back to the Missing Persons Unit."

Chapter 11

Jake and Hayley hadn't got married, although the idea had been discussed.

Hayley had spent the morning in the bathroom vomiting; she had done that every morning for the last week.

She knew she was pregnant. She was late and her boobs were hurting and the morning sickness practically gave it away.

She hadn't told Jake; she didn't really know how to. While she was ecstatic, she knew he was still coming to terms with everything that had happened at the cabin all those years ago.

Maybe it would be a good thing.

Maybe it would help get him out of his slump.

She had been working at the Children's Hospital for over 12 years and had recently been promoted to head of the ICU.

Most of the time she enjoyed her work, but sometimes it was hard. For some reason, the last 14 months had been particularly hard.

She'd had a five-year-old come through the ICU, although this was nothing new. Kids were often in there with leukaemia, heart conditions and injuries.

This incident, however, was desperately sad. Ryan was an everyday child, just started school, fought with his siblings. His mum and dad were hard-working responsible people. The kind every kid would love to have as parents.

* * *

From all reports, Ryan was very friendly, smart and well liked amongst his classmates. He had made lots of friends. As any boy does when they are making their way in school, he had play dates. Friends came over and played on a Saturday or after school. Then he would go to their house; it was the way it worked. Joan, his mother, thought nothing of it when Ryan asked if he could go and stay at his friend Josh's house, after all, she had had Josh in her house.

She dropped him off and arranged with Josh's mother to pick him up at lunchtime on the Saturday. All seemed fine. Little did she know that it would be the last time she would speak to her boy.

At 7 am the next day, she received a frantic phone call from Josh's mother. "Oh my God, you have to go to the Children's Hospital now. The ambulance is on its way. Ryan needs you!"

"What happened?" Joan asked, now in a panic of her own. "What's going on?" she asked again.

"Please, just go to the Children's, I will meet you there."

Joan got dressed and rang her husband, who was already on his way to work. "Hi, babe, you're up early." But before he could finish, the frantic voice, half-crying and half-speaking, came through the speaker.

"Reece, something has happened to Ryan, he's on his way to the Children's Hospital in an ambulance. Paula hasn't told me what happened, just said it was urgent and to get to the hospital."

"I'm on my way there now," he said after a slight pause.

Reece had pulled his car over. He had no idea what had happened or if Ryan would be ok. One thing he did know was that he had to stay calm. He turned his car around and headed for the hospital.

When he walked through the doors to the emergency ward, he saw Paula sitting in the waiting area crying. "Where is Joan?" he asked.

"She's with Ryan just through there. I am so sorry," she said, but Reece didn't wait for her apology. He raced into the emergency room itself.

The triage nurse escorted him to bed 11. Joan was sitting on the edge of Ryan's bed, holding his hand. At first he looked ok. It looked as if he was asleep.

"What happened?" Reece asked.

"He fell in the pool, no one noticed. He was dead when ambulance officers arrived. They revived him. He had been dead for almost 30 minutes."

* * *

He had remained in a coma ever since, the parents still going in every day to see him. Each and every day they prayed for a change that never came. There was no eye movement, no finger that twitched, no toe that moved.

Nothing; just a lifeless body.

Yet the parents continued to visit. Tomorrow would be his seventh birthday and his first in hospital. There would be no celebration, although Hayley was sure the parents would bring cake and gifts. The parents always held out hope that a new toy might connect with him, somewhere inside, wherever he was trapped.

Hayley and Jake had made a rule not to bring their work home with them. Both of them were concerned that eventually the darkness would consume them both if they lived it 24/7. At home, they tried to put their other worlds aside and concentrate on the more positive aspects of their lives together.

Despite her best intentions, Hayley struggled to set aside the sadness she had over Ryan, but true to her promise, she kept her sadness to herself.

She hoped Jake couldn't sense her sadness although she thought he must. She lay awake, wondering how and why these things happened to the most innocent people of all, children.

Chapter 12

To the wider community, Senior Superintendent Mike McLeod was an outstanding member of the police force. However, the few people who had seen his dark side had a different story to tell.

Mike was not on duty tonight but he was working for a boss no one else knew he had. He sat in the driver's seat of the Black Chrysler 300c that had been provided for him. He was parked on a dirt road just past the gates of the Learmonth cemetery and had been there since 10 pm.

His delivery was due at 10.15. He had been asked to collect and then deliver the goods to his employer tonight. He did as he was asked, without question.

Lights appeared in the distance. This would be his man, Mike thought. He checked to ensure no lights were following him. He was in the clear. As the van headed towards him, the driver toggled the lights in a quick flash. The van moved closer, before slowing to a complete stop.

Mike sat in the car and waited for the van driver to exit before he made his move. The driver exited and stood at the front of the van in between the headlights. It was the Joker.

Mike opened his door and walked towards the fat balding Joker. He looked like something you would normally see at a fancy dress party. Mike was dressed as Batman, well, only from the neck up and minus the cape.

Mike wasn't much taller, maybe just a couple of inches, but he was a lot fitter and well built, plenty of muscle he could use if he needed to. He would probably suit being Batman.

"You got the goods?" Mike asked.

He had met the man several times before but names were never discussed. Everyone that worked in 'the loop' as they called it, stayed anonymous and wore masks.

"You got the envelope?" the fat Joker asked back. Mike pulled a folded yellow envelope out from his inside jacket pocket and handed it over.

Beau thought he had met this man several times before. Surely no two guys were built like this one. He assumed Batman was the Priest's muscle, someone to do his dirty work when required. Beau walked forward and took the envelope from the large Batman.

He had no fear of this man, he had fought plenty bigger than him and had still won. Several times in the joint the gangs had come for him. They thought he was slow and stupid because of his stutter; many thought he was retarded. What they didn't know was that anytime he fought he went to some other place inside himself, somewhere animalistic.

Beau walked to the back of the van and came back dragging a small shape with a rope attached around their neck. The head was covered with a black bag. Beau handed the rope to the big man.

"Is he what was ordered?" the big Batman asked.

Beau nodded, turned back towards his van.

By the time he was in reverse, the boy had been loaded into the back of the black car. Beau wondered if this delivery was for the Priest himself or if he was destined for another buyer.

Was the Priest in the back waiting for his delivery? Beau wondered.

Beau took the envelope and opened it, quickly counting to ensure he hadn't been short-changed. Even though every deal had been correct thus far, it was always best to double-check.

Closing the envelope, he folded it under his seat. Five thousand dollars was his cut. Not bad for a few minutes' work. The Priest had always told him never to pass up on an opportunity, and that he would always have buyers for undamaged goods.

Beau usually picked up the goods as ordered, however, if any other opportunity presented itself, sometimes he just couldn't resist.

The Priest had only three rules.

1. Wait a minimum of two days before transporting to ensure there is no heat.

2. No names.

3 Always wear masks, common ones at that.

Mike loaded the boy gently into the black seat of the Chrysler, ensuring that he didn't hit his head on the way in. This was common police procedure, an everyday habit he was unaware of.

Once inside the car, Mike removed his mask. The inside of the Chrysler had been specially fitted. Separating the front and back seats was a dark glass electric window. The rear seat could lift up if required, providing enough room to hide someone. All the locks were controlled from the front, and there were hidden cameras in the lining of the roof and in the wall that contained the glass separation panel. Alongside the cameras were listening devices.

All products on the way to and from delivery remained hooded and with their feet and hands bound.

Quite often, Mike would hear the hooded children counting the turns, some even counting the time. Others would be a mess from the start to the finish of the trip. If Mike ever heard them counting, he would purposely go around the block a few times or drive a longer, more confusing route. For the smart ones, he would play a loud CD of traffic noise, trains, dump trucks, police sirens, the whole box and dice.

Mike wasn't a paedophile; in fact, he was happily married. Delivering for the Priest was just a job. He simply helped out with the deliveries and the clean-up if required and his reward was money, lots of it.

Chapter 13

Father O'Riley walked the halls with his Bible in his right hand and his gold cross hanging around his neck. Every night, he would start his nightly prayers at 8. He would go from dorm to dorm.

Each dorm had four beds, two on each side of the room. Each bed had a night table beside it. At the end of the room was a communal closet with enough space for all four children. The night table had a top drawer which housed the Holy Bible. Above each bed hung a cross with Jesus on it. On the table was a statue of the Virgin Mary.

Father O'Riley used the same prayer every night in every dorm.

"Children, are you ready for your nightly prayer?" he would ask. Most times the children would already be waiting in silence, kneeling beside their respective beds.

Father O'Riley stood in the middle of the room, Bible open in the palm of his left hand. He began and the children joined in, in chorus:

Be present, O Lord our God,

At the end of this day I thank You most heartily for all the graces I have received from You.

I am sorry that I have not made a better use of them. I am sorry for all the sins I have committed against You.

Forgive me, O my God, and graciously protect me this night. Blessed Virgin Mary, my dear heavenly mother, take me under your protection.

St. Joseph, my dear Guardian Angel, and all you saints of God, pray for me
     AMEN

At the end of the prayer, the father would perform the sign of the cross. "Bless you, my children." The children would repeat the sign of the cross and climb into their beds. They were allowed to read for a further 15 minutes but then lights had to be out.

When he had finished in the St Therese wing, he headed to the end of the hall, past the night station and west down the St Alexius wing. Then he headed to the two wings that had been allocated to the Wards of the State; and other sources. The St Paul wing held the boys and St Abigail housed the girls.

He would save the boys' ward for last. Both wards had only single rooms; there were no dorms, no groups of four. This was because these were often abusive and violent children, or children who had been abused and needed time to accept the Lord into their lives, before they could be assimilated into the dorms. Some children would only be there for days before being moved on.

Father O'Riley finished in the girls' rooms, leaving them to read their Bibles.

He was expecting a delivery. By now, his new arrival should be safe in his new room in the St Paul wing. There should be five housed there now, four from the State and one from his own delivery service.

He never interfered with the ones from the State or any of the orphans. There was simply too high a risk of getting caught. He had done that once before and it had nearly brought him undone. The boy, 11-year-old Jonathan Lucas, now lay buried at the south-east corner of the cathedral. Father O'Riley told authorities Jonathan had simply run away. He was believed because children often did, although they were usually found. Children running away from a boys' home attracted a state-led police investigation that lasted months. Father O'Riley's only saving grace was that they never found the body, and Jonathan had a previous history of running away which added weight to the father's story.

After the investigation ended, he decided those children who were under his care had to be his biggest asset and they could no longer be used to fulfil his inner demons. Having many children speak highly of you would always help, if he was ever questioned in the future.

He found the best way to satisfy his own requirements was to have his desire shipped in and when he was done with them, they would either be sold or disposed of.

After all, he had plenty of buyers that didn't mind damaged goods, as he called them. They would still fetch between $7,000 and $15,000 each. This one had already been sold and would be delivered in the morning.

He performed his usual nightly prayer for all the ward children, and then went into his new arrival's room.

"Hello, my child," Father O'Riley said as he entered, his face hidden by a hood and a mask.

The boy wondered why the man was dressed as a priest.

"Help me! I've been kidnapped, by a man in the van. Please help me," the boy replied, shaking and in tears.

"No, my son, you haven't been kidnapped. The man works for me; you have been chosen by God to serve him," Father O'Riley replied as he approached the boy, who was standing in the back corner of the room.

"What is your name, my child?" he asked, now standing within touching distance.

"Stevie," the boy answered, shaking in fear and crying. "I want to go home."

"This is your home now, my child."

The Priest closed the door behind him.

Chapter 14

The next morning, Austin woke early, as he had done every day for the last few years. He lay there watching his wife sleep, holding her tightly, her head resting on his chest.

He stroked her hair and kissed her forehead as she held him tighter in her sleep.

He had slept well, by his standards. Four or five hours, only two bad dreams that he could remember. Maybe the others would show their faces later as the day developed.

The alarm on the bedside table flicked over to 7 am and on cue, the radio came on. Without even a lift of her eyelids, Sarah tapped the button and sent the clock back to sleep.

She snuggled in tighter.

Making the most of her sleep with her man.

By 7.45, they had again made up for lost time and then showered together.

Sarah had decided to give Mikayla the day off school so she could spend the day with her father. After all, the school year was almost finished. Only another week before summer holidays began.

They sat and ate their eggs and bacon breakfast as a family for the first time in over six months. And they enjoyed every second of it.

"So, I was thinking we could go to the movies today or the park? Have some lunch out," Austin said.

Before Sarah could respond, Mikayla piped up, "I want to go to the movies, see *Frozen!*" she said, all excited.

"*Frozen* it is," Austin replied.

Their morning was relatively lazy. The movie wasn't showing until 11.30 and they had nothing that needed to be done before then.

They pulled out of their garage at 10.45, leaving them plenty of time to get to the movies and enough time to queue for the popcorn, ice-cream and drink.

Austin couldn't remember the last time he had had ice-cream. More than six months, at least.

* * *

After spending five hours travelling the country and making his delivery to Batman, Beau gave himself a treat and slept in. He only had a few odd jobs to do for the local real estate agent, and they weren't booked until the next day, Saturday morning. The last thing he wanted was stay at home and put up with his mother mouthing off all the time. He could hear her now, "Don't you have something useful to do?"

He decided to head out to the movies to see *The Hunger Games* and grab a burger afterwards. He had to try to think about how and where he would find another girl.

Beau had always gone to the movies alone, not because he enjoyed being on his own but simply because he had no friends. He found it relaxing, but it was also a great place to locate suitable targets for the Priest. He had been asked to produce an F7 within the next two weeks, so he was on the look-out more than normal.

He always went during the day. He figured it looked less strange being at the movies by yourself in the middle of the working week than it did on a Saturday night when everyone was out with friends. However, the main reason was parents always took their kids during the day, not at night.

Today was a school day so pickings would be slim.

Beau got a bucket of popcorn, a drink and a choc top. For 11 am, it wasn't the most ideal food in between meals. Beau sat in the lobby nibbling at his popcorn while he waited to be admitted. The lobby was getting busier as more movie sessions neared. That was when he noticed her; she was beautiful, big smile, big brown eyes, hair plaited, cute outfit. He would get a lot for her. Maybe he could bump the price up. The Priest would have to pay more for her. Once he sent her photo, he would be able to ask for more. He glanced away so as not to get caught staring at the young girl. He especially didn't want to get noticed by the rather large and muscle-bound beast who was walking with her. Obviously her dad, he thought. A lady who was obviously the girl's mother accompanied the girl and her dad. The resemblance between mother and daughter was incredible.

They walked past and sat opposite in the foyer, the mother and father talking and holding hands as they sat. The girl was spinning in circles, singing, "I'm going to see *Frozen, Frozen,* for me! How much longer is it?" she interrupted her parents.

"It starts in 20 minutes," her father answered without breaking off the conversation with his wife. The usher came out and asked Beau for his ticket. He held his popcorn with his thumb with the same hand that was holding his drink. He passed the ticket trying to prevent the drink or the popcorn from spilling.

The usher ripped it and returned half to him. Beau knew he had about 110 minutes before *Frozen* finished, taking into account the later start. He figured he wouldn't get through all of *The Hunger Games,* because he had to find out more about this girl. He couldn't let this opportunity pass. There would always be another session of *The Hunger Games,* part two. He set his iPhone to vibrate in exactly 98 minutes.

The film had just started to get exciting when the phone vibrated in his pocket. Beau made his way to the exit. The doors to theatre four where *Frozen* was showing were still closed. Beau took the opportunity and quickly visited the men's room.

For 12 long minutes, Beau sat in the foyer and made out that he was waiting for someone, scrolling through his phone. Pretending he was dealing with important business.

When they left the theatre and walked past him, he inconspicuously took several shots of the girl.

They strode through the foyer, the girl holding tightly onto her father's hand. He looked even bigger than before. Had he grown while watching the movie? The girl was singing. Her voice was soft and angelic. It was a song he had never heard before. He figured it was from the movie they had just watched.

Do you wanna build a snowman?
Come on let's go and play
I never see you anymore
Come out the door
It's like you've gone away
We used to be best buddies
And now we're not
I wish you would tell me why!
Do you wanna build a snowman?
It doesn't have to be a snowman.

Then she started up again. She was so pretty. He had to know where she lived. He was a little concerned that the dad was so protective: hawk-like eyes, looking everywhere. Beau followed them out to the car park. He lit a cigarette as he watched them head towards the car. He thought it was safe now to continue his pursuit. He removed his keys and fumbled through them as if looking for one key in particular, and he saw them hop into a black SUV. Beau made out the numberplate and typed it into his phone.

He copied the number-letter combination into an open message, added two words and pressed send.

Address required

The phone vibrated back.

Why?

Beau typed the second part:

Order for M

He watched as the ... hovered.

Again Beau's phone vibrated.

Will do

Beau waited in his vehicle for them to leave in their SUV. He followed, but ensured it was at a safe and inconspicuous distance behind.

Chapter 15

"You need to come now. I think I've killed him." The voice on the end of Mike's phone quivered.

"I'll be right there. Don't touch anything."

Mike turned to find his wife Jemma standing directly behind him. "That sounded urgent. Who killed who?"

"You know I can't discuss work, hun. No one is dead but I do have to go."

He kissed his wife who was still in her morning gown, then quickly headed over to his two sons and pecked them both on the cheek. They were two and they were adorable, born only minutes apart. Identical twins, Brock born first and Clay second.

He rushed out the door as they sat in their matching highchairs. His wife had already begun to wipe up the crumbs from the floor beneath them.

Mike hopped into his car. The story for his wife was that the black Chrysler had been bought with an inheritance. In reality, it had been given for services rendered to the church. Services like this one, services that his wife had no idea about.

Had she known what he had been doing and what his true reason for doing it was, he knew she would leave him and take the twins with her.

He couldn't have that. He'd see them all dead before that happened.

The Priest was waiting outside the Ward of the State wing where

Mike had delivered the child not more than 12 hours ago.

"What's happened?" he asked the Priest.

"He was being difficult, trying to fight me off. At first it was fun, you know how I like a bit rough play. But then he got serious and really violent."

Right about the time you tried to butt fuck him, Mike thought.

"Then what happened?" Mike asked.

"I hit his head against the wall. Blood spurted out, and he collapsed," the Priest said.

"Have you checked his pulse?" Mike asked.

"No, I just left. I'll need you to dump him if he's dead."

"Understood," Mike responded. "I'll go check on him first, just to make sure we're not jumping at shadows. Does he still have his hood on?"

"Yes," replied the Priest, "I could see blood soaking through it," he added.

With the boy's hood still on, Mike had no need to cover his face with his standard Batman cowl. He slipped into the room, closing the door behind him.

The boy didn't move.

Didn't even stir.

He was sprawled in the top right-hand corner of the bed, head twisted at an unusual angle.

Upon first appearance it didn't look good. The Priest might be right.

Mike approached the boy, slowly knelt down beside the bed and felt the boy's wrist.

There was a pulse. It was there and it was strong.

Mike was sure he would be ok. He walked over to the basin that was bolted against the stone wall of the room. Cupped his hands and filled them with water. He carried the water back to the boy and splashed it over his face.

The boy moved and groaned, slowly at first.

Then he obviously remembered where he was and what was

happening and frantically began kicking out.

"Stop now and be quiet or I will slit your throat where you lie."

Mike's voice was not loud or angry, it was very cold and matter-of-fact.

That scared Stevie very much.

He stopped fighting immediately.

"What are you going to do with me?" he asked, confused.

Stevie could not see the person sitting over him, although he could feel the water and the cool air through the hood. Other than that, he had no idea where he was or who he was with.

"I'll be back for you later," Mike said as he made his way to the door. Stevie could hear a bolt and then the turn of a lock a few seconds later, then the closing of the door.

Where is he going to take me? Stevie wondered, as he sat curled up in the corner of the bed. He could feel cold rough stone against his right arm and palm.

"He's alive," Mike said.

The Priest was leaning against the wall of the corridor, rosary beads in hand.

"Good, I think it's best we ship him off. I'll make the arrangements, can you make the drop? It will either be tonight or tomorrow."

"Just send me the details as per usual and I'll collect him and drop him off."

"Mike, before you go, I have another job for you."

Mike turned and faced the Priest. "What type of job?" he asked.

"A buyer has reneged on a deal; he needs to know he can't do that to us." The Priest spoke calmly.

"Do you want a reminder so he goes ahead with the deal, or am I setting an example?"

"Just a warning he needs to take delivery next weekend, otherwise an example will have to be made of him."

Mike nodded, "Send me his number I'll follow the rest up. The message will be delivered by the end of the weekend."

Chapter 16

I had taken Jake's advice and ignored my feelings about the case, but it continued to haunt me.

Three children, all taken in broad daylight. It wasn't right and I couldn't let it go. Maybe the fact it was kids was what tormented me most.

As a child, I had spent a lot of time in hospital and had seen a lot of other children come and go during my stays. Some would stay only a short time and go back home to normality just days later. They were the ones I was envious of. Then there were the others that came in but didn't leave. They died all of a sudden, their lives over. Extinguished like a new flame before it had a chance to become a fire.

I had survived. I was their envy; they had just wanted to live.

There was the little boy I recalled who suddenly fell over one day, and then the next and the next until soon it was every time he walked. He was just six and he wanted to be a policeman. Within weeks, he couldn't walk and six months later, he was dead. I saw his funeral on the news. The Make a Wish Foundation fulfilled his wish of becoming a police officer and ensured he was buried with full police honours. A year later, I was in hospital for another stint when his brother came in suffering the same fate as his older departed brother. He died too! Life is cruel!

I had driven to the home of Stevie Bradley without even knowing how, my mind on auto pilot while it visited the ghosts of my past. Memories I had hidden deep down.

I knocked loudly and then stood back from the door. The door opened but the security door remained closed. "Can I help you?" the lady asked.

"Mrs Bradley, I'm Detective Brodie Foxx from Homicide. Just wondering if I could ask you a few questions regarding Stevie?"

"Do you think he's dead?" She began to cry. "Have you found him?" I could hear running from the other end of the house. "What's wrong, hun?" the male voice asked. "It's the police, Homicide."

I quickly said, "We haven't found him and we have no reason to think that anything has changed. We're still looking at it as a missing person."

"But you're from Homicide?"

"Please, Mrs Bradley, if I could just have a few minutes of your time, I can explain."

She unlocked the security door. "Of course, excuse me. I don't know what happened to my manners."

Her crying stopped almost as quickly as it had started. It was obvious she was in a state of shock and she had no way of dealing with how drastically her world had changed. Their world as they'd known it had changed forever, and they did not know how to move forward.

I stepped inside their house, which was dark, blinds drawn, TV on. Mrs Bradley was still in her dressing-gown despite it nearing lunchtime. Makeup was no longer a concern. Everything in this lady's life had stopped and tomorrow would never come until there was closure.

"Thanks for your time. I just wanted to ask you some questions. I'm investigating some links between Stevie's abduction and other missing children cases."

"Are the other children dead?" Mr Bradley asked, nervously awaiting my answer.

"No, we haven't found them yet. But they may be connected and if that is the case, we might find a lead into all of them. Did you notice anything unusual leading up to the morning of Stevie's disappearance?" I asked them.

They looked at each other and shook their heads. "Nothing we can think of," his mother said. "It was just like he vanished off the face of the earth. All they found was his ball in the gutter and they only knew it was his because it has his name written on it. He did that to stop other kids from taking it at lunchtime."

"May I look in his room?"

The parents nodded and led the way down the even darker hall. They opened a door. I guessed this door had been shut since Stevie was taken. Except for when the Missing Persons Unit had asked to view it.

Stevie was into basketball for sure. His walls were covered in posters. There was Chris Paul, Kevin Garnett, Lebron James, Kevin Durant. I stood taking it in. His bed was in the corner, desk against the wall with a computer. Photos of friends stuck to the walls next to the posters. Basketball ring attached to his cupboard door. There was a ball sitting on his bed, the one I assumed he had taken to school that day. It sat there waiting for him to return and play with.

"Was he on Facebook?" I asked.

"No, we thought he was too young. He played PlayStation online but that was with his friends."

"Did you ever hear him talking to people he didn't know; names you didn't recognise?"

"No, I knew them all. It was a very select group of friends."

I closed the door and headed back out to the lounge. The Bradleys followed. "I'm going to walk his route to school and I'll be in touch if I come up with something of interest. Thank you for your time."

I turned and headed for the door, then I stopped. Something registered in my memory from a case I had read about years ago. "I asked you earlier if you noticed anything unusual. Let me rephrase that.

Did you notice anything normal but also a little odd, out of place?"

It was like a lightbulb going off. His mother answered immediately, "About a week before, I noticed a van parked down the road. It had a phone logo on the side, but it wasn't for a phone company. Anyway, I remember seeing the same logo, possibly the same van, one other afternoon, except it was parked three streets over. I just happened to pass it on the way home."

"Did you see the driver?"

"No, I didn't pay any attention to who was driving it."

"I'll follow that up but it was probably nothing. If you have any questions please call me any time."

I handed her my card and headed out the front. I needed to re-create Stevie's last movements.

I stood at the bottom of the reserve, ready to cross where he had crossed through the reserve, and looked up. I could see the street at the other end. I set my watch and walked. It took me 53 seconds to walk to the top. It might have taken Stevie less than that. I looked at the houses either side of the reserve. Both were single storey; unlikely they would have seen anything. Across the road were two more single-storey homes and one double storey. The double didn't have great views of the reserve. According to crime scene reports, none of the other residents had seen or heard anything, but I would ask again anyway.

Now, I had to test my theory. I headed back down to my car, started the engine and drove past the reserve at 40 kilometres an hour. I pressed start on my watch and without having to speed, I had reached the top of the reserve with 25 seconds to spare.

I figured that if he had been dribbling the ball, Stevie might have taken a little longer to reach the top. He might have even lost his dribble, which would have extended even more the time available to the suspect. The suspect had 25 seconds minimum to park, lie in wait and then make his move. He knew the area; he knew the connecting streets; he knew Stevie's route. Had someone seen Stevie at the bottom of the reserve they would have had enough time to drive around and cut him off.

Providing one thing.

Our suspect knew how to get there first.

Was our unsub the man with the van?

I knocked on both the single storey front doors, with no luck. There was no one home.

I tried the two storey across the road. A lady answered. I introduced myself and showed her my badge. "The morning the boy was taken. Were you at home?"

"Yes, my children go to the same school. I drop them off." Her voice was soft but matter-of-fact.

"Did you see or hear anything unusual?"

"No, I was busy getting my own two ready for school, and that's a task and a half on some mornings. When we drove out of the driveway, I saw the ball lying in the gutter and I thought nothing of it, to be honest. When the police came by in the afternoon and I found out that the ball belonged to the boy, then I realised all that time he had been missing and my heart sank. I knew he hadn't run away, so did the police. If you run away, you take the ball with you."

She was a lovely lady. Someone you would like as a neighbour.

The phone in her house began to ring in the background. "Is there anything else, Officer?" she asked.

"No. Thanks for your help, I'll get back to you if I need anything else."

I sat in my car thinking things over. Jake was right as usual. The case wasn't a homicide and it wasn't mine. I had to suggest that Missing Persons take this over but first, I had to be sure the cases were similar.

I headed to the street of the second missing child, Chloe Henderson. I had to know if the MO was the same for the boy and the girl. I just had to know.

Again, I made that dreaded knock. I hated it because I knew the parents would automatically fear the worst. "Mrs Henderson, I'm Brodie Foxx from Homicide." I placed my hands forward, palms down, as if to say, calm down. "Firstly, I don't have any news on your daughter, I'm just reviewing the case. May I come in?"

Mrs Henderson let out a big sigh of relief and clasped her hands together, dish towel held tightly between them. She was dressed in around-the-house clothes. Maybe since the abduction of her daughter, appearance had lost the importance it had once held.

"Of course, please, may I get you a drink?"

"No, thank you. I can't stay, I just have a few questions for you if that's ok? Sorry to bring all this up again, but I'll be asking you some questions that you may have been asked several times. I'm trying to stay fresh and look into this as if it just happened."

I removed my pen and unzipped my folder.

"I do it this way to make sure I come to my own conclusions without the influence of other officers or any case file notices. Does that make sense?"

"You're the expert," she replied with a small smile.

"On the morning Chloe disappeared, can you tell me what time she left home?"

"She left at 8.20 as she did each morning. It took her about 20 minutes to walk to the school. It was only five streets away, three this side and two the other side of the highway."

"When did you know that she hadn't made it to school?" I asked calmly.

"Her friend Jasmine rang at around 4 pm. She asked if she was ok. It was then I knew something was wrong." Her eyes were beginning to well up.

"The worst part is Chloe almost made it to the school. She was only 80 metres away from the school. How did she get so close without anyone seeing her? How is that possible?" She looked at me as if I could provide the answer to a question that might never be answered.

"I don't know but we're doing everything we can to find out. Can you show me which way she walked?" I opened Google Maps on my phone. She pointed with her finger, following the streets three prior to the highway, then two after. The last led to the back gate of the school. It was less than 180 metres away from where she was last seen. How she had vanished from this spot was unbelievable.

"Police told me she was seen by the owner of number six. He was out sweeping his path; he swears it was her." Mrs Henderson was mopping up her tears with a tissue she held scrunched up in her left hand.

'No. 6 Elmer Road', I scribbled.

"Would you mind if I look in her room?" I asked nervously, expecting that this would bring on another waterfall of tears.

She didn't answer, only gestured me to follow.

It was at the end of the hall, furthest from what seemed to be the master bedroom.

Her room was typical of any 12-year-old girl's room. There were the latest dolls and plenty of drawing and craft material on a small table in the corner, including a do-it-yourself bead set, lid open with a half-finished project. "I thought it was best I leave it for her to finish when she gets back," said the mother from the doorway behind me.

"That's best," I said, not turning. I could feel a tear in the corner of my eye begin to well.

There were photos on the walls, selfies as the kids called them, of her and her friends pulling faces and making pig noses, tongues out.

"You know that I tidied this room but when I realised she was gone and wasn't coming home, I tried to get it back to just how she had left it. I think it's close but I know it's not how she had it. Is that the craziest thing you've heard? A mum wanting her daughter's room messy again?"

"No." My voice croaked. "It's not crazy, it's what I would want too." The tear dropped this time.

"I even say goodnight to her every night as I pass on my way to bed."

I had no response. I wouldn't know what I would do, so I just smiled gently.

The room was as if time had stopped and hadn't restarted.

It had become the waiting room, waiting for its child to return.

Chapter 17

Mikayla had grown so much in the time Austin had been away. It didn't show a lot in her size, but her maturity and confidence had changed a great deal. Sarah had done a great job with her. Austin couldn't believe she was 11.

They pulled up at the pancake parlour and sat at a table. The place was relativity empty but it was a week day after all. Austin assumed tomorrow would be a different story.

Beau watched them enter the restaurant, waited a few minutes and then entered himself. He sat at a table close enough to eavesdrop, but not close enough to raise suspicion.

Austin didn't usually eat a lot of junk food but he decided to let his strict diet go today. He ordered the steak with potatoes on buckwheat pancakes and salad.

His daughter ordered something called 'Alice in Wonderland', while his wife ordered Hawaiian crepes.

His wife had been talking his ear off, as if she had saved everything she had wanted to tell him. Now she was just opening the vault door and letting it all out.

He liked listening to her sweet soft voice. It was better than the heavy artillery fire he had become used to. She gave him all the family updates. Her sister Debbie was planning on leaving her husband, thought he was cheating on her with a floosy from the office.

Austin nodded and wondered how he had become so distant, so indifferent to problems that other people considered dire. To him this was incidental compared to the bigger troubles of the world.

Maybe it would have more significant if it affected him directly. His line of thought was broken as the phone in his pocket began to vibrate. Very few people knew this number; very few people knew he was in the Special Forces. To most people, he just said he was in the army. If anyone tried to find him, then they would end up receiving one word back: Confidential. Only the general could access his file. They kept the identity of all personnel in the Special Forces secret to avoid terrorist reprisals. You knew the people in your regiment and your superior, but that was it.

He swiped across the green answer button. "Austin, is that you?" the voice at the other end of the phone asked. A smile came across Austin's face, a smile his wife hadn't seen enough of lately.

"Yes mate, it's me, how are you?" Austin replied. "You still working in the Melbourne office?"

"I have a couple of days off next week. Would you like to catch up and go fishing at the lake?" the voice replied.

The 'lake' meant Beechworth, a small Victorian country town and once home to the now empty yet apparently haunted lunatic asylum. It was also famous for having the prison that had once housed the famous bushranger Ned Kelly. Marcus and Austin had done several fishing trips between tours.

"I'd love to but I've just got back from tour and I really want to spend some time with the family. Thanks anyway."

Beau's ears pricked up. Tour. Perhaps a navy or army man, he thought. That would explain his physique.

Austin was about to say his goodbyes when Sarah nudged her husband. "Go," she mouthed.

"Hang on a moment…what day were you thinking, Marcus?" Austin asked.

"Leave Monday morning, come back Tuesday night, stay the

one night," Austin repeated so that Sarah could hear. She nodded, waving her hand in agreement.

After a slight hesitation, Austin agreed. "Sounds great, but you're driving. What time are you picking me up?"

"Five am."

"Man, it's like being back in the army again!" Austin replied before hanging up.

"Are you sure you're ok with this?" Austin confirmed with Sarah.

"It's fine, you need to relax. About time you enjoyed life a little."

"But I just got back. I think I should be home. Mikayla will get upset."

Sarah grabbed her husband's hand. "She will be fine and so will I, it's only for one night. Go, enjoy, end of discussion."

"Ok thanks," Austin replied, smiling. He knew there was no point continuing a discussion he could not win.

Their meals arrived. Mikayla's Alice in Wonderland was fairy bread on pancakes with ice-cream and chocolate sauce. Way to dress it up, Pancake Parlour, he thought.

He dug into his potatoes that were covered in bacon bits, sour cream, cheese, and chives. They were divine and the steak was amazing. Was the food extra-good, or was it the fact it was one of the few decent meals he'd had in months?

Sure, the food in the army would get you by, but it was nothing like this.

Ahh, so you are an army man, Beau thought. That news aside, he had just learned that the girls would be alone Monday night. That would be his opportunity. He had everything he needed. He left the money on the table along with his half-eaten pancakes and headed out.

* * *

Beau received the one-line message with the address.

It had only taken a matter of minutes. Beau didn't know where or how they got the information and he didn't really care. He assumed the Priest had connections.

He decided to survey the area of his chosen child, but not until Sunday afternoon.

Sunday he would have more time to plan for Monday night. He had to get the planning right. The father was only away for one night.

He didn't want to upset the Ukrainian Monster any more than necessary. It sounded as though waiting a week for part one and then another week for part two was already upsetting him. Beau didn't want that but in this case, it couldn't be avoided.

Tales of the Monster had been rife throughout Port Phillip Prison. The main story told from prisoner to prisoner involved two 'employees' who had thought to turn State's witness and testify against the Monster's extensive operations across Australia.

Despite being under guard and with new identities, they were found one frosty winter's morning only weeks before the trial was due to commence. The four police guards were given Colombian neckties, while the informants were found in a burnt-out vehicle on a remote beach in NSW.

According to police, the fire had been set from the inside. They had been burnt alive. The van and its contents were then set alight from the outside while the cries of the burning men came from within.

The underworld said that the Monster had insisted on lighting the fire himself. He wanted to see their eyes as he struck the match in front of them.

Beau closed his phone and headed home. He needed some sleep before he was to make his delivery after work tomorrow and as he was visiting the Monster tomorrow night, he had to make sure he had his wits about him.

Chapter 18

Jake sat down in his usual spot for his Friday afternoon therapy session.

"So Jake, how have you been this week?" was the first question Salma asked.

"Same as always," Jake replied.

"You still having the dreams?" Salma asked.

"Yes," Jake replied.

"How many times did you have the dreams this week," she probed.

"Three out of seven."

"Jake, it's time I was frank with you. You've been coming here on and off for over 10 years and you increased your number of sessions a few months ago, but I can't help you if you don't tell me what the main concern is. Each week, you answer the questions, say you're ok and then give me nothing. If you want to start to heal, Jake, then you need to talk to me." Salma paused and waited for Jake to respond. She would wait until the end of the session if need be.

It took over three minutes before Jake finally spoke.

"The issue I keep coming back to is life. How do I plan for the future with Hayley when I know there are people out there who lie awake planning evil acts? Acts that I don't know about. Acts that I can't control..."

Salma interrupted, "I'm sure that in your line of work that is not a new feeling?"

"No, it's not, not at all, but before that, I assumed I might get hurt by doing my job, not that others would. Since the cabin I don't feel like I can protect them any more."

"Them?" Salma questioned.

"Hayley is having a baby. I guess she's about 10 or 12 weeks."

"You mean she hasn't told you?" Salma frowned.

"No, she hasn't, but she forgets that I'm a detective. She's afraid of how I'll take the news."

"And how will you take it?" Salma asked immediately.

"I'll be rapt," Jake said, "but how would I be able to protect them from all the evil? What if there's another Mason Belic? Brodie thinks there are hundreds of them roaming out there."

"Jake, you need to see the good in the world too. There are people out there like you making it safer for the rest of us. You'll never be able to control all the bad ones and you'll never be able to predict crimes. All you can do is your best, and you have to make your peace with that."

Jake sat deep in thought for a moment.

"I used to think fate was good or bad luck that just happened to people, but the whole Mason case made me realise that there are people who interfere with fate and send it in a whole new direction."

"But don't you see the flaw in your argument? You could say that about things that are not evil in the least. Let me give you an example. A driver of a truck leaves for work on a cold Wednesday morning. It's been raining with heavy thunderstorms most of the night before. The truck driver's power goes out. As a consequence, his alarm doesn't go off on time and while he isn't late by much, he leaves for work five minutes later than he would have if his alarm had gone off. Before you ask what this story has got to do with the price of fish, let me finish.

"Due to being late out the door, the driver decides to skip breakfast and go to McDonald's drive-through on his way to the first job. By the time he receives his meal, he's further behind schedule by two minutes."

She sipped her honey and lemon tea on her desk.

"As he's eating his McDonald's in the truck, his concentration is slightly distracted. He doesn't see the light change and goes through a red light. His truck hits a car crossing the intersection. He kills a mum and two children. Every day he blames himself. But the purpose of the story is that fate sometimes consists of several little things. If it hadn't stormed the night before, he would have left on time, he wouldn't have needed to stop. If the queue at the drive-through had been one car longer or one car shorter he would have either made the light or most likely not been the first at the lights. Sometimes there is no one to blame, some things just are, you understand?"

Salma paused, taking another sip. "Now, I agree there are those who plan evil acts, but that is why we need people like you. Without an army of good the world will fall into despair."

Jake nodded.

"Before you go home I want you to write a list of all the good qualities you have and all the reasons you became a police officer. Then I want you to go home and tell your beautiful wife Hayley why you are glad to be having a baby."

Jake nodded again.

This time, Salma thought she saw a glimmer of acceptance in his eyes.

Chapter 19

Mike received two texts from the Priest, each from different numbers. Both were received in the hour after he had left the Priest.

The first was a time to deliver the boy and collect the sum of $50,000. The delivery was set for tonight. Midnight. Usual place.

The second text was a number followed by: *Give warning. Confirm delivery next Saturday.*

It only took him 20 minutes of looking through the LEAP Victoria Police database to match up the number to a person. The photo that appeared on the screen was an individual called Neil Figal.

Figal had spent eight years in prison for three separate incidents. Two were for indecent assault of a minor and one was attempted kidnapping.

Good information for Mike to have.

He had to work today and tomorrow, but he had Sunday off. A good time to pay him a visit. A good time to deliver a warning.

Mike had managed to spend the evening meal at home with his wife and kids. It was a time he really enjoyed. His wife again questioned him about the morning phone call and what she thought she had heard.

"So who was killed?"

Mike knew the best way to lie was to mix it with a little truth. "The call this morning was from Father O'Riley. He was concerned that a young ward of the state who was sent back to his family had been killed. It was a rumour he had heard through the congregation. We looked into it. The young fella is doing fine and it was obviously some unfounded rumour. Jemma, remember you can't say anything. I could lose my job if you do."

Jemma nodded. "Well it's good to hear all is ok. That's the problem with a town this size. Too many rumours from bored housewives." She placed her hand on his and smiled.

"I need to head out tonight," Mike said. "I've had complaints from the council about people dumping rubbish at the cemetery. I told them I'd check it out myself."

"Can't someone working tonight do it?" Jemma asked, disappointment ringing with every word.

"It will only take an hour. I promise I'll be back by 1 at the latest."

Mike finished his dinner, bathed his twins, read them a story each, and managed to relax a little and watch some TV with his wife, although neither of them watched. It just provided background noise while Jemma discussed the latest events. The most important was Christmas, which was only three weeks away. What were they going to get the twins?

Chapter 20

Beau knew he would be on the road for the next 24 hours. He might have a sleep on the way back but until the drop was made, he would be wide awake.

He locked the shed from the inside and slid the train set from vertical to horizontal. He opened the trapdoor. He removed the red ladder and placed the two hook ends into the specially crafted holes to hold it.

The ladder reached all the way down except for the last 50 centimetres. Beau put on his standard joker mask and then headed down the ladder with a hessian sack tucked into the waistband of his grey tracksuit pants.

He approached Chloe's cell for the second time in days. "Looks like someone loves you. Your ransom has been paid. Put this on," he said, handing the sack through the bars. Chloe did as she was told. Soon she would be home: she just had to play it cool for a little while longer.

She pulled the hood over her head and darkness fell.

She heard the lock undo and the cell door open and an instant later a hand grasped her elbow.

She felt the rope tighten around her neck.

"Need to go up the ladder. Now I will guide you," he said to her. He placed her right foot on the first rung. "Now you move your other foot."

Chloe lifted her left leg but missed on her first two attempts, then clunk, the toe caught the metal rung. She managed to hold it there, preventing herself from slipping off.

She only missed two rungs for the rest of her trip up the ladder. The second and last miss hurt her the most. She had become over-confident and her knee clipped the rung above. She grimaced, not that Beau could tell; her hood hid her anguish.

Beau already had the rear doors of his van open. He ushered her into the back, sat her on the same side as the sliding door, on the floor, then looped and tied the rope to the welded metal hoop.

He folded the rope in two and threaded the loop through the metal hoop. Then he removed the rope from Chloe's neck and pulled the loop through, creating a slip knot before replacing the original loop back around Chloe's neck.

He locked both doors from the outside using the key. The windows in the back of the van had been highly tinted. He placed the ladder back and returned the train set to the original position. Down below was one boy, the one the media had called Scott.

Beau hit the road for the Monster at five minutes after 11 o'clock on Saturday morning.

Chapter 21

Tyler had cased the house several times over the past few weeks but he had decided that Monday would be his day. He had thought it best that he break in while the mum was out collecting the girl from school.

In the 15-minute window he had while she was out, he would have enough time to find and crack the safe, bag the loot, sneak out to the back door, jump the back fence, and sprint across the neighbour's back yard and down their drive. Their front fence was not only lower, but it was brick and easier to scale. Simple job.

If he got caught, what would be the worst that would happen to him? Another six-to 12-month stint in Port Phillip. He had decided to take a small weapon, not a gun but a butterfly knife. That way he would be protected if the big guy he had seen with the lady was more than a friendly visitor. He would at least be protected.

It couldn't be the husband, who according to Jack his cellmate was away at war. But he wanted to be prepared.

If he got this score he would be set for the next two years, according to his informant. The hardest part was getting rid of the goods but now that Jack had set that up with Mr Lee, he was good to go.

The way it worked was 60% went to Tyler and 40% went to Lee. Out of his 60%, he offered to put 10% in a safety deposit box for Jack until he was released.

Tyler put Rocky in the back of the car and cranked the window. He watched.

The man was still there. What the hell was going on? Who was this guy? Maybe he was on weekend leave, that could be a possibility, Tyler thought.

Tyler started his car. He had no choice; guy or no guy he was all set to do the job and come Monday he would ensure it was done.

Chapter 22

Beau arrived at two wrought-iron gates with one word written across them in big bold letters. 'PALANOK'.

To the right side of the gate was a long brick wall with built-in camera, buzzer and speaker. Sitting to the side of each gate was another camera. This was no ordinary house, it was something a king would live in, Beau thought. He only saw four other houses in the street. This was a very exclusive house in a very exclusive street. Beau guessed that each house was on acreage, most likely five-acre lots.

Beau had put on his Joker mask on arrival at the gates. Now he wound down the driver's side window and pressed the button. "Yes," the voice replied in a strong accent, which Beau assumed was Russian. He wouldn't have known the difference between a Russian and a Ukrainian. "I have a delivery for Mr Pavlychko." Beau was very glad the word 'Monster' didn't slip out of his mouth.

"Take off the mask," the voice replied.

"Can't do that, sorry. Does he want the delivery or not?"

* * *

In normal houses, the rumpus room was for the family to enjoy activities such as billiards, darts and table tennis. Igor Pavlychko's rumpus room was more often used for business and drinking.

Igor was known by the outside world, incorrectly, as a Russian crime boss with a quick temper prone and to violent rages. Usually resulting in someone's death. He was in fact a Ukrainian crime boss and there was a big difference: Ukrainians were more violent and less tolerant.

His three business associates, as he called them when introducing them to someone new, were the only three people on this earth he trusted. Too many other people wanted him dead, either to take over his business or to remove his business.

Alexi, the Monster's most senior guard and trusted ally at six foot eight, sat on the right side of the sofa. On the left sat Shevd. He was not as big as Alexi but still a big guy, at just under six foot four.

Shevd was a more skilled killer than a brute fighter like Alexi was. Alexi would kill you up close and personal while Shevd would kill you without your even realising he was near.

The man standing at the intercom was the Monster's third trusted ally, known only as Andrei. He had unknowingly saved the Monster from an assassination attempt by a rival drug cartel while they were in the Ukraine.

It was after this that the Monster had organised their lives in Sydney and set up the lifestyle they all wanted.

It was believed that prior to his chance meeting with the Monster, Andrei had been fighting the Russian invasion in his home province of Crimea. During the war with Russia, he killed over 65 Russian soldiers, leading fellow officers to name him Andrei after Ukraine's worst serial killer, Andrei Chikatilo.

When they had first arrived in Sydney, drugs were 90% of the business, with local prostitution filling the other 10%. The business was now more than drugs. Igor found he had a liking for prepubescent girls. He also discovered they were a hot item on the domestic and international markets, and they sold well, extremely well.

Over the past five years the trafficking part of the business had become half his business. He now employed several local suppliers;

the priest of a church in Ballarat was just one. Not only was the Priest a paedophile, he was a paedophile hungry for cash, and as a middle man you could make a lot of money. Igor also liked the fact that it removed him from the dirty work. For doing the dirty work, Igor paid the Priest well and sent through the occasional toy-boy to keep him happy. Igor knew the Priest had his own supply chain and he was sure that this Joker was at the top of it.

Igor made sure he never met the delivery people. He left that to his men to handle. Anyway, it was unnecessary for him to be there, and the fewer people who knew of his existence, the better. The last thing he wanted was to be fingered by some two-bit paedophile delivery man trying to downgrade his sentence.

* * *

"The Joker won't remove his mask. Do you want me to go take care of it?" Andrei asked.

"It's ok, send him in," said Shevd.

"We will teach him some manners; the boss wants his delivery," Alexi replied. Then he communicated back through the intercom, "Let him in."

The gates buzzed and began to open. Beau drove the van up the long, tarsealed driveway, lined with pine trees and gums. The brick fence, measuring a metre and a half with 50-centimetre wrought-iron spikes atop it, ran from the gates along the property boundary. Every four metres there was a brick pillar two metres high.

By the time Beau reached the homestead, he had driven over 500 metres. In front of the house, the drive opened up into a circular turnaround area, in the middle of which sat a large concrete fountain.

Two men in suits stood at the door at the top of the terracotta steps. They looked like secret service agents.

Beau slowed the van and shut off the engine. He unloaded the cargo, holding the rope and leading Chloe up the front stairs.

"Here to see…" he addressed the suits but before he could finish his sentence, the smaller of the two said, "Follow me." Then he opened the door and led the two of them inside the expansive home. The other suit stayed outside at the doorway.

The front door opened into a large tiled foyer. Off to the left was an expansive lounge with an open stone fireplace. To the right was what looked like a second lounge but there were only two chairs, both high-back Chesterfields, one opposite the other. To the right of each chair was a side table with an ashtray and a wooden box. In the middle of the two chairs was a chess table with some pieces lying face down on each side of the table, while others were placed across the board in various positions.

Beau did not understand the game or why anyone would waste their time playing. He found the combat missions on *Call of Duty* more fascinating and a lot more fun.

Beau followed the suit through a hallway past an in-house gym and into some type of games room.

Alexi stood. "Remove the mask," he said in a thick accent.

"I've been told to keep it on when dealing with clients," Beau replied calmly.

"Do you think we are clients? We pay the Priest, who I assume pays you. We are your bosses," Alexi said.

Beau paused, unsure what to do. This guy was huge, at least 6 foot 5, built like the Hulk. A real-life monster. Was he about to disrespect the Monster? He thought better of it. If push came to shove, he wouldn't be able to match him for brute force. He was sure this must be the notorious Monster. Made sense, he thought. The other two were too small.

Behind the Monster, two men were sitting on the sofa. One was about six foot while the second man was a little taller, maybe 6 foot 2.

One on three would be suicide.

His thoughts were interrupted by more talking; another voice, a stronger accented voice.

It was the six-footer who spoke.

"He told you to take off the mask. You don't want him to ask you again."

Beau had summed up the situation and thought it best to do as asked.

He removed the mask, revealing his bald head. The wisps of hair on the sides had fluffed up with sweat.

"Now show us your licence," Alexi demanded.

Beau frowned, but did as he asked.

"You have family?" Alexi asked.

"Just live with my mom, my deadbeat dad is dead, well, as far as I know he is."

"You work for the Priest, yes?" Alexi said, confirming his own statement.

Beau nodded.

"You realise two girls were required?" the other seated man asked.

Beau nodded again. "He just told me yesterday. I have a second one almost ready."

"This is not acceptable to us. You understand?" the seated man continued.

He stood for the first time, and put his hand around Beau's throat and began to squeeze. "I don't think you understand that we run this show."

Beau didn't reach for the gun tucked into the back of his pants. Pulling it out now would surely end his life.

"You come in here with your mask, and then you bring half the deal. Who the fuck do you think you're dealing with? We're not some drug-fucked paedophiles who don't care about their stock or its quality."

His grip stayed firm around Beau's neck. He was finding breathing increasingly difficult.

"I think it's time to send a message to the Priest. Maybe we could mail you to him. Would that send a message?"

Beau thought the guy was going for his gun, but instead he pulled a knife and pressed it against his eye.

"Wait," he said. "What I have is very special. One more week and she will be yours. I have a photo of her on my phone."

The guy withdrew his knife and took Beau's phone from him.

Shevd released his grip from Beau's throat and handed the phone to Alexi, who was towering over him. The man took the phone and disappeared down the rear of the home and returned a few minutes later. He replied with one word, but it wasn't a word Beau recognised.

It sounded like 'fin eel'; maybe it meant fine or finally. Beau couldn't be sure.

Who had he shown the photo to?

The big guy turned back to face Beau. He placed the phone back in his jacket pocket.

"You tell the Priest we pay $40,000 total. That girl must be here by Saturday night," Alexi said in his thick accent.

"Now, you don't deliver, I will see you personally and I will take your eyes and the eyes of anyone else close to you," Shevd butted in. "Do you understand?"

Beau nodded.

The man Beau took for the Monster had returned to his seat on the couch.

Shevd took two steps back and folded his knife and replaced it in his pocket.

Beau turned to head for the door.

"Where do you think you're going?" the man leaning next to the intercom asked.

"Show us the merchandise, we need to make sure she is what we ordered."

"I can't have her see my face."

"Don't worry about it, you will never see her again."

Beau removed the rope and then the hood and bowed his head. No matter what they said, the less the girl knew about him, the better.

The girl stood there barely clothed, mouth taped, face red and fringe wet with sweat.

She looked at the men sitting on the couch and immediately began to fret.

"You satisfied?" Beau asked without looking up.

The Monster nodded. Beau turned towards the front door; he had been here way too long already.

His delivery moved to follow him, arms outstretched, crying as Beau left.

Better the devil you know, hey girl, Beau thought to himself.

She would be desperate at the idea of being left with three guys who looked ready to have their way with her. Especially when one was the size of two.

After all, Beau had not touched her.

By the time Beau reached the door, they must have removed her tape because he heard her scream. The scream was followed by an almighty slap. Hand across her face, Beau thought.

Twenty minutes later, in his van heading for Melbourne, he was still fuming. "Fucking Russians," he muttered to himself. "Who do they think they are? Speaking to me like that." The guy with the knife hadn't fazed him. He had seen his type before. All threats, most likely a lousy fighter. He could probably beat him and the guy standing by the intercom at the same time, if it came down to a fight for life or death. But the big guy, presumably the Monster, there was no way. He was bigger than anything he had ever seen in jail.

Beau began to think about the following week. That delivery might be his last. They might decide to terminate him once they had the goods. He had to ensure he made the delivery but more importantly, his best chance of survival was to get the girl- at any cost.

Chapter 23

Mike collected the boy just after 11 pm. The delivery had been arranged for midnight at the cemetery, a secluded and private spot for such a transaction.

He had been waiting for 13 minutes, according to the clock on the dash. It was now 11.53 pm and soon the man who was due to collect would be here.

Mike could see the boy in his mirror. The glass privacy panel was down and the boy sat shaking, nervous. The Priest had left him in a pretty bad state. His eye-socket might be fractured, not to mention the abuse his body had taken. Mike doubted the Priest had restrained himself after knocking the boy out. He'd probably put him in that state during the rape and kept going until he was finished.

Lights in the distance shone through the front windscreen, breaking into Mike's thoughts. The car turned at the crossroad, disappeared for a few seconds and then the lights reappeared.

The driver stopped about 10 metres away from where Mike was parked. Mike exited his vehicle and stood next to the front right tyre. The boy remained in the back of the car.

The driver of the other vehicle turned off his engine and shut off his lights. He was wearing no mask; he was in a suit and tie, looking very professional. It was if he was here to buy a new car.

He looked like a typical paedophile, sleazy and slimy. The suit didn't fool Mike for a second. It just made him look like a crim ready to face the judge.

He was tall with thick black hair, narrow eyes, almost Asian in appearance. His nose was small and pointy, his frame thin and wiry. He was probably stronger than he looked, but there was nothing about him that concerned Mike.

"Evening," the gentleman said. "Are you wearing a Batman mask?"

"What I am wearing is none of your concern," Mike answered. "What *is* your concern and what should be your only concern is, do you have the cash for the purchase?"

"Yeah sure." The man in the suit reached into the passenger side of his vehicle and removed a large bag. He walked forward and handed it to Mike.

"Your licence?" Mike held out his hand.

The gentleman seemed stunned. "What do you need that for?"

Mike stared at him and repeated, "Your licence."

"I think I will just take my money back and leave," the gentleman said, ignoring Mike's second request for the licence. He reached for the envelope, his fingertips clasping the corners, before they were wrenched downwards towards his own wrist.

"I suggest you show me your licence, now," Mike said.

The gentleman laughed. "Is this hand thing you're doing supposed to hurt me?" he said, half-jokingly.

"No, it doesn't hurt, not until I do this." Mike pushed the elbow of the arm he was holding against his stomach and pushed his hand down, hard.

Excruciating pain travelled up the gentleman's arm.

"Now, are we getting that licence?"

The man nodded. "Ok, ok, please stop."

Mike released his grip a little, but not enough that he couldn't reapply it in an instant if he had to.

The gentleman handed his wallet to Mike, who removed the licence and took a photo of it with his phone, then handed it back.

"Now, Mr Ian Welling. I know where you live. If the money is not all there I will come for you. If at any time in the future you allow the boy to escape from whatever dungeon you and your rock spider mates plan to keep him in, call me immediately and we will find him."

Welling nodded.

"Don't wait. Call immediately," Mike emphasised.

"You won't have to worry. We have a room all set up for him. He will be secure," Welling replied.

Mike nodded. "Now I will get the boy and you will put him in your car. Under no circumstances do you remove the hood until I am gone. After that, it's up to you. Then you will go back to doing what you do and you will never see me again."

"Agreed," Welling said. He was all smiles now. Such a sleazy smile.

Mike removed the boy from the back of the Chrysler and led him out by the rope around his neck.

He handed the rope to Welling. "All yours."

He didn't like Welling much and given the opportunity, he would enjoy ending his life.

Chapter 24

After dealing with Welling, Mike was looking forward to issuing his warning to Neil Figal the next day.

Figal, French heritage, Mike guessed.

The drive to Preston was a good hour and a half.

He arrived in the middle of Sunday afternoon, unannounced.

At his doorstep.

He knocked, his four usual quick raps.

A small man arrived at the door dressed only in a pair of shorts and a dirty (once white, now grey) singlet.

"Yes?" the small man said with a slight touch of a French accent.

Mike considered Welling a sleaze, but he had nothing on this guy.

This guy was a lot smaller, a lot thinner, definitely on some sort of drug. Ice, most likely. His left arm was full of holes and his skin was scratched to pieces; his eyes were dark and recessed, half sunken into his skull; his teeth were yellow. He was dirty.

"You Mr Figal?" Mike asked.

"Maybe, who the fuck are you?" the short man asked.

His right shoulder was leaning against the door frame and his right arm was out of view. Mike knew he had a weapon concealed on the other side of the door. His first thought was a baseball bat, but he immediately dismissed that from his mind. He was too heavily involved in the drug scene for a bat to provide adequate protection. Mike's next thought was a gun, most likely a shotgun.

"I take it you're Figal. That shotgun you have beside the door won't help you. If you keep fucking around..."

Figal had no sooner raised the shotgun from the floor than he felt pressure on his ribs. "I'd show your other hand right now," Mike said. Figal released the gun and placed his right hand against the door jamb.

"The Priest has asked me to ensure you're ready to take delivery of the goods on Saturday night. He doesn't like to have orders cancelled. Now, I can see that you probably don't have the money to pay for the order, so here is what I will do for you. You will pay a cancellation fee of $5,000 within seven days. You will deliver it to me where and when I ask."

"I ain't giving you fucking 5k man, no way, tell the Priest to go fuck himself."

Mike didn't wait to see if he had finished speaking. He whipped the shotgun up from the man's ribs to his chin, clipping him on the jaw with the barrel.

Figal jolted backwards with the hit and probably would have fallen had Mike not had him by the belt with his left hand.

"You don't understand, Figal. I was told to come here and make sure you follow through with the order. Now, I'm giving you a break, I'm letting you off. If I go back and say you said 'get fucked', he will send me back. If I come back, there will be no more warnings, it will be the end you. So I am giving you an out and the out is $5,000."

"What, you think I'm stupid? You think I won't just move once you leave? You would never find me again."

With the gun firmly pressed against Figal's ribs, Mike reached into his back pocket and flashed his badge. "I bet you're on parole and I bet if you run I'll find you."

Figal couldn't believe that a crooked cop was shaking him down. What the fuck.

"Now how much of that can you pay today?"

"I don't have any money, I swear, I just bought a hit," Figal answered.

Mike knew this was a lie. If he had just bought a hit, it would be running through his veins, right now. He figured he was coming off a three-day bender and was almost ready to buy again. He would be cashed up.

"I will be in contact with you in seven days. You better have the money when I ask for it or there is nothing I can do for you."

Mike removed the shotgun from his ribs and pivoted as if he was about to turn away, then without warning, his pistol came down. It was fast and ferocious. This time Mike wasn't holding him to protect the fall. Figal stumbled backwards and fell into the hallway. Mike stepped through, took him by the throat and whipped him again. He was out.

Mike rifled through his pocket and found his buyer's roll: $1,700 in total, all in hundreds. He took the shotgun and left the residence, closing the door behind him.

It was a quick call to the Priest on the drive home, only a matter of a few sentences. Most of his calls to him were like this.

"He has no money. He's agreed to 5k, I have $1700 with me."

"What do we do with the goods?" the Priest asked quietly.

"We could always get $3,000 for a weekend with the Judge. Holidays are coming up and the Judge is always looking for some play toy to take up to the lake house."

"But then what do we do with it?" Still quiet, almost whispering.

"Maybe we give it to the Monster, to try and smooth over the relationship. He could always use it on the plantation," Mike suggested.

"Sounds like a lot of trouble for us, Mike. Might be time to just cancel the order."

Cancel the order was code for killing the child. The Priest very rarely resorted to this. However, occasionally things went wrong and loose ends needed to be tidied up. Mike had cleaned up a lot of the Priest's loose ends in the past, but he had planted enough evidence over time to ensure he wouldn't be the only one going down if anything ever went wrong. As his dad had always told him, don't paint yourself into a corner. His other saying was, don't burn your bridge while you're standing on it.

"I think we can avoid cancelling the order. Five thou isn't a bad return, plus we need to gain some bonus points with Monster."

"All right, but if M doesn't want it, you'll need to cancel the order."

With that, the call went dead, and Mike continued on his drive back home to his wife and twin boys.

Chapter 25

As always, Marcus was punctual and reliable. He arrived at exactly 3 am so that they would get to Beechworth at 6, be out on the water by 6.30, and be talking about Afghanistan and the boys by 6.45.

Fishing had never been the purpose. When he and Austin had first started going on trips to Beechworth, it was to relax between tours, to try and forget all that they had witnessed, as well as spend time with their mates away from the war zone.

If war had taught them one thing it was mateship. It was part of their creed to 'never leave a man behind'. They had respect for one another and they had their backs. That was what made the SAS so strong.

Today though, it was just the two of them. Marcus had been injured in the last tour and sent home and Austin had now retired. They had been best mates in the battalion. They had gone through their induction training together and been on all their tours together. The only tour they had not gone on together was Austin's last.

During the three-hour trip to Beechworth, they discussed everything from politics to music, anything except the war. Their conversation centred on Marcus' new line of work with ASIO, Australia's secret service.

"So, what is it you do exactly?" Austin asked.

"Because I know you understand the meaning of 'classified', I can tell you," Marcus answered. "I'm a glorified computer hacker for the government. My technical title is 'security analyst'. I follow suspected terrorists, networks, Facebook accounts, bank accounts, religious leaders, money trails, weapon purchasers. All online. I also do phone taps, but they're getting smarter, using handwritten notes to pass messages now, and I can't hack a note. But that's just the terrorist side of things. I also work on government security. Making sure government sites are secure. The last thing we want is some nutter hacking into the prime minister's travel itinerary."

"So you can look into anyone's personal files?" Austin asked.

"If you give me a name, I can give you everything on them. Same with an address or a licence plate." Marcus continued, "It's different from the war. Not only are we trying to fight them over there, we're now trying to quell the uprisings over here as well."

Austin nodded. He didn't want to go into a discussion about Marcus' injury. The topic was still raw. He could see that Marcus had a severe limp and thought it would remain that way for the rest of his life.

Marcus had arranged a boat, rods and equipment to be ready at the cabin upon their arrival and in accordance with his plans, they were out fishing at 6.45 am. The sun was rising, the wind was cool without being cold, and the temperature was pleasant.

The water was calm and their boat hardly broke the surface as it floated on the lake. Rays of sunlight bounced off the water. The lines dangled, free of nibbles. Not that capturing anything made any difference; they would put it back, regardless. The wee craw fishing lures were not working today.

Marcus sat at the bow while Austin was at the stern, one arm resting on the throttle handle. Marcus passed him an egg and bacon roll and a cup of coffee. The coffee was hot and the egg and bacon roll still warm. Both went down with delight.

It took longer than the usual 15 minutes, but the war conversation raised its head eventually. It was Marcus who said, "In case I haven't said it enough, thank you," he began.

"You don't need to thank me; you would have done the same," Austin replied.

"I know, but if you hadn't come back for me, they would have killed me," he reiterated. "Do you have dreams about that day?" he asked Austin.

"Sometimes," Austin replied, staring out at the lake. "Sometimes I dream that by the time I kill them and get to the Humvee, it's on fire and I can't get you out."

Marcus sipped his coffee, "Sometimes I dream you don't come back and I'm stuck there and I burn to death. Luckily, neither of those things happened. You came back."

"Sorry I was so long. I had to kill six Afghani soldiers to get to you. It wasn't easy, you know. But you never had to worry, you knew I was coming back, we were both coming home or we were both dying there, I was never leaving," Austin answered.

"Excuses, excuses," Marcus joked.

"How is the leg coming along?" Austin asked.

"I'll have the limp forever, but as the doctors say, a limp is better than no leg. I was lucky. Had we driven over the antipersonnel mine directly, I would have lost both my legs. So in a way, I'm lucky we just clipped it," Marcus replied.

"You seen much of the others?" Marcus asked.

"No. All of them except Leeroy were going back. Like us, Leeroy retired. I think he lives up north Queensland, so I doubt we'll get to see him much. The others should be back by June, so we'll need to plan another trip after that. By then, it'll have been 18 months since we were all together," Austin replied.

The line on Marcus' rod began to buzz as it was taken by something. Marcus quickly placed his coffee and roll down to attend to his possible catch.

They spent until lunchtime fishing, then went for a round of golf. It was a relaxing day and it was not until the third hole that Austin realised how much he had needed this. Sarah had obviously seen that.

Their lunch was just a quick bite at the clubhouse between the front nine and the back nine.

Their real meal was tonight. It was a prime Angus T-bone weighing in at one-and-a-half kilos. Dubbed 'the Texan', it was named after the US State of Texas. It came with baked potato and a side salad. If you ate it all, the rest of your table ate at half price. Both Marcus and Austin had never finished the meal. However, tonight could be the night.

First, they had to finish their lunch and work up their appetite before they tackled the Texan.

Chapter 26

Tyler had planned to wait until the lady of the home went to pick up her daughter at 3 pm from school. This trip usually took 15 minutes, but half an hour if they went to the shops after. He had not seen the man at all today. He must have gone back on tour, just a weekend stopover perhaps.

He would need all of the 15 minutes to cut the cameras and disable the alarm, locate the safe, and get the jewels.

The gates opened. The lady's Mercedes drove out, turned down the street and drove out of view.

Countdown.

Tyler drove around to the back of the home to the neighbouring street. He parked two houses down from the target's rear neighbour. He knew they would be at work and there was no gate to scale to enter the property. They had an open drive that led directly to the back yard. The drive was empty, just as it was supposed to be. Tyler pulled down his balaclava, scaled the back fence and sprinted across the back lawn. He was at the back wall of the house within seconds. He cut the two lower cameras with ease. It was the higher ones that would prove the challenge. He had to do them from the inside. He went to the rear laundry door, placed the bump key inside, a simple trick he had learned on the inside. He had bump keys for four and five tumbler locks. He tried the four-tumbler lock key, placed it in the lock and hit and turned. Nothing. Hit and turn, nothing. Hit and turn, nothing.

He tried the five-tumbler key. Placed it in the lock, hit and turned, nothing. He did it again with the same result. What was he doing wrong?

This was eating into his tight schedule.

"Come on Tyler," he muttered to himself.

Still nothing.

Then he remembered the O-ring. It stopped the key from bobbing in and out. He fumbled through his pocket. How could he have forgotten it? His fingers clasped it and he quickly removed it and slid it down over the key.

He stayed with the five-tumbler key already in his hand, placed it in the lock and followed the same steps as before. Bang. He hit the key with the end of the screwdriver and turned the lock. The door opened.

Now the race was on. He had to turn off the alarm. He had 30 seconds. It had already started beeping the second the door opened. Beep, beep, slow and regular at first. Tyler closed and locked the back door behind him. He sprinted towards the internal access door to the garage.

There it was, right on the wall where it was supposed to be. Now to enter the code. The master code, 1739, the four corners, starting top left, finishing bottom right.

Beep, beep, beep, the alarm continued, now beeping a little faster. "Fuck!" Tyler hissed.

He knew the prisoners had been fucking with him. Lies mixed in with half-truths. Some type of initiation, he thought.

He was going to go down for this if he didn't get out and soon. The alarm was about to sound any second. He headed back towards the laundry door, then stopped. Lies with half-truths. Was the safe a half-truth? Tyler changed direction quickly and headed for the stairs. Beep, beep, beep, very fast now. Soon the siren would scream out. He headed for the master bedroom, removed the screwdriver from his pocket, ran into the back of the robe. There it was. The box that sent the signal from the alarm to the security firm. Tyler stood on a suitcase and reached above the shelf. He cracked the case in one quick motion.

Once while studying videos on bump keys, he had come across how to deactivate and reset an alarm. Tyler removed the case and pulled the red wire. The alarm sounded for an instant before being silenced. He looked for the safe in the bottom of the robe. Nothing, another fucking lie. Then something shiny grabbed his attention. It was a bolt. The safe had been bolted here to the floor once upon a time but must have been moved. But to where?

He checked his phone; 3.11 pm. Only four minutes before her return. He was way behind and time seemed to be running extra fast.

Tyler raced down the stairs, nearly tripping on the step third from the top, regaining his balance by grabbing the railing. A vision of him lying in a pool of blood at the bottom of the staircase when the wife came home flashed through his mind. He headed straight to the study. He looked behind a painting of a colonial style picture of early settlers. No good, just wall.

Where would it be? Why would they have moved it?

Tyler's phone beeped, telling him 3.13 pm. Two minutes until her return.

The bolt flashed into his mind again. What had the safe been bolted to? Chipboard. Why move it? Too easy to pick up and take away. Needed to be bolted to something stronger. Concrete. It had to be here somewhere, but where?

The floor was all smooth, nothing bolted to it.

Tyler looked under the desk. Nothing, just a filing cabinet to the right-hand side.

Then he looked at the desk and cabinet again. The desk was deeper than the cabinet. Something was behind it.

Tyler moved the cabinet, just sightly, so he could see behind it.

Jackpot! There it was, bolted onto the concrete slab through the carpet. Wouldn't be able to pick this one up. Good thing he knew how to crack it, but that would take time, time he didn't have now. On cue, his alarm sounded at 3.15 pm. He could hear the gate moving. She was back, right on schedule. *She* was on schedule but he was behind.

He was out of time and empty-handed.

What was he going do now?

Leave with nothing?

He had an idea, but he had to act fast.

He needed to reconnect the alarm and then get up into the manhole. Tyler slid the cabinet back to its original position and sprinted up the stairs. He reconnected the wire, tapped the cover back on with the handle of the screwdriver. He could hear the alarm beeping as if it had just been set. It was counting itself down 30 seconds and then it would be rearmed.

He made sure everything looked undisturbed, as best he could in the limited time he had.

The garage door had opened and the engine was switched off and they were coming inside.

"Wait honey, we need to check the mail," Tyler heard as he lifted the lid of the manhole. He stood on a shelf with bath towels and pulled himself up into the roof cavity. As he dropped the lid back into place, the alarm sounded its final beep.

He let out a huge sigh of relief.

The stroll to the letterbox gained him only 30 seconds but he needed every one of them.

Now all he had to do now was wait. Wait until they were asleep, then he would have all the time he needed to crack the safe.

Then an awful realisation came to him.

He had left his screwdriver in the master bedroom. He couldn't leave here without it. Even though he was wearing gloves, he had used the screwdriver without them. His prints would be all over it.

* * *

Beau sat inside his van waiting for an hour to pass since the last light, in the top right corner of the home, went out at 11.30 pm. No doubt the master bedroom. It had only been out for half an hour. He had to be patient a little longer. He had not seen the man from the movies, so this confirmed he had gone away, and that was a good thing.

His plan would go to perfection and the girl would be his. He had to get her, otherwise the Monster would end him, he was sure of it. Now that the Monster had seen a photo of her, he could not substitute her for another if this went wrong.

Beau had done his research on her house. The back way was the easiest but there were cameras. He would have to put his paintball skills to the test.

His plan was simple: first, cut the power. Most cameras stopped recording once the power was cut. Very few had an uninterruptable power supply attached. But he had to get to the house itself in order to cut the power. Next, he would need to hit all four back cameras with orange paint from his paintball rifle. It was state-of-the art, had cost him almost $1,500, the infrared telescopic sight a large chunk of the cost.

Beau snuck past the car parked in the drive directly behind the girl's house. It was hard to use the scope while he was wearing his joker mask, but he managed it.

He stood on the fence, aimed up at the bottom camera but noticed the cable was hanging. It had been cut. He scanned across to the other lower camera. Same deal, cable cut. He scanned up to the top camera. The top one was intact, as was the one on the other side. Possibly they'd had an attempted break-in and hadn't yet had them fixed. Didn't matter, wasn't his problem, just made his job easier. Only two shots needed. He doubted the rifle would be powerful enough to break the camera. He only needed the paint to cover the lens.

He scanned again, his finger resting against the metal trigger. He slowed his breathing and squeezed. The paint ball flew, hit its target and splattered paint over the camera. There was no crack. Nothing broke. Everything was going to plan. He scanned the telescope across the home and repeated the process. Fifteen seconds later, he was over the fence and heading for the back door.

With his rifle slung over his left shoulder, Beau used his screwdriver to apply pressure on the lock, while with his right shoulder he pressed against the door. He was having trouble seeing. The mask kept slipping. With all the cameras disabled, he removed the mask and placed it in his back pocket.

Soon enough, the lock popped and the metal lock and screws fell to the floor, clunking on the tiles of the laundry floor as they landed.

Chapter 27

Sarah always took a couple of nights to get used to sleeping by herself again.

Every time Austin left for duty, the week after was always the toughest.

The clunk downstairs immediately startled her from whatever light sleep she had managed to find. She sat upright, frozen, listening for the slightest sound.

Nothing.

A stair creaked ever so slightly and she knew someone was in her house. Someone was coming up the stairs.

Her thought immediately turned to Mikayla. Her bedroom door was shut, she was hopefully asleep. Sarah grabbed her phone and called the police. She hopped out of bed and hid in her wardrobe, hoping she could tell the police what was happening without being heard.

"Police Emergency," the voice on the line answered.

"Someone is in my house."

"Address ma'am?"

Sarah replied as quietly as she could.

"A patrol car has been dispatched, ma'am. It's on its way. Do you know where the person is, ma'am?"

She listened. Nothing. "No, I'm not sure."

She stood in her wardrobe shaking, listening for any sound, any clue as to the intruder's whereabouts. Then there was another creak, not a step this time. This time it was a door opening. The door to her daughter's room.

She could hide no longer, she had to act. Phone still in hand, she turned to leave when a silver object on the shelf caught her eye. Before she had assessed what it was, or even thought about who it belonged to, the screwdriver was in her hand and she was heading out of the bedroom.

Her daughter's scream filled the whole house. It was only one but by god, it was a good one. A scream to be proud of!

By the time Sarah was on her landing, she could see a man descending the stairs carrying Mikayla in a bear hug with one big paw over her mouth.

"Put her down and get out of my house!" she yelled and ran towards the intruder.

She threw herself at the man as he reached the last step, grabbing at his jacket. Her phone flew from her hand, coming to rest at the bottom of the stairs. Now she had dropped her phone and lost her grip on the intruder. The intruder was heading towards the back door. This was no robbery. This was a kidnapping.

Mikayla tried desperately to free herself from her captor's grip.

After a failed first attempt, Sarah jumped on her daughter's attacker as he neared the back door.

The attacker held the girl in his left hand and reached over his left shoulder with his other hand. He grabbed the woman by her hair and rammed her face and forehead into the back of his head, like a reverse head butt. After three quick reverse butts, he felt the woman slide off his back.

Beau turned to see her slumped on the floor, screwdriver still in hand. She had seen him so he had no choice.

"Don't hurt my mummy!" Mikayla screamed as he raised Sarah's limp unconscious body up off the tiled floor. Beau answered the child's screams with a back-hander that sent her sprawling across the room. The sound of the leather glove against her skin ricocheted throughout the room.

Mikayla heard her mum scream and then thud to the floor, the screwdriver she was holding now embedded in her throat. The man was still holding her mum. What had he just done, had he killed her?

"Mum!" she screamed, before his big paw covered her mouth again. "Scream again and I will kill you. Do you understand?" he said carefully, as he moved his hand down from her mouth and placed it firmly around her throat. "I will snap your neck just like a chicken."

Her tears turned to anger. Her mum was dead and this man was taking her. But why? Was this a dream, a nightmare? She would wake soon.

Wake up, she begged herself, but the nightmare continued. The big guy flung the back door open and rushed out into the night air. It was cold. The wind was blowing and it was icy. For a big guy he was really moving. She could see her house getting further away. As he ran faster, she bobbed around in his bear-like grip.

They reached the back fence and before she knew what was happening, she was airborne and free-falling. The fence came and went under her as she flew through the air. She let out a small scream that was cut off when she thudded to the earth. Before she had even regained her breath, she was back inside the bear grip.

Now he was sprinting down the street and they approached a white van. He removed his hand from her mouth and threw her inside. Sliding along the metal floor, she crashed to a stop when she slid into a wire mesh frame. The door slammed behind her.

Seconds later, they were moving, fast at first, sharp corners. She rolled from one corner of the van to the other as the van skidded sideways.

This was no dream, she had just been kidnapped and her mum had been killed. Where was he taking her?

She couldn't see anything. Everything was blacked out including the view to the front driver's cabin. She tried to count the streets.

She started out well until she took a tumble and then missed a few after that.

Twenty minutes later they were still driving, at normal speed now. She could hear the bells of a train crossing. A few seconds later she could hear the train pass, then the bells stopped and they continued driving. Soon after, they came to a complete stop and the engine was cut.

The driver's door opened and closed. Soon he would come for her, or so she thought. She heard a loud dragging sound followed by slamming, as if metal had hit metal.

She moved towards the back doors of the van, slowly, so her movement wouldn't be noticed, if he was still around. The steel mesh was also on the inside of the van doors. There were two large metal plates where the handles should have been. She assumed they were there so no one could open the back doors. But she would still try. She had to.

She placed two fingers in through the metal mesh and wiggled them down behind the metal cover. She could feel what she thought was the plastic door handle but she couldn't get her fingers to the edge to pull.

She was trapped.

* * *

The girl's scream startled Tyler, who had drifted off to sleep in the roof cavity. His watch was set to vibrate at 1 am, but the scream beat him to it.

The cries of "Put her down and get out of my house!" brought him back to reality.

Who else was in the house?

Maybe the man had returned, a custody dispute perhaps. He reached for his butterfly knife, which was in his back pocket. It was hard to grip with the gloves so he took his right glove off and threw it into the crawl space of the roof.

Maybe the husband or ex-husband had come back for the girl.

Whatever it was, the commotion had stopped and he had to get out of there as fast as he could.

Tyler raised the lid of the manhole and peeped out. No one was there, no one he could see anyhow. He waited a few seconds and peeped again and again. Still no one. He lifted the lid enough to slip out. There were no sounds. From the top of the staircase he could see a mobile phone on one of the lower stairs glowing. It was still on, still calling someone. As quietly as possible, Tyler stepped down slowly, taking care not to use the rail so as not to leave fingerprints with his right hand. Was there still someone in the house? As he came to the phone, he saw the number on the display. Triple zero. The police would be on their way. He had to get out of here now!

From the bottom of the stairs he could see the tiled hall that led from the front entrance, and the back dining and kitchen where he had entered. Slumped in the middle of the tiles directly in his path was a body, the mum's body.

Tyson's ears pricked up at the sound of distant wailing sirens. He could study the scene no more, he had to leave and leave now. Tyler darted around the body and out through the open rear door. He sprinted across the back yard as if he was in the trials for the Olympics. He had never run so fast. His heart felt as if it was going to explode. He was anxious, sweaty and dismayed at what had unfolded. What the fuck had just happened?

It wasn't until 20 minutes later when he finally felt comfortable with the distance he had put between himself and the property that a shocking thought hit him for the second time that night. Like a baseball bat to the nuts. He had left the screwdriver at the property. He then reflected on the scene: a screwdriver had been protruding from the mum's neck. Couldn't have been, could it?

"Fuck!" he screamed, bashing the dash of his car and rocking back and forth in his seat. "Fuck, fuck, fuck!" he continued screaming.

Chapter 28

Nothing worse than being woken by a ringing phone at 3 am.

"Hello?" I answered.

"Sorry to wake you, buddy, but we have a homicide." Jake's familiar voice.

"What do you mean 'we'?" I asked. "I'm on cold cases, not homicides."

Jake took no notice. "They believe it's a child abduction gone wrong."

I sat bolt upright. "What do you mean an abduction gone wrong?" I asked.

"It's not clear yet but early reports are a girl may have been taken from her room. I thought you would want to get involved early. It may be related to the others," Jake replied. "I'll text you the address. Get there as soon as you can."

"I'm leaving now," I answered, already half dressed.

Jake had hung up.

Being in Kew, Jake would have got there first, but not by much. When I arrived, several officers showed me through to the rear of the property where the crime scene had been established.

I pulled out my torch and my notepad. It hadn't taken me long to establish my own system when examining a crime scene. Although it sometimes went against standard protocol, I liked to walk myself through the scene before getting all the information from the offi-cers. That way my first impression was mine, not someone else's.

Gloves, torch and notepad, my tools of trade. The torch was

slimline and lightweight, so I could hold it under my arm if I had to. The first thing I noticed when escorted to the rear of the property by the uniforms was the surveillance system. There were four front cameras, one side camera and four rear. The rear ones had been painted with orange paint, and on the ground was a skin of paint. I asked the uniforms to pick it up and bag it, have it ready for examination. There were other skins near the other cameras as well.

When I examined the cameras, I could see that the cables to the two lower ones had been cut at the connection point. When I got to the door, it was already being dusted for prints. They had collected the broken pieces of the lock for individual testing at the lab.

Inside a lady lay in her nightgown, lifeless on the cold tiles. The positioning of her feet was of particular interest to me. It looked like 'dead man fall', which meant she was dead before she hit the ground. Her legs had crossed on the way down. This could have been because she'd died suddenly. I was guessing she had been beaten, lifted up, stabbed in the throat, and then dropped.

I made my way to the bottom of the stairs. Jake was questioning a neighbour, with a uniformed officer taking the statement. We exchanged nods and continued with our tasks. There was an evidence marker, number six, sitting next to a phone on the second bottom step. I'd noticed evidence markers up to 27 as I passed the rear doors and was sure there were more yet to be found and marked.

I walked wide of the phone and headed up the stairs.

At the top, three doors were ajar, the closest a girl's room. At the landing end of the staircase was the master bedroom.

I started there. I wanted to leave the girl's room until last, because that was where I would need to focus most of my attention. The master bedroom looked like any other. While the bed sheets were messed up, there didn't appear to be any evidence of a scuffle in this room.

I walked through to the en suite. All was neat and tidy; again, no signs of a struggle. I looked into the wardrobe on my way past. It looked normal enough. I noticed the alarm box was on the wall above the robe shelf. I had almost walked past when I noticed a scratch and a dent.

Better to be safe than sorry. I'd hate to miss a vital clue. I waved my torch over it. Definitely scratched on the lip. It could have been done on installation, I supposed. There was also an indent under the scratch, which made me wonder if the lid had been tampered with. I called down to a uniformed officer to send the fingerprints unit up once they had finished with the door, and then headed to the girl's room. The night light was still in the on position although with no power, there was no glow. The doona still covered most of the bed. I touched the bed. Hell, it was still warm.

I sat on the corner of the bed. Who would do this? I wondered. Was it the same person responsible for the other three kidnappings? If so, this was a big concern. He had become desperate. While the others had been taken from the streets in broad daylight, this one was worse because it showed me the criminal had evolved from opportunistic to targeting his prey. Tonight he had shown he was willing to do whatever it took to acquire his prey.

If he was targeting them, I needed to know how. Maybe he was a neighbour. As soon as I thought of that possibility, I discounted it. It was unlikely that an unemployed man who took kids from the street in a van would be able to afford to live in such an affluent area.

Which led me to wonder, how had he targeted this one? Maybe this was different from the others. Maybe this was a kidnapping or a ransom ploy gone wrong. Whatever it was, it was too soon to try connecting them. I had to find some stronger evidence before I could consider them related.

I sat looking at the room. It was now another waiting room, a room waiting for the return of the person who brought everything here to life. Nothing upset me more than seeing a child's room full of possessions lying idle. Barbies sat in their house and their cars, soft toys on a shelf above the foot of her bed, clothes were laid out on a seat, obviously ready for the day ahead. The lamp that would normally bring the cut-out characters' shadows to life, dancing on the walls as the shade slowly spun around the globe, stood still.

I sat there staring into emptiness. I was praying not to a god but to a higher being. My prayer wasn't for me, it was for time and more of it. It suddenly registered that I had better speak to Jake and get a full briefing.

Halfway up from the bed, I saw it. How had I missed it? How had they all missed it?

Maybe, like me, they hadn't thought of it. I walked out of the girl's room, half stooped over, not taking my eyes off it.

In the linen press there were towels strewn over the floor.

"Officer, bring me a chair." I switched my flashlight on and examined the messy linen closet. I worked the torch up. The lid of the manhole was three-quarters of the way off. The section not obscured by the cavity looked as if it had dirty marks, maybe prints. I shone the torch across the cupboard from celling to floor. The two bottom shelves had dirty marks on them, maybe from a shoe. An officer arrived with a chair. I didn't want to disturb anything that had been left behind. I stood on the chair and looked inside the cavity. It was dusty but empty. No girl, but someone had been up here recently.

I asked Forensics to make sure they searched the roof space immediately, just in case she was there. It was standard procedure to check the whole scene for a missing child, yet there was no harm in stating the obvious.

Forensics had finished at the rear door. The lock had been torn right off. Springs and metal lay across the tiles, every piece marked with a numbered cone detailing its evidence number.

I stepped through the doorway and headed to the back of the home. It was dark. I could see the cameras but only just. I shone my flashlight on the back wall of the house. The cameras were covered in orange paint.

I walked across the yard to the back fence. Luckily, the rungs were on this side. I stood on the bottom rung and looked into the neighbour's yard and saw what looked like orange casings. I shone my torch across the top of the fence. There was some orange paint on one of the palings, and what appeared to be a strand of green hair.

I called an officer over, and asked him to wake up the neighbour and ensure the back yard was secure until the forensic technicians had a chance to completely check the scene.

* * *

Jake had seen all he needed to have a fair understanding of what had happened here tonight. Someone had broken in to rob the place and had been confronted. That confrontation had ended in Sarah Campbell's death. Her daughter either witnessed the attack and had been taken to be disposed of later, or was taken in order to extort money from the family.

It seemed to Jake that the intent of the home invasion was more likely that of robbery than of kidnapping. Robberies had been rife in the area over the last few months.

Jake had finished speaking with the neighbours on both sides. Neither had seen or heard anything out of the ordinary and both described the victim as a very nice and easy-going neighbour.

Only one of the neighbours had met the husband. Apparently, he was away a lot with work. Apparently, he had been back all weekend but no one had seen him since Sunday night.

Jake decided it was best to try and contact him, find out where he was and what his movements had been over the last day or so.

The neighbour told him the husband's name was Austin.

Jake cycled through Sarah's recent calls and found a call from 7.30 Monday night only five minutes long, an outgoing call to Austin.

Jake's thumb hovered over the number before pressing on it. It rang three times before it was answered. "Babe, is everything all right?" the half-panicked, tired voice asked.

"Is this Austin Campbell?" Jake asked.

"Yes, what are you doing with my wife's phone?"

Jake paused. "My name is Detective Jake Miller. I'm with Homicide. We were called to the property by your wife. Upon our arrival we have found her deceased. I am sorry."

There was a stunned silence on the other end.

"I am ringing to ask, is your daughter with you? She's not here at the house and we're desperately trying to ascertain her whereabouts," Jake said.

Austin was clearly upset. "No, she's not with me, I'm away on a fishing trip with a mate. We're up in Beechworth and it'll take me over three hours to get back. I'll be there as soon as I can."

"We'll still be here when you get back. I can organise a police car to drive you back. Save you driving at this time if that helps you out at all?"

"It's ok, my mate will drive, we'll leave now."

Jake hung up the phone.

"Listen up people: we have a missing child believed kidnapped. Please put out an APB for her." He moved over towards me. "Well, if what he's telling us is true, he didn't do it. He's away on a fishing trip up state. They're checking the phone towers to confirm he is where he says he is and we're having both calls examined; the call I just made and the one his wife made at 7.30. He would have had time to get here and kill her but not enough time to get back."

"How did he sound?" I asked.

"Genuinely distraught," Jake replied. "What type of person does this, Brodie, what type of person steals a child from the safety of their bedroom?"

"Clearly whoever did this was desperate. But we may be looking at a different offender to that of the other kidnappings. The others were more opportunistic, don't you think?" I asked.

"It appears that way," Jake replied. "Forensics have a lot of work to do here. Feel like a coffee? I have something important I need to tell you."

Concerned and quizzical, I accepted.

Chapter 29

When Marcus woke to thumping on his bedroom door, he instinctively knew something was wrong. He opened the door to a man who looked void of all life, whereas hours earlier, he had seemed full of life.

Austin had been crying. "Mate! What's wrong?" Marcus asked.

"Sarah's been killed and Mikayla's missing."

"What? How?" Marcus asked, trying to register what he was being told. "Oh my god," were the next words out of his mouth. "What happened?"

"I don't know, I just had a call from Homicide. They were called to my home and found Sarah dead and Mikayla missing. I really need to head back home now, if that's ok."

"Of course, no problem," Marcus answered, already throwing things into his duffel bag. "Meet at the car in two mins," he said.

Austin nodded and headed back to his room.

It took Marcus a little longer than two minutes. By the time he got to the car, Austin was already waiting.

"Mate, it's raining; why didn't you just wait on the porch?"

Austin shrugged. "Let's just go."

They drove in silence. Every time Marcus looked over to speak, he noticed Austin blankly staring out the window into the darkness.

An hour in, Austin finally spoke. "I'm going to find who did this and kill them and anyone else who had anything to do with it."

"Buddy, don't go doing anything stupid, they might find Mikayla, she will need you, now more than ever," Marcus replied.

"Can you get me my kit?" Austin asked, ignoring Marcus' warning.

"Don't go down that path, now is not the time to be making these decisions, let the police do their job," Marcus said, almost pleading.

"Can you get me my kit?" Austin repeated.

Marcus nodded.

"I can organise for it to be sent to Melbourne for reassignment and just not reassign it."

"Good, get it done. The sooner the better, I don't have much time. They better not hurt Mikayla." Austin returned his focus to the dark emptiness outside the window.

Marcus knew if Austin had been at home, Sarah would be alive and Mikayla would be asleep in her bed. Marcus knew it was just cruel fate, but he couldn't help feeling responsible. He was the one who had pressed Austin to go on the fishing trip.

Marcus turned slightly towards him. "I am sorry man. It's my fault, you should have been there. I took you away on this dumb fishing trip."

Without turning, Austin answered, "Don't blame yourself, the only people who are responsible are those who did it and they're the ones who'll pay."

"Whatever you need," Marcus said.

"What will the police learn about us when they do our background checks?" Austin asked.

"Police will get 'army employed, honourable discharge' in your case. The ASIO and SAS part will remain confidential. The only people who will ever know about the status of ASIO employees like us are the general and the prime minister and the defence minister. We're covered by the highest classification in the country, that's how we stay safe from terrorist reprisals," Marcus said.

Austin didn't speak again for the rest of the trip, but Marcus knew that he was thinking about poor Sarah.

Chapter 30

Jake and I sat down at the local McDonald's, the only place open at 5 am.

I was eating a McMuffin and Jake was drinking his coffee.

"So what did you want to tell me?" I asked, full of curiosity.

"After this homicide I'm going to retire from the force."

"What? Why?" I asked.

"I don't think I'm making a difference anymore, maybe I never was, maybe I've just woken to the realisation that justice no longer exists."

"You're one of the best cops that has ever been."

"Maybe. You know Karl and Amanda from when we were kids?"

"Yeah, I remember it well," I replied.

James Mitchell had been sentenced to 20 years for the murder of Karl and Amanda when they were children. He stole the car they were passengers in. He'd convinced the jury that he didn't mean to kill the children, that he couldn't even remember doing it because he was drug affected.

"Mitchell is likely to get out of Northview at Bendigo. He'll probably be declared no longer a threat to himself or society. I can't believe he was found not guilty by reason of insanity. What's the point, seriously?"

"How do you know he's getting out?" I asked.

"Salma told me, she's on the advisory board. She's one of the psychiatrists who makes the decisions and she said they're having trouble finding fault and they can't just keep him in there. He's been out on visits to his mother's for months."

"Maybe he has got better, maybe he was insane?" I proposed.

"Let me tell you, he was acting, he was full of shit. What many don't know is that at the time he was arrested he was living with his cousin. Police found an eight-year-old boy strapped to a bed in the spare room. He had been raped dozens of times and he'd been there five days and was close to death. Luckily, the boy survived. Spent two months in the hospital and was mentally scarred for life but he survived. Kidnapping was added to the sentence for Mitchell. He didn't care, he was too busy acting the loon trying to avoid life sentence for the murders. The kidnapping charge was the least of his issues. His cousin, what was his name?" Jake tapped the table, trying to remember. "Anyway, he was just as big a scumbag, he had raped the boy too, but the police were so keen to send Mitchell away when Ian..." Jake turned his head to the left and looked up as if searching his brain for the last piece of the puzzle, "that's it, Ian Welling. When Ian offered to testify, his charge of rape was pleaded down to a short sentence for accessory after the fact for the kidnapping, but he was just as bad. Two scumbags, both hooked on drugs, both child molesters, both under 25." Jake shook his head and sipped his coffee.

"Is that what this is all about, a light sentence, a plea deal?" I asked.

"No...possibly...to some extent, I'm not really sure," Jake answered. "Our work gets undone. We catch whoever is doing these kidnappings and he'll run around like a loon and he'll get off, or be sent to a farm, or plead it out for a deal.

"After Ian did his two years, he raped a boy in a park, he got seven, was out in five with good behaviour. Good behaviour! He raped two kids before he was 30! Good behaviour shouldn't be an option. But it is."

Jake took a deep breath.

"Plus Hayley is having a baby, she hasn't told me, but I think she's afraid that I won't want it."

"Do you want it?" I asked straight out.

"Of course I want it, I was just hoping the world would be better, but it only seems worse. I don't understand the world anymore. Look at all the kidnappings and murders we have piling up."

His coffee was almost finished.

"We work our asses off and the courts send them back out to us a few years later," Jake continued. "Now we have terrorists on the streets, the world's gone mad. I don't feel I'm making a difference anymore," he repeated, swishing his remaining coffee around in his mug. "Maybe it's that I don't want Hayley to get that phone call. I never used to care about what happened to me but since I found out I'm going to be a father, I'm shit scared of getting killed doing this job."

"What will you do if you don't do this?" I asked.

"I've been offered a job at Professional Investigations. It's $100,000 a year and fewer hours."

"Are you going to find taking photos of guys cheating on their wives exciting enough for you?" I asked Jake. I had finished my McMuffin in four bites. They didn't seem as big as they used to be. My hash browns were cold. I should have eaten them in the reverse order.

"Probably not, but I won't be disappointed with the outcome all the time. I think they would be happy to take you on too, if you wanted to come," Jake responded.

"Thanks mate, but it's not my cup of tea, I love working the cold cases. It's where I'm best suited. So when are you leaving?" I asked.

"Not sure yet, I think I need to give four weeks' notice." Jake paused.

"What do you think of the murder?" he asked.

"I'm not sure Jake, I don't know if it was a kidnapping gone wrong or a burglary that turned into a kidnapping, in an attempt to get some ransom. It could be either."

Jake's phone buzzed. The caller ID came up as 'Pete IT'.

"Hey, Pete, what you got? Ok, good to know, we'll be back in five." He hung up. "They've accessed the computer and the crowd that stores the security footage. Let's go have a look." Jake slid out from behind the table.

"Maybe it'll explain the orange shit on the cameras," I suggested.

"It might even provide us with a killer," Jake said.

Even though the ride back to the Kew crime scene was short, it gave me a bit more time to ask Jake about the one positive piece of information our chat had provided.

"So do you want a boy or a girl?" I asked.

"Not fussed," he said. "The name I have will suit both."

"What's that?" I asked.

"Indiana," he replied.

"Like Indiana Jones?" I questioned.

"Yep."

"That's awesome, what does Hayley think of it?"

"She doesn't even know I know she's having a baby."

"If she didn't tell you she's having a baby then how do you know she is even having one?" I questioned.

"I'm a detective, it's what I do."

"Ok, do me a favour. Before you say anything else to anyone else, talk to her, please."

"It's ok Brucey, we're going out for dinner tonight. I'll tell her I know and it'll be all good," Jake said.

* * *

By the time we arrived back at the crime scene, Jake had switched back into detective mode.

In the study, Pete sat at the desktop playing feedback from the various cameras.

"Come and look at this," Pete called out as he noticed us enter the property.

"What have you got?" Jake asked.

"I was going back through the cameras and at 12.30 the top left back goes black. I think that's the paint. If at the same time we look at camera two, we can see a small reflection from what appears to be a scope just over the back fence."

It was hard to make out and identifying someone from this footage would be impossible. But it at least gave us the time the suspect entered the property.

"What time did the victim first call dispatch?" Jake asked the Forensics team.

"Twelve forty-three," one of them answered almost immediately.

"Ok, cameras out just after 12.30, phone call 12.43, all seems to fit. What time did the officers first arrive?"

"Twelve fifty-two," the same man answered. Obviously it had been his job to detail the calls made to establish a window.

"So we have nine minutes from call to arrival, during which a lady was killed and a girl taken. Let's get filling in those nine minutes, people," Jake ordered.

Chapter 31

It was after 7 am and Austin Campbell was sitting in front of us. He was clearly devastated, as any loving husband and father would be, and both Jake and I ruled him out as a suspect immediately.

"We are sorry for your loss," Jake began. "Our biggest concern right now is to establish where your daughter is. So any information you can provide us could be vital. If you need to stop at any time, please just let us know."

Austin nodded.

"We are aware that you have just returned from duty in Afghanistan and that you have now retired after four tours."

Again Austin nodded.

"In the last few months had Sarah raised any concerns about home security?"

"About six months ago she installed a security system, a monitored one. She had some jewellery in an upstairs safe and there had been some break-ins in our neighbourhood so I suggested she get an alarm system installed. Anyway, she told me that when the guy came he suggested moving the safe from the robe to the study so it was more secure and at the same time further away from her. That way if someone ever did break in, they wouldn't be confronted and they would just take what they'd come for and leave. We took his advice and had it shifted. As far as I know, no one has ever attempted to break in. Sarah was only concerned because of what had been happening in the area," Austin said.

"Austin, we're of the opinion that this may have been a break-in and your wife disturbed him. Rather than leave empty-handed, we think he took Mikayla for a ransom. It means he's less likely to do her harm if he thinks she's his pay cheque," Jake suggested.

Austin nodded.

"The good news is we've collected a lot of evidence, we have a weapon and several prints as well as two possible shoe prints. They've been sent to Forensics for analysis."

"Well, that's a good start," Austin said. "What do you want me to do?" he asked.

"We might need you to appear in an interview, it may help keep Mikayla alive. When you do, just remember that every time you mention your daughter, mention her by name, invite a ransom, because that way if we're wrong we might at least give him the idea that he could score big. If he isn't planning on keeping her around, he might see the benefit." Then Jake asked him, "If we organise the interview, would you be happy to do it? We really need it done as soon as possible."

"Please. Whatever will help get her back," Austin said.

It was only 45 minutes later when Austin found himself sitting in front of dozens of cameras at the St Kilda Road police station.

"Thank you all for attending the press conference," Jake said to the media. "Overnight, Victoria has suffered one of its most heinous crimes. A young mother was murdered and her daughter has been taken from inside the family home."

He stood aside for Austin, who was visibly upset. The recent events had begun to take their toll.

He began, "I would like to say to the person or persons responsible that what's done is done. However, you have the opportunity to prevent the situation from getting a lot worse. Mikayla is only 11 years old. It's important that Mikayla is brought back to me. If you have Mikayla, please just drop her at a street, don't hurt her. Mikayla is all I have left. I am open to paying a reward for any information leading to her whereabouts and her safe return."

Jake held up a photo of Mikayla. "Any information on Mikayla's location will be handled in the strictest confidence. Let me just add this: if you have information on this crime but had no direct involvement in it, you will be offered immunity. Please call Crime Stoppers with any information, no matter how small or insignificant you may think it is. Thank you," Jake finished, before stepping away from the media desk.

Austin left the interview and sat down in an office cubicle at the heart of the Homicide division. He sat there, head in hands, trying to keep the worst thoughts away. He knew he had to stay strong but he didn't know if he would be able to.

He remembered something Marcus had said. "She needs you."

He decided to keep saying that to himself until he had her back.

Whatever it took, he was getting her back.

Chapter 32

Beau had been disciplined as usual. He had kept his mask on, but on entering the girl's home, he had taken it off and placed it in his pocket. Usually he would have kept it on, however, he was scared the big guy from the movies, her father, might be there and if he was, he didn't want his vision limited.

He had seen him leave but he couldn't be sure he hadn't returned and he couldn't afford a surprise attack.

* * *

He had never killed before, well not on the outside anyway. Once, on the inside, he had been forced to show his mettle and set an example of what happened to those who thought he could be used as a sex toy.

As with most new inmates, the weak ones were targeted, eyed by the gangs and then when the opportunity presented itself, attacked. Attacks usually happened in isolated areas of the prison so the attackers were not interrupted by prison officers. On occasion, officers were paid to walk in the opposite direction.

Beau had been on the inside for only two weeks when he first noticed he was being watched. He had drawn the attention of the gang known by all other inmates as the 'Husbands', because those they targeted would become their 'wives'.

Beau suffered a close encounter where he was nearly raped by the

Husbands in the toilet block, only to have the assault broken up by an uncorrupted guard. The fact that Beau had been incarcerated for child molestation only made the target on his back bigger.

Beau understood the prison world and knew that he would never be free from attacks. He also knew if he put up a fight, people might think twice before attacking him again.

Beau remembered it as if it was yesterday. He was finishing a job in the laundry room where he had been stacking the shelves of the laundry cupboard. The shelves were six feet high and four feet wide and they were enclosed within a steel cage so that the goods would not be stolen.

He was on his last shelf when he noticed the guard at the far end of the hall nod and walk away from his post. The guard at the entrance at the other end of the hall also left his post. Beau instantly knew something was up and prayed it wasn't going to be about him. But then he knew. Three men, all members of the Husbands' gang, approached him. The three of them all working together would get what they wanted, and what they wanted was a turn. Luck was with Beau on that day. He would normally have said God was with him, but Beau knew there was no god, especially in a place like that.

The first one entered the cage, with the second man about three metres behind him. The man was bigger than Beau and so Beau did the only smart play he had available. He went on full attack. His first move was not a punch or a kick, but a head butt. The top of Beau's forehead matched perfectly with his attacker's nose, and the force of Beau's strike was ferocious. The man went flying backwards, his body slamming against the door of the cage, forcing the door closed and his Husband mates trapped outside. It was difficult to open a door with a dead weight behind it. Even though Beau's attacker was bigger, he was in no state to offer assistance to his gang members trying to enter the cage. His nose was spread across his face from the head butt and his vision was blurred. Before he knew what was happening, Beau had him up against the gate. Beau had fed a piece of packing wire through the cage door and he now pulled it tight around the man's throat.

Beau pulled the packing wire tight so it cut into his attacker's throat. His two gang members could only stand and watch.

The blood trickled at first and then as the wire really began to cut deep, it flowed. The two remaining gang members remained circling outside the cage like a pack of half-scared, half-hungry wolves, trying to work out if there was going to be a meal or not.

The standoff continued for another three minutes before being broken by a new shift of laundry workers walking in. Both the men on the outside fled the laundry, as did Beau as soon as the Husbands were out of sight.

One thing was certain: no one would talk about who had killed the gang member. Everyone's privileges were restricted for two weeks, but still no one spoke. A message was sent to Beau through his cellmate. It was clear and simple.

'You're dead.'

Just as his murder of one of the Husbands had angered them and moved him to the top of their hit list, it had not gone unnoticed by other gangs, especially those who wanted to keep their prison virginity intact. The death in the laundry room sent his whole cell block into lockdown, all privileges were withdrawn and every-one was confined to their cells 24 hours a day. No one was going anywhere until answers were found. Of course, no one would talk, no one would snitch. You snitched, you died. Eventually, life in the prison would just move on.

During the lockdown, his only visitor was an elderly priest. "I hear the Husbands have you high on their wanted list," the priest muttered.

"In prison, everyone wants something from you," Beau replied.

"I could have you moved away from the Husbands into a special rehabilitation program for the remainder of your sentence. A nice prison far away from here. Do you believe in God, my son?"

All Beau heard was 'away from the Husbands'.

"Yes, I believe in God," he answered. He would believe in aliens if it kept him alive.

"Good. I will take care of the details," the priest said, leaving Beau alone once more.

After he left, Beau wondered what the priest might want in exchange.

* * *

This time, however, it was an innocent woman who hadn't deserved to die. But getting caught would have meant death for him. There would be no way he would be able to avoid the Husbands for another jail term, or satisfactorily explain to the Monster he was empty-handed and without the girl he had promised.

He drove the van back to his home, opened the shed and moved the train set. Then he opened the hatch and took the red ladder down from the wall.

It was a routine he knew well.

He placed his mask on, not for her, she had already seen him, but for the boy who was still below.

He had taken a sack from under the driver's seat. Before he removed her from the van, he needed to cover her face. The less she saw of the surroundings, the better. Beau walked to the back of the van, opened the rear doors and placed it quickly over her head. She went to scream at the sight of his mask but thought better of it when Beau raised his massive hand ready to slap her again.

He took the piece of rope, placed it over the hood and guided her down to the cell. He placed her in the same cell that held the Monster's last delivery. He didn't speak to either of his current captives.

He removed her hood, closed the gate behind him and disappeared up the red ladder.

Chapter 33

Austin booked himself into a hotel, hoping he might be able to get some sleep.

Forensics were still at his place and according to detectives, would be there for quite some time. The idea of sleeping in the same house where his wife had been slain didn't appeal, although he knew he would have to go back eventually.

Sleep was well overdue, but the events of the worst night of his life prevented it. He had lost his wife and his daughter. Although he didn't yet know the fate of his daughter, the unknown was killing him more, yet at the same time the possibility of her being alive was the only thing keeping him going. He needed to take matters into his own hands, find his daughter and those responsible.

But where would he start?

He decided the only lead he had might be at his fingertips. What did the surveillance cameras show? Nothing, maybe something? The police had been interested in looking at them. The good thing about storing information on the Cloud was it couldn't be stolen or confiscated, even though he guessed his house computer may have been taken as evidence. Best of all, information on the Cloud could be accessed by any computer, tablet or iPhone anywhere in the world, as long as he knew the site and the password, which as the owner, he did.

There was a computer bank in the lobby of his hotel for $2 per hour. It would do.

He got up and made his way downstairs, then began reviewing the film from the 2 am mark on the camera, working his way backwards. As he wound back in the evening, the cameras went from black to light, from nothing to vison. Suddenly there was a picture and he could see something through one camera. As he rewound, a splatter disappeared and then the same thing happened with the second rooftop camera. Then he could see a man on the fence, a man with a gun. There was no other disturbance. However, there was a fault; the two lower cameras remained blank. Austin checked the time: 8.41 pm. They were still out. He rewound the day further to 6.12 pm; they were still blank.

The front cameras showed nothing of interest and the two working back cameras remained free of clues.

He rewound further and decided to continue rewinding until he saw something, anything. Then he saw the most beautiful sight in the world. It was his wife and daughter, checking the mail, just after 3.15 pm. They had just arrived home from school. The back camera remained out.

He rewound further. They hopped back in the car and disappeared down the road backwards. The gate closed. Then he saw it.

The back camera came to life and a hand moved away from it. Then the other camera came to life. It too had a hand move away from it.

Then he saw a second unknown man. Austin watched this at normal speed. He could rewind more later if he needed to.

Just after 3 pm, he saw the man jump over his rear fence. He was of average height, neither particularly tall nor particularly short. He was reasonably bulky, although compared to Austin nearly everyone was puny. The cameras did not show a close-up, not that a close-up of a balaclava would be of any help.

Austin didn't know what happened to the man after the second camera went out. He seemed to vanish. He switched to the side camera. He was hoping the man in the tape wasn't aware of its presence. It was positioned high up near the eave, semi-obscured by a conifer, and it would be almost impossible to cut.

Austin clicked on the live view. The camera was still actively recording! He could see Forensics looking at the door. He selected the recorded file from 2 am, just as he had done with the others.

He began to wind it back. It started off with no one in sight, just his side path at night with a couple of shrubs blowing in the wind. Just after 12.30 am, the same time as the other cameras had been shot at with a paintball, a second man appeared at the side door. He was bigger and fatter than the first man who had cut the cameras at 3 pm. And he was wearing a joker mask.

Were they working together? Austin wondered. Maybe one was doing some casing work for the other. Then the man removed the mask. Austin zoomed in. He couldn't see his face because his head was down while he concentrated on the lock. It didn't take the man long to break into the house. Austin played the tape at normal speed; three seconds it took him to bust the door down.

Three seconds didn't provide much by way of identification, apart from his size. Five seconds later all the cameras went blank. Power been cut, Austin thought.

So the man with the joker mask jumps the fence at 12.30 am after shooting at the cameras with paint.

Then the guy busts in the door.

Cuts the power, so there's no footage of him leaving.

Austin wound the camera back again to 3.13 pm. The other man appeared at the side of the home. He took longer to get into the house and he was still wearing his balaclava.

There was footage of him entering but not leaving. Austin double-checked the footage, then triple-checked. Definitely no footage of him leaving.

Austin wondered if they had left together. Were they in on it together? He had better call the detectives.

But first he had one more call to make, to his security company.

Austin provided his security details to the receptionist and was transferred to the security department.

"Security," a man answered.

"Hi, I need to check my security from yesterday. I'm wondering if anyone tampered with the system."

"Let me have a look for you, Mr Campbell." There was a short pause as the man checked. "The system was activated at 8.30 am and then deactivated via pin code at 10.47." Makes sense, Austin thought. Sarah probably dropped Mikayla at school, did some shopping and then came home.

He paused. Austin could hear him typing at the other end of the phone.

"It was then reactivated via pin at 2.57 pm. Then there was a four-minute period when no signal was being received, between 3.11 and 3.15 pm."

"What does it mean?" Austin asked.

"Could be a couple of things. Most likely cause is that your home lost power," the technician replied. "The alarm was rearmed without a code just after 3.15 pm, which tells me the power must have come back on. It was then deactivated via pin code some 30 seconds later."

"What else could it be?" Austin probed. "Could it be a faulty wire in the box?"

"Someone who knew what they were doing could have removed the wire inside the main control box and reconnected it to bypass they system," the tech answered. "But it's highly unlikely. To do so they'd have to have an understanding of how these alarm systems work. They'd have get to the wire inside 30 seconds. Not likely," the tech said. "I'd say you had a power outage," he confirmed. "Is there anything else I can help you with?"

"No thanks, that should do. If I have any other questions I'll get back to you."

Austin hung up and leaned back in his chair. What had the first guy been doing, and why had he hidden in the house for so long?

Surely they must have been working together. It must have been planned.

What were the odds of two different criminals working the same target on the same day? Two million to one?

Now it was time to contact the detectives.

Chapter 34

Jake wasn't surprised to receive a call from Mr Campbell. He assumed it would be to check on the progress of the investigation. When, however, he offered new information, Jake was taken aback.

What information could it be that he didn't know already? Was Mr Campbell involved in the murder of his wife? Had the guilt got to him? Was he going to confess?

Jake doubted it, but he had to know what the man knew.

Jake came over to my desk and hovered over me. "Mr Campbell wants to see me, says he has information, might be worth you tagging along."

"Sure thing, I need time to think anyway," I replied, closing the file of Scott Western. "Did he say what information he has?" I asked as we headed to the elevator and down to the underground secure parking.

"No. He just says he has information," Jake answered.

"Interesting."

We met Mr Campbell in the foyer of the Hilton and then followed him to the lobby to a row of computers. He clicked on the screen. There were eight squares all showing different aspects of his yard.

"This is the footage from the cameras at my house last night," he said.

"Mr Campbell," Jake interrupted, "we have already gone through the footage from last night."

Austin clicked on a small link that said '2'.

A new page loaded showing one more square, the side of his house.

"Then why has there been no footage of this man?" Mr Campbell pointed to a man at the door wearing a joker's mask.

Jake looked at me and I looked at him.

"What camera is that?" Jake asked.

"It's the side camera, most people don't think I have one because it's partially hidden by the pencil conifer we have growing next to the gate. If you're looking for it on the web, it's also hard to find because the page holds the first eight cameras only," Mr Campbell explained.

We bent in to get a better view. Mr Campbell went through the footage again. He was correct; it looked like a fat man wearing a joker's mask. He then wound the footage to earlier in the day. Another man appeared in the camera's view.

This was a skinnier, smaller man than the one we had just seen wearing the joker mask. This one was in a balaclava.

"What time is this?" Jake asked.

"Just after 3 pm," Mr Campbell replied. "I don't have any footage of either of them leaving, which leads me to suspect they both left after...after they killed Sarah."

"Can you go over them again please, Mr Campbell."

We took several more looks at them. I now knew where the green hair that I had found on the fence came from. It was from the joker's mask.

However, with his mask removed, we could see nothing of use.

"You're the psychologist, what do you think?" Jake asked me.

"I agree with Mr Campbell. It seems unlikely they were operating separately, but one thing doesn't add up. Why did the second guy break in if he already had someone else on the inside?" I asked.

Both Jake and Mr Campbell could offer no explanation.

"Also," said Mr Campbell, "I rang our security company. They told me there was a four-minute outage between 3.11 pm and 3.15 pm. Their interpretation was that it was likely due to a loss of power."

"I doubt that, but we can check with the power company," Jake said without hesitation. "I think the first man removed the cable and then reset the alarm. It's a trick many burglars use. Usually they enter the premises, disconnect the alarm, take what they're after, and then reconnect the alarm just as they're leaving. Not only does this stop the alarm from going off, more importantly, when the owner comes home the alarm is still armed and there's no sign of a break-in. In some cases, it's days before people realise things are missing. Crims often do this when stealing credit cards. They take the credit card and go spending," Jake explained. Then he continued, "Thank you for this valuable information, Mr Campbell. We'll keep you updated on any developments. If you have anything else you find or think of, please let us know. Once Forensics have finished, I'll call you so you can move back home. Should only be another day, or so."

Mr Campbell stood up and shook Jake's hand and then turned to me with his hand held out. I accepted and shook it. Mr Campbell didn't let go, instead he asked, "The other kids that went missing, has any ransom been demanded?"

"No," I answered, "no one has sent in a ransom note."

"Then why do you think this guy is going to demand one?" Mr Campbell asked.

"Because this abduction is different from the others. This abduction was done from the home. The others were carried out on the street. We feel that maybe they broke in, were disturbed, didn't have time to get whatever they were after, so instead took your daughter," I replied.

"But it's just a theory," Jake added.

"Yes, it's just a theory we're going off," I confirmed.

Mr Campbell finally let go of my hand. "Ok then, well, we will soon see," he said.

We turned to go back to the station when he spoke again.

"Just so you know, there is no way in hell I am going to sit here while my daughter is out there somewhere. I will do whatever I can to bring her home."

Jake turned, "It's best not to get involved in a police investigation. The best thing you can do is stay home in case they call with the ransom demands. Getting involved could only hinder our investigations," Jake said.

"I can't do that, Detective. Getting in your way is my least concern. I will do whatever it takes to bring her home."

Not only had we been made to look inept by the Forensics team because they had missed an entire camera, we now had a dad challenging our work.

Jake didn't bother to reply. He understood Mr Campbell was upset and there was no point trying to tell him otherwise. After all, if he wanted to walk the streets, how could we stop him?

"Ok," Jake said to me, "so we have two men we need to identify, and that's where we start. Once Forensics run the prints through the database and we get the results, we'll will be able to compare them to the footage."

Chapter 35

Beau hadn't slept past 11 am in years, however, the sleep debt owed from the weekend and Monday night had caught up with him. Even when he woke he was still tired. If it hadn't been for the fear of the police knocking on his door and the evidence still sitting on the passenger seat of his van, he would have stayed in bed for a few more hours.

Instead, he got dressed and was headed out to his shed when his mum stopped him in the kitchen. "Where did you get to last night?" she screeched.

"Went to the movies," he responded automatically. "What's it to you anyhow?"

"While you were out, another girl was taken, this one from her home, and I know how much you like young girls," she replied.

Annabelle leaned into the corner of her kitchen bench, one cigarette in her mouth and another at the ready in her fingers. "You better not be up to no good, ya hear me, because you'll be out on your ass quicker than you can say jack rabbit."

Beau reached into his pants, removed the ticket stub. "I was at the movies. See? The 11 pm session of *The Hunger Games* part two." Beau had bought the ticket not to convince his mother, but to provide an alibi just in case the police ever asked. He brushed his mother aside and headed out to his shed.

"Aren't you going to have breakfast?" Annabelle asked him with her head poking out the door, ciggy still in her mouth.

"I'll get something later," he called back without even turning to face her.

Beau unlocked the shed, and locked it again from the inside. He flicked on the TV, removed from his bar fridge a bottle of milk, smelt it – not off, but on the edge – took two paper bowls, two plastic spoons, and two mini packets of cereal from a cupboard built into his work bench.

He removed the red ladder from its hanging spot on the wall and leaned it against the work bench. He turned his train set, revealing the trapdoor, unlocked it, placed the ladder into its usual position. He put on his joker mask and put the bowls, cereal and spoons in one hand and the bottle of milk in the other. He held the ladder, the milk handle hooked around his thumb.

When he arrived at the bottom, the girl screamed, while Scott remained silent, lying curled up in a corner of his cell. "Don't know why you're wearing the mask. I've seen your fat ugly face!" Mikayla screamed at him.

Without speaking, Beau placed the bowl and milk on the gravel path, opened the cell, stepped inside, and grabbed Mikayla by the throat. "Unless you want to end up like your mother, I suggest you keep your mouth closed."

Mikayla grabbed at his hand. It was firm and strong. Even using both hands she couldn't pry his fingers away. She was struggling to breathe. This was it. She would die like her mum. Tears rolled down her face. She began smacking his leathery hand. Suddenly he released her and air flew into her lungs, causing her to cough. She dropped to the floor, trying to regulate her breathing.

Slumped in the corner, Mikayla watched as the Joker bent down to pick up the bowls, cereal and milk. This was her chance. Something inside her called 'run!' She didn't hesitate, she didn't think, she just ran. Like a professional runner, Mikayla was off. She pushed on the big man's hip as she passed him on the path. Being stooped over, he lost his balance and fell. Mikayla didn't look to see if he had gone over or not. Her attention was squarely on escaping. Her hands clasped the old red metal ladder. At first her legs couldn't agree on which one was moving first, so for an instant, she stood there motionless, then her right leg decided to take charge and step up.

At any moment she expected the Joker to grasp her foot or to feel a hand on her shoulder, but there was nothing. Surprisingly, she was free. She reached the last rung; still nothing. She gathered herself out of the hole and searched for the door. She saw what appeared to be a door off to the side. Sprinting, she reached for the handle, arm outstretched. The tips of her fingers withdrew at the touch of cold metal. She pulled down on the handle and pulled again. The handle turned all the way but the door resisted and remained shut. Mikayla pulled again, nothing. She looked up. There was a bolt with a padlock through it, "Nooo!" she cried.

"You thinking of going somewhere?" the Joker asked, half muffled by his mask.

"Please, let me go. My dad will be looking for me." Tears began to well but the fear of being beaten dried them up before they began falling.

"You shouldn't have run; you've made me mad now."

Mikayla looked for a way out. She could only see one other door, a big sliding metal door big enough for cars to go through. It had big bolts top and bottom and was also padlocked.

She could see no way out of the garage. There was no way out of this mess. The Joker was upon her now. The mask didn't scare her; it was the gaze from the dead-looking eyes that lay behind it. She tried to prepare herself for the beating she was about to get. He grabbed her face, squeezed her cheeks with his fingers and squeezed hard. Her cheeks touched each other and her mouth was deformed like a fish. She was ready for the rest, but nothing came. Instead, he eased his pressure and took her by the hair. "If you try to escape again, I will kill you," he said slowly and deliberately, "regardless of how much they're paying for you."

Who is paying for me, she wondered, who was he talking about?

Chapter 36

When James Mitchell killed the two children, pleading he couldn't remember doing it, the truth was that being drug affected had made the killing so much more intense. He remembered every second of it. Some days he lay in his bed reliving it.

James knew if he ever got caught he would do his best not to go back to jail. Being declared clinically insane was both good and bad. The bad was he had to deal with all the 'nutters', as he called them, walking the hallways. The good was it was like a free motel, just with padded rooms for the naughty ones.

It had been hard playing the part and selling his version, but he had done so from the moment he was arrested and he'd laid it on thick. His main defence was that the 'shadow people' had made him do it. He could hear them and sometimes see them, usually when he was going to sleep. During his questioning, he asked the detective to protect him from the shadow people, that they would be coming for him.

His hardest task was still to come. Now he had to prove that he was no longer insane. How long that would take was anyone's guess, but it didn't matter to him. Anything would be better than being constantly raped and beaten in jail. Most prison inmates didn't take kindly to child molesters, let alone ones that killed as well.

He had spent 20 years in Northview at Bendigo, the high security home for those found by a court to be 'not guilty by reason of insanity', held there by the Commonwealth until it was deemed suitable for him to return to society.

Everyone at Northview had been good to him, no one had tried to rape him. It was better than prison. He had decided to wait several years before even showing a sign of improvement, then he would phase in and out. Sometimes the shadow people were there, sometimes they were gone, sometimes he could comprehend what the doctors were saying, other times he would accuse them of being involved and trying to plot his death.

For the past five years, he had exhibited stable behaviour; no mood swings, no imaginary shadow people, no voices, all calm. He had become a model patient. He could be good when he had to be, and now he had to be. He needed out. Inside, his monster was back and growing stronger, day by day, week by week, his hunger for children stronger than ever. The constant news reports of the missing children over the last few months had fed his monster's hunger.

Chapter 37

Hayley had decided tonight was the night to tell Jake. She stood beside Ryan's bed, distraught at the sight of the motionless boy.

She was holding a stuffed Garfield in her hand and she leaned over and tucked it under Ryan's arm, patted his sweaty head, leaned in and kissed his cheek. "Here is Garfield. He needs your cuddles," she whispered. Of course, there was no response.

She had asked Jake if he would be able to make dinner tonight, if she booked somewhere. He'd said that after seven would be best.

Hayley cleared her mind of her personal issues and went about taking the morning obs. By the time she returned to Ryan, his family had arrived for the day, hoping their bedside vigil would bring him around.

"Excuse me, do you know how my son got this toy?" his mother Joan asked.

"I bought it for him," Hayley responded. "I hope you don't mind, I just thought something new to cuddle might help."

"Don't be silly, Hayley, of course we don't mind. Thank you so much, you're such a sweetie," Joan responded.

She leaned down and placed the Garfield back in the bed with Ryan. Then she walked over to Hayley who was standing at the end of the bed, chart in hand, and threw her arms around her, saying a simple, heartfelt "Thank you."

Hayley had got to know Ryan's parents over the time he had been in hospital. They didn't deserve this; no family did. They were good people and had they been there, Ryan wouldn't have drowned.

It always seemed that fate only visited the innocent, not the guilty.

"The doctors will be around shortly. After they've been, I'll give him his sponge bath and freshen him up a little. Maybe then we could even put on some of his favourite music and have that playing for him," Hayley said, smiling.

Joan nodded, "That would be great. Thank you." There was no smile to accompany the nod.

Hayley had never seen her smile. Who could blame her? It wasn't as if the current situation called for it. Maybe she would never smile again. If Ryan died, she doubted it.

Chapter 38

After our meeting with Austin Campbell, Jake rang ahead to Forensics asking to meet with Grace, the head. She had taken over from David in the spring of 2009, when David had passed away. She was great at her job and even though she was easy going, she was tough on her crime scene investigation team to ensure its integrity.

Grace met with Monique (our chief of Homicide), Jake and me in the conference room. She had already gone over the crime scene report supplied by her team. "Hi guys..." she began.

Jake interrupted her, "Your technicians made us look like idiots."

"Jake, I've spoken to them about thoroughness and how they need to be on their game every scene. They understood they made a mistake, Jake, they can't do anything about it now," she continued.

Jake calmed himself.

"Ok, let's move forward," Grace said. "I have good news. We have the match from the fingerprints on the screwdriver and on the manhole. I've reviewed the footage from the side camera. Based on the arrest records and the fingerprints we found at the scene, we have a match." Jake was about to say something. She held up her hand. "There's more. We also found a glove in the roof cavity. The fingerprints found on the manhole and the screwdriver are the same. There's also a match to a partial print on the back door."

She slid a file across the desk to us.

"Tyler Parsons was convicted and sentenced for B&E. Looks like he's back to his old tricks, except this time he's added murder and kidnapping to his repertoire."

Jake finished flicking through the file and passed it to me. Grace was right; the prints matched the screwdriver and the manhole, and the video footage showed an extremely close resemblance to the photo of Tyler when considering body size.

Jake thanked Grace for her report. He then turned to Monique. "We need to organise SWAT to clear Tyler's house. Then we'll need Forensics to look for any sign of Mikayla in his car or house," he said.

"We already have a sample of Mikayla's hair from the brush in her room, so if we find any, we'll have a comparison back quickly," Grace answered.

It was 35 minutes before SWAT was ready to clear Tyler's home. We had been waiting outside his house for 15 minutes before Sal from SWAT came across the radio to let us know they were two streets away.

"Looks like he's home," Jake told him. "There's a car in the drive and it's registered to him, but we haven't seen anyone yet."

"Satellite shows three exit points, one at the front, one at the rear and one on the left, so we'll send four in from the back, two on the left-hand side and four at the front. Once we have him I'll give you the all-clear so you can enter," Sal said.

"Hey Sal! We need this one alive. He has an 11-year-old girl somewhere and he's our only lead."

"Will do our best, Detective, but can't guarantee anything. If he opens fire, we'll have to take him down."

Less than a minute later, the all-clear came through from Sal.

We entered the property. This time there were seven Forensic's technicians following us in, led by Grace herself.

When SWAT had entered the house, Tyler was sitting on the couch, eating a bowl of spaghetti.

We walked through the door to find he was cuffed, spaghetti stains all over his shirt and the rest spread over the lounge room floor. They removed him, placing him in the back of Jake's squad car.

Jake and I immediately began searching the house for signs of Mikayla. We came up empty-handed. I decided I had to talk to Tyler now. If we waited until we were in the interview room at the station, it could be too late.

I opened the rear car door and knelt in the doorway. "Tyler, you need to tell us where the girl is. Whatever happened at the house we can sort out later. Where is she?"

He didn't answer, just sat there silently staring out the window.

"Tyler, do you want to go inside for the rest of your life? They'll throw the book at you if you don't help us."

Tyler said, "I don't know about the girl or the dead lady. I had nothing to do with it."

"Tyler, if you had nothing to do with it, then I will help you, but you need to help us first. Where is the girl?"

He gave no response.

"Tyler, who was the other guy you were working with? Tell us who the big guy was."

Still nothing. This wasn't working. He wasn't giving me anything, so I had to change tactics.

"Obviously you want to protect him, but so far it's your prints on the screwdriver. Right now, you're going down for the lady's murder and now you want to go down for the girl too? If we can't find her, we'll charge you for both their deaths. We don't need a body to charge you. Do you understand? Tell us who he is, don't go down for something you didn't do."

Tyler looked up. "I don't know who he was, I was hiding in the roof waiting for the mum to go to sleep so I could have a crack at the safe. Then I heard screaming. I panicked and ran. She was dead when I left. I never saw the guy or the girl." Tyler was shaking.

"You expect me to believe you don't know the guy you were working with? If what you say is true, that she was dead when you left, then how come the screwdriver has your fingerprints on it? How could it have been used to kill her, Tyler?"

Tyler shook his head, "I must have dropped it, and the other guy picked it up and killed her," Tyler said, still shaking his head.

"Tyler, the only prints on the screwdriver are yours and the victim's. Quite a coincidence, wouldn't you say? How does he pick it up and kill her and not leave any prints?"

Tyler looked up, "He must have had gloves on."

"So you're telling us that you dropped your screwdriver and the other person picked it up and killed her, and it was this other person, who you don't know, who took the girl as well?"

Tyler nodded. "That's the truth."

"You must be the unluckiest burglar of all time."

Tyler mumbled, "I am."

"Tyler, if what you're saying is the truth, why didn't you come in and see us? Why did you flee the scene that night?"

Tyler rocked back and forth in his seat, "I didn't think you'd believe me."

"This is your last chance to tell me the truth. Come clean. Who are you protecting? Where is the girl? You'll be looked on favourably by the courts if you help us find the girl."

I waited for Tyler to speak. If I spoke now I'd lose for sure.

He replied, "I've told you what happened. It's the truth. I'm only telling you the truth. I can't tell you what I don't know."

"I can't help you if you don't help me. We know you're not telling us the truth. You're going back to the police station where you will be formally charged for murder and kidnapping as well as breaking and entering."

I shut the door.

Tyler began to cry.

"Read him his rights, then take him to St Kilda Road," I instructed the officer accompanying him. "We'll be back there to question him again soon."

Jake was still searching the house. "Did he tell you where he put the girl?"

"No," I responded.

"Arseholes never do; they rarely tell you where their victims are. Even years later when the trial is all done and dusted, they still don't."

"Some psychologists believe they enjoy the control," I replied.

"What did he say?" Jake asked as he walked the back yard looking for any freshly dug ground.

"He said that the other guy killed the mum and must have taken the child. He said he was in the manhole, heard a scream, went to leave the house, and saw the lady dead on the floor." I stopped walking. "Normally, I'd say it's crap, but on that video the two entered at different times. Maybe they weren't working together."

Jake turned and eyeballed me, "They were working together. Don't doubt yourself."

"If they were, then why would he go down for something he didn't do? Why wouldn't he just give him up?" I asked Jake.

"Jail is better than death. If you rat out your boss, maybe he'll kill you and your family," Jake said.

"We could protect him," I fired back.

Jake laughed.

"You have to understand, Brodie, some of these people are connected, sometimes giving up someone just isn't worth it!"

I looked at Tyler's dog in the yard. It was a gorgeous boxer, practically still a puppy. He had the best of everything, best bowls, best bed; the lead hanging in the doorway was leather. Hanging next to it was a winter jacket Tyler obviously put on him on his walks. Most likely the dog slept inside with Tyler, same bed, would be my guess.

Maybe that was my way in.

Chapter 39

Austin had seen the two men in the video footage and he knew his daughter's time was running out. He couldn't decide if they were working together, and if he was honest with himself, he didn't care. He would chase them both down and he wouldn't stop until he found them.

The man who had killed his wife had his daughter. He had little doubt that Sarah had died trying to prevent Mikayla's abduction.

Still sitting in the hotel lobby at a computer terminal, Austin scrolled through his phone contacts and pressed the green call button to Marcus.

"Hey buddy, how you coping?" Marcus answered sombrely.

"I need my kit," Austin said.

"It's on its way to you, everything you need."

"I also need information on the following missing children." He reeled off one by one the three names he knew of. "I also want some tracking devices as well as bugs. I need to find this guy and I'm running out of time."

"I'll send it to you today. I take it you're staying there tonight?" Marcus asked, confirming what he already knew.

"I'll be here until I get my kit and then I'm gone until I find her," Austin replied as if it was going to be a sure thing.

The ability of Marcus to provide him with what he needed in such a short time shocked even Austin. Two packages arrived at his room within two hours. The first bag was his kit. It contained all his weapons. Marcus had done the smart thing and removed the uniform, replacing it with some casual clothes in a suitcase with two false bottoms. Austin unzipped it and removed the jacket and jeans, a pair of black shoes and a belt.

He flipped the bag over, unzipped the other side. It contained a laptop bag, a phone and a set of keys. He removed the items, placing them all on the bed. He opened the laptop bag. In one slip was a MacBook Air, in the other were three folders, each with a name printed on the lip. It was a dossier on each kidnapping. Austin could have got all the information from the internet himself but it would have taken him a while. In the front of the bag was the laptop cable.

He turned the phone on. A text message came up.

It was from Marcus.

Laptop has email address only we can view. If u need anything checked email/text me

In bag four trackers to place under a car & follow on GPS. I've set them into yr phone. Numbered 1 to 4. Most I could organise in limited time. Also a jammer – blocks central locking to get into car to plant device

Keys for government car. Been checked out 4 weeks for repairs.

After that will be reported stolen

Will help you as much as I can. If u get caught doing something illegal you're on yr own. I'll say u went rogue and all our communications will be deleted

Austin typed a reply.

Do whatever you have to do, I understand

Five seconds later he had deleted both messages.

Austin then removed the false bottom of the case. There were two identical handguns, both SIG p228 9mm, holding 12 rounds each. It was a light handgun, better for going house to house and in hostage situations.

Then there was a Walther P99 semi-automatic pistol holding 16 rounds in the magazine, a machine gun H&K G36 with five 30-round clips, and finally an L96A1 sniper rifle fitted with the Schmidt & Bender telescopic sight and with one 12-round clip.

There were three titanium suppressors, two for the handguns, one for the sniper rifle.

Finally, were his knives, both kukri. He had used them in Afghanistan. They were designed to kill. Unlike a standard kitchen knife that struggled to cut tomatoes, these would cut through flesh as if it was paper.

Marcus had done a good job. Good thing he wasn't a terrorist; he could start a one-man war with weapons like these. If all went to plan, Austin wouldn't need to fire a single shot.

The phone rang, startling him at first, then he realised it could only be Marcus.

"Hey," Austin answered.

"Turn on the news," Marcus said.

Austin fumbled with the remote that was sitting on the bedside table in the shade of the lamp. He clicked the remote several times and found the Sky news channel. 'Man in custody for Campbell murder', read the caption.

"I'll call you back," Austin said.

He picked up his own phone and dialled Jake's number.

"Have you found my daughter?" he asked, without waiting for the normal exchange of pleasantries.

"No," Jake said. "We're still looking. The man we have in for questioning said he never saw your daughter. We're trying to validate his version of events."

Another caption scrolled across the screen.

'Man identified as Tyler Parsons of Victoria.'

"Is the man you have Tyler Parsons?" Austin asked.

"Austin, I'm trying to find your daughter. Let me get back to you as soon as I have solid information I can share."

Austin replied sheepishly and somewhat apologetically, "Ok, sorry," and ended the call.

He picked up the other phone and called Marcus back.

"The police won't confirm who it is," Austin said, "but if the news sources have named the person of interest, it must have been confirmed. Otherwise they could face a massive legal bill."

"I've emailed you Parsons' criminal history, it's all thefts. No rape convictions or child abuse of any kind. So murder and kidnapping would be new for him," Marcus said. "If you want my suggestion, I'd start looking for links between the other kidnapping cases and Mikayla's," Marcus added. "It'd be foolish to dismiss the possibility Mikayla's isn't linked to the other three. Maybe he had a reason to break in and take her."

"Maybe you're right, perhaps there is a reason we don't know of yet," Austin said. "Maybe I need to go back to the beginning."

Marcus spoke again. "So we agree? We both think it's possible that Mikayla's kidnapping is related to the others?"

"Forget the fact that they were different circumstances for a second because really when you think about it, all the kidnappings were slightly different. Maybe they were all targeted? Maybe he planned to strike when he did?" Austin said.

"Maybe he planned to break in because he knew you wouldn't be home or he saw you leaving?" Marcus suggested. "Can you remember anyone watching you over the last few days?"

Austin thought about that. Had he noticed anyone out of the ordinary?

Was it out of the ordinary to be at the movies alone, like the fat guy he saw on Friday?

Was it out of the ordinary for the fat guy to go to the Pancake Parlour for lunch, just like they did?

Was it out of the ordinary to park near the movies?

Did he park?

Or just fumble for his keys?

What car did he get into? Did he see him get into a car or just stand in the lot?

What car did he get into?

Austin couldn't remember. Maybe because he didn't see him get into a car.

Was the big guy the same guy as on the tape? Possibly; maybe.

"Austin, hello?"

"Sorry," Austin replied. "Someone may have been watching us at the movies. It may have been the bigger guy in the surveillance footage," Austin replied.

"The bloke with the joker mask?" Marcus asked.

"Yeah…maybe…not sure," Austin answered.

"Well it's a start," Marcus replied.

Maybe the best place to start looking for Mikayla was with the other lost children, Austin thought. Time was ticking and as each hour passed, the chances of finding her alive were diminishing. It had been 12 hours already.

After the first 24 hours, the chance of finding her alive was 50%, and each day after that was 2% less.

Chapter 40

By 2 pm, we had searched Tyler's house thoroughly twice through. We had uniformed officers going over the property a third time, just in case anything had been missed.

Tyler sat in interview room four. He remained cuffed. Looking at him through the mirror, we saw he was sitting still, head down and emotionless.

"So, what do you think?" Jake asked me.

"I know I've said it before, but I don't know why he would be protecting someone. Why wouldn't he just give him up?"

"Thick as thieves," Jake replied.

"Maybe he doesn't know the guy. Maybe he's telling the truth?" I posed to Jake.

"You saying two different guys hit the same place on the same night? I doubt it. We already calculated the odds of one in a million," Jake said.

"One in two million," I corrected him. "I keep thinking about the back door. If your guy's inside, why do you need to break in again? It's not logical."

"Maybe we give him a polygraph? Let me see how I go. Fresh person, fresh approach, and then we'll offer the lie detector test."

"Sounds good," I replied, ready to go in. Jake grabbed me by the shoulder and held me back.

"Did you write notes on what he said in the car?" he asked.

"No," I answered. Jake rolled his eyes, ever so slightly. "I recorded it on my phone though, does that help?" I asked, pushing Jake towards room four.

We sat down opposite Tyler. Jake introduced himself. Before asking him any questions, he asked if he was thirsty, if he needed to go to the bathroom or if he wanted something to eat. Tyler asked for a can of Coke.

"So, Tyler. Just before we start, please be aware you do not have to answer any questions without your lawyer present. You have been charged with breaking and entering at this time. This interview is being recorded. Do you want your lawyer to attend this interview?"

He shook his head.

"Please answer yes or no for the recording."

"No!" he replied firmly.

"Can you tell me what happened on Monday 10th December and Tuesday the 11th?"

"Well, I broke into the house at about 3 pm. I switched off the alarm using my screwdriver to pop the case in the master bedroom. And then I went looking for the safe."

"Ok, then what happened?" Jake's tactic was never to ask another question until they were finished with their story. He believed this gave them enough rope to hang themselves with.

Tyler continued. "It wasn't where it was supposed to be, so I did a quick search and I found it in the study. Except while I was there, the lady came home. I heard the automated gate."

"Ok, then what?" Jake asked.

"So I had to rush to reset the alarm so it would still be good when she walked in. Otherwise she would know something was up and I'd get caught. The alarm was rearmed and I was up in the roof before she entered the house. My plan was to wait till 1 am when they were asleep and then go for the safe. Then at 12.30, maybe a little after, I heard screaming, the girl screamed. It startled me. Woke me up. I think I'd been dozing and then the lady said 'Put her down!' or somethin' and 'get out!'. But I don't know to who she was talkin' with."

"So what did you do?" Jake asked calmly.

"When I heard no more screaming, I got out my knife. I had one in my pocket. I remember throwing my glove away, so my knife didn't slip. I climbed down from the roof and went downstairs. Her phone was still on the step and I walked past it, it was glowing because the rest of the house was dark. I saw the lady on the tiles. I didn't stop 'cause you guys were on your way. Then I ran out the back and jumped the fence and then I was in my car, gone."

"Do you know who this other person was?" Jake asked, still very calm and unemotional.

"Man, I never saw the dude and I never worked with him. I work alone."

"You would agree it would be rare to have two people rob the same house at exactly the same time who were not working together, would you not Mr Parsons?"

"I don't think he was robbing the joint. He had no reason to go upstairs. He could have got to the safe from downstairs," Tyler replied.

"You said earlier that you went to the master bedroom for the alarm and the safe wasn't there. Why did you expect it to be there?" Jake asked.

"That was the word in prison. It was supposed to be in the robe," Tyler replied.

"But it was in the study, wasn't it?"

"Yes," Tyler answered.

"Maybe the other guy got the same info you got, that's why he went upstairs?"

"I suppose, but I didn't hear him come past me," Tyler added.

"But you were asleep, maybe you missed him?"

"Nah, I would have woken up, I wasn't sleepin' that heavy," Tyler answered.

"Ok, can you clear something up for me?" Jake asked, going through the photos of the crime scene.

"Is this your screwdriver?" In the photo Jake showed, the screwdriver was embedded in the lady's throat. Jake had done the right thing by the family and concealed her face with a Post-It note.

"Might be, I can't be sure," Tyler answered.

"How did it get in the lady's neck?" Jake asked.

"I don't know, I was up in the roof," Tyler replied.

"Where I have an issue is that the screwdriver only has two sets of prints on it: yours and Mrs Campbell's."

"Maybe I dropped it. I can't be sure," Tyler answered. He had almost finished his Coke and maybe it was the caffeine or the questions but he was starting to fidget.

"You know what I think?" Jake began. "I think you went in to rob the house, as you say, while your partner waited outside. When you didn't come out, he waited in the car until it was dark, then he went in to see what the fuck had happened to you. But in doing so he woke them up and when you had to leave empty-handed, you went for the girl as ransom. But on your way out, the mum tried to stop you, and one of you killed her!"

"No, no, not at all. No, that's not what happened!" Tyler rebutted.

"Tyler, I have been doing this for a long time and the evidence doesn't lie," Jake replied. "Now, I can help you. Tell us who the other guy is and where the girl is. If you help us find the girl and if you didn't kill Mrs Campbell, then we will help you. You don't want to go down for two murders you didn't commit, do you?"

"Two? Who else is dead?" Tyler asked.

"What do you think will happen to the girl if we don't find her?" Jake asked.

"I don't know who he is, I swear." He thumped his hands on the table. "Fuck, how many times do I need to tell you the same shit?" he said, frustrated.

"Will you do a lie detector test?" Jake asked.

"Hell yeah, cause I'm tellin' the truth, no problem," Tyler replied.

"Ok, we will organise that. Sit tight. Is there anything else you need, another Coke?" Jake asked.

"Yes please, and somethin' to eat. You guys messed up my leftover spaghetti this morning." Tyler pulled up his shirt to show the stain from the spaghetti sauce.

Jake got up to leave.

It was the only time I spoke in the interview but I wanted to leave him with something to think about.

"Maybe you should think about what's going to happen to your dog if you go away. We'd have to send it to the pound, and they never find another home for them so within two months he gets the green needle. Just think about that and if you remember anything let us know."

I didn't wait for the response.

We left the room. Jake turned to me, "Did you just threaten to have his dog killed if he didn't give up information?" Jake asked, almost laughing.

"Possibly, it's been a long night."

Chapter 41

Austin could wait no longer. He had to start looking. He had spent the last hour reading the files on the three missing kids while he was waiting to hear back from the cops. No call had come. He could be waiting a while yet.

He would head out and do some investigating of his own. He arrived at the residence of the Bradley family just after 1 pm. At first, he sat in the car and looked around. This could be any street in any suburb. He knocked quietly on the door, not loudly like a police officer.

A dishevelled woman in a dressing-gown appeared at the door. She was wearing no makeup, had not done her hair and didn't look like she cared. Her face was drawn, and her eyes had heavy dark rings underneath. Sleep had obviously evaded her.

"Hi, my name is Austin Campbell, my daughter was kidnapped and my wife was killed." Austin got straight to the point. "I was wondering if I could ask you some questions to see if there is any connection between our children's abductions?"

"Oh my God. I saw you on the news. Please come in, you poor thing," she said, giving Austin a hug as he passed through the doorway.

"Your son Stevie was on his way to school when he was taken?" Austin asked.

She nodded, "His basketball was found at the top of the park so we assume that he was taken from the court that meets the other side of the park."

"Did he normally walk to school?" Austin asked as they both took a seat at the table.

"Tea?" Mrs Bradley asked.

"White, no sugar please," Austin replied.

She flicked the kettle and removed the cups from the shelf above the stove.

"I was supposed to drive him, but I had a migraine that day," she replied. "He had walked two days that week and most of the week before."

"Do you think someone had been following him?" Austin asked.

"The police asked me if I had noticed anything out of the ordinary, but I hadn't, except I had seen the same van a few times over the last week."

"How did you know it was the same one? They're a common vehicle," Austin said, sipping his tea. It was good and strong.

"I don't for sure but it had the same yellow logo on the side. It was some type of phone company."

"Do you know which one?" Austin asked.

"No, I'd never seen it before. I've looked for it everywhere since."

Austin pulled out a pen and a piece of paper. "Could you draw it?"

She took the pen and paper. Austin took another sip of his tea.

A few seconds later, she slid the paper back. The logo wasn't so much a phone as an old-style phone receiver. Austin folded the piece of paper and put it safely in his shirt pocket.

He then turned his questions from those of an investigator to those of another concerned parent. "How are you coping?" he asked.

Mrs Bradley suppressed a cry. Then she looked herself up and down. "You can probably tell, not very well, I hate myself, it's my fault. If I had been ok that day, he would be here with me now."

Austin, who had almost finished his tea, gently touched her hand.

"I need you to listen to me. It's not your fault. The person who did this is responsible and I tell you one thing; I will find him, I will not stop until I know who took them! But you need to do me a favour."

Mrs Bradley frowned, hesitated, "Ok, what do you need?"

"You need to stay strong, because if I bring your boy home, then I don't want him to see you like this, ok?" She nodded, and began crying.

"How can you stay so strong?" she asked.

"I need to be strong for her, I need to be strong for all of them. Whoever did this has unknowingly made it my mission and I won't stop until I find them."

"I hope you find the bastard that took them. If you do, what will you do?" she asked.

"End him," Austin said without hesitation and with total conviction.

It was the first smile that Austin had seen from her.

"I will stay in touch with you. I wouldn't advise telling the police I was here; they aren't too happy about that. I'm poking around," Austin said as he stood ready to leave.

"I found them of little assistance anyhow. I'm glad that you're out there looking. Thank you."

Austin kissed her on the cheek, and headed back to his car.

Time was ticking.

Chapter 42

Monique Keller was my third police chief in 10 years and she was by far the most driven. The last two had been men who were past their prime, where Monique was still hungry to kick ass. While she took cases very personally, she was strong enough to handle the burden.

Monique sat on the driver's side of her desk while Jake and I sat on the side that usually meant we were in trouble. As usual, she was dressed immaculately today, in a dark blue pant suit, her gun holstered to her right hip. Her red hair was tied up in a complicated looking ponytail.

"So gentlemen, tell me, where are we at with the Campbell murder? Has the suspect provided any further information?"

"We've interviewed him three times. His story is the same, nothing's changed."

"Do you think he's telling the truth?" she asked.

Jake and I exchanged glances.

"Well, Detectives, you must have some thoughts."

Jake answered, "We both think that he may be telling the truth. The reason we say that is Forensics found no evidence of the girl in his house or his car. Only evidence we have is the fingerprints on the screwdriver and the back door. The two main questions we can't yet answer, but that give weight to Tyler's version, are, why would someone who was working with someone else lock them out, and why would one person enter so many hours after the first if they were working together? He's just finished doing the polygraph with Dr Swan, so those results might lead us somewhere. Either way, we need to find the other offender to find the girl."

Monique picked up her phone, pressed four digits and spoke. "Have you finalised the results of Tyler Parson's polygraph? Great, bring them by my office." She hung up. "Raymond will be here in a few minutes. Let's talk about this other suspect. What are we doing to find this guy?" Monique asked.

Jake sat forward. "We've put out the footage of him in the mask, asked for anyone who may know this person to call Crime Stoppers. We've mentioned the paintball aspect. I wouldn't imagine many people would have that combination. We're also still going door to door but until we have more to go on, we are where we are." Jake sat back in his chair.

"Do you think this is related to the other kidnappings?" Monique asked.

"I'm not sure at this point. It's something I'm considering. This seemed well planned, while the others appeared to be more opportunistic. Although having said that, the perpetrator may have planned the others. Maybe their best time was on the way to school?"

I added, "Maybe he changed his MO in this case because Mrs Campbell drove Mikayla to and from school. So there was never any opportunity to strike. That's my best guess anyway."

"I think we start working these. If they are connected and we get a ransom note, then we reassess. Whatever, don't mention to the media that they're connected, or the whole city will go into a panic," Monique said. "You studied at the behavioural science unit in Quantico," she said to me. "How many serial kidnappings did you study?"

"In most of the cases I studied, the children were murdered soon after the abduction. Ransom is very rare," I replied. "That's why I think they're connected."

"Do you think they could still be alive?" Monique asked.

"We haven't found a body in any of the cases. So I would think they are still alive, especially if they're being taken for the purpose of sexual gratification. Either that, or we just haven't found them yet," I replied.

"Maybe they're being sold?" Jake chimed in.

"It's possible. However, I'd say if they were younger that would be more of a possibility. A two-year-old for example won't remember they were abducted. Someone desperate for a child will pay for a two-year-old. They can be raised by someone else and will never know what happened. But an 11-year-old, they will remember being taken," I said. "It's possible that we could have a paedophile who's not fussed on gender and it could be possible that he's keeping them somewhere. But I think we need to be prepared for the worst."

"Don't they usually go for one gender or another?" Monique asked.

"There was a case I remember studying in Quantico. The man was Lewis Lent. He kidnapped a girl from near her house then a month later, a boy from a movie theatre where he worked as a janitor. So a single offender can have desires for both," I said.

"Come in, Doctor." Monique waved in Dr Raymond Swan.

He stood at the side of her desk where he could better see us all.

"What was the outcome?" Monique asked, her chair squeaking as she twisted around to face him.

"Technically, he passed. But when we discussed the fingerprints on the screwdriver, there were inconsistencies. He passed when I asked him if he was working with anyone, if he killed Mrs Campbell and if he knew who had killed Mrs Campbell.

"The only question that he didn't pass on was 'do you know why your screwdriver was found in the victim?' He answered no but the graph suggested this wasn't truthful. So he didn't fail but it wasn't a pass either. He knows more than what he's telling us, but if I were to go to court, I'd have to say it's a pass."

Raymond placed the results on the desk, and Monique immediately handed them to Jake.

"Well, Detectives, I suggest you go look under rocks. Do whatever you have to do to find this guy and the kids."

Chapter 43

It was just after 3 by the time Austin arrived at the home of Chloe Henderson. He knocked in the same quiet way. Mrs Henderson answered the door and asked, "Can I help you?"

At first glance, Austin knew this lady was holding it together a lot better than Stevie's mother. She was wearing makeup and was reasonably well dressed. Hell, she was dressed.

"Mrs Henderson, my name is Austin Campbell and as you may have heard, my daughter was taken last night. I think the kidnappings may be related. Do you mind if I ask you a few questions?" Austin asked.

"I recognise you from the conference, how are you holding up?" she asked as she opened the door.

"I'm trying to stay busy so I don't dwell on it," Austin replied.

She offered Austin a tea or coffee but he declined. He explained he had just come from the Bradley's home. She had heard of the other cases but had never sought to communicate with them. She hadn't thought she would be able to handle it and so she was suffering alone. Being a single mum, she relied on her parents and the police to provide support.

Austin listened intently and when Mrs Henderson said something of interest, he made the occasional note in his notebook. It wasn't until she showed Austin into Chloe's room that he realised his daughter's room was sitting at home waiting for her to return. It hit him. Tears began to well up in his eyes but as the emotions began to flow, his mind ticked into military gear. Stay focused on the mission, the mission, bring them home, he reminded himself. He took a deep breath and moved away from the door.

"Can you tell me about the last person to see Chloe?" Austin asked.

"I don't know much more than what the police told me," she answered, suggesting that what she knew was insignificant.

"What was that, if you don't mind sharing?" Austin replied.

"They said that the man at number six, Mr Lubic I think his name is, was apparently out sweeping his path when he saw her walk by. When he looked again, she was gone. A hundred and eighty metres more and she was at the school gate."

"Did they ever mention a van or any vehicles?" Austin asked.

"No, the police are at a loss, a total loss." Mrs Henderson shrugged.

"What was the name of the street where she was last seen?" Austin asked.

"Elmer," she answered almost instantaneously. Another note for his book. "Do you think they are related, Mr Campbell?" she asked.

"Yes I do, until something shows me otherwise. I will search until I find them."

"If you find the prick that took my daughter, hurt him for me, make him suffer before you hand him in," she said.

"I don't want to upset you any more than you are already, but if I find him I won't be handing him in, that's for sure," Austin replied.

"That suits me even better." She led him to the door.

"Good luck!" she called as he headed down the path.

He was back in the security of his own car. It was almost 4 pm. Time was ticking. He thought it was best to follow up the lead on the last person to see Chloe alive. The Lubic man at number six Elmer.

Then he would visit the home of the missing Scott Western.

Chapter 44

Mikayla sat back in her cell. She was still surprised she hadn't been beaten or hurt for trying to escape. The music continued to play some type of slow rock, she couldn't make out the song, it was just all noise.

"How long have you been here?" Mikayla asked the boy who sat back in the far corner of his cell.

"Shhh, he will hear you."

Mikayla pointed her index finger to the celling. "He can't hear us, he has the radio on too loud."

Scott listened intently for a few seconds. The girl was right, the music was loud, he would never hear them talking if they were quiet.

"I don't know how long it's been," but then he looked at his wall and began counting, "I've had 24 breakfasts, but I don't think I've been given breakfast every day, so it might be longer."

"Do you know what's behind the red door?" Mikayla asked.

"It's a bedroom. He takes you there and takes photos of you and he sends the photos to people. When I first arrived, there was a girl he took in there, I think he did things to her, there was a lot of screaming."

"What happens to them after that?" Mikayla asked.

"I dunno, I guess he sends the photos to your family so they pay." Scott shrugged.

"Why are you still here if everyone else has paid? Why haven't you been sent home yet?" Mikayla asked.

"My parents don't have the money, they wouldn't be able to pay…I just want to go home," Scott said, starting to cry.

"When my dad buys me back, I'll make sure we pay for you as well so you can go home," Mikayla said, trying to stop his crying.

* * *

Stevie had been chained to the bed for three days now. He'd had very little to eat or drink.

The room was plain, nothing out of the ordinary, nothing different from a standard bedroom in a normal house. There were curtains over the window and a door. In the corner opposite the bed, there was a TV. It was on the cartoons, as it had been for the last three days. He thought he had seen the same *Scooby Doo* cartoon every day, sometimes twice.

He thought he was going home when the man with the mask put him in the van, but when he met the Batman he knew it wasn't true. Then he met the Priest with the strange opera mask. He had seen it once before on a poster of the *Phantom of the Opera* billboard in the city.

Even though he couldn't remember it in detail, he knew the Priest had hurt him. If it was anything like he had been through in the last three days, he was glad he couldn't remember it fully.

The last three days had been hell. At first they just took photos, then they crawled into bed with him. Every time they did, he went somewhere else, usually into the cartoons on at the time. He would imagine himself solving a mystery in *Scooby Doo* or killing Yo Sammity Sam with Bugs Bunny. He visited a lot of cartoons in three days.

He had only been in the room for three days but he knew it like the back of his hand. He knew all its little secrets, all its little intricacies. Like the curtains. They must have been bought specially for this room and likely for this purpose. Even though they were new, they were thin enough that any light behind them would make them transparent, except the light never changed, so Stevie was pretty sure the window must be boarded up.

He knew it took his kidnappers exactly five steps from the door to the bed.

He knew there was a daddy long-legs spider in the far corner above the bed. It must have been comfortable because it hadn't moved in two days.

In three days, he had worked out that there were hidden cameras in the room, one in the smoke detector and one behind the mirrored door, opposite the bed. Even though he couldn't see it in the middle of the night, he could hear it, even above the TV.

His wrists were burning; the skin had been broken by the handcuff. He could see a red tinge from the bleeding around the edge of them.

He lay on a bare mattress, in just his briefs, shivering. Yesterday had been hot, but today was cold, and he felt it. He had no blanket, not even a sheet. Goosebumps had formed all over his body. His lips were dried and cracked and his throat hurt. He was desperate for a drink. When was the last time he'd had one? He couldn't remember.

As he lay there breathing what he thought would be his last breaths, one thought entered his head. Ellie Davis and her beautiful smelling hair, and that wonderful exotic perfume, and those lips that one day he wanted to kiss for real, to see if they would be as soft and beautiful as he imagined.

That smell, her smell, it was all that kept him going.

As if on cue, the man that he had only seen in a suit or naked walked through the door. He was holding a glass of water in his right hand and a plate of sandwiches in his left.

Stevie began to salivate just at the thought of eating and he licked his lips. They stung as his tongue ran over the cracks. The man placed the plate and glass on the table at his right-hand side. He didn't speak, he simply sat on the bed and undid Stevie's right cuff. He then stood and headed out, but before he got to the door, Stevie spoke. "Thanks for the food and drink, sir." The man paused for a few seconds, as if contemplating a response.

Stevie knew what would happen when they tired of him or wanted something else to video. He had seen on the crime shows what usually happened to the missing kids. Often they would be found dead and were soon forgotten when the next one went missing. He knew if he was to stay alive he had to try and befriend them; get them talking. Maybe get them to drop their guard.

The man in the suit was the nice one, if there was such a thing. It was like choosing between two monsters. His name was Ian.

The second man was called Bill. He was home all the time and had a drug issue. He was a few inches shorter than the man in the suit, scruffier, not quite bald but with thinning hair. He was always in tracksuit pants and a singlet, which looked to be the same ones every day. But the worst thing about him was that he was dead-set mean. The meanest, angriest man Stevie had ever seen. It seemed that he didn't just want to rape but he wanted to watch him suffer. He'd noticed the needle marks on Bill's left arm, which looked like a swarm of mosquitos had attacked him.

Ian left and locked the door and as soon as the bolt sounded, Stevie got stuck into the food. He sipped the water. He needed to savour it.

Stevie sat on the bed eating peanut butter and jam sandwiches, watching cartoons, and for the briefest of instances he felt like a kid again.

Chapter 45

Mr Lubic answered the door. He was a tiny man, dwarf-like in stature. "Hello," he said in his thick accent.

"Mr Lubic, I was hoping you could help me. I'm Austin Campbell. My daughter was kidnapped and it may be related to the kidnapping of the girl who was taken while walking to school near here. Can you show me where you last saw her?"

"Yes, yes, terrible it is, come I show." He took Austin out the front of his house and stood on the footpath, "I was standing here, I sweep, I look in that direction," he said, pointing to the start of the street, "girl was walking, I see her coming closer and closer, as I sweep. As she walks past she is very close to me, so that's why when police ask me I am sure it's her. We were only few feet apart. She is not paying attention as she passes by, she is on the phone, moving thumb up and down, doing whatever they are doing. The wires are in her ears, I could hear the music as she passed."

"Did you see her go all the way to the school gate?" Austin asked.

"No, my phone rang and I hurried to answer it. When I came back out she was gone, I thought she was in school grounds. Didn't think any more about it."

"How long were you on the phone?" Austin asked.

"About thirty seconds. It was hospital, confirming my appointment next week. I said yes and hung up and then I was back out. I even remember looking up road to school, before I began sweeping again. The street was empty."

"Would you mind helping me for a few minutes? I want to walk from the point she reached when you went inside."

"Yeah, sure no problem," he answered.

Austin began walking towards Lubic. "You're going too fast. She was walking slow, because she was playing with her phone."

Austin slowed down his pace. "Is this better?" Austin asked.

"Better," Lubic answered.

The two men re-enacted the scenario as before.

When Lubic returned from inside, Austin was five metres from entering the school gate.

"Ok. Let's do that again. This time I want you to take an extra 15 seconds inside." They ran the test again. This time when Lubic returned to his sweeping, he looked up as he had done that day, and instead of seeing nothing he saw Austin on the path inside the gate heading for the oval.

Austin made his way back to Lubic. "You could still see me, and even if you were inside another 15 seconds, I still wouldn't have been out of sight."

"No, I could easily see you, I have a lot of carrots, grow them fresh out the back. Good for eyes."

"Are you sure we have the timing right? Could it have taken you longer? Could it have taken you longer than you recall?"

"No, no, it was very quick call. I think the first time was even a little too long. I went inside, pick up phone, say 'hello', they say 'Mr Lubic,' I say 'yes,' they say 'it's Helen here from Monash Medical Centre just confirming your appointment at 10.30 Thursday.' I say 'yes, no problem,' she say 'I see you then.' I say 'thank you' and I hang up."

"You came straight back out. You didn't go to the toilet or get a drink?" Austin asked, trying to eliminate any potential complications to Mr Lubic's story.

"No, I came straight back out," he said emphatically.

"Ok, ok, just confirming," Austin said. "You know that means someone took her from the street?" he said, gazing down the street where she had vanished.

It was an unusual street, he thought. The left-hand side was all standard residential development, while on Mr Lubic's side, it was one-acre blocks. Five hundred metres beyond the back fence ran the high-tension powerlines.

"There are a lot of criminals around these parts. They let out the sexual offenders and for some reason they let them live close to a school," Lubic said. "You know, in the village where I grew up, you touch kids, they cut your balls off. They need to have that here."

"Had you noticed any cars or anyone acting strangely that morning or even the days prior?" Austin asked.

"No, everything was the same. The only cars I saw that morning were dropping kids off."

"Thank you," Austin said before he leaned in to shake his hand.

Mr Lubic held his hand. "I hope you get her back; I hope you find them both." He let go of Austin's hand and headed down his driveway to his front door.

Austin sat in his car trying to imagine what had eventuated. He asked himself was it likely that someone drove up while Lubic was inside on the phone? It was such a small window of opportunity that Austin doubted the chances.

He picked up his ghost phone and dialled the only number stored in it. "I hope you're not ringing me to clean up a mess?" Marcus answered.

"You know that I don't leave a mess," Austin said. "Looking for some information. What do you have on registered sex offenders living in the Elmer Road area of Bayswater?" he asked.

"It will take me a few minutes to access that database. I'll call you back," Marcus replied.

The phone call ended.

Austin sat in his car wondering if it had been a lucky or a planned abduction.

He must have dozed off because he saw his wife smiling at him at the airport, and he kissed her. Had the ringing phone not butted in, he might have had one more kiss.

"You're not going to believe this," Marcus began, "there are 15 registered sex offenders within a two-kilometre radius! And there's one in the very same street. It's the second-to-last house according to the satellite map. His name is Beau Delacroix. He lives with his mother. He did a two-year sentence for attempted abduction of two girls in a park. He was released only four weeks before the first child disappeared."

"You're right, I don't believe it, but I did expect something similar," Austin responded.

"He was interviewed as a witness in regard to Chloe's disappearance. He said he had left before that and arrived at his first job at 9.15. His alibi checked out, although it's impossible to know if he left when he said he did or if he was two minutes later. His house and garage were searched. There was no evidence of her anywhere. But he remains a suspect. As do five other sex offenders in the area."

"I might go pay him a visit," Austin said. Before hanging up, he remembered to thank Marcus for his assistance.

* * *

Austin had briefly thought about pretending he was a detective for this next visit, yet he suspected they would recognise him from his TV interview. Everyone else had, so he dismissed the idea.

He walked up the driveway of the house at number 18 Elmer Road. It was built of older style clinker brick, which suggested it was an original house and had been there for decades. Austin wondered if, in fact, it might have been the original farmhouse before the land was subdivided. The driveway went down the side of the house and led to a large freestanding garage, a big one, possibly for six or eight cars.

Austin approached the security door with the mesh falling away in the corner. He rapped his knuckles on it three times. Instead of sounding like knocking, it sounded like he was trying to bust the door down. Maybe he'd rapped a bit hard.

The door opened and the cigarette smoke made him cough. It was disgusting. He carried on regardless. "Sorry to bother you. My daughter was kidnapped and I was just looking into Chloe's kidnapping to see if there might be any links. Do you mind if I ask you some questions?"

The woman at the other end of the cigarette was old, wrinkly and had skin the colour of a potato sack. The smoking had aged her, that was certain. She was a masculine looking woman, the kind you expect to see in hillbilly horror movies.

She drew on her cigarette again, "Yeah, I saw ya on the news the other mornin'. Not good losing a kid, but I don't know how I can help ya."

"I just wondered if you had seen anything on the morning the other girl vanished, that's all."

"I'd love to help but as I said to the coppers, I wasn't even home, dole money had come in and I was doing me shopping," she said.

Austin immediately imagined her gambling.

"Was anyone else at home, your husband perhaps?"

"Don't have no husband, I fucked him off long ago. Useless fat heap of shit he was."

"No kids?" Austin asked.

"No, live here all by my lonesome. I have to go now, I have something on the stove. I hope you find your girl," she said.

Austin knew there was no husband but wanted to see if she was protecting her son. According to her, she had no son.

As she began to close the door between them, a white van pulled into the driveway and drove past them down to the back shed.

"Who's that?" Austin asked, followed quickly by, "I thought no one else lived here?"

"He's never home, so it's like I'm by myself. That's want I meant." She closed the door before Austin had a chance to ask any more questions.

He walked down the step and back onto the driveway, his eyes remaining firmly on the man in the shed.

He headed directly for the big sliding door.

As he reached the entrance he could hear loud music playing. It sounded like INXS.

"Excuse me," he said. The man had his back to him and continued to unload something from the top of his van.

Austin tried again, "Excuse me!" This time he said it a lot louder. This time the man turned.

"Whatever you're selling, we don't want any," he said, continuing to unload.

"I'm not selling anything. I want to ask you some questions about a missing girl."

The man stopped his unloading and came to the entrance of the garage.

"Who you looking for?" Beau asked.

"I just wanted to ask you some questions about the morning the girl disappeared. Do you remember that morning?" Austin asked.

"I've told you guys everything I know," Beau answered. He had recognised Mikayla's dad the moment he drove past him in the drive. He was praying the father wouldn't recognise him from the movies.

"No, I'm not with the police. My daughter was kidnapped yesterday and I'm trying to see if there was maybe a connection between her kidnapping and Chloe's, the girl who was kidnapped on her way to school," Austin replied.

Austin tried to compare the man standing in front of him with the man in the mask. Could it be the same guy? Definitely the same build. Could be the same person, could be a hundred other fat guys. Austin knew one thing; he had met this man before, somewhere.

"As I told the police, I left probably five minutes before the time she would have passed my house. I saw her on the other corner of the highway. Apparently some guy saw her in this street. I don't know who, but he was the last to see her."

Austin got the feeling something wasn't right.

"The cops think I had something to do with it, but I said how could I have if someone else had seen her after me? They checked out the job I attended and the time I arrived and left," he added without prompting.

"I never suggested it was you; just wondering if you had seen her at all," Austin said smiling, "and you did, so that helps greatly. Sorry, how rude of me, I'm Austin." He offered his hand for shaking. "Beau," the man replied, as he took Austin's hand and shook it.

"What do you do for work?" Austin asked.

"I'm a handyman. Work everywhere really. I have a big day ahead tomorrow. Really need to get this van unloaded," Beau replied.

"Yeah, sure, sorry," Austin replied. He scoured the garage for anything that might have belonged to his daughter, but there was nothing. He was about to turn and leave when Beau stepped behind his van, leaving the side in clear view.

It read 'One Call Handyman'. Underneath was a picture of the handle of an old phone receiver. He had no doubt this was the logo Stevie's mum had seen.

And he still couldn't shake the feeling he had seen this guy before.

Chapter 46

Hayley and Jake had not been out to dinner in months, but it felt like years to Hayley. They had never been more distant from each other than they were right now. Hayley hated herself for keeping secrets, and tonight she was going to tell Jake she was expecting their baby.

Jake came directly from work and they met at the Crown Casino. It had an abundance of restaurants to choose from. They decided on Chinese. It was expensive but worth it. They chose the seven-course banquet. The courses were small but by the time they hit the fried ice-cream for dessert, they were struggling to finish it. Even Jake had trouble fitting it in, but he would always find a way.

"Jake, there's something I've been meaning to tell you."

Jake put his hand on hers. "It's ok, I know." He paused. "I know about the baby and I'm ecstatic."

Hayley looked utterly shocked. "How did you know?" she asked.

"I'm a cop, remember?" Jake replied. "You might be thinking I've been a bit distant lately, but it wasn't intentional. In fact, I was distant because I was trying to get some things straight in my own head." Jake took a deep breath. "I've decided that I'm going to leave the force and do private detective work."

Hayley sat there, even more shocked. "But you..." She paused, trying to understand. "You love that job," she continued, "why would you quit?"

"I do love it, but I love you and Indiana more."

"Indiana?" Hayley questioned.

"Yeah, Indiana, our boy, or girl, that's going to be the name," Jake said, smiling.

"Ok, let's discuss the name later," Hayley began. "Why are you quitting the force?" she asked again.

"It's because I love you and I don't want you getting that call, the one that says I'm not coming home. Call me selfish but I don't want to miss any of our future because some drug-fucked crim got lucky and shot me. Plus, I can't do my job properly if I'm worrying about it every day."

Their first course of spring rolls arrived but neither of them even looked at them.

"I'll give my notice soon. I just want to help Brodie clear some cases first. Also, they need time to replace me."

"You're irreplaceable, honey." Hayley laughed. "Whatever you want, that's ok with me." She smiled, and it seemed to say 'thank you'. Maybe deep down she had wanted him off the force too. Maybe Jake knew her better than she knew herself.

They spent the rest of the dinner talking baby. What they needed, what colour the baby's room should be and of course the name came up again, several times. Jake was sure she was accepting it as a boy's name. If they had a girl she would need a bit of convincing.

They decided not to find out the sex of the baby. They were happy with the surprise. He had almost eight months in which to convince her, if that's what it took.

Chapter 47

The air was crisp and salty. A gentle breeze broke the heat. The warmth from the sun on his back filled his soul. Water flowed over his feet and retreated with each wave. He walked along the beach like a man at peace with the world. "I love you," a voice next to him said. He turned. Sarah stood there, shining. The wind caught her hair, her hand touched his. She smiled and pulled him in. He had never seen her look so beautiful. She nestled her head under his chin. As he hugged her, he looked up the beach and could see Mikayla in the distance. She was drawing a heart in the sand with a stick. Above the heart was the letter 'I', below was the letter 'U'.

He turned his gaze back out to sea, smelling the ocean with every breath.

"You need to save her before it's too late," Sarah said to him.

"She is just there," Austin replied. He was still enjoying the hug.

"Look again," she whispered.

He turned back towards the beach where his daughter had been drawing in the sand.

She was gone and there was no heart. Instead was the word 'HELP!'

Austin felt his wife disappear in his arms.

Save her, before it's too late. The words rang in the air.

Austin awoke crying. He was sitting in his car. 'Save her, before it's too late,' still rang loudly in his head. Had he been asleep or was it a vision? He couldn't be sure. Whatever it was it was vivid. Was it a snapshot of heaven? While he didn't believe in heaven, he was sure he had already been to hell, or as close to it as he wanted to get.

Could it have been his wife's spirit? Could she be caught in the in-between? Many cultures believed the spirit would be trapped between earth and heaven if business remained unfinished.

Austin pondered the possibilities for a moment and then concluded that with the sleep deprivation and the tragic circumstances of the last 24 hours, it was most likely to have been a dream. The message was clear, however; he had to find her before it was too late, and time was running out.

He had parked the car at the end of Beau's street. While he had strong suspicions about Beau, he couldn't focus all his effort on one suspect. He had to make sure he looked at every possibility.

His cell rang, and Marcus flashed up in the caller ID.

"Hey," Austin answered, sluggish and tired.

"I'm just ringing to let you know the police have arrested Tyler Parsons. It's only for B&E, but more charges are expected. I managed to find the name and address of his last cellmate. His name is Jack Taylor. It might be worth making a house call. I'll send you an email with the details."

"Yeah, ok. It'll be my next stop. Any news on Mikayla?" Austin asked.

"Nothing. Sorry," Marcus replied.

"I'm getting more and more convinced her kidnapping is related to these other disappearances. Something big is going on here," said.

"Whatever you need, I'll get it for you. Keep me updated."

"Thanks buddy. I'll let you know how I go at Jack's."

Austin hung up. During the whole time he had waited outside Beau's house, while he had been awake, his eyes had been focused on the driveway. Staring at it for over four hours. No movement.

Before he moved on to Jack, he needed to be able to track Beau. That way he would always know where he was.

The idea of breaking in to his shed to plant the tracker had crossed his mind. He also wouldn't mind another look inside that shed.

Chapter 48

I had to follow up the two remaining leads. One was the first kidnapping, Scott Western's. I wanted to go and speak with the parents. The other was the last witness to have seen Chloe Henderson, Mr Lubic.

As I neared the Western's house, one thing struck me; the similarity between the areas. Not a geographical similarity, a suburban one. All the abduction sites were the same: quiet neighbourhoods, normal suburbs, normal kids. This person was a master at blending in.

I knocked and this time, a man answered. He was tall, but not quite as tall as me, about six foot two. He had a barrel chest, broad shoulders, toned arms, and he looked as if he dedicated a fair amount of his time to the gym.

I introduced myself. "I'll get my wife," he answered, without even introducing himself.

Moments later, a blonde lady appeared at the door. "How may I help you?" she asked in a bright cheerful way that I hadn't expected. I was taken aback.

I explained how we now believed the cases were connected and I was going over each case to see if we could find a common thread that might give us a new lead.

Mrs Western showed me through to the dining/kitchen area. I stood in amazement; the feeling I had interpreted as cheerful was in fact determination. This woman had thrown herself into searching for Scott and I had just entered ground zero. They had made posters and maps. The maps had a red pin with the words 'Last Seen' in the colour ledger at the bottom.

From the look of it, they had been doing an investigation of their own. She sat at the table and offered me a seat opposite. As I moved the chair to take my seat, a white cat darted from under the table into another room.

"So, Mrs Western, could you tell me what happened?"

"Audrey, please," she replied.

"Audrey," I repeated.

"It was like any other school morning. Scott got up, had brekkie, packed his lunch and headed off to school on his bike."

"Now, the school is Sunbury State Primary, just six streets over, correct?" I asked.

"Yes, that's the one. He always rode his bike to school. He loved riding his bike, he was always on it, even after school he would be out the front riding it until dark."

"So on that morning, there was nothing unusual. Scott went to school as normal?" I asked.

"Yep, I went on with my day, thinking he was in class. All that time he needed me and I didn't know... It wasn't until lunchtime when I went up to the shops for some groceries and I saw his bike on the footpath. At first I thought I must have been mistaken so I went and checked the bike. It looked like his. I rang the school, and they told me he wasn't there, that they thought he was off sick. They had no reason to think otherwise.

"I stood there on the side of the road staring at his bike while I waited for the police. I had no idea what to do. It was like I was in a haze, but at some point in that haze I knew falling apart would be of no benefit to Scott and I had to stay strong," she explained.

She leaned in across the table.

"Neville, my husband, on the other hand, it's torn him apart. They were really close. He just mopes around. I was hoping he would be influenced by my positivity, but it's like he's resigned himself to the worst," she said, sounding sad.

"Could you make us a cuppa, darl?" she called out to him.

Without a word, Neville heaved himself out of his recliner and turned his eyes away from the TV. His walk was slow and it seemed to take him a huge effort. By the time he had placed the cups on the bench, he had sighed several times, as if to protest his chore to his wife.

"How would you like your coffee?" she asked.

"I'd prefer a tea, if it's not too much trouble," I replied.

"Of course not, how would you like your tea?"

"Just white, thank you."

Neville begrudgingly walked over, placing the cups on the table. He even made a second trip, this time placing a plate of biscuits on the table.

"Audrey, did you notice any strange cars or vans hanging around the neighbourhood before Scott's disappearance?"

"No, everything appeared normal."

"Scott didn't mention strange cars or a van following him in the days leading up to the abduction?"

"No, and he would have said if he'd noticed someone. I always told him to be aware of stranger danger," she said.

She had several more sips from her cup, chewing a biscuit between sips.

My tea was hot and strong, just the way I liked it. The biscuits were only store bought but they were chocolate chip and moreish. It was a good thing Jake wasn't here or they would be demolished.

"Audrey, do you mind if I look in Scott's room?"

"Not at all, I'm sure he would love you to see it," Audrey said.

She stood up from the table, cup of coffee still in hand, and headed back past the front door through a lounge where Neville had retaken his seat in front of the TV.

Scott's room was bright and clean and based on the rest of the house, this was probably how he had left it the morning he'd left for school.

His shelves displayed several statues, which looked like figurines from various video games. There were also sports trophies on the shelf and several posters on his wall. One was labelled 'Black Ops 3', whatever that was, and the other 'The Last of Us'. I assumed these were other video games.

It was another waiting room, waiting for its child to come back and return it to life.

"Does Scott have a Facebook account?" I asked.

"No, he isn't old enough. A few years off for that yet," she said.

She finished her coffee.

"What do you think about a private detective, Mr Foxx?" she asked.

"Some are good, some are bad, some just in it for the dollars. I know we haven't found anything yet but rest assured, we're throwing everything we have at this case. We want to solve these crimes," I replied.

"Thank you, but it's been six weeks now and with every new missing child, Scott gets forgotten about just a little bit more," she said.

"No one will forget, and all of us at the station are working hard. If anything, the new cases are providing leads. We are hopeful they will lead to a connection between all of the abductions. Keep up with your posters and promotion of Scott, it's always good to get his face out there as much as possible," I said.

I handed her my card, "If you think of anything, please, let me know, no matter how small."

It was almost dark when I reached the solitude of my car.

Mr Lubic was next.

But he would have to wait until tomorrow.

Chapter 49

T he man at number 18 obviously wasn't going out tonight, Austin realised, which meant one thing. He had no choice but to break in. He decided the best way was around the back. Going down the drive and past the house was just too risky. He would have to enter through the reserve at the rear with the high-tension lines running through it.

Austin drove to the end of the street and turned left. He parked his government SUV at the kerb. He opened his bag and removed his knife and pistol. He also took his case of lock picks. He had noticed the padlocks on the side door; they were good quality, yet nothing he couldn't bypass.

The grass in the reserve was knee high. The lines overhead buzzed. His head hurt. How they were ruled safe was beyond him. He had no doubt that in five or 10 years, there would be a class action proving they were responsible for tumours and brain cancer. An Erin Brockovitch-type case.

He passed Mr Lubic's back yard, and could see him seated at his dining room table eating spaghetti for one. He must be lonely, Austin thought.

He made his way down the row of houses. The large shed at the rear of number 18 stood out like a lighthouse.

The lights in the shed were off, but the ones in the house were still ablaze.

Normally, he would wait. But time was one thing he didn't have a lot of. He was hoping that any noise he made would be drowned out by the TV in the house.

Austin climbed the fence and waited. No one stirred. He moved slowly to the side door and again waited; again, nothing stirred. He began on the bottom lock. This was a risk, as he couldn't watch the door at the same time as he was crouched. So he had to be quick, and quick he was. It took him all of 15 seconds before it was open. With the top lock, he could keep one eye on the house while he fiddled. After opening the bottom lock, he had found the secret, and the second one was open in less than 10 seconds.

Austin inched open the door, listening for any creaks. It was quiet for the first few centimetres and then the tin door gave its first cry of angst. Austin waited. Still all quiet in the house. He pulled the door faster, hiding behind it, and waited. Still all quiet.

Austin pinned the door against the shed wall so it wouldn't bang shut with the wind. That would certainly send the fat guy running.

The darkness of the shed would normally require a torch, but Austin had his night-vision goggles with him. His first task was to plant the tracker on the van. Then he would look for clues. He made his way to the van and removed the tracker from his pocket. He slid it under the van and placed it between the axles.

He slid back out, checked the door. All clear. There were drawers and cupboards under the work bench. He rifled through them looking for anything; children's backpacks, clothes, anything that might disclose if he had taken them and where he had put them.

There was nothing. To the far right there was a train set with locomotives, mountains, stations, and people. He had his own little world on the train board. Yet there was nothing that suggested he was a kidnapper. Above the bench were tools and a red ladder. Again, nothing screamed kidnapper.

He had expected more. Then a thought came to him. He hadn't checked the van itself. It was reversed in so the rear doors were at the work bench end. He carefully pulled on the handle of the rear door. The van was unlocked. He looked inside. The back was clear except for two large 'U' bolts bolted to the floor, halfway between the back door and the cab. Then he noticed the doors were caged, as was the cab.

The back of the van was like one big cage. Could this be how he was doing it? Once the children were in here they would be trapped.

He quietly closed the back door and went to check out the cab itself. He opened the passenger door. It was full of junk food, packages, notes, an invoice pad; nothing incriminating. Austin flipped open the glove compartment. One empty eye stared back at him.

A mask.

A joker's mask.

Rage filled every vein of his body. His hand went to his gun. He was ready to kill. Then a thought interrupted his rage. If you kill him, how will you find her? A gun to his head might make him talk? But if it didn't work, the kidnapper might never go to her again, he might just leave her where she was to die. The risk was too great. He had to follow him from afar. There was no guarantee the Parsons guy hadn't taken Mikayla. After all, Austin hadn't yet been able to find anything that led to any of the missing children.

If this guy had taken the kids, then where the hell was he keeping them?

Without warning, he was blinded. Someone had switched the shed lights on.

"Who's in here?" a loud, deep voice called out.

Austin slid down the van and scurried noiselessly to the front. He removed his knife. He heard the fat guy move to the back of the van. Austin stayed low and circled him.

Beau had come to check on his cargo before he turned in for the night and he'd noticed that the side door was open. He also noticed the locks hadn't been cut, but picked. What were they looking for? Were they just looking for gear to hock, or were they poking around in his other business? Either way, he was going to find out and give them a hiding they wouldn't soon forget.

The back of his van was wide open. He poked his head around the corner of the door expecting to see someone sitting in there waiting for him, but it was empty. He clasped the door ready to pull it shut when he was struck. Something or someone struck him on the back of the head and everything went black.

His thumping head was the first thing he noticed when he regained consciousness. He touched the back of his head. There was a big lump and the skin had broken, although there was only a little blood.

Beau got to his feet, looked around, couldn't notice anything missing. When he had ensured he was alone, he locked himself in as he always did before checking on his prized possessions.

Chapter 50

For the first time since Stevie had been kept there, he'd finally had a night where he wasn't abused. Maybe it was the fact that the captors were too high or too tired. Either way he was glad.

The only downside was he had not been given any food or water since yesterday lunchtime. He had lost track of the days. Today could have been any day, but he thought possibly Tuesday. He had counted two mornings since Bill had requested the Sunday night special. Even though Stevie had never seen the sun, the cartoons were an indication of how much time had passed.

Stevie had purposely saved his water. He would only have a sip every hour or so but no matter how hard he tried to ration it, it simply wasn't enough. Ten minutes after he had sipped it, he was craving another sip. Despite the water he'd had, his lips were still cracked and dry because he was so dehydrated.

Then the pains came, pains in his stomach, a craving for any form of nourishment.

The captors had been hitting the drugs pretty hard. The last time he saw them they were still high and they had been that way for at least a day.

Stevie heard the lock turn and then the door opened. "I'm ready for some morning fun, how about you?" Bill stood there in the doorway, naked. Stevie begin to shake at the thought of what was about to happen. "I need to go to the toilet," he said softly, "please, I'm busting."

"You better hurry the fuck up." He took a set of keys that hung on a nail on the outside of the door.

Bill walked over, one hand playing with the keys, the other playing with his cock. He unlocked the cuffs. "There you go, hurry back." Stevie stood up, his legs turning to jelly. He hadn't walked in hours. He swung his legs over, planted his feet on the carpet and was about to stand when he was restrained. Bill put his arm across his chest from behind. "Remember: try to escape and I will kill your family." He licked his ear. Stevie stood, headed to the bathroom. It was filthy. There was vomit to one side of the bowl where someone had obviously thrown up but missed. He did his business, trying not to vomit himself. He rinsed his hands, ducked his wrists under the cold water. They stung, badly, but only at first. After a few seconds the water calmed them. He quickly put his face under the dirty tap. He drank like there was no tomorrow, guzzling as much as he could. A trip to the toilet was a rarity for him. Who knew when or if he would get another.

When he arrived back at the bedroom, Bill had fallen asleep. "What the fuck took you so long?" Bill asked, one eye now wide open.

"I was just freshening up," Stevie replied.

Bill patted the empty space next to him. Gesturing him to come.

The morning hell with Bill, luckily, didn't last long. Maybe it was the drugs, whatever the case, he was glad.

Stevie lay in bed watching the morning cartoon as usual. Scooby Doo had made his standard appearance.

He could hear Ian and Bill eating. He guessed it was eggs and bacon by the smell. God, he would give anything for a slice of bacon.

He tried to listen to their conversation. Often, the jingles and theme songs of the cartoons prevented him from hearing what they were saying. However, this morning their conversation was louder, the men were almost arguing. Something was going on.

"We just can't let him go," Ian said.

Stevie's ears pricked up.

"I'm not saying we fucking let him go, I'm saying we can't keep him much longer, plus he's starting to get boring, he doesn't even fight back anymore," Bill said.

"So, what you're saying is we kill him?" Ian asked.

Stevie heard that loud and clear.

"Yeah, just strangle him and dump him up the bush. No one will ever find him. If we bury him," Bill answered.

"That's how my cousin James got caught, got high, went for a drive and went crazy," Ian replied.

"We will bury him," Bill repeated.

"A dingo will dig up his fucking bones, scatter them all over the fucking bush and then some girl guide on a field trip will stumble across a leg bone. Next thing there's a search party, they find the body and a piece of fucking hair or DNA that links him to us. I watch *NCIS*, you know. That's how they get caught," Ian added.

"Don't panic, before we cover him over, we pour bleach all over him and then we burn him. Once the fire does its work, we fill in the hole," Bill said.

"Ok, so when are we doing it?" Ian asked.

"Kill him Friday, bury him Friday night," Bill suggested.

"What do we do until Friday?" Ian asked.

"We party. Take a couple of days off. We go on a bender, enjoy ourselves and on Friday our heads will be clear. Then we get rid of him," Bill said.

"Ok, we start the bender tonight, but come Friday, you better not fuck it up," Ian said.

Stevie had just heard his fate decided over eggs, bacon and morning coffee. In about three days' time, he would be dead. He had to get out of here and maybe the bender would give him a chance. He only needed one…even half a chance would do.

Chapter 51

Chloe had spent the last two days coming to grips with knowing that she was no longer going home. She had been sold to a monster and she was living with a man she only knew as Igor. He was a small man with cold eyes, and she had feared him instantly. She had been raped more times than she could count and it wasn't just the raping, it was the beatings that went with it, either from him or from his goons.

She was told she was free to roam the house but that if she tried to leave, she would be killed and so would her family. Igor told her she would end up like the other girls.

Igor's guards watched over every part of the house 24 hours a day.

On the second day, she was moved to his country house. Until then, she did not know he had another house. Soon after arriving there, Igor raped her again. This time, she fought. Igor bashed her, then he had his goons take her to the cellar. It was no ordinary cellar. This one was more like a dungeon, accessed via a secret door in the library. Chloe couldn't see a lot, with her face bruised and her right eye closed over, but she could make out being carried through a series of underground tunnels that led to a big brick room. In the room was a single chair.

The big man that they called Alexei or Alex plonked her in the chair. She was semi-naked, blood had dripped down from her face and onto her chest, her vision was blurry, her cheek stung, in fact her whole face was in pain. She had been hit hard.

As she landed on the chair, it rocked and almost tipped over.

Alex chained or cuffed her hands, she couldn't tell which, but she could feel the cold metal against her wrists. She moved her fingers around, and then she felt the links in the chains. The chains were tight and her wrists hurt.

Alex took her by the hair to raise her slumped head.

"Keep your head up," he demanded in a strong accent.

She did as she was asked.

She could see Igor standing in front of her.

He was holding a small blade in his hand.

What was he doing? Was this it? Was she about to die? Her tears flowed and panic set in. Without warning, Igor slashed her already aching face. This was it; this was how she was going to die. He was going to cut her to pieces.

"Turn your head and look at me," Igor commanded.

Chloe turned to face him.

"Now if you fight again, I won't stop cutting you," Igor said.

"Hang her in the next room."

Alexi dragged the chair under the archway and down a tunnel into a second room.

Igor ordered Alexi to unchain her hands. Then he placed the chain around her feet instead. He smiled and dragged her off the table by the chain. Her head clipped the edge of the table as she swung downwards. He put the chain over a spare hook that hung from the beam.

Something bumped into her or she bumped into it.

She turned her head to see what she had hit. She screamed.

It looked like a body. It was hanging by the feet and it was covered in blood. It spun as it hung, and when it stopped spinning, Chloe saw that it was a girl, just like herself, except her hair was matted with dry blood. She was obviously dead. Her face was frozen as if she had died in fear, her eyes wide open.

Chloe's body filled with fear; she wanted to run, but she couldn't move. She didn't want to look, but she couldn't look away. Even when she closed her eyes, she could still see the hanging girl.

She couldn't breathe. Something was wrong. What was happening to her? Why couldn't she breathe? Panic had set in.

"Relax," Igor said. "This is what we call an example. If you want to stay alive, then I suggest you don't fight me," he said.

Chloe nodded in understanding.

"This one fought. The choice is yours, I will leave you here to think about it."

"No, don't leave me here," Chloe cried out.

But she was left hanging next to the dead girl.

Their eyes met as they swung.

Chapter 52

I'd been hoping for a good night's sleep, yet I had a feeling I wouldn't get one for a while. So many questions kept entering my head.

In the dark, surrounded by silence, I let my subconscious answer the questions with the first thought that came to me.

Why haven't we received a ransom?

Because it was a kidnapping, just like the others.

Are they all related?

MO suggests it's likely.

Is the van linked?

Yes.

Is Tyler telling the truth?

You know he is.

I believed in my natural instincts and the first response of my subconscious was usually reliable and correct.

If my subconscious was correct, then I needed to find evidence that either supported my thoughts or led me to someone else. Either way, until we found who was responsible, we had little chance of finding the kids.

* * *

It was just after 9 am when I arrived outside Mr Lubic's home.

He was already out the front tending his garden. He was busy planting some shrubs just outside his front window as I walked down the drive.

"Mr Lubic?" I called.

His head turned and he looked up. "Yes?" he answered.

I flashed my badge. "Do you have a few minutes to answer some questions?"

"This about the girl again?"

"Yes, it is."

Mr Lubic stood. "I am going to have a cup of coffee, would you like one?"

"Tea, if you have it?" I replied.

He nodded and headed inside.

I followed.

"What can I help you with, Detective?" Mr Lubic asked.

"I've just taken over the investigation and I wanted to speak with you myself. See if any detail was missed or if you remembered something new?"

"Like I told the guy yesterday, I saw her walking and when she was approaching, my phone rang. I went inside for 30 seconds and when I came outside she was gone," Mr Lubic explained.

"Did you say the man yesterday?" I queried.

"Yes," Lubic replied.

"Was he a policeman?" I asked, confused.

"No, he was the father of the other girl. He called in to find out what I saw, exactly. He was a hell of a nice guy. I hope he finds his daughter," Mr Lubic answered.

"He came to see you?"

"Yes. Said he was following up some leads. We even did a test of how far she would have walked while I was inside on the phone. Funny thing, the police never asked me to do that…do you want to know the result?" he asked me, but didn't wait for me to answer. "She wouldn't have made it to the school, not even if we added an extra 15 seconds to the call. So I should have seen her when I came out of the house."

"We know she disappeared between here and the school, is that what you're saying?" I asked.

"No, after running the test, he believes she disappeared between here and number 20 and never even made it to the school gate," Lubic said.

He placed the tea in front of me at the kitchen bench.

As I added the milk, I pondered my next question.

"What did he do after he left here?" I asked calmly.

"He went door knocking as far as I know. Sat in his car for a while. Some people were not home I guess, then he left. You don't think he is involved, do you?" Mr Lubic asked.

"No, he is not involved. He's just trying to find his daughter," I answered.

"I think he is trying to find them all. I think he has made it his mission," Mr Lubic replied.

I didn't respond.

"Let's move on to why I'm here. I have read your statement." I passed him a copy and he began to read it.

"Does that still ring true, nothing that you think needs adjusting?" I asked.

"No, that's what happened. It's still fresh. I may be old but I'm still dealing with a full deck, if you know what I mean," Mr Lubic said, tapping his head.

"I don't know if you were ever asked this or not, but did you notice anything unusual that day?" I asked.

"Man yesterday asked me that but not the police," Mr Lubic replied.

"What was your answer?"

"No, just a normal school day."

"What about a van? Did you see any vans around, white ones?"

"Every day the man at number 18 drives one. He's a handyman," Mr Lubic replied.

'No. 18 has a van,' I scribbled.

A girl vanished in a 30 to 45-second window when this elderly man was inside and no one saw anything.

My only new piece of information was that number 18 had a white van.

My next stop, number 18.

Chapter 53

Austin was certain he had found the person who had taken Mikayla. Only problem was he doubted he still had her and from the brief search of his garage, if he did, it was somewhere else.

Austin was going to play his meeting with Jack one way, and one way only. He was going to hope that the unwritten rule of crime applied. Children were off limits.

Austin pressed the doorbell and waited. According to Marcus, Jack had just been released and was living at this address with his sister. Austin was assuming he hadn't found work yet.

His wait seemed like an eternity, but finally the door was answered, but not by Jack. A woman stood in the doorway. Her long, dark, curly hair was flowing in the wind. She was wearing jeans shorts and a white blouse. Her perfume hit him immediately. She was smiling from ear to ear, happy and pleasant. "How can I help you?" she asked.

"Is Jack here?" Austin asked.

"He's asleep as per usual," she replied, still smiling. "Are you the police?" she asked as if expecting them.

"No, my daughter is missing and he shared a cell with someone who may know her whereabouts. I really would like to talk to him."

"I'll go wake him," she replied.

She left Austin standing in the doorway.

"Jack, get your butt up. Someone is here to see you!" she shouted. She pounded on his door with her fist. "Jack, get up. Someone is here."

She returned to the front door after few minutes of yelling and banging.

"He's coming. Did you want to come in?" she asked hesitantly.

Austin could sense her concern and declined the offer. "I will wait here. I'm sure you have things to do."

The lady smiled but didn't insist.

Austin knew he had made the right decision. She was probably put out enough, having her brother just out of jail living with her. Last thing she would want was his mates calling over or worse still, unannounced strangers.

If the man who arrived at the door was Jack, he was shorter than his sister and that was rare. Maybe they had different fathers, Austin thought.

"Do you know Tyler Parsons?" Austin asked immediately.

"Yeah, what about him?"

"He broke into my house. Cops say he killed my wife and took my daughter," Austin said.

"Why you asking me? Cops have him. Go ask him," Jack said.

"You did time with him. I want to know about him," Austin replied.

"Look man, I dunno, you'll just have to ask him," Jack repeated.

Austin took a breath, "Can you help me, please. The police seem determined to say he did it, but I just want to find my daughter," Austin said.

"All right, I'll tell you what I know," Jack said.

He drew a cigarette from the packet, held it in his sleeve and lit it. He leaned against the brick pillar of his sister's porch.

"I shared a cell with him in the last 12 months of his sentence. The 11 months prior, he shared a cell with a guy named Neil Figal. He was French, I think. Anyway, he was in for the rape of a 12-year-old boy in a shopping mall. Figal was doing the last year of a four-year sentence. Let me just say that other prisoners don't do you any favours when you share a cell with a paedophile. One of the gangs had a particular problem with peds, and most of them assumed that Tyler was one of them. I don't know if you've seen the guy, but his looks don't do him any favours in dispelling the rumours. He's 25 and can hardly even grow a beard. Just looks like a person who would, how would you say, venture down that path."

He squashed the butt of the cigarette against the post between his thumb and forefinger before flicking it into the garden bed.

Before he began his next sentence, he had lit up and begun to suck on the end of another cigarette.

"Anyway, there's a motorcycle gang called Death Angels. They have a reasonably big contingent on the inside as well as the outside. The Death Angels have a huge problem with peds on the inside and they pride themselves on making their lives hell."

Jack stopped to let out a cough that sounded like his lung was about to be ejected. He thumped his chest a few times with his fist and then continued.

"One winter's morning last year several members of the Death Angels heard of Figal's mall escapade and offered Tyler a way to prove he wasn't one of them. It was simple: he had to send Figal a message from the Death Angels and if he did, they would lay off him. I don't know exactly what happened in the cell that night, but it resulted in Figal being sent to the infirmary and Tyler to solitary. Figal never came back into the main population. He had to be placed in lockdown. When Tyler reappeared, I was his new cellmate. We hit it off straightaway. He was in there for B&E. He'd never hurt anyone, he just wanted to get rich. The beating he gave Figal was not in his nature, it was foreign to him.

"Having been around, I taught him a few tricks of the trade and gave him some names that could get him set up on the outside. So I believe when he robbed your house, he was just after some cash or jewellery. He would never take your daughter or harm your wife, that's not him. If he was caught in the act, he'd just make a run for it."

Jack sucked the last of his second smoke and sent it away into the garden bed, which was obviously his own little dumping ground.

"That's what I suspected," Austin said. Having received that information, he was ready to leave. Now, he could focus on the man with the van.

Austin held out his hand to thank Jack but before he could, Jack spoke. "Before you leave, I have something else you might like to know."

Austin removed his hand, "Such as?"

"Tyler told me that Figal mentioned to him they now had a supplier of kids. They sent in their order via text and then the order was completed and delivery arranged. It made him sick. Figal didn't say who the guy was, only that a priest held the kids until delivery was organised. He said kids were sold anywhere from $10,000 to $50,000. It might be worth you seeing this guy. Whoever took your daughter may have sent her to this priest."

Austin had always imagined that his daughter had been kidnapped by a paedophile and was being held in a hotel room, or a house somewhere. It had never crossed his mind that she had been kidnapped and on-sold.

"If you want good news, I think she's alive somewhere. If I hear any more, I could give you a call."

"Do you know where this Figal guy lives?" Austin asked.

"Wouldn't have a clue, but you seem like a resourceful guy, after all, you found me," Jack replied.

Austin handed over his private mobile number. "Thank you again," he said.

He extended his hand for a second time. This time, Jack took it and shook it firmly.

As Austin headed back down the driveway towards the gate, Jack called out, "Good luck!"

Austin waved to acknowledge his well-wishes.

He called Marcus. Apparently, finding Figal might be a little harder than Austin had first hoped. He didn't even have time to put the key into the ignition when his private phone rang and the caller ID came up as private.

Chapter 54

Less than a minute after leaving Mr Lubic to enjoy the rest of his morning tea, I knocked on the door of number 18.

A burly man who could have once been well built but had let himself go was in the driveway working on a van.

"Excuse me, sir," I said, flashing my badge as I approached.

"Yeah?" he said.

"I'm Detective Brodie Foxx. I'm investigating the disappearance of a girl who went missing…well, we believe she may have even gone missing from this street," I said.

He wiped his hands on his overalls as he approached. "I won't shake your hand. Mine are dirty. I'm Beau," he introduced himself. "What do you guys want now? I've already spoken to you guys several times. Do you wanna take me in for another lie detector test I suppose? Don't you guys fucken speak to each other?"

"Yes we do, I have the file here. I'd like to go over a few things if I may. It's been plonked on my desk. Just want to ensure everything's been done properly," I said.

He looked uneasy and in my book, that moved him up on my suspect list.

"Well, can we get on with it? I need to fix me truck and if I don't, I got no job, you understand?"

"I understand, I'll be quick. On the morning she went missing, you were home until 8.45, is that correct?"

"If that's what it says, then, yeah. I can't remember. But it sounds about right."

"Did you see the girl as you left?"

"I didn't notice her in particular. There were a lot of kids walking to school. You guys rang my job. They said I was there, you even checked my house, my van. I had nothing to do with it," Beau said.

"About the van. How do you explain the traces of bleach found all over the floor?"

"As I said, at the time, I was doing painting. On the trip home from the job, some of the bleach spilt and it took me a good hour to clean it up. Stunk to high heaven for a week."

It was plausible. But I had my doubts.

"What about the steel mesh you have in the back, why do you have that?"

"Just to hook stuff onto, tie wood to when I'm taking it to jobs. Sometimes I even have to take my Bond saw to jobs and it's heavy and if I don't chain it in, the fucker slides everywhere." Then he added, "You should be following up on the dirty old man that supposedly saw her walking this way, maybe he was the last to see her for a reason."

"We're following up all leads, Beau, we're just trying to eliminate you as a person of interest. Well, I think that's all. Thanks for your time," I said.

I put the photos of the van back in the file and turned to leave. Before I did, I had a revelation, maybe it was a voice, maybe it was the investigator in me nagging at me.

Check out the van for yourself, my internal voice said.

I turned back, "Is that your van?" I asked, pointing down the drive.

"Yep."

"Do you mind if I have a quick look?" I asked.

"You guys have done that already, but go ahead," he replied.

As I walked down the side of the van, a cold shiver went down my spine. I knew instantly this guy had just become number one on our list, not just for the disappearance of Chloe Henderson but for all of them.

I couldn't let him know I thought there was any connection.

What made me shiver was the logo on the side of the van. It was a big phone with the words 'One Call Handyman' and below that, a picture and a phone number.

I took a photo of the logo. I needed to show this to some people. Thoughts were racing through my head. Definitely needed to organise another search warrant.

I walked further down the driveway, stuck my head in the shed. I was looking for Mikayla, not that I was telling him that.

"If you want to look through the property again, you'll need a search warrant," his voice came from over my shoulder.

"No need for that," I replied.

"I'd like to make a formal complaint," Beau said.

"What about?" I asked, thinking police harassment.

"The dad of the latest girl to disappear was here yesterday, asking me all sorts of questions and then last night, he broke into my shed and hit me on the back of the head," Beau said.

Classic deflection procedure. First Mr Lubic and now Mr Campbell, I thought.

"How do you know it was him, did you see him?" I asked.

"Well no, but who else would it be?" Beau asked.

"Unless you saw him, I can't really do much, but I will have a word to him about his visit."

"Typical fucking cops," Beau replied.

"Thanks for your time," I said.

The logo was exactly what was described to me by Stevie's mum, coincidence maybe, but unlikely.

I rang Jake but had to deal with his voicemail. While I waited for his return call, I rang Mr Campbell.

"Hello?" Austin answered.

"Austin, this is Detective Brodie Foxx, can you talk for a few minutes?"

"Sure," Austin replied.

He sounded as if he was expecting horrible news so I said hastily, "I have nothing new to report, so don't panic. I'd like you to come into the station. Around 3? There are a few issues we need to discuss."

"Yeah sure, I'll be there," Austin replied.

As soon as I hung up, Jake rang back and I filled him in on the van's logo.

"While you're on your way back to the station, I'll organise a warrant," Jake said.

Chapter 55

By the time I got back to the office, it was nearing 2.30 and Jake had just received word that the warrant had been partially approved. We had requested permission to plant listening devices as well as for a physical search of the two vans, the house and the shed.

However, the judge only approved the physical search, his reasoning being that having a van that was seen at one kidnapping and that resided near another was not enough evidence to suggest that they were responsible for the crime. He could thus not approve a listening device.

We had organised for Forensics to come with us on the search, with both Beau's vans to be impounded for 24 hours and analysed in the crime lab. I had just put the finishing touches to the paperwork and sent it to the captain for execution when my phone rang. Mr Campbell was in reception. He was early. "Jake, he's here," I said.

Jake was on the phone, so he pointed to interview room one.

I met Mr Campbell in reception. "Come through, would you like a coffee?" I asked.

"No thanks," he said.

I ushered him into interview room one. It was small, with a desk, three chairs and the standard two-way mirror.

"Am I in trouble?" he asked.

"No, we're just short of space around here," I replied.

I sat down on the side with two chairs, and he sat on the one opposite me. The chair next to me remained empty.

"Jake will be joining us in a second, he's just finishing up a phone call."

Jake entered, offering his apologies.

"Mr Campbell, we've asked you here today to give you an update on the investigation," Jake said. "We've arrested Tyler Parsons for breaking and entering. While he admits to being in your house, he told us that he was in the roof so he could rob the place in the early hours of the morning."

Austin wasn't completely sure that Beau was responsible, but he knew one thing: the more pressure the police put on him, the less chance he would have of being led to Mikayla. His biggest risk right now was Beau going underground, and leaving Mikayla to die of starvation.

"He claims he never got a chance to rob the safe and he never saw the man that he claims killed your wife and took your daughter," Jake continued. "He says that your daughter's screams startled him. He waited in the roof until the commotion was over before leaving and on the way out, he found your wife dead."

"Do you believe him?" Austin asked.

"We can't be sure. The lie detector test was inconclusive," I replied. "We're only 68 hours into the investigation of Mikayla's disappearance and your wife's murder. We have hundreds of leads that we're continuing to follow up. During the investigation we've also been looking into the possibility of Mikayla's abduction being linked to the other missing children."

"I thought you felt it was a ransom and it wasn't related? Isn't that what you told me?" he asked.

His temper had begun to rise. The whole situation was getting to him and I could see it.

"Stay calm, Mr Campbell, we're doing everything we can to find Mikayla."

He sat back and relaxed a little.

"During the investigation it came to my attention that you have been conducting something of an investigation of your own," I said.

He was about to speak when I raised my hand and then Jake butted in.

"Now we can't stop you looking for your daughter and we can't stop you interviewing people, but just be sure you don't go breaking any laws when you're doing it."

Campbell knew what Jake was referring to but just in case he hadn't got the hint, I knew Jake was about to explain it to him plain and simple.

"Mr Delacroix claims his shed was broken into the night you visited him. Do you know anything about that?" Jake asked.

"I know it's a bad area. I went and asked him some questions. He said he was at work; him mum was there and she verified it. I will do anything to find Mikayla. The other missing girls are the only lead I have. What else am I going to do? I can't put up posters forever."

"We know you're not going to stop looking but if you find anything, you need to tell us. Our suggestion to you is not to go breaking into places looking for your daughter. If you have any suspicions you want followed up, call us. No point getting yourself put in jail. You can't look from there," Jake added.

"Will do. I don't have anything that will help your investigation," Austin answered.

"Before you go, we're about to conduct another search of the residence, the shed and the two vans Beau Delacroix has on his property, so I don't want you to be surprised when you hear it on the news," I said.

Austin was halfway to the door but decided to sit back down.

"If he has her and he is holding her somewhere else, if you search there and he goes underground, Mikayla could starve to death, all of them could."

"We know it's a risk, but he has no other property we know of. If he has them, they're probably there. If we don't find them, then we can probably eliminate him as a suspect."

"Eliminate him? Why?" Austin replied. The anger had returned.

"We won't have any reason to think he's involved," Jake said.

"He's been sighted at two kidnappings!" Austin replied.

"Both of which were indirect. We've searched his property and van previously and they were all clean. He has undergone a lie detector test in the past and it was inconclusive. We simply have nothing to tie him to any of the abductions. We've struggled to get a warrant this time around, and in the eyes of the law, coincidence doesn't equal evidence," Jake replied.

We stood up, telling Mr Campbell we would stay in touch.

Austin stood again, ready to leave. He had a million thoughts going through his head. Should he tell the police about the mask? Surely they would find it. What if the fat guy found himself under constant surveillance and went underground with Mikayla left starving somewhere? Austin knew if he mentioned the mask, he would be admitting to breaking and entering and he would be held overnight at least. Tomorrow was Thursday and he could afford no time in jail. He still had a few leads to follow up.

He kept quiet.

"Thank you," he said as he left.

Chapter 56

Three unmarked cars and a van all arrived just after 4 pm. Jake and I were in one car; the other two were occupied by members of the Missing Persons Unit and uniformed officers. The van held Grace and three members of her Forensics team. Jake was first onto the property, warrant in hand. As he knocked, three members from the Missing Persons Unit split up. One followed Jake, the other two headed straight for the shed.

I followed Forensics into the garage. We were prepared to cut the locks but Beau was happy to let us in.

"Detective Miller is giving your mother a copy of the search warrant if you want to see it?" I said.

"It's fine, Detective. I have nothing to hide, please look around," Beau replied.

"We need to impound your vans. Should only be for 24 hours," I said.

"I have work on Friday. Jobs to do, so I better have them back by then," Beau said.

"We will do our best," I said.

Forensics took the keys and drove the vans out to the street where the tray trucks were waiting.

"Do you mind if I keep working on my locomotives while you look around?" Beau asked.

I looked over his shoulder. He had a big board set up with

mountains, a town and several stations. He had the works. There were locomotive parts spread out in one corner of the board, obviously the one he was repairing.

"Sure, no problem. Just don't interfere with the search." I began to look through the cupboards. They were full of things that a kidnapper, or a handyman, would use: duct tape, rope, cable ties. Our biggest problem was we didn't have anything to compare to. As none of the kids had been recovered, it was impossible to know what these items had been used for.

We confiscated everything.

My hopes were resting on finding some of Mikayla's hair or DNA in one of the vans.

Jake received a rude response from Beau's mother. "This is police harassment. My boy hasn't done anything. He's been a good boy."

Jake didn't even respond. He handed her the warrant, headed past her and went straight for Beau's room. If he had any souvenirs from his victims, Jake doubted that he would keep them out in the open in front of his mother. He would do what a teenager would do with a packet of smokes. Hide them at all cost, or cop a belting.

Jake opened the first drawer of the three-drawer side table. There was a pile of dirty magazines, pens and a few odds and ends. Nothing of interest. The next drawer held socks and undies. Jake removed it, emptying the contents onto the floor. Again, nothing of interest. The bottom drawer held football cards, dozens of them, just dumped there. Again Jake upended the drawer and the cards fluttered to the floor.

Jake left the drawers all askew and the contents where they lay. He lifted the mattress off the bed. Nothing. Under the bed was another stack of magazines and a video tape, marked XXX. Jake tossed it aside. He picked up the pile of magazines and flicked through them, hoping something incriminating would fall out.

Nothing did.

Jake moved over to the robe. It consisted of one shelf with hanging space below. On the shelf were some DVDs, not porn, and a stack of CDs. The shelf itself was relatively empty. An old shoe box sat in the other corner. Jake's hopes rose, only to be disappointed by a pair of worn Blundstones.

Nothing, he thought, there's nothing fucking here.

"I hope you're going to clean all this up?" Mrs Delacroix yelled. She was standing in the doorway and smoke was drifting into the room as she spoke.

"I am sorry, Mam, we are not a maid's service," Jake replied.

"You fucking pigs are all the same," Annabel replied.

Jake left Beau's room alone and headed for his mother's, taking extra time in upsetting her room. After the pig comment, anything goes, he thought. By the time he had finished, it looked as if a three-year-old had chucked a tantrum in there.

Jake checked kitchen cupboards, cereal packets, Milo tins, anything and everything. He checked the sofas, both in the cushions and down the back.

Jake had not been looking for the girl. He doubted she would be here; all he was after was a sign that Beau had once had her. But there was nothing.

By the time the whole crew had finished, they had searched the home top to bottom including the roof cavity. It was clean.

Jake was hoping they'd had better luck in the shed.

"You got anything?" he asked me.

"No." I shook my head.

I looked over at Beau. He didn't even look worried. Too calm for my liking. Even an innocent person gets upset when the cops are searching your home. It didn't faze him in the slightest and that made me think he knew we wouldn't find anything. Not because there was nothing to find, but because he had removed it or hidden it. Clearly, something was wrong with this picture.

PART TWO

The Priest, the Cop and the Judge

Chapter 57

Father O'Riley had received a text. It was only one word but he knew exactly what it meant.

HEAT

He picked up the phone and called the man he always called when things got a bit sticky and requested a meeting with Mike. He didn't want to do this one over the phone.

Mike came over as soon as he could and sat across the desk from the Priest.

"I need you to fix a problem," Father O'Riley said.

"Don't you always," Mike said. "Who hasn't paid us this time?"

"It's more serious than that, I'm afraid. Our supplier is under pressure from the police."

"What do you expect me to do? I can't go putting myself into the investigation. That'll only compromise our position," Mike replied.

"I want you to send them on a different path. Give the dogs a new car to chase, so to speak," the Priest said.

"So you mean stage an abduction. Using the same sort of car. Take the attention away from our supplier?"

"That's exactly what I mean," the Priest said.

"What car does he drive?" Mike asked.

"It's a white van," the Priest replied.

"What do you want me to do with my catch?" Mike asked.

"I have no orders to fill at the moment and therefore no use for any goods. So what you do with it will be up to you," the Priest said.

"I don't kill children," Mike replied.

"You may not have a choice," the Priest responded.

"I always have a choice," Mike replied.

"Do you? When the goods are not delivered to the Monster, what choice will you have then? What choice will your family have and those beautiful twin boys? Will they have a choice?" the Priest said.

"The Monster doesn't scare me," Mike replied.

"I believe in God, and the Monster is the closest thing to the devil I have seen here on earth. Maybe you should be afraid," the Priest countered.

"I will sort it out. Don't you worry. Maybe after Beau makes this delivery to the Monster, we get ourselves a new supplier."

"I think that is a certainty," the Priest agreed.

"Leave it with me. I'll make sure a kid is taken care of and I might even have a way of putting our mate Figal in the frame."

Chapter 58

James Mitchell had spent more than enough time in this nuthouse. He needed to get out. The desire to kill was growing stronger every second. He only had one more review to pass, and that was with the board that oversaw the hospital.

He wanted to be back where he could satisfy the urge that was growing inside. Even without the drugs to feed it, the monster had continued to live inside, and now it wanted out. He had managed to keep it quiet in the corner of his mind while he had visitations with his mother. Soon, his monster would refuse.

* * *

Salma looked through her notes several times. She had to make her decision by 5 pm. Other members of the board were doing the same. Reviewing a criminal who had been found not guilty of a crime by reason of insanity was not about now finding him sane, it was more about eliminating any reasons he would still be considered insane or a threat to himself or society.

The facts were clear to her. James had been out on visitations with his mother at weekends and even for weeks at a time. He had been off his antipsychotic medication, his voices and delusions had disappeared years before, and any reference to the 'shadow people' had vanished close to a decade before. If his case was before the court today, she would not be able to find him insane. Had he still shown the signs he had displayed when he was arrested, there would be no doubt at all.

After deciding her own stance, she read through all her colleagues' reports and was pleased to find they agreed with the diagnosis and thus the conclusion to release Mr Mitchell.

Salma began to type her report.

She concluded that Mitchell should remain on the Sexual Offenders List but that in her professional opinion, he no longer posed a threat to the community.

Chapter 59

Finding a white van was easy enough. Taking a kid off the street would be a more difficult proposition. It wasn't something you did on a whim. Mike knew that he had no real choice, despite what he had said to the Priest. If the choice involved angering the Monster or not, you chose not to, every time. At five foot five, the Monster hadn't achieved his reputation because of his size. He was a vicious killer who had been rumoured to kill an enemy's entire family, including their children and the grandparents.

Mike didn't want to kill a child, but what else could he do? Take him to the country and let him go? What if he came back and was able to identify him? That wouldn't work. What was he to do? How was he going to kill a kid?

He left his car in the parking lot several rows down from where he had taken the van. Now all he had to do was find a kid, boy or girl, it didn't matter. He drove the streets of the local neighbourhood; the surroundings were all unfamiliar. He was hours and hundreds of kilometres away from his home town. He was now in the Joker's territory. The streets were all the same, houses crammed next to each other, rarely a difference between them, cars in the drives. Kids were in school, well the good ones were. It was the ones who decided not to attend that he was looking for.

He put some distance between himself and the shopping complex where he had found the van. He had passed through dozens of suburbs, the names of which he could no longer remember. It was late morning and at this rate, lunchtime would come and go and he would be no closer to fixing the Priest's problem. The longer he drove the van, the more chance he had of getting caught.

A sign caught Mike's attention. Northland Shopping Centre. Surely an opportunity would arise. He drove around to where the cinemas were located, hoping to find some kid heading in alone. Every kid he saw either had a mate or a girlfriend with them. Taking two was out of the question. Double the problem, double the risk and double the guilt. No one ever took two at once; no one except the Beaumont killer. He'd taken three off a busy beach. How had he done that? Confidence, nothing more, Mike answered himself.

He decided to park in the lot outside the cinema and wait. It was a safer option than to keep driving around. He sat watching, cap on, head down. Mother after mother passed the van and occasionally a group of children, but never a single child. He had his clipboard up. Whenever an adult walked past, he held it in front of his face as if he was working.

He emptied the contents of his wallet into his jacket pocket. Preparing for the ambush.

He was about to try another location when he saw a boy. He guessed he was about 12. He was walking towards the van, about 15 car spaces down from where Mike was parked. His hair was dark brown and it was spiked so he looked taller. Mike guessed he might have wagged school for a girl, a date maybe, maybe his first ever. He was dressed nicely in jeans, shirt and a red jacket.

This was his chance, and he might not get another.

Mike got out, opened the side door, dropped his wallet and kicked it under the van, just enough so it was out of sight.

Now he waited.

The boy got closer. Seven cars.

Three cars.

"Excuse me?" Mike said.

The boy stopped, turned, unsure if he was being spoken to.

Mike took a quick glimpse around for witnesses. None.

"Yes?" the boy answered politely.

"Can you help me?" Mike asked.

"What with?" The boy was hesitant.

"I dropped my wallet and it slid under the van. I'm so clumsy. I've just had an operation and I can't get it, I really need to get my daughter's birthday present."

The boy stood in front of the van, being careful to keep his distance. He crouched. He could see the wallet; the man was telling the truth.

"Yeah, sure mister. I'll get it for you," he said, moving around to the side of the van. He bent down and collected the wallet.

"Here you go." He handed it to Mike.

"Thank you," Mike said. He took the wallet with his left hand and pushed hard with his right. The boy flew back, through the open door of the van. Mike had punched the boy hard in the face, twice. The back of the boy's head hit the floor of the van and bounced back with the next punch, which was even more vicious.

The boy lay on the floor of the van with blood flowing liberally from his nose and mouth. Pain was shooting up his face. His eyes were watering.

His vision was going blurry. What had happened? He couldn't be sure. He heard the door shut. Now he could feel the van moving, he wanted to run, he needed to get out, but he couldn't even see the door, let alone move.

He was dizzy, he could taste blood flowing down his throat.

They were travelling faster now, but his vision was still hazy.

Where was he going? Had he been taken? His eyes flickered between light and dark, until darkness came.

Chapter 60

Grace went over both vans with her team, there every step of the way, more hands-on than she would normally have been. She knew her team would be thorough, but she wanted to ensure every box was ticked.

But after going through the vans, they had nothing; not a hair, not a fibre, no bloodstains, not a single fucking thing. She could tell the van had been cleaned regularly and with bleach. Bleach was a killer's best defence against any trace evidence and this guy knew it. She had heard the story of the spill, but this was no spill, this had been used methodically and carefully to remove anything left behind. She thought he must have hosed the back, scrubbed it, then bleached it and hosed it again. She was hoping for some trace evidence that had caught on his clothes and been transferred to the front cabin, but there was no such luck.

* * *

It was early afternoon when Grace came into my office. Jake was standing by her side like an eavesdropping schoolgirl, trying to get the latest gossip. I could see it in his eyes; he was hoping they'd found something.

"What did you find?" I asked.

"Nothing. They were both clean. He's used bleach all over the place. He was covering up something," she replied.

"Unfortunately, using bleach is not a crime," I replied, although we all knew I was just stating the obvious.

"What about the house? Did they find anything there?" I asked.

"No, it was clean, no trace of any children in the house or garage," she replied. "If he has them, he must have taken them somewhere else."

"Why don't we ask him to do another polygraph test?" Jake interjected. He'd done one for us when Chloe Henderson had disappeared.

"Why would he agree? He passed the first one, I don't think he'd volunteer for a second," I said.

"It was inconclusive," Jake corrected me immediately, "I think it's worth a try. How about we bring him in for questioning, put some pressure on him and see where that leads?"

"Nothing to lose," I agreed.

"Let's keep the vans here while we question him," Jake said. "It'll make him think that we found something."

"Let's go get him," I said.

I picked up my folder and car keys and we headed for the elevator down to the car park.

We drove to Beau's. At first we sat in silence, which was unusual for us. Then Jake spoke. "We have our ultrasound in six weeks and we'll find out what we're having."

"How are you getting Hayley to accept the baby's name?" I asked.

"It will be Indiana. She'll agree, she's warming to it," Jake replied.

I wound down my window even though Jake had the air-con on. I had been feeling sick of late. I wasn't sure what it was, but something wasn't right. I had made an appointment to see my specialist and until I knew more, I would keep it to myself.

"You ok there, Brucey?" Jake asked.

"Yeah mate, I'm fine, just feeling a bit sick in the guts," I replied, trying to wave it off.

"You're probably hungry and it's way past lunch. Do you wanna grab a quick bite before we pick up Beau? It's not like he can go anywhere." Jake laughed.

"No, it's all good, I'll be ok," I answered.

Truth of the matter was that eating was the last thing I wanted to do.

"What do you really think is this guy's involvement? What does your gut tell you?" Jake asked.

"I don't know, my gut says he's involved, but my head asks for the evidence. There isn't any, so my brain tells my gut that it's wrong and to look elsewhere," I replied.

"Ok, so your gut says it's him. Now why would there be no evidence?" Jake asked.

"Because it's not him?" I answered.

"Ehhh! Wrong," Jake replied, making a buzzer sound like a wrong answer in a quiz show. "Think. How did you find Mason?"

"Esmeralda found him," I responded, referring to the psychic who had confirmed the identity of the serial killer.

"No. Think. You were led to him because he made a mistake and killed someone he knew. Correct?"

"Correct," I replied, "but what's this got to do with Beau?" I wasn't sure where Jake was heading.

"Maybe Beau knew the girl who walked past his door every morning? We didn't find any evidence of Mason at his home. He had a secret place. Maybe Beau has a secret place too?" Jake suggested.

"You think he's keeping them somewhere else?"

"Possibly."

"I'm sure they don't have any other property. Where would he take them?"

"Maybe he has a house elsewhere that's not in his name. Maybe he has a sick and twisted friend. Hell, that Cleveland guy had three girls in a room for 16 years, one even had a child and the neighbours knew nothing of it," Jake replied.

"I don't know about Beau being able to keep four kids in a house undetected, especially when he's elsewhere. But we agree on one thing: they are alive somewhere," I answered.

"Let's bring him in for questioning and we'll see what he has to say for himself," Jake said.

Chapter 61

James Mitchell didn't have many visitors and the few who came were usually family. But when his cousin was sitting opposite him in the visitors' room, he was the last person James had expected to see.

"What the hell are you doing here? Do you know I'm about to get out?" James asked.

"Yes, that's why I came," Ian Welling replied. "We've set up a surprise for your homecoming, one specially delivered by the Priest," Ian continued.

James knew that it was possible their meeting was being recorded. "I'd love to see the Priest again if I get out, but it's unlikely I'll be able to spend time with you, Ian, due to our past. I hope you understand."

Ian knew exactly what he meant by saying 'see the Priest again'. He wanted an order.

"How are things on the farm?" James asked.

"Still having trouble with the wild pigs up there. They're becoming a big nuisance. Need exterminating," Ian said.

James knew all too well that wild pigs meant cops.

"I'll be able to give Dad a hand on the farm if need be," James replied.

"That'd be great, I'm sure he'd appreciate the help. I hope I'll see you up at the farm at some stage," Ian replied.

He stood and left.

James sat in the visitors' room alone. Thinking.

The pigs were still causing problems.

Had they ever stopped?

In the whole time he had been here, he had learned one thing. The pigs had put him here.

Finally, he would make them pay, one by one.

Chapter 62

Austin knew Beau was out of action for the day, so chasing other leads was his next best option. He was waiting for Marcus to come up with Figal's address. He had given Marcus the details the previous night. Jack had told him he had a supplier. Austin knew if he found the supplier, he would be one step closer to finding his daughter and hopefully, the others.

Marcus had told Austin he couldn't risk going back into the office late at night. He had taken a lot of risks already and if he got caught searching things he wasn't supposed to be searching, the whole operation would be in jeopardy. Austin knew without Marcus' intel he would have to rely on the police and that was simply not an option.

The clock on the bedside table clicked over to 11.30 am. Austin sat on the bed, which remained made. He hadn't slept in it lately; he just lay on top of it when the urge to sleep became too great. He had dreamt of Sarah every time. The same dream over and over. Every time, Mikayla was walking ahead of them on the beach and every time, he and Sarah were happy. Then Mikayla was gone and Sarah began to fade. She cried out for him to find her before it was too late. Not only did he dream the same dream, he woke up exactly the same way, staring at an empty beach, listening to the screams of his dead wife. Every time he woke, he was in a cold sweat.

He sat taking in the view of the city and the world below carrying on around him. He had not gone home since the police first called him. He couldn't bear the thought of stepping inside that house again. He had been in contact with Sarah's parents; they understood. Her father made him promise that when he found who had killed Sarah, to make it painful. No doubt about it, was Austin's response.

Usually he was a patient man, but the wait for Marcus' call was driving him insane. He wanted to be on the move, finding out what Figal knew about the so-called delivery man.

Another 15 minutes passed before his cell phone began to jump off the bed.

"Sorry I took so long, but I had to ensure my system hadn't been breached," Marcus began. "The only Figal I've found is a Neil Figal. He was Tyler's cellmate only for two months. In for kidnapping and molestation. He has an address in Prahran listed as his permanent place of residence. You got a pen?" Marcus asked.

"Sure," Austin replied.

He scribbled the address and collected his already packed bag from the floor.

He was getting close; he could feel it in his bones.

Chapter 63

Stevie had noticed a drastic change in the way he was treated, especially by Bill. He no longer tried to hide his drug problem. He had been injecting on the bed and throwing the needles into the corner of the room. Last night, Stevie had been forced to lie still as Bill sprinkled and sniffed white powder off his stomach.

Stevie couldn't remember the last time he had eaten. It might have been the morning he overheard their plans to kill him and bury him in the woods. Since then, he had spent every waking moment trying to figure out a plan to get out of there. He knew if he was still there Friday, he would be dead.

He sat on his bed, cold and shaking, busting to go to the toilet and desperate for a drink. He had considered drinking his own urine but the thought of it made him feel sick. They were always willing to let him go to the toilet. He guessed it was only so they didn't have to clean up the mess. Every time he went, he guzzled as much water from the tap as he could handle.

The frequency of the attacks increased, and the brutality also increased. Not only were they high and drunk at the same time, they seemed to be continually feeding themselves with more white powder, needles and vodka. Stevie hadn't slept since they'd discussed their Friday plans, but neither had the men. Whatever it was they were taking, it was fuelling them. He had worked that out.

"We're almost out of C, and we used the last of the H last night.

I want to speedball tonight. Can you get me some more H?" Bill asked.

"You better slow down, you'll overdose if you keep going," Ian replied.

"I know my body, just one speedball for our last night with the boy. Then we'll get rid of him," Bill replied.

"Where am I supposed to get the money for the H? I'm down to my last grand and that was meant for rent."

"Just give me 500 for the H and I'll get you some cash next week," Bill replied.

"How are you going to get me some cash next week? You're unemployed," Ian said.

"I have my ways, don't you worry," Bill replied.

"I don't want you hurting anyone to get the money," Ian said.

"Ok, I promise no one will get hurt," Bill said.

Ian handed over the 500 and Bill was immediately on the phone to his dealer.

Chapter 64

It took Austin just over half an hour to reach Figal's. From the kerb it looked like a house belonging to a low-life. The lawns were unkempt weeds, as high as a man's knees. The windows were filthy and the blinds were closed. The driveway had an old Toyota sitting under the small freestanding carport. Austin thought it must be at least 20 years old, with faded paint and bald tyres. It would be lucky to get a road-worthy.

He crossed the front lawn, the weeds whipping his ankles as he walked. The man who answered the door was a small, dishevelled, unwashed scumbag. Looked like he was high. "What you want?" he asked. The door was cracked open just enough to see through the door. The security chain hung above the man's chest.

"I'm looking for Neil," Austin said.

"I'm Neil. Did the copper send you to rough me up for reneging on the deal?" Neil asked.

"No one sent me. I have a business offer for you," Austin replied, confused.

"You a cop?" Neil asked.

"No, far from it, I'm hoping you can help me," Austin said. "Tyler told me to look you up," he added.

"How do you know Tyler?" Neil asked.

"Friend from inside," Austin answered.

"Hold on," Neil replied.

Figal closed the door so he could unlatch the security chain.

Austin noticed that inside was like outside, only dirtier and darker. The TV was buzzing with some porn movie and the table consisted of an ashtray, a lighter, some cigarettes, a spoon, and some needles.

Neil lay down on the couch and went back to watching porn. The couch was old and dirty. It looked like something that he had picked up off the street.

"Watch this chick, she's amazing," Neil said.

Austin didn't even glance at it; he was here for one reason only.

"Do you want to sit down?" Neil asked.

"No, I don't plan on staying long. I was just after some help."

Neil reached under the couch cushion he was lying on and removed a black pistol.

Looking down the eye of the barrel, Austin remained as calm as ever. It wasn't the first time an enemy had pointed a gun at him.

"Now, tell me who sent you, was it the cop?"

Austin raised his hands, "I told you, I don't know anything about a cop, Tyler sent me," Austin replied.

"You see, that's where your story hits a snag. Tyler beat the shit out of me on the inside and we aren't exactly friends. So I will ask again: who sent you?"

"It was one of Tyler's previous cellmates while you were in protective custody. He told me about you," Austin replied.

Neil just lay there staring at Austin, finger on the trigger ready for action.

"I'm looking for people who might have bought a girl recently. My friend said you told Tyler you had a contact? I'm looking for my daughter."

"Empty your pockets, put everything on the table," Neil demanded.

Austin followed Neil's orders, placed his keys, some loose change, a knife, and his wallet on the table.

"Big blade, not wise to bring a knife to a gunfight," Neil said. "Take your clothes off," he instructed.

"What? Why?" Austin questioned.

"I wanna make sure you're not wearing a wire," Neil replied.

"How many times do I need to tell you I'm not a cop?" Austin asked.

"Till I believe you," Neil scoffed.

Neil began to flick through Austin's wallet, then he paused. Austin knew exactly what he was looking at. It was a photo of Mikayla.

"You're her dad, you were on the news," Neil said. "Did you come here to kill me?" he asked. "Because you're barking up the wrong tree there, I didn't take her."

"I just told you I'm looking for my daughter," Austin repeated. "Anyway, I know you prefer boys. I'm not here for you, but I just want your contact, and I'll pay you for it," Austin answered. He threw $500 on the table. "All I want is your contact."

Neil lay on the couch, shocked at the cash and at the stranger's brutal honesty.

"The cop I was asking you about, he was sent from higher up the chain, if you get my drift, he was sent to punish me because I reneged on my order," Figal said.

He placed his gun on the table and handed the photo back to Austin.

"Why did you renege on the order?" Austin asked him.

"Can't afford it at the moment," Neil said, counting the cash.

Austin knew why. He was spending all his cash on drugs. "How do you place an order?" he asked.

"Well it isn't like McDonald's, that's for sure. I was given a name and number on the inside and once they check out your credentials, they contact you. I would say they have the copper do the check first, then once satisfied, they get in touch."

"This copper, you know what station he's from?" Austin asked.

"It wasn't like he left me his card, he flashed his badge, told me I owed five large, had a week to pay it, then he near broke my nose and took my roll, took my enforcer too," Neil replied.

"What about you ring your contact. Say you want to place another order for a friend. Then I help you out with the cop?" Austin said.

"Once you're done with them they wipe you. I have no doubt when the cop comes back for the money, he'll be here to rub me out. They don't like loose ends," Neil answered.

"So, what are you going to do when he comes back?" Austin asked.

"I have this." He indicated the black pistol. "Self-defence, I guess you'd call it. I tell you what, I'll give you my contact's name for $500 and his phone number for another $500. The rest is up to you," Neil offered.

Austin agreed, dropping another bundle of cash on the table in front of Neil.

"But let me warn you. They recognise you, they kill you," he added.

Austin thought about what other options he had. He could kill him, he thought, but where would that get him?

"What do they do with the kids they take?" Austin asked.

"They sell them to people like me," Neil said.

"Who's your guy?" Austin asked.

"His name is Ian Williams or Welling or something like that. I can't remember exactly," Neil said.

Neil was busy going through his phone, looking for the number, Austin assumed.

"Put this number into your phone." He read out the 10-digit mobile number.

"He did a stint in Barwon two years back. If he's changed his number, it's because he had heat on him," Neil said.

Neil then removed a small bag of white powder, placed a little of it in a cut-out plastic bottle, added water, and watched the powder dissolve. Then he poured out a spoonful. His thumb scraped the lighter to life. Neil's eyes widened as the concoction boiled on the spoon. He drew the boiled substance into the syringe. He repeated the boiling process two more times.

He had all three needles lined up ready to go.

"If you want to have a shot, it'll cost you $50. That's on top of the $1,000. If not, get your shit and fuck off out of here, let me enjoy my afternoon."

Austin had what he came for. He took his belongings and left Neil to ruin his life even more. Good riddance, he thought.

Chapter 65

Mike could see in the rear-vision mirror that the boy was out cold. He drove the van at normal speed through the traffic, trying to think of a place where he could dump him. He knew he had crossed the line when he took the child, and once that line was crossed there was no going back.

In his mind there had always been a difference between them and him. He was the cleaner, the man who fixed problems and cleaned up after the Priest. For that, he was paid well. He had always been able to separate himself from them. Now he was the same as them. He had joined their depraved world and he would surely pay.

Mike shook the thought from his head. He needed to concentrate on the task at hand. He pulled over in an isolated side street, Googled 'Northland' in his phone and then clicked on 'maps'. He pinched the map to get a broader view. Then he saw it, 'Billabong Sanctuary'.

It was connected to the Yarra River, a secluded place only about 20 minutes away, located just behind a golf course. In the early afternoon with kids at school, it was likely to be deserted.

Worth a shot, he thought.

He drove slowly out of the side street and towards the reserve.

His only worry was the boy waking up. He didn't want to be stopped at the lights with a kid screaming in the back. He had ensured all the doors were key locked so escaping was not an issue, but noise might be. He had thought if he woke he would turn the music up as loudly as it would go.

By the time Mike reached the first golf course, the boy had begun to stir. Luckily he was only a minute from the reserve entrance. The road turned to gravel, and the ride became bumpy. Mike swayed from side to side, with the occasional jerking forward when the van hit a pothole. The equipment in the back rattled around as tools shifted from side to side.

Mike drove the van a long way down the road, near the water. The van beeped as he reversed to the water's edge. He stopped and got out and scanned the area. No one around. The section of the second golf course that adjoined the reserve was tree lined, with large pines providing a screen. The only real concern were people walking around the reserve.

Mike looked in all directions as he made his way to the rear of the van. There was no one about.

It was as clear as it was going to get. He opened the rear van door, just one, and grabbed the boy by the feet. He pushed his feet together and slid the black cable tie around his ankles and then pulled hard. The boy screamed in fear. Mike leaned in and took him by the jacket. The boy did everything in his power to fight back and Mike was impressed. He even wished there was another way.

Mike rolled him over, pushed his knee into the boy's back. He clasped both the boy's hands together behind his back and held them tight in his left hand, and cabled them with his right. He pulled it tight. He grabbed an old oily rag from the shelf and used it to gag his mouth. He knotted it tight, catching some of his hair in the knot. He tied the hands the same way as the feet, and then tied the hands to the feet and to each other using a long piece of rope that had been used to tie down a wheelbarrow in the back. Now he needed something heavy.

There it was, a crowbar. He attached the crowbar to the rope with more cable ties. He rolled the boy back over. His expression was one of immense fear, his eyes wide and terrified.

"I'm sorry mate, you were just in the wrong place at the wrong time."

The boy tried to speak but Mike had no idea what he was saying. Maybe that was a good thing. It was hard enough as it was.

Mike took the boy by the ears and lifted his head, ramming it into the metal crowbar tied behind him.

The boy's lights were out almost instantly.

* * *

The freezing cold water brought him around. He was shocked to find himself sinking. Had he been thrown in? He couldn't remember it if he had. Even underwater, Samuel could still taste the oil from the rag in his mouth. Now it was being flooded with dirty dam water. Samuel bit down hard on the rag, quickly cutting off the water. He held his breath. He tried to kick. If he could kick, he would be able to get to the surface. He pushed hard with his legs. The rope between his legs and his hands held tight. Samuel could feel the steel rod that went from head to toe. If he could just free himself from it. He clasped the cold wet metal pole and pushed down hard, trying to feed it through. It moved. It was moving. Adrenaline pumped through his veins, he was going to get out of this. Suddenly there was hope. It had to happen quickly, he couldn't hold his breath much longer. Soon his body would force him to breathe. Samuel kept feeding the pole through. Suddenly, it would go no further, it was stuck.

His fate was sealed.

He opened his eyes. He could see the light filtering through the murky water. It was a beautiful view, a fitting one considering it would be his last, he thought.

I wish I had gone to school, Samuel thought, as the water began its final journey into his lungs.

Chapter 66

Mike tried to forget what he had just done, but he thought no amount of time would let him forget. He stood watching the boy sink to the bottom of the dam. After four minutes, he knew it was done.

He didn't need to look up Google on his phone, he knew where he was going. He had been there before. Best part of it, his destination was just minutes away. If all went well, he would be home just after dinner and no one the wiser.

Fifteen minutes later, Mike parked the van in the driveway behind a faded old Toyota. He took the cloth that was sitting on the passenger seat and began to wipe the dash, steering wheel, gear stick, and door handle. He wiped the outside of the door handle and the back doors before heading through the carport and towards the back door.

Mike was prepared to break the door down, but before he kicked it in, he turned the knob just to check. Lady luck was on his side. He moved quietly through the laundry. The TV was on, as was the stereo, which was pumping music. Mike looked through the kitchen and saw Figal lying on the couch. There was an open bag of coke on the table and two empty needles, one still full of mixture.

He had obviously used one shot of coke, perhaps done a line and then soon after, injected the other shot. Now they had worn off and he was on a downer, and sleep was his body's way of coming down.

Mike removed a separate injection from his inside jacket pocket and put his knee on Figal's chest, instantly waking him.

"What the fuck are you doing, you bastard!" Neil yelled. "I don't have any cash. It's not due yet!" he continued.

Mike didn't reply; he didn't speak or even acknowledge his presence. He could feel Figal try and lift him off, but he knew he wouldn't have the strength from underneath. With one knee into his chest and the other knee pinning Figal's right arm to the couch, Mike was free to inject his hot shot, a lethal drug combination, into Figal.

He stayed on top of Figal until his eyes rolled back into his eye sockets. It looked like he was turning into a zombie. He started to foam at the mouth and his body began to convulse. Mike got off him and stood by the couch and waited for the convulsions to stop and for his lungs to close and his heart to stop. The hot shot was a guaranteed overdose.

It took only three minutes for Neil's body to stop shaking. Mike leaned over and felt for a pulse. There wasn't one.

He wiped the syringe he'd used and then placed it in Neil's left hand. Then he let it drop to his side.

Mike then spent the next five minutes planting evidence: hairs, carpet fibres. He even found an old sleeping bag in the hallway closet that he threw into the van. He took Figal's shoes and banged them together inside the van front cabin. Finally, he took the tissues from the coffee table and threw them on the passenger side floor.

* * *

By dinnertime, Mike was sitting across from his wife and twins. What he had done today would haunt him in this world and the next but if he wanted the money to keep flowing in, he had to keep the Priest safe. Fifteen thousand a month was a retainer he had become accustomed to and he could no longer live without.

His wife smiled at him the same way she always had. How

horrified she would be if she knew the truth. What would she think if she knew what he had done? He could keep the lies to himself; no one would have to know. He would take the boy's murder to his grave.

He had to.

Chapter 67

"Do you know why you've been called to this meeting?" Salma asked.

"No, not really," James Mitchell said.

"The Board of Northview can no longer find reasonable grounds to hold you here for ongoing treatment. We believe you do not need any further treatment. This is a meeting to discuss the specific conditions of your release back into society."

"Ok," James nodded.

"I will list the conditions and then we will go through them one by one. Ok with you?" Salma added.

"That's fine," James answered.

"Your release is subject to the following. You undergo weekly drug and alcohol testing. You provide us with a permanent residential address. You no longer associate with known sex offenders or people with a criminal background. You maintain an ongoing therapy plan with an approved therapist. You provide an undertaking to return to Northview should you notice any change in your condition.

"Do you have any questions?" Salma asked.

"I have a couple," James said. "How do I not associate with my family? Some of my family are convicted felons."

"We have excluded your family. However, with family like Ian who came to see you the other day, even though they are family I would suggest you associate with people that are more appropriate.

Is there anything else?"

"No, I understand. You want me to live out there like I have been in here, clean," James replied.

"I'm glad you understand the effect that drugs and alcohol could have on your mental wellbeing," Salma said.

"I don't want to go back to what I was. I've come such a long way and I want to stay like this," James lied.

"That's what I expected. You've done very well in turning your life around. You should be really proud of yourself," she said.

"Who do I have to see for therapy?" James asked.

"Any doctor you choose. As it is a condition of your release, it is paid for by the government."

"Can I choose you?" James asked.

"No, sorry, I only see patients at the hospital. I don't have a private practice. But if you tell me who you're seeing, then I can call them occasionally to keep updated on your progress. Would that be all right?" Salma asked.

"You would do that for me?" James said. He couldn't believe she hadn't realised he was playing her.

"Sure, I want to see you succeed in life," Salma replied. "Do you understand all the conditions as I have put them to you?"

"Yes," James answered.

"Do you understand that they form part of your release?"

"Yes," he answered again.

"If you will just sign here and initial here," Salma pointed to the places on the contract where he needed to sign.

James signed without hesitation.

Chapter 68

Beau had been in the interview room for more than three hours. His constant responses of 'no comment' were becoming trying.

"Beau, we know you're involved, tell us what you know," I said.

"No comment."

"It's not just coincidence that you were near to both of the abduction sites," Jake said. "We're searching your house now, so why don't you just tell us? We're going to find the evidence."

Beau sat in silence.

This wasn't working; he was staying quiet and I needed to try a new tack.

"You know, the only thing I really want to know is, how you took Chloe on her way to school without anyone seeing? How did you do that?"

Beau looked up and smiled and for a second, I thought I was going to get the answer. Just for that second. I thought he was going to crack. Then he repeated the words, "No comment."

I knew then that we wouldn't get anything. Even if the children were alive, he would let them die even if he was in jail. We would never get anything out of him.

I knew from his smile he had done it and he would love to brag about it, but previous experience had taught him to stay quiet.

"If you tell us where the children are, it will help you at sentencing," Jake said.

"We're taking a break. Can I get you anything, a Coke or a coffee?" I asked.

"No thanks," Beau replied.

We left the recording running, hoping we would catch a slip, but unfortunately for us, Beau sat there staring into space with that insolent smile across his face.

"What do you think?" Jake asked.

"He's dying to tell us but he just doesn't want to get caught. We didn't find any evidence in the searches. I don't think we can hold him much longer," I said, stating what we both knew.

"I agree. I think he had something to do with it. Maybe we could ask Monique for a surveillance budget?" Jake said.

Monique had the phone glued to her ear but she motioned us into her office as we stood in the office doorway.

After about five minutes, Monique hung up her call. "So where are we at?" she asked.

"We have diddly-squat, no confession, no evidence, but our guts tell us he's involved somehow. Every question we ask he says 'no comment'," Jake said.

"Has he asked for a lawyer?" she asked.

"No, he's just playing the silent game. We were hoping we could get a surveillance budget?"

"Firstly, what sort of surveillance order do you think the judge will give me with no evidence? I don't have just cause to get approval for wire taps or recording devices, especially after the searches turned up nothing. Secondly, my boss won't approve the man hours required for 24-hour surveillance, not on what we have. I suggest you go find more evidence. I'll rephrase that: go find some evidence."

Jake sighed, looked at me and nodded towards the door.

"Detectives," Monique called out.

Both of us stopped and turned.

"Don't get fixated on that suspect. If the evidence isn't there, it may be because he isn't involved."

Jake nodded.

"You have until Friday, that's all I can authorise. If you don't find anything in that time, I want you to investigate other leads."

"That's just over 24 hours," I said.

"I'm stretching it at that, Detective. I can't have all my resources following a guy for weeks, when it may not be him. If we're seen to be focusing on the wrong guy, the media would have a field day and I would get the sack."

I opened my mouth ready for a response when I was cut off.

"Time is ticking, Detective."

Jake grabbed me by the shoulder and we headed back to the interview room.

"Wait," I held Jake back. "Both of us think this is our guy, that he has them and is keeping them somewhere, which is why we haven't found any evidence or any bodies, right?"

"Correct," Jake replied.

"So we need him to drop his guard. At the moment, he's feeling he's the number one suspect, so he'll stay well away from wherever he's keeping them."

Jake nodded, more out of politeness than understanding.

"If we tell him we've crossed him off our list, he might just lead us to them."

Jake nodded.

"You organise his van from the compound and I'll go and give him the good news," I said.

I sat opposite Beau Delacroix. We needed evidence and we needed him to give it to us.

"Sorry to take so long, Beau. I know this has been a stressful time for you, but I'm pleased to tell you we've be able to eliminate you from our suspect list."

I watched Beau's body language and everything about it was wrong. Normally, people are relieved, but Beau came across as confused, unsure how this could be. This only increased my suspicions.

After he had calculated a response, he replied civilly with, "Well, about time."

"Your van is being brought around from our depot and will be out front in a few minutes. You can wait in the foyer."

Chapter 69

Chloe had swung next to the dead body for several hours. The smell was so bad she had vomited twice. Since being admitted back into the house a day and a half before, she had complied with everything she'd been asked to do without complaint. She never wanted to go back down there again.

She knew that the cellar was where they all ended up once the captor was done with them. The girl she had seen swinging from her feet had obviously bored him.

Igor wasn't at the house the whole time. Sometimes she would see him and the other three baddies, as she thought of them, leave by helicopter from a back paddock. In the front paddock was a large shed full of dogs. On the days she was locked in her room, Chloe would look at the woods at the back of the property. Depending on the time of day, she would see an older man with grey hair and black boots open the dog-house and let them run around for a few minutes. He would blow his whistle and all the dogs would exit the building like a wild pack. There were all different types of dogs. She recognised a few. There was a Rottweiler, a German Shepherd and a Doberman. The old man would then enter the building with a wheelbarrow and broom. Chloe guessed he was cleaning up their mess and feeding them. Usually he attended to them morning and afternoon. The man seemed to be working quickly today. The dogs had only been out for a short while when the man reappeared. Normally he took longer to do the job.

There was no helicopter yet. Maybe it would come later, she thought. It had left with the four men the day before but as far as she knew, they had not returned. The security men still stood guard. She could see one of them standing to the left of her window under the verandah. He too was watching the dog-man work. The bottom of the paddock abutted the woods. From the house to the wood was only four paddocks away but it seemed like miles. Chloe guessed it would only take two minutes to run from the house to the woods and out of sight of the house security. Was running into the woods her way out?

That might be the easy part. Getting out of her room and out of the house was a whole other complication.

Sometimes, when Igor had his way with her, she would stay in his bed. Early one morning, she had got up to use the toilet and quietly peeked out the door. No one seemed to be on guard and the door was open. She thought about running then, but was too terrified. She would take the chance if it ever arose again. Maybe when Igor returned, he would want her to share his bed. Maybe she could pretend to fall asleep and hope that he would let her lie there. Then she would have to wait for him to fall asleep.

If she was caught, she knew she would also be made an example of for the next girl and be left hanging in the cellar. But if she didn't escape, she would more than likely die in the cellar, one way or the other.

Chapter 70

Hayley sponge-bathed Ryan every morning. While she bathed him, she would talk to him and squeeze his hand, hoping for any response, a flutter of the eyes or a squeeze back.

Nothing ever seemed to work but Hayley followed the same routine regardless. Even when she took his obs, she would tell him how her day was and always pass on a funny story, if she had one. Today, she was telling him how Mr Kelvin had been walking around the hospital with the back of his gown open and it was flapping in the breeze showing his bare butt to everyone in the area.

She was hoping it would cause a smile, but there was nothing.

Ryan's parents were still visiting, but the 24-hour bedside vigils had changed. Their new normal had started. They had accepted that their world, while now very different, could not stop. They still had a daughter who had to go to school and they still had bills to pay, jobs they had to get back to. Both had used all their holiday and sick leave and while both their bosses were kind and compassionate, after a month of leave they needed their employees back at work.

Hayley had finished the sponge bath when the doctors made their usual rounds. Today neurologist Professor Alice Wise had her team with her, including her new intake of interns.

She flicked through the chart and began to describe Ryan's condition. Each intern took his vitals and studied him for sensory responses. They also looked for bed sores and muscle deterioration. "Now, who can tell me what a good Glasgow coma scale rating is?" Several students put their hands up, eager to gain the attention of Professor Wise. The professor pointed to one of the students. "Eleven to fifteen," a redheaded man answered." "Correct," the professor responded. "Now, after conducting the sensory tests, what would you give as a score for this patient?" The same red-haired gentleman raised his hand but this time, Professor Wise selected a different student.

"After reviewing the patient and finding no response to any of the key testing areas –no verbal response, no motor response, no pupil reaction, no limb strength – I think it would be a four." "Well done, correct. Based on that score it is very unlikely that the prognosis would be a favourable one. It is likely that Ryan will never come out of his coma."

Hayley heard all of this and even though the information was correct, it was too soon for the parents to get the news of the most likely outcome. That conversation would have to happen soon and it was never one the doctors liked to have.

The doctors left and Hayley made her way back over to Ryan's side. His sweet innocent face was motionless and unresponsive. "You find your way back home; your parents need you," she said to him calmly.

Chapter 71

Jake had been keeping an eye on Beau since his release from custody. We had 24 hours to find some answers and I was out chasing some answers of my own. I was used to specialists keeping me waiting for hours on end. But my GP had always been good and he definitely broke the mould.

"So, what can I help you with today?" he asked. He was a polite doctor, in his late 50s with grey hair. English background but only a slight accent. He wore bifocals and looked at me over the top of them.

"I'm feeling nauseated all the time," I said.

He put the blood pressure cuff on my arm.

"Are you still eating normally or have you lost your appetite?" he asked.

The cuff went tight for a few seconds before it slowly released the air and the pressure.

"I get hungry, but I just feel sick. Do you think it's something bad?" I asked.

"You always fear the worst, don't you. It could be any number of things. I wouldn't worry just yet," he replied.

I was a worrier, but I had bloody good reason to worry. I had been sick from the moment I was born. Hell, my parents had been told I wouldn't make it past three weeks, but I'd always been a fighter.

"Let's take some bloods. That will rule out a few things and hopefully narrow it down. Have you been feeling lethargic at all?" he asked.

"Yeah, a little during the day. Sometimes after lunch I just want to sleep, but I've been working long hours at the moment."

"You may need to consider slowing down. You're not fit and healthy like the other officers. You keep going like this, something will have to give and that something will be your health," he replied.

"I can't stop. I have to solve this one. Too many kids are being hurt, if it costs me my life so be it, I won't stop," I replied.

"I'm not suggesting you stop. I'm just saying slow down a bit, get some more sleep. Remember, you can't save anyone if you're dead."

I took the slip he handed me and headed out to a second waiting room, where I took a number from the wall and sat down to wait to be called.

Being number four, I assumed there would be three people ahead of me but when the nurse came out and called "number three" I was pleasantly surprised.

I hated having blood taken and the one thing I could never do was watch as the needle went into my arm. The nurses at these centres were usually first-go masters, and this time was no exception.

I'd experienced many a time when four tries had still not been enough and thought that some of the nurses seemed to feel that if they wiggled the needle around under the skin, they might hit the vein. I often wondered during these episodes if they thought they were digging for oil?

There was no digging required this time.

Chapter 72

Jake had been watching Beau's house just on two hours before a call he least expected came in. It was Monique. "You won't believe this, Jake," were her first words.

"What happened?" Jake asked.

"Another boy was taken today from Northland. We need you to get on it now," she said.

"What about Beau, do I stay on him?" he asked.

"Forget him, this happened while he was in custody. It's obviously not him. I need you to come back to the office. We have some leads I need you to follow up."

When Jake got back to the station, the place was buzzing. He walked through the auto double doors to see Monique in her office madly waving to him, her phone attached to her ear as usual.

"Hold on," Monique said to the person on the phone, and then pressed a button and placed it on her desk.

"We've found a child's body. Could be the boy that was taken today. Here's the address." She waved a piece of paper at Jake.

Jake opened the folded sheet of paper which read Billabong Sanctuary Northland.

* * *

Jake rang me on his way to Northland. I met him at the top of the road at the scene. The latest development surprised me. I was sure we had our man, I was sure Beau was him. Even though we had nothing to prove my theory, I didn't like to go against my gut instinct. I thought it through some more. Could I be right and wrong at the same time? Could Beau be involved but be working with someone else? Maybe there were two of them.

I didn't dismiss the idea totally, but the possibility of two kidnappers working together didn't feel right.

I followed Jake's car down the dirt track. It was getting on dusk and Jake had his headlights on.

When we pulled up, Forensics were already on the scene. Instead of Grace in attendance, it was Philip, one of her more senior forensic analysts.

I will never forget the first time I saw the dead boy. It was an image that will stay with me for the rest of my life. He had already been removed from the water. He was lying on his back, and his legs and hands were bound, crumpled beneath him. His eyes were wide open as if bewildered at what he was seeing. It didn't seem to be a look of fear, but more one of amazement. Had he seen what was on the other side?

I often wondered where the spirit went when you died. One day I would find out.

The boy's hair was filled with dirt and sand. There was a twig stuck behind his ear, like a spare pencil. His skin was wrinkly and bloated, with blotchy patterns all over his face, neck and hands.

"Was he dead before he was dumped?" I asked Philip.

"Unfortunately not, he was alive when he was put into the water. He suffered an excruciating death. Drowning is a horrible way to go. Once your lungs fill with water, the body goes into convulsions before the victim becomes unconscious and eventually dies."

"A golfer spotted him floating in the dam early this evening," Jake said. "He'd been weighed down with a crowbar. Police divers recovered it after they dragged the body from the river."

Philip continued, "From what I can establish so far, during the boy's convulsions, the cable tie holding the crowbar broke. But by that stage it was too late for him to swim to safety."

They gently moved the waterlogged body into the plastic bag.

"Did you find his shoes?" I asked.

"They weren't on him when we took him out. Police divers have looked in the dam for them, but haven't found them. They could still be down there somewhere," Philip answered. "We need to get him back to the lab to undergo further tests. The longer he's out here in the elements, the less chance we have of collecting anything of substance. Water is our worst nightmare," Philip said.

"We'll meet you back there. You taking him to St Kilda Road I take it?" I asked.

Philip nodded.

They loaded the boy into the van and headed away from the scene. Jake was already walking back to his car.

I stayed to survey the area and saw that tyre moulds and shoe casts had already been taken. What a horrible crime, a boy with his whole life ahead of him, taken and thrown while alive into a dam, how inexplicably disgusting, I thought.

I knelt down, hands resting on my knees. I looked at the water and then up to the fading sky. Wherever the boy was, I was hoping he was at peace.

"You all right, Brucey?" Jake asked as he realised I wasn't following him.

"No, not really, who would do this to a child?" I asked.

"That's what we have to find out, mate," Jake replied.

"God help him when we find him," I said.

Chapter 73

Stevie had watched Ian and Bill go from acting like 'normal' people to completely crazy. They switched from being abusive and evil, to caring and jovial, and then back again. He didn't know what mood they would be in or what was in store for him each time they entered the room.

He knew they had done with their drugs and now they were finished, he noticed they were getting sleepy and continually trying to wake each other up.

It had been a few hours since he had last been raped and from what he could tell, both the kidnappers had fallen asleep. His door was shut but they had not locked it the last time they had left. He remained cuffed to the bed with his right hand, his left hand free. Although he could still only reach from one side of the bed, now he had a free hand, he would be able to rummage through the drawers that had previously been out of reach.

He started with the right-hand side, hoping he would find a screwdriver or a paperclip. He had two options: pick the lock of the cuff, or unscrew the bar that ran through the cuff.

He rummaged through the first drawer. There was a coin. He thought about using it on the screw that held the iron bar to the bed but realised it was too wide to fit the screw. There was nothing of use. He quietly slid the drawer shut again and moved on.

The next drawer was empty.

Stevie rolled over to the other side of the bed. This side was a lot harder to search, as he had to reach across his body.

This time he started with the bottom drawer first. Inside were a couple of old magazines and a notepad. Again he slid it closed quietly.

There had to be something. This last drawer was his last hope. Surely there would be something in here he could use.

He slid the drawer open but it only opened a few centimetres before it got stuck. He pulled harder but the angle didn't help and the drawer didn't budge. He reached his hand in and slid it across the bottom of the drawer. A sharp pain hit his pinkie finger. He wondered if he had been stabbed by a used needle.

He pulled his hand out and inspected his finger. It was bleeding but it seemed more a cut than a prick.

He sucked the finger and dived his hand back in again, a little more carefully this time, padding the bottom of the drawer. This time there was no sharp pain, only the cold touch of metal, something thin and sharp. It was only a couple of centimetres long but it could be of use. He slid his fingers over it again, trying to lift it out, but he couldn't grasp it. Stevie slid the object towards the front of the drawer, using the front panel of the drawer to lever it up. He clasped it between his fingers.

He slowly withdrew his hand and the object shone. It was a blade of some sort. He immediately knew that even if it wouldn't help with the cuff, it might help with the bed screw.

He knelt on the bed and threaded the blade into the head of the screw. His only luck of the day was that the screws were not the Phillips head type. Stevie applied some pressure, praying that the blade didn't break before the screw moved.

The screw stayed put and the blade remained intact. He applied a little more force. It moved slowly at first, then turning it became smooth and easy. Stevie removed the blade from the head of the screw and used his fingers to unwind the remainder.

He then put the blade into the second screw head. It was all that remained between him and being free from the bed. He turned with what he thought was the same amount of pressure as before, but this time the blade snapped, flew up into the air and fell down onto the back of the bed. Stevie realised he had just enough blade left to grip onto. If he lost any more of it, he wouldn't be able to apply the pressure required. He threaded the broken blade into the screw head and turned it again slowly. Then he increased the pressure, paused before adding a little more, then another pause and more pressure, pause, pressure. This method went on for several tries, until finally the screw gave up its fight.

Seconds later, the screw was in his fingertips and he had slid his cuff down and over the free end of the metal rod.

He quickly screwed the rod loosely back in place so that there was no risk of it slipping and making a noise. Dressed in just his jocks and a white t-shirt, Stevie crept towards the window and drew the blinds. The window that had once been there was now boarded up, as he had suspected, and only a few thin bars of light filtered through. There was no way he would be able to get out that way without making a racket. Even though it was filthy, the carpet felt soft between his toes. He made his way over to the door, hoping the floor wouldn't creak as he walked around the room.

The door was shut; he had no way of seeing where Bill and Ian were. If he opened it, would they see him? Would the door squeak if he opened it? Had it squeaked before? he asked himself but he couldn't remember. It was something he had never noticed or thought about until now. How had he not noticed? Maybe he had been too pre-occupied about what was coming to notice any noises. He had no choice but to try it. He held the small broken blade in his hand, poised ready to unleash whatever damage it would inflict. He had wrapped the spare cuff around his right wrist as well, so it wouldn't dangle or hit on something as he tried to escape.

He turned the knob and pulled on the door just enough to create a crack. He had only a limited view through the crack, but he couldn't see anything. The house was in darkness.

He opened the door a little further. This time, the door let out a groan as the crack widened.

Stevie expected to hear one of the men come running down the hall towards him, but no one came. The house remained quiet and dark.

His feet moved briskly and quietly as he tiptoed across the carpet.

He paused at the end of the hall, staying as still as possible. He even tried to calm his breathing. He wanted to have no noise to impair his hearing. With everything within him as calm and as quiet as possible, he stood and listened.

He could hear the muffled noise of the TV coming from his own room, and the sounds of another TV coming from the left. Once his eyes adjusted to the darkness, he poked his head around the corner of the hall wall and studied his surroundings. The first thing he noticed sent his head recoiling around the corner. He had made out a pair of bare feet hanging over the edge of the couch. He didn't know which one of his captors they belonged to. He calmed himself once again, put his head around and listened. He was hoping for some snoring. At first he didn't pick it up but within a second the noise was unmistakable. It was low, but it was there. Whoever the feet belonged to was asleep.

He had two choices: head for the back door past the sleeping man with the bare feet, or head towards the front door, towards the unknown. He was hoping the feet belonged to Bill, and that Ian was somewhere else entirely.

He decided to head to the front. The last thing he wanted was to risk waking the devil while it slept.

He tiptoed across the kitchen tiles. The floor was sticky and the bench was a mess, with most cupboard doors ajar. He caught a glimpse of the knife holder sitting next to the stove and thought about taking one of them for protection, but the thought of staying in the home longer than he needed to prevented him from taking it. He heard talking coming from the other side of the kitchen. He was hopeful it was a radio or a TV, and not people. He poked his head through the door. The lounge was on the right, and another bedroom door was on the left. It was ajar but he could not see inside. The TV in the lounge was on and it looked to be the source of the talking; some sports show. There was no sign of the other man. Had he gone out? Was he in the room, just feet away? Was he sitting on the lounge couch?

The longer he waited, the more chance he had of getting caught. He had to go for it, now. There was no benefit in waiting. He took a breath and prepared himself.

He moved quicker than he ever had before, or so he thought. The lounge room came and went and before he knew it, the cold metal door handle sat firmly in his hand. He turned it and pulled; there was no resistance at all. It flew open in his hand and had he not had his wits about him, it would have flown wide open into the wall behind.

Beyond the door was a mesh door, a security door. He pulled on the handle. It didn't move.

"Hey Bill! The boy, he's trying to escape, quickly, the front door, Bill!" someone hollered. At the sound, Stevie could see a man approaching from the bedroom. He flicked the snib and tried the handle again. It flung open and the cold night air rushed in. He stepped out onto the porch before a hand grabbed him tight, the fingers digging into his neck.

"Quick Bill, he's getting away!" Ian called again.

Stevie spun to try and break the hold. As he turned, he saw and then felt the impact of Bill's elbow being thrust into his face. The pain was sharp at first, then he felt nothing.

When he woke up, Stevie knew where he was he before his vision returned. His hands were both cuffed above his head, and the bar that he had just removed was back.

"Where did you think you were going?" Ian asked.

"Home," Stevie replied.

Bill climbed on the bed and sat on Stevie's torso. "Let's just kill him here," he said.

"No, not here," Ian replied.

Bill didn't listen. He grabbed Stevie by the throat, and began to squeeze.

"Bill, not here!" Ian yelled.

"Bill, stop!"

Bill didn't stop. If anything, he squeezed harder.

Ian could see he was killing the boy.

"William, if you kill him here, we get caught."

Bill released a little at first and then totally eased his grip. He felt the boy beneath him gasp for air. By the time he climbed off the boy, he was breathing again. Even though he was unconscious, he was alive, for now at least.

A loud noise rang through Ian's head and it took him a few seconds to come back to reality and realise it was their own doorbell.

Bill turned towards him and they stood staring at each other.

Chapter 74

Within two hours of watching the boy's lifeless body being loaded into the coroner's van, we knew who he was and had a fairly good idea of how he had ended up in the bottom of the dam.

He was Samuel Sadiq, who was born in Australia and had grown up in his large family with five sisters. His parents owned the local café and life had been good to them all. Samuel enjoyed school and had been doing well, but today was a special Thursday, it was the day that the new James Bond movie was due to be released and he couldn't wait to see it. Two of his friends had also skipped school to see it with him. Their plan was to meet at the cinema for the 1 o'clock session. When Sam didn't show, both Ben and Nick thought he had chickened out and they went ahead without him.

When Ben found out that it was Sam who had been found dead, he thought he had better come forward. Although he knew he would cop a hiding from his father, he decided to tell Sam's parents about their movie plan.

Jake and I had gone to the Sadiqs' and we were sitting in their living room. "Hi Ben, I believe you have some information for us?" I asked him calmly. He looked nervously towards his parents who were sitting with him.

"I am sure your parents will go easier on you if you tell us what happened," I said.

"We all agreed to skip school so we could see the new Bond movie. It came out today. We were meant to meet at the movies at 1 pm, that way we would all be back home at 4."

"Did you see Sam at all today?" I asked.

"No, he didn't show up. We thought he was sick or he'd chickened out. We didn't think much of it. I tried texting him, but he didn't reply."

"So you watched the movie and what did you do when you got home?"

"I rang Sam to tell him about it, but his sister told me he hadn't arrived home from school and they'd rung the school and he hadn't been there all day. So I told her we were meant to meet at the movies and he didn't show up," Ben said. "Now he's dead and it's my fault, all because I wanted to see the stupid movie." Ben was crying now, filled with guilt and sadness.

"Ben, you can't blame yourself, you've been a great help. We will find who did this," I replied.

I took a piece of paper from my notepad and wrote 'CCTV, mall', and passed it to Jake.

Jake took the note and headed outside while I finished up with the family.

The Sadiq family were distraught, as any family would be when they lose a child. In situations like that, the only thing you can do is find the person responsible and make them pay. Anything you say seems insignificant.

I joined Jake outside a few minutes later.

"How did you go?" I asked.

"The mall management will have some techs there within 30 minutes to go through the footage. Do you think we need to search all of it?" Jake asked.

"Possibly, did they say how many techs they were sending?" I asked.

"Four," Jake replied.

"That should be enough, though it still might take a while," I said.

"Did you get a photo we can use for comparison?" Jake asked.

I nodded. "It's in the file. We better get going if we want to meet them there."

Chapter 75

Austin stood on the porch in the dark. He had just rung the doorbell. He knew they were home; he could hear the TV. He pressed it again.

He was counting on these guys being as willing to sell information as Neil had been.

Seconds later, he made out movement inside the home. Moments after that, the door opened. "Can I help you?" a middle-aged man asked.

"I was looking for Ian, Neil sent me. He said you would be able to help me," Austin said.

"Don't know any Neil, sorry you're mistaken," Ian replied.

"Neil Figal," Austin repeated. "You were friends down in Barwon."

"Oh yeah, you mean Figal, yeah, what about him?" Ian replied.

"He said you have a contact who can get me a very exclusive product," Austin replied.

"How do you know, Figal?" Ian asked.

"I did a stint with him myself. Let's just say we all have similar interests. I'm after the contact, the one you use they call the Priest," Austin replied.

Ian looked directly at Austin, then behind him, and even down the street a little, as if to check he was alone. "Come in," he said as he unlocked the security door.

Austin stepped inside. He knew one thing instantly. Crims didn't make good housekeepers. The place smelt, and there was drug paraphernalia everywhere. They were not hiding their addictions.

"Bill, we have a visitor," he said to a man who appeared from a back room wearing track pants and a singlet that had once been white. His pants were low and almost falling off his arse.

"This is…sorry, I didn't get your name?" Ian said.

"Wayne, but most people call me Al."

"How do they get Al out of Wayne?" Bill asked.

"My last name is Alfred. So I guess Al just stuck," Austin said.

Bill chuckled to himself. "It's better than mine. I got called Worm by all the girls."

"Girls can be cruel," Austin answered.

"They're fucking dumb sluts, is what they are," Bill said.

Austin saw the sudden change in Bill's personality and they had only been talking 90 seconds.

"So, why you here?" Bill asked, unaware of the conversation Ian had already had in the doorway.

"He's after the Priest's number, says he knows Figal from down the Bay," Ian answered on Austin's behalf.

"Why didn't Figal give you the Priest's number?" Bill asked.

"He said he'd had some recent trouble with the Priest because he cancelled an order, and now some cop was after him," Austin replied. He even raised his hands as if to say, I don't really understand.

"Apparently you'd be able to hook me up for a price?"

Ian and Bill looked at each other.

"$5,000 large and maybe we can point you in the right direction," Bill replied.

Austin removed a wad of cash and counted out $2,500 dollars, placing it on the coffee table in front of them, just as he had done at Figal's.

Then he returned the remaining funds to his pocket. "I'll give you the balance when I get the details."

"How do we know you're not a cop?" Bill asked.

"You don't, I can't prove it. I can only tell you I'm not a cop," Austin replied.

"Ring Figal," Bill said, pulling a revolver from the back of his pants. "You look like a cop," he said.

Bill pointed the gun at Austin's head.

Austin remained calm.

"Ask him if he knows of Wayne here," Bill continued.

Austin panicked a little on the inside. He had made up his name on the way over. He hoped Figal would catch on. He would, wouldn't he? If he didn't, Austin was a dead man.

Ian selected a number in his mobile and held it out, speaker on. It rang, and rang. Then click, 'You've called Figs, leave a message.' Then it beeped.

"He was pretty high when I left. Suggested I fuck off and let him enjoy his afternoon," Austin said quickly.

"Oh fuck, he could be out of it for days," Ian said.

"Still doesn't prove he's not a cop," Bill said.

Austin removed his shirt and handed the gun sitting in his belt to Ian. "You have my weapon. I'm not wearing a wire. I'm only asking for a phone number. Even if I was a cop, which I'm not, you can't go to jail for giving me a phone number," Austin said. "Think about it," he added.

With both their guns pointing at Austin, Ian and Bill looked at each other. "It's just a number," Ian said.

Bill nodded.

"I told Figal if I got the number, I'd help him with the cop if I could find out who he is. Do you guys know him?" Austin asked.

Ian shook his head, "No, but I reckon the Batman is the cop," he said.

"The Batman?" Austin questioned.

"The Batman does the delivery. It's a guy in a Batman mask," Ian replied.

"So why do you think this Batman is a cop?" Austin asked.

"When I got my last delivery he asked for my licence," Ian said.

"That doesn't prove he's a cop," Bill said.

"No, but it was also the way he held my wrist. I've had a cop do that before. Last time I was arrested, actually," Ian said.

"Fuckin' pigs," Bill added.

"Friends have told me some got their deliveries direct from a guy in a Joker mask," Ian said.

Austin knew about the Joker.

Soon the Joker would know about him.

Chapter 76

Jake and I met the mall staff at 6.30 on the Thursday evening. They had called in two of their senior CCTV specialists to help look for evidence of Sam.

They colour copied the pic I had given them from the file and pinned it next to each screen with Blu-tack, then began their search.

Our guess was that Sam had spent the morning at the shops until the boys' 1 o'clock movie began.

"What would you have done before a movie when you were 12?" I asked Jake.

"You know that answer, Brucey," Jake replied.

I did know that answer, which was 'eat'. It reminded me of the time Jake had consumed a full family meal, including four burgers, four fries and four drinks before a movie and was still hungry enough to order popcorn.

"Can we check the food court from 11 to 1 first?" I asked the CCTV specialists.

"We normally start with the toilet areas. That's usually where kidnappings happen," the security guard replied.

"I think you'll find most rapes happen in the toilets but most abductions happen from the car park. I think what my partner is trying to establish is if he even made it into the mall," Jake replied.

The security officer accepted the request and forwarded the instructions to his colleagues to search the cameras from the food court.

Only a few minutes in, one of the officers said, "I think I've found him, here, ordering at KFC at 11.47 am."

I stood up to compare the footage to the photo. Jake was leaning over the other side of the security officer when his phone buzzed.

Jake stepped aside and I heard him answer, "Miller," in the background.

The image in front of me looked like Samuel.

"Brodie, we have to go," Jake called out.

I turned away from the screen, wondering why we needed to leave.

"They may have found Sam's offender," Jake explained.

I turned back to the security guy, pointed to the screen. "This is him. I want you to find out where he goes every step. Then I want you to copy it, so it flows like a movie. Can you do that?" I asked.

"Yes sure," the officer said, "now that we've found him, he'll be easy to follow."

"Make sure you don't erase any of the footage by accident," Jake added.

"Don't worry, Detective, it's all backed up in the Cloud."

"Thank you," Jake said.

"We'll send an officer down to collect it," I said as we left.

"You seemed extra nice today?" I said to Jake.

"They had to come back into work when they'd only just finished for the day. They were doing us a favour," Jake replied.

"So what do you mean we might have him?"

"They found a stolen van in a guy's driveway. Apparently he's a known sex offender and there's evidence all over the place."

"Let's go question him. Find out what the fucker has to say for himself," I said.

"We can't, he's dead, overdose," Jake replied.

"You're fucking kidding me, right?" I asked, even though I knew he would never joke about a case.

Then it hit me: why would a man steal a van to kidnap a child, only to drive it home and overdose? Something smelled and it smelled bad.

Chapter 77

Austin was standing in Ian and Bill's lounge, still half-naked and still with two guns pointed at him, one of them his own. "Isn't it entrapment if I say I'm not a cop, but I am?" Austin asked Bill and Ian, who again exchanged dumbfounded looks of uncertainty.

"Can I put my shirt back on now?" Austin asked.

Ian picked it up off the floor and handed it to him.

"If you don't mind, I'll feel safer if I hold on to the piece until you leave," Ian said.

"Sure, no problem, I trust you," Austin replied.

"Here's the number. You need to text your order in a specific format and he'll text you back with a price. If you don't use the format he won't even respond."

"How will I know the format?" Austin asked.

"I'm going to tell you, fuck-head," Ian said, laughing. "You need to put M or F and then the age of the goods. That's it; nothing else, no other information. Then you'll get a price and a date. Just before the date sometime, even on that day, you'll get your delivery instructions. Do you understand what to do?"

"Yeah, sounds easy enough," Austin replied.

"Now, this next piece of info is for your own benefit. I heard of a buyer who turned up to the drop and tried to negotiate. I heard he was cut up, fed to some guy's dogs in New South Wales, someone they call the Monster."

"I don't plan on negotiating," Austin replied.

"I don't know how true this, but I don't plan on testing it," Ian said.

Austin followed through with his end of the bargain, placing the balance of the money on the coffee table. He was about to ask to use the bathroom so he could plan his next move, when Bill interrupted him. It couldn't have worked out better.

"Do you want to see the quality of the product? We have one here now if you want to take a look," Bill said.

Ian's eyes widened; he was furious, and Austin had noticed.

"Are you fucking insane? What if he's a cop?" Ian asked.

"I'm not a cop, I already told you that," Austin said before Bill had a chance.

"Then we fucking kill him," Bill answered.

Bill pointed towards the hallway, motioning with the revolver.

"Follow me," he said.

All Austin could think was, please let it be Mikayla and please let her be alive.

He followed Bill past the kitchen.

The smell and the mess were disgusting. He could see the home-made drug kit lying on the table in front of the second TV.

Bill entered the hall.

Austin could see the shiny lock, high on the outside of the middle door. He knew right then that they were keeping someone.

Possibly Mikayla.

What if it was Mikayla?

Then Austin wondered what would happen if they opened the door and his daughter was on the other side. Sure, he would be able to stay in character, but there was no way she would. The first word out of her mouth would be 'Daddy'.

He knew what the consequences would be for them both if that happened.

He couldn't risk it, he had to act now.

Chapter 78

The suspect's home was only a few minutes from the mall and several blocks from the victim's residence.

Jake parked on the opposite side of the street. We both got out and as was custom, we surveyed the scene before we went any further. I noted there was an old Toyota in the drive under the carport and a van sitting in the driveway behind it.

Police tape had been put up across the whole front of the property, from one neighbour's fence to the other.

Jake lifted the tape and stepped under it, then held it up for me. The back doors of the van were open and Forensics were going through it. Grace looked up. "You might want to start inside the house, there's more in there. We're almost done. I'll come and get you shortly when we're finished."

Jake led the way and I followed. We crossed the lawn, which was well overdue for a mow, and went in through the front door. Jake flashed his badge at the officer standing in the open doorway, and then we stepped inside.

Two steps inside into the lounge, we stopped. A short balding man lay dead and naked on the couch. He had foamed at the mouth. One of the Forensics guys was looking him over.

"OD?" Jake asked.

"Looks that way," the Forensics officer replied.

I looked at the syringes all lined up on the table, all used. I noticed a syringe down the left-hand side of the couch, as if it had fallen out of his left hand. I looked at his left arm; it was full of holes. Then I looked at the right; there was only one.

I asked the doctor to pick up the syringe from down the side of the deceased and place it on the coffee table, and then I compared the syringes. Three were the same type and brand, but the one on the couch was different.

"Why do you think he changed arms?" I asked the doctor.

"I was wondering that myself. Normally, they only change when they're having trouble with a vein, but the veins in his left arm seem reasonably good considering the high use. So I don't know. Maybe he had a bit of trouble with his last shot?" he theorised.

I wandered through the house. There were more syringes in the top drawer of the bedside table, together with spoons and several lighters. These were to provide for the late night or early morning fix. Why was his last hit in a different syringe? I asked myself again.

Grace came in.

"I have some things that I need to show you," she said.

I followed her outside to the van.

"What have you got?" I asked.

"I found a pair of child's shoes and from the description the parents gave, I think they belong to Sam. I have a jumper on the passenger floor which belongs to the deceased in the house."

"How do you know it's his?" I asked.

"It's the matching jacket from the pants on the floor in the lounge. There are also muddy shoe prints on the driver side floor and the back laundry floor. They both match the shoes at the back door. Finally, I have hairs. I have no doubt that they will belong to the deceased."

"Sounds like an open and shut case," Jake replied. He had followed me outside.

"It does, doesn't it? But among all this incriminating evidence, I've found very little from the boy, and no prints from anyone. None belonging to Sam and none belonging to the deceased," Grace said.

"I'm not sure what you're getting at?" Jake replied.

"I have enough incriminating evidence for a conviction 10 times over. But why would you wipe down all the prints, yet leave hairs and jumpers and shoes all in the van?" Grace questioned.

"Maybe he came home, was halfway through cleaning, and needed a fix. Got carried away and OD'd. Who the hell knows, but this is a person who has kidnapped kids in the past."

"Possibly, just seems unusual," Grace replied.

"Everything about this case is fucked-up, Grace, starting with a boy thrown into a dam alive," Jake said.

Jake left us at the van headed back into the house.

"Don't worry about it, Grace, he's not upset with you. All these missing kids are starting to get to him," I said. "I have a few questions about this case too, something doesn't feel right," I said.

"Like what?" Grace asked.

"Well, who steals a car to commit an abduction and then parks it in their own drive? Who uses a different syringe and arm for the fatal dose? Why is this kid found within hours of the kidnapping and the others are still missing? Like you, I think it seems odd," I said.

Grace looked at me. I could see she was pondering the questions I had posed.

"But also I think we need to consider the fact that the drugs may have affected the suspect and the scene is odd because we're not dealing with a rational human being," I added.

"Let's just keep an open mind for now and see what the investigation and the science tell us. After all, I have a lot more left to analyse," Grace said.

"Agreed," I answered, "although it's going to be difficult getting answers from a dead suspect."

Chapter 79

Austin was now standing less than a couple of metres from the bedroom door, between the two paedophiles. He towered over both. They each had a gun, yet he knew he was in control, he had the advantage, he just had to be precise. The SAS had taught him precision, and in a few seconds he would put it to the test.

A trained soldier notices everything. Austin had already noticed that Ian, who was in front of him, was beginning to handle his gun in a manner that would render it useless when he needed it most. He was holding it by the butt, his trigger finger no longer in the trigger guard. Also, Austin had flicked the safety off when he'd handed it over.

Bill, who was in front of him, held his gun well but he was in the wrong position to keep himself safe. Ian needed to be armed and ready should an attack from behind occur. He was the one in position to prevent what was to occur, but he was not ready.

Austin's only dilemma was psychological: did he kill them both or leave them alive? Killing them would be justified, simply for what they had done to the child behind the door. If that was Mikayla, death would be a certainty. If he left them alive, he would be identified and then questioned by the police, at length he assumed. That would certainly prevent him from tracking Mikayla and that couldn't be allowed. If he let them live, he wondered how long it would be before they were out of jail and doing this to someone else's child.

Poised to strike, Austin waited for Bill to reach for the bedroom door handle. Then he struck. He grabbed Bill around the neck with his left arm, and spun his body to face Ian. Bill was now his shield. Bill tried to ram Austin into the wall to break his hold, but he only succeeded in breaking the plaster.

Ian was fumbling with his weapon, trying to place his finger back on the trigger.

Austin had Bill's arm well under control. He wasn't trying to wrestle the gun from him, he only wanted Bill to fire it. After all, Bill shooting Ian was better than Austin doing it.

Ian pulled the trigger, only to be answered by a click rather than a loud bang. Austin watched as Ian fumbled for the safety. By the time he had located it, it was too late. Bill's gun had exploded, and Ian was flying backwards through the air, his gun leaving his hand as he thudded against the wall. Blood flowed from the right side of his chest.

Bill was nearly unconscious in Austin's hold. Austin crouched down, Bill's neck still firmly held by his elbow. He removed his blade from his boot and without further thought, slit Bill's throat, from ear to ear.

Sending blood spraying, like a garden sprinkler.

Ian screamed like a girl.

Austin walked over, picked up his piece.

"Wait here, I'll be back to deal with you," Austin said.

Not trusting that Ian would obey his order, he lifted Ian's foot with one hand and kicked down on his knee with the other, hard and forcefully, shattering his kneecap instantly and sending another girly shriek from him through the house.

Austin opened the bedroom door, hoping to finally see Mikayla again. When he saw the boy, he was disappointed and happy at the same time. He recognised Stevie immediately. His mother would be ecstatic at his return.

"Stevie, it's ok. I'm here to help. I'm looking for my daughter, Mikayla, she was taken just like you, have you seen her?"

The boy sat there shaking.

"Stevie, I need you to help me otherwise I can't find her. Please, she needs your help," Austin begged.

"I never met a Mikayla, I met a Chloe and a Scott. The Joker took them, like he took me." He paused.

"The Joker?" Austin asked.

"Yes, he had us hidden in cells. He used to come down on a red ladder, then take us to the room with the red door and take photos of us and send them to someone."

"Did the Joker bring you here?" Austin asked.

"I don't know. I was in a car for hours and then in another car for even longer," Stevie replied.

Groans came from the outside the door.

"Don't worry about him, I'll take care of him. Have you ever seen someone dressed like Batman?" Austin asked.

"No, only like the Joker," Stevie replied.

"Now, I'm going to get you out of here, but I need you to promise me you didn't see me because I need to keep looking for my daughter. If the police question me, I can't be out looking for her," Austin said. "Can you do that for me?"

"I promise," Stevie replied.

Austin walked back to the bedroom doorway, took Bill's keys, bank roll and mobile. He threw the keys to Stevie so he could unlock the cuffs.

"I'm going to close the door so you don't have to see this," Austin said.

"No, don't go, please don't!" Stevie cried.

"Stevie, it will be ok, you're safe now," Austin replied, still standing in the doorway.

Stevie stopped crying and began undoing the cuffs.

Austin knelt down beside Ian. His breathing was shallow. He

hadn't been hit in the heart, but it looked as though his right lung had been punctured and it would be filling with blood.

"I will give you a choice, a quick death or a slow death, your choice. Either way, you die here today."

"Please don't, please, I will stop," Ian began.

"Save your begging for God for when he judges you," Austin replied. "What do you know about the Joker?" he asked.

Ian frowned, confused. "I don't know anything about a Joker, I only met the Batman, I swear," Ian spluttered.

Austin knew he was telling the truth.

"Does the Batman work for the Priest?" Austin asked.

"I think so," Ian replied.

"Who does the Priest work for?" Austin asked.

"I don't know; I don't think he has a boss," Ian replied.

His breathing was becoming shallower, his time for answers was running out.

"Everyone has a boss, tell me who it is and I'll make it quick," Austin said.

He placed the knife that had slit Bill's throat against Ian's.

"I don't know, I swear. Wait, the Batman mentioned to me a person called the Monster. He told me he would protect me if the boy escaped," Ian replied.

"Thank you," Austin said.

He slit Ian's throat, left to right. He stood out of the way, so as not to be covered in spray, and then he opened Stevie's door.

"Come here," Austin said.

Stevie walked towards him. Bill was slumped in the doorway.

"Step over him," Austin said.

Austin led Stevie along the hallway and they headed for the front door. He wiped Bill's phone and handed it to Stevie.

"I want you to stay here until you count to 100 then you step outside and walk across the road to the neighbour's and call the police. If they're not home, use this cell phone. You don't need to worry about these two anymore. They're dead. Just look ahead and count, do you understand?" Austin said.

"Please don't leave," Stevie begged.

"I promise I won't leave until you're safe, I will be watching you until the police come. Ok?"

Stevie nodded.

"Now count," Austin said.

"One, two, three, four," Stevie began. He did as he was asked and did not look back and went outside as soon as he hit 100 and stepped out into the street.

Austin waited in the safety of his vehicle and when he saw a lady in an apron take him inside, he knew Stevie would be safe, but true to his word, he stayed until the police arrived.

Chapter 80

When another double murder call came in, I looked up to the sky to see if it was a full moon tonight. This one spiked my interest a lot. Initial reports were that one of the kidnapped boys had been recovered.

There was a full moon and it looked as though I would still be awake when it disappeared and the sun took its place.

"What the hell is going on today? Why are we finding these guys now?" Jake asked.

"I don't know if we're finding them, or if their organisation's imploding, but I agree something's going on," I replied.

The call gave us an address in Brunswick, another suburb that was renowned for low-life scum, like many others it seemed.

Jake placed the address in the sat nav and we headed straight from the Neil Figal crime scene to the Welling one.

When we walked in, we saw it looked like any other drug house in any other suburb. There were empty bags, needles and powder on the table, and the kitchen was a mess, full of the evidence of drug use.

Another overdose, I thought.

Then I saw the mess in the hallway, the blood sprayed wall to wall. The first victim had been identified as the owner, Ian Welling. According to police reports, he'd had several convictions for kidnapping and child molestation as well as some minor drug-related convictions.

The other man slumped in the doorway was still being formally identified, but it was believed to be Ian's lover, Bill Halstead. Jake and I were both scribbling down notes. We believed it was good to collect our initial thoughts prior to Forensics delivering the scientific evidence.

Jake stepped over the slumped body in the doorway and entered the room. I followed. The empty cuffs on the bed were the first thing I noticed, and I am sure that struck Jake too.

It took a while for me to register the noise in the background and it wasn't until I heard the laugh of Woody Woodpecker that I looked up and saw a TV set on the Boomerang 24/7 cartoon channel. Something you might do if you were keeping a child.

I pointed at the TV with my pen and Jake nodded. He was studying the bedside table as well as the bed and the cuffs. Then he moved over to the bodies and looked at them. "Forensics are here," I said.

He looked up.

"Ok, let's go interview the boy," Jake answered.

"He's across the road, with Child Services," I replied.

We walked to the neighbour's house where three women were sitting in the lounge room. Stevie was sitting in an armchair by himself, wrapped in a blanket and sipping a hot chocolate. Ambulance officers were assessing him and hooking him up to what looked like an IV. He was probably dehydrated.

Jake walked over and sat on the floor in front of him. He wanted to be lower to seem less threatening. I took a chair from the dining room table and placed it on the carpet next to the ambos. I knew if I sat on the floor I would look like a turtle on its back trying to get up again.

Jake opened his notebook.

"Hi Stevie, I'm Detective Miller but you can call me Jake. And this is Detective Foxx, you can call him Brodie."

"Stevie, can you tell us what happened?"

"Do you want me to start at the start?" he asked, sipping his hot chocolate.

"If that's what you feel comfortable with, Stevie," Jake replied.

"I was walking to school when someone dragged me into a van. I was locked in the back and I couldn't get out. We drove for a while, I have no idea where we were going, I couldn't see out."

He stopped and had another sip of his chocolate.

"I guess it was about an hour, but when we arrived, I had a bag put over my head. I couldn't see anything, I was pushed down a hole, I landed on gravel and there were cells, like a jail either side of the path."

Stevie was using his free hand to show how the cages were on both sides.

"At the end of the path was a red door. He would take us there to take our photo and then he would send the photo to someone. When he took my photo he rang someone about me. I could hear him say I was a good-looking lad."

"Did you ever see the person who took you?" I asked.

"No, he always had a Joker's mask on, or I had a hood on," Stevie replied.

I could see he had finished his hot drink. "Would you like another? I asked.

"Yes, please," Stevie replied, jumping at the offer. "I didn't stay in the cages for long, a few days maybe, then I was taken to meet another man. I remember leaving the van and sitting in another car. It smelt nice. The man who drove the car took me to a place. I don't know where or what it was but it was like an old castle on the inside with wooden doors that had old handles on them. I was sitting on the bed when a priest with a mask on walked in. He tried to rape me but I fought him off."

"What sort of mask was he wearing?" I asked.

"I don't know. It only covered his eyes and half of his face," Stevie said. "I can tell you, he was old. His hands were wrinkly and his hair was grey," Stevie added.

"Was the mask like the one in *Phantom of the Opera*?" I asked.

Without waiting for his response, I Googled it on my phone and showed him the picture.

"Like this?" I asked.

"Yes, sort of," Stevie replied. "Then the man who took me there picked me up and took me to someone else."

"So the man who took you to the priest and then picked you up again, did you see him at all?" I asked.

"No," Stevie replied.

"What about the car?" Jake asked.

"No, I always had my hood on," Stevie replied.

"And you have no idea where you were taken, just that it was an old building?" Jake asked.

"Yes," Stevie confirmed.

"Did you see the man who held you in his car?" Jake asked.

"No, I had a hood on. The next time I could see, I was here. The man that took my hood off was Ian. They locked me in the room, put handcuffs on the bed and they did bad things to me. They were going to kill me tomorrow, and bury me in the woods."

Stevie had handled the whole experience really well, up until this point anyway.

"How do you know that?" Jake asked.

"I heard them say they were getting sick of me. They said the best way not to get caught was to dig a hole and burn me in it, before burying me."

"So, how did you escape?" Jake asked.

Stevie had been waiting for this question.

This was where he had to keep his promise, and keep it he would.

"I was trying to escape, using a blade I found in the drawer. They used it to cut the drugs. Anyway, I took the blade and I was unscrewing the screw in the bed that held the bar to the bed when I heard the doorbell ring. Then there was arguing, it was hard to hear what it was about with the cartoons on. I heard someone say, I think it was Bill, he was always an angry man, something like, that's the last time you screw us.

"Then I heard what sounded like fighting, people throwing each other around into walls, then after it stopped, the bedroom door opened and a man I had never seen before threw me the keys. I could see Bill lying on the floor, I didn't see Ian till I left the room."

"Did the man who threw you the keys say anything to you?" Jake asked.

"He said, 'you're free', and told me to count to 100 before leaving. Which I did."

"What did this guy look like?" I asked.

Truth mixed with lies, Stevie reminded himself.

"He was tall." True. "He had red hair and a beard here." He pointed to his chin. False. "He was really pale." False. "That's all I really remember of him," Stevie said.

"What about when he spoke. Did you notice any accent?" Jake asked.

"No, he sounded normal," Stevie replied.

"We have some photos of people we need to show you. Can you tell us if you have seen them before?" I asked.

I showed him the photos of Beau and Tyler.

"Do you recognise any of these men?" I asked.

"No, I don't, but I had a hood on or they had a mask on. The big one could have been the Joker but I can't be sure," Stevie said.

"These people," Jake nodded in the direction of the Child Services staff, "are going to take you to the hospital now, and then take you back to your family. We'll come back to ask you more questions tomorrow. Make sure you get plenty of rest."

"Have you found any of the others?" Stevie asked.

"Others?" Jake questioned.

"The others in the cells," Stevie answered.

"You never told us you saw others in the cells," Jake said.

"Both Scott and Chloe were there when I was there, but I got moved first," Stevie explained.

"So they were still there when you left?" I asked.

"Yes, I was last in, first out, Scott had been there the longest."

Jake took a pen and a spare notepad from his inside pocket. He handed them to Stevie. "Between now and tomorrow I want you to write down anything you remember, no matter how small. Ok?"

Stevie nodded.

As we left the house, Jake turned to me. "Looks like we're in the middle of a big spider-web."

"Agreed. Let's go see what Forensics have come up with."

Chapter 81

“So, is this how you repay your mother?” Annabelle asked, cigarette in mouth.

“I have no idea what you’re talking about,” Beau replied.

“Maybe this will help?” His mother threw the object at him. “Good thing the coppers were searching you and not me!” she said. “Just as well the police didn’t find it,” she added.

She put up your hand to prevent Beau from speaking.

“I know you’re involved in those kids somehow, so don’t fucking lie to me anymore. Whatever you’re doing, get out of it, now.”

“Mum, I have nothing to do with it, I swear,” Beau answered, still fiddling with one of his engines.

“Don’t treat me like an idiot, I know where you keep them, I know where the money comes from. Get rid of them now. If you don’t, they’ll catch you. We have enough to tide us over for a while,” Annabelle replied.

Beau realised he had been treating her like an idiot. She knew exactly where the money had been coming from and exactly what he was doing.

“Ok, I’ll get out of it,” he replied.

Annabelle flicked the cigarette into the dirt and headed back into the house.

He wanted to get out but there was no way out. The Monster wanted him dead. The army man would too if he knew his girl was still down below, and he knew the Batman despised him. Tomorrow, he had to make two deliveries, one to the Batman and the other to the Monster.

If he made the delivery to the Monster, he would certainly wind up dead. He'd never leave. Maybe he would be fed to the dogs, which was what he heard had happened to a dealer who tried to screw with the Monster.

He had spent two weeks trying to come up with a way out, but no ideas had come. Maybe this would be the end of the line for him. Death was what he deserved for what he had done, and he knew it.

Maybe, just maybe, if he provided the army man with the delivery address, he could deliver the girl to the Monster and let him deal with the Monster. All he had to do was stay out of the way.

It was a chance, but a chance all the same.

Chapter 82

Austin only heard about the child murder and the suspect's overdose when he arrived back at his hotel room. He had still not dared to venture back home, not until he had Mikayla.

They were saying that Figal had kidnapped and killed the boy and then died of a drug overdose. One thing Austin knew for sure; he hadn't kidnapped any boy that day, because he had been there with him. Figal couldn't have been where they said he was. His death sounded like a hit. Austin didn't know who had ordered it, although he suspected the Priest and the Batman were involved.

Tomorrow was Sarah's funeral. He assumed that the police would be there although with all the recent deaths including the missing child's, he doubted the presence would be as large as it might have been.

Austin called Marcus. He wanted to know what he could find out about the man they called the Monster.

The phone rang a few times before Marcus answered.

"Hey mate," Marcus answered, always trying to stay upbeat for the sake of his friend.

"I need to know if you've ever heard of a guy called the Monster."

"We had tracking on a guy in New South Wales two years ago nicknamed the Ukrainian Monster. We thought he was bringing in illegal weapons, but they found nothing. I know local police had been investigating drug rumours, but ASIO pulled out when there was a lack of evidence," Marcus replied.

"I heard through a source he was buying and selling kids. Find out what you can. I know who the Joker is. He has Mikayla somewhere. I should go and confront him," Austin said.

"Mate, I don't know. He was questioned by police for eight hours and he gave them nothing, so why would he tell you?" Marcus asked.

"I have better negotiating techniques," Austin said.

"Torture is not a technique, is it?" Marcus said.

"It's often the most persuasive," Austin replied.

"So when are you going to persuade him?"

"I have a few other leads to follow before I get to that point. But it's tough knowing he's involved."

"You sound undecided," Marcus said.

"I am. Because if I show up again, he might close up altogether and then I'll never find her," Austin replied.

"What time do you want me to pick you up tomorrow for the funeral?" Marcus asked.

"The service is at 1 pm."

"Ok, I'll be at your hotel at 12. It'll give us time to talk on the way."

"Thanks, mate," Austin said.

The suit he had sent to the hotel cleaning service had been returned immaculately pressed and ready for what tomorrow held.

He ordered himself a steak and vegetables from room service. It had been a long time since he had eaten a full meal and his stomach was craving a decent feed. It was good. While he ate, he watched the news. The media couldn't get enough of Stevie's 'miracle survival', as they put it. Reporters were interviewing neighbours asking stupid questions like "how did you not know they were holding the boy?" "Didn't you see anything suspicious?"

The head of the Missing Persons Unit praised Stevie, and said this would hopefully lead them to the other missing children.

"We will not stop until this investigation has uncovered the whereabouts of all the missing children, and the people responsible will be held accountable."

Austin didn't have much faith in the Missing Persons Unit or in their spokesperson, based on the results. So far he had one; they had zero.

After hearing the same news repeatedly, he switched channels. He needed to rest his mind, although he doubted whatever he watched would do that. Sport was usually the best. Since being stationed in Afghanistan with troops from the USA, he had discovered an enthusiasm for NFL and baseball.

Austin flicked to ESPN. The NBA game of the day was on, Golden State v OKC. Steph Curry was doing his thing and Russell Westbrook was trying not to be outdone. Amazingly, he had OKC in touch with the rampaging Warriors.

Sleep came quickly to Austin as it had on several occasions over the last few days. He found himself on the beach again, yet his family was nowhere to be seen. He headed up the beach, the waves rippling against his feet as he walked along the shoreline. A light breeze blew and he breathed in the salty tang. He heard birds squawking in the distance. Seagulls, probably. He felt the warmth of the sun on his face.

In the distance he could see a figure; it was kneeling. He couldn't make out who it was from this distance but as he drew closer, he could see it was Stevie, in his stained white t-shirt and underwear.

"Stevie, is that you?" Austin asked as he approached.

"Yes, thank you for saving me," Stevie said. "I am sorry you couldn't save your wife." Stevie was looking at the gravestone that was erected on the beach in front of him.

"It's not your fault. I will find the person who did it and they will have a gravestone of their own."

Austin bent down to tend to the weeds that had sprouted in front of the stone.

"Why are you here, Stevie? You should be at home with your family," Austin said.

"I need to tell you, time is running out, people will start to panic after today."

The earth groaned, and a second grave began to build itself from the earth, like a jigsaw puzzle putting itself together. Within seconds, it was standing next to Sarah's.

It read 'Mikayla Campbell'. He stopped reading; he couldn't bear the pain.

"Not much longer now," Stevie repeated.

Austin tore his eyes away from the grave and looked back to where Stevie had been, but his body was fading. Then it disappeared.

Austin woke in his usual cold sweat. The basketball was still on, and Curry had just sent it into overtime from a deep corner three. He turned the TV off and slept, his mind emptied of all the horrors of the past week.

Chapter 83

We were standing outside the home where Stevie had been kept waiting for Forensics to finish.

"What do you think went on here?" Jake asked me.

"Based on what the boy said, it was a turf war over drugs or a drug deal gone wrong. There was arguing. Maybe they were buying more drugs and felt they got ripped off, maybe they were going to kill him with the boy and he fought back, killed them both," I replied.

"Why would he let the boy go, considering the kid had seen him?" Jake asked.

"You know, code of honour with some crims, won't hurt kids. Until we find him, we won't know why he let the boy live."

"Hmm, I don't know. It seems wrong to me," Jake replied.

"How so?" I asked.

"I don't understand how it ended in the hall. I don't believe the boy's story for some reason. It seemed too detailed, too specific."

"I'm not sure why you're having trouble with this, Jake. To me it adds up. Ian and Bill were on a three-day bender and ordered some more of whatever. They accused the redheaded man of short-changing them on the deal. There was a scuffle and they lost. He opened the door, saw the boy and threw him the keys. Told him to count to 100 before leaving. Which he did. I think it rings true. But if you think something is wrong, then I trust you," I replied.

Grace had left the Figal scene to come and join us at the Welling one. Today her department was being pushed to the limits. She approached us and said, "I've reviewed the scene here and just wanted to discuss the initial findings with you guys. The evidence suggests that the two men had a scuffle with an unidentified third man, at which point Bill fired his .38-calibre weapon, hitting Ian in the right upper chest. We're waiting on Ballistics to come back, but we believe it's the same gun. Then during this scuffle, both Bill and Ian had their throats cut. From their wounds, it appears it was the same knife. That's why we think there was only one man. Ian was left to bleed out for a few minutes prior to having his throat cut. We also noted his kneecap was smashed, most likely during the scuffle."

"How do you know the Welling victim was left to bleed out?" I asked.

"There was an excessive amount of blood around the gunshot wound. Had his throat been cut soon after being shot, we wouldn't have found that," Grace replied.

"What do you think the man was doing, while Welling was bleeding out?" I asked.

"Ransacking the joint, would be my guess," Grace replied.

Chapter 84

The rain had kept Chloe awake. She had always been scared of thunderstorms but up here in the mountains they seemed worse, ferocious, alive even.

She heard the helicopter arrive and the three men returning to the house. She was terrified; he would be coming for her. She wasn't sure what she was more afraid of, the storm or Igor.

The only benefit Chloe noticed was that once the rains came, the security guards withdrew, to where she wasn't sure, but they were no longer standing watch where they had been. Had they moved inside? Maybe they were in the gatehouse?

They were answers she needed to know.

The sooner the better.

She crept out of her bed and turned the door handle. Igor had never kept her locked in. He trusted her fear and he trusted his men to keep her in the house.

The door creaked a little. She waited, but no one came. She stepped into the hallway and swiftly made her way up to the entrance of the large family room, where she could hear men talking, laughing, but not in English. It was a language she had heard in the house before, but she didn't understand it.

The man who usually stood guard outside the family room door was not there. She needed to check if the guard who usually stood outside the master bedroom was there, and so she turned and headed back past her own room and towards Igor's suite.

The only way she would be able to tell if he was there was to go in. If she went in and woke him, who would know what might happen.

She opened the door. He was asleep, she could hear his breathing. It was slow and steady. She walked past the bed, and made her way through the large open hexagonal space. It was a room that belonged in a castle. She slowly opened the door that led to a patio where she had once had breakfast. His guard was not there. No one was out there. Maybe this was her chance, maybe she was looking for an opportunity that was now right in front of her.

She placed her right leg out the door while she contemplated her opportunity. Her nightie was getting wet from the rain. She slid her back through the small gap in the door and was ready to follow with her right leg when a large crack of lightning hit a tree just beyond the dogs, and it burst into flames.

She jumped back and almost screamed with fright from the lightning crack and before she realised, she was back inside the room with one wet leg.

"Are you going somewhere?" a voice said from the bedroom.

"I was coming to see you. I hate thunderstorms. Will you keep me company please?" Chloe asked.

"Sure, come in here," Igor said.

He pulled back the sheets for her to climb in.

Chloe took a step, then realised her leg was wet. "I just need to…" She pointed to the en suite bathroom.

He nodded and said, "Hurry up."

She realised her nightie was wet and her only option was to dump it on the en suite floor, or have him discover that she had been out. How would she explain?

She reappeared in his room, without her nightgown.

"Can you keep me warm?" she asked. "I hate the rain, especially bad storms with lots of thunder and lightning."

"You know, my grandfather used to believe that there was a single god called Perun and it was Perun who would throw down lightning and thunder when he was angry at the world," Igor said.

"Why would God be angry?" Chloe asked.

"Some people believed he got angry if you had done wrong, or not prayed enough. So when the thunderstorms came, people saw them as a warning. If your village was hit by lightning, people would think that you had angered Perun," Igor explained.

"Did you believe it?" Chloe asked.

"I believed what my dad told me when I was young. I learned as I grew older that this world has no god."

He began to touch her, as he always did.

She closed her eyes and realised she too was learning that this world had no god or if it did, it hadn't shown itself.

PART THREE

The Monster and The Spider's Nest

Chapter 85

It was raining. Austin thought it was God setting the tone for the day ahead.

As he stepped out of the hotel lobby and into Marcus' black SUV, which was identical to his, the rain hit the windscreen like a million tears falling from heaven.

Since Afghanistan, Austin had found it difficult to reconcile his life and his religion. He believed in God and that one day he would stand before Him and be judged. However, he didn't believe in the Ten Commandments. He simply believed that as long as he lived an honest life, he would be ok when he stood before God.

Then when he first killed in Afghanistan, he asked the USA soldiers how they thought God considered their killing in war. One soldier told him that it was for the greater good. Killing evil was allowed, and the killing of terrorists was protecting the good of the Afghan people. The theory of the greater good made sense.

Maybe he was right, maybe he was wrong. The Bible could be interpreted a million different ways and when his time came, Austin was ready to meet his maker.

He was sure that Sarah was one of the good ones.

"Did you find out anything about the Monster?" Austin asked Marcus.

"Hi, how are you Marcus? Thanks for the lift," Marcus replied sarcastically.

"I'm sorry, mate. I haven't been normal lately, I just can't even think straight with Mikayla still missing. I don't want to go today, I know that sounds crazy but Sarah would want me to be out there looking for Mikayla, not at her funeral," Austin said.

Then he turned his attention to the rain hitting his window.

"I will know more today hopefully," said Marcus. "As I said last night, New South Wales police are still investigating him. I rang a friend in the New South Wales organised crime unit. He's going to get back to me as soon as he can establish where the investigation stands. I wish I'd never invited you to go fishing. I wish I could go back in time and change it all. I just don't know how I can best help you, other than getting Mikayla back for you." Marcus was clearly distressed.

"We've been through this," Austin said. "It's not your fault. It's no one fault, except the Joker and whoever he works for. You know that, we both do, and I'll set it right soon."

The church was already filling an hour before the service. Aunts and uncles, army friends, Sarah's work colleagues, Mikayla's school friends. By the time Austin and Marcus arrived 30 minutes before the service, the church was full. Any latecomers would be restricted to the steps of St Michael's.

The reverend was an older gentleman who had known Sarah and her family for years. He was a close family friend and had conducted baptisms for both Sarah and Mikayla.

"How you holding up? Any word on Mikayla?" Father Doyle asked Austin as soon as he arrived at the altar.

"I'm holding myself together. I need to be strong for Mikayla although there's been no word on her yet, Father," Austin replied.

"Stay strong. The Lord is with you in these trying times."

Brian, Sarah's father, and Helen her mother, both hugged him. "How are you coping, dear?" Helen asked. "You haven't been back to the house yet," she added.

"I'm ok, I just want to find Mikayla and I won't go back home without her, I may never go back. I am so sorry I wasn't there to protect her," Austin said as the tears welled up.

"Oh darling, don't blame yourself," Helen said, hugging him again.

Father Doyle called for everyone to be seated.

The whispered conversations ceased and people who had been standing in the aisle sat down. Austin sat in the front row with Helen on one side and Marcus on the other.

Sarah's nieces and nephews moved down the aisle, quietly handing out the order of service booklets to any who had missed them.

'In loving memory of Sarah Jane Campbell, 1977–2014.'

Below the date, a large photo of her, in happier times.

Father Doyle led a hymn and then said, "Before we begin the service, the church and Sarah's family ask us all to remember Sarah as she was and not to dwell on the evil act that took Sarah from us. We are here today to celebrate the life of Sarah Jane Campbell who has now returned home to our Lord and Saviour the Father."

Sarah's father Brian went up to the lectern to read the eulogy.

He stood proudly in a black suit with a red tie, his hair neatly brushed across his forehead.

"Sarah, you were and will always be our angel.

"From the day you were born, you were full of laughter and love. Nothing was ever too much trouble for you, you showed more kindness to strangers than some struggle to show their own family.

"You and your sister Heather both shared a love for living and a kindness for your fellow man that is rarely seen.

"You were a beloved wife, a fantastic mother and most of all, a wonderful daughter who I was lucky to call my own.

"While you were taken from us all way too soon, I pray you're at peace, and although I shall never see that cheeky smile again, I will hold you in my heart forever.

"Love you, Scare Bear."

By the time he left the lectern, he was inconsolable.

Father Doyle returned.

"I had the pleasure of performing Sarah's baptism when she was a girl. She attended mass in this very church. She could sing like the angels. I was lucky enough to conduct her marriage ceremony when she wed her husband Austin. I was then delighted to perform Mikayla's baptism. While to many, myself included, Sarah's loss seems like a tragedy that we cannot comprehend, we must have faith that the Lord our Father has a bigger plan for all of us.

"Whilst we will weep, we should take comfort in knowing that Sarah is with our Lord. I would like to take this opportunity to say a prayer for the safe return of Sarah and Austin's daughter, Mikayla."

After the service, only immediate family and Father Doyle went to the grave site.

"Ashes to ashes, dust to dust," he began.

Austin faded away from the words and became fixated on the coffin. He remembered their wedding day, the birth of Mikayla, the love they shared, all the loving glances that had passed between them that had meant so much more than words could ever say.

He would miss his wife, every day. Finally, he realised the life he had known was gone forever.

Chapter 86

Beau had spent Friday at home in his shed preparing for the night ahead. He knew the probability was that he would not return home, even if he managed to escape the Monster's clutches.

He had decided not to run. What good would it do him? He couldn't outrun the Monster, and even if there was a chance, running wasn't his style. He had also decided not to give the army man the Monster's location. After all, what was in it for him? There was a small chance he would be allowed to leave the Monster's place unharmed and with the payment he'd receive for the girl, he'd have a shitload of cash. He had no intention of passing it over to the Priest this time. He was going to start a new life for himself.

He took his mother out for lunch. Nothing flash, just the local pub, extra cheap meals. It was a good feed and he needed it, with the long weekend in front of him.

They arrived back from the pub around 1 pm, which gave him a good hour to prepare before he had to leave for Ballarat. Beau had an 8.30 pm appointment with the Batman and he had to have completed his delivery to the Monster's by Saturday night, although he was considering dropping her off early, on Saturday morning. That way, the Monster might be less inclined to kill him.

With the news in overdrive about the discovery of the boy, he had called the Priest, asking to drop off Scott earlier and head for NSW.

The Priest agreed that he would be better off in NSW than staying home. Beau reassured him there was no way Scott knew him or where he lived, and he had nothing to worry about.

Beau doubted the Priest believed what he was saying.

Beau turned on his train set and drove all of his locomotives into their rail yard, possibly for the very last time. When they were all in and secured, he pulled the lever to move the train table sideways.

Moving aside the mat, he unlocked the four padlocks, lifted the trapdoor, placed the ladder down the hole, and put on his Joker's mask.

He descended the ladder with two ropes and hoods in his right hand and the keys to the cells in his left.

"Good news. You're both going home. Both ransoms have been paid," he said to the children.

Mikayla and Scott were curled up in their respective cells, terrified. As the Joker descended the ladder, their fears increased.

He passed the hood and the rope through the cells.

"Once they're on, I'll unlock you."

Since her escape attempt, Mikayla had been wary of the man in the mask. He had threatened her with death, and every day she was worried that he would see his threat through.

She had never believed they were going home, and even when they put on the hoods ready to be moved, she believed in her heart she was heading for her death.

They were led up the ladder and into the van. The two children sat together against the side and for the first time in a week, Mikayla touched someone other than the Joker. They held onto each other tightly. He had been trapped there longer than she had and was desperate for someone to cuddle. She could feel her hands being cuffed and then heard him cuff Scott's hands too.

They listened as the Joker got into the front seat and started the van.

The radio came to life.

"No matter what, we stick together," Mikayla whispered.

"Always," Scott replied.

The music was turned up, suddenly the truck slowed, she thought she heard muffled talking, and then the music was back up.

The van was moving. Everything was dark because of the hoods.

"Mikayla?" the voice from the front of the van called.

"Yes?" Mikayla replied.

"Could you take your hood off, if I asked you to?"

"I think so."

"Take it off but if I hear any commotion back there, I will stop the van and it will be the end of you, do you understand?" the Joker said.

"Yes," Mikayla replied.

"I have food in the back. You will be able to reach it. Take your hood off, untie Scott's hood but leave it on. He will be able to eat with it on."

She could smell the hamburgers through her hood.

"It's a long drive," the Joker explained.

"I thought you were taking us home?" Mikayla queried.

"I am, but the drop-off point is different. No more talking, just eat and then the hood goes back on. Got it?"

"Got it," Mikayla replied.

"Can't wait to get the Monster's money and go fishing," Beau muttered to himself.

Chapter 87

Jake and I arrived at Stevie's home. He showed us where he had been walking when the driver from the van took him, which was from the top of the path. We walked back to his house with him. He seemed a lot calmer than he had been the day before.

Mrs Bradley, who had been totally detached, had come back to life. Having her boy back was a much needed early Christmas gift. She was busy in the kitchen, making tea and coffee, slicing cake and putting biscuits out. His nanas and aunts were kissing and hugging Stevie and asking him how he was. He didn't give them much. He always answered with a "fine" or an "ok".

It was a defensive answer to prevent further prying questions. I had done the same after one of my horrific hospital stays. Family would ask, "how are you, how are you feeling, glad to have you home", when all I wanted was to push the memory of it all as far back in my mind as possible. I thought Stevie would want his experience boxed and filed as far back inside his head as it would go.

His mum kept him within sight. If her gaze left him for a second when she poured a cuppa or cut a slice of cake, it returned immediately after to check on him. If he moved or went to the toilet without her knowledge, the fear came flooding back.

We sat in another room, in privacy, to question Stevie again. We had asked his mum to join us while we questioned him but he wanted to talk to us alone, and she accepted that.

"Thanks for talking to us again, Stevie," Jake began.

"That's ok," he replied.

"You said yesterday that you saw both Chloe and Scott who were being held in the cells near you. Can you draw a sketch of what the cells were like?" Jake asked.

"I did, in the notepad you gave me yesterday," Stevie replied.

Stevie opened the pad and showed us the drawing. There was a pathway down the middle and cells on each side. He had put a 'C' in Chloe's cell, an 'S' for Scott's and an X for his own.

Under the drawing were two other words:

Red ladder.

Blue train.

"What does red ladder and blue train mean?" I asked.

"Every time he came down to feed us or take photos, the red ladder would drop down first. We all used to freak every time the ladder dropped. Sometimes he would say we were making too much noise, so he would hit us or make an example of one of us. One day when we were talking, I thought we were whispering but we must have been too loud. He came down and gave Chloe a hiding like I have never seen. I thought she was going to die that night. It was horrible, and we couldn't even help her," Stevie said.

Jake looked at me. We both knew to tread carefully. Stevie was at breaking point.

"Do you think you were underground?"

"I think so, but I couldn't see dirt because the walls were plastered. It was like a room."

"And you mentioned a blue train. What can you tell us about that?" Jake asked.

"I remember one day he came down with his Joker's mask on and he was dancing around showing us his shiny new train. It was bright blue. I asked him did he like trains and he said, 'This isn't a train, it's a locomotive'," Stevie said.

I looked at Jake but could see he hadn't realised the connection I had made.

"That's all we need, Stevie," I said.

Jake stayed seated and couldn't work out why I was suggesting we leave already.

"Let's leave Stevie to enjoy his day, hey Jake?" I gave him a significant look and then said to Stevie, "If we need anything else, we'll be back in touch, ok Stevie?"

Before I was seated in the car, Jake started, "Why the fuck are we leaving? I have heaps more questions!"

I put my finger up. "Wait a minute, mate." I was flicking through the files, then I reached for the yellow envelope and tipped the contents into my lap. They were photos of the search of Beau's house.

One of the rooms.

Several of the van. Where was it?

One of the yard.

One of his mum's room.

There! The one I was looking for, the shed. I handed it to Jake.

I kept looking through the photos for the other one I wanted to show him.

"What! A shed? This helps me a lot," he said sarcastically.

"Look on the wall," I replied.

He looked in the background and squinted.

I handed him another.

"On the table, at the station," I added.

It was like looking at a cryptic picture. You don't see anything until someone asks you to look hard.

Once he saw the ladder, he knew what I knew.

Beau was involved.

Chapter 88

Chloe now knew the best time to escape was during a storm. The guards retreated indoors. Her only issue was conquering her fears and heading out into the storm.

She had managed to endure the night with Igor with only one horrible episode. Usually, there were multiple episodes, but he had fallen asleep straight after. She was left awake, sobbing, to listen to the rain and ponder her escape.

She did not get out of the bed, although she contemplated running for it several times. She thought about running into the storm, down past the dogs and over the fence into the woods. She thought about the lightning hitting the tree on the edge of the woods, earlier in the night. Would that happen to her? Would she attract the lightning? She knew people got hit by lightning and most died, but she wasn't sure what attracted the lightning to people. Was it just bad luck? She wasn't sure and she wasn't going to find out tonight, anyway.

She finally managed to fall asleep and the next morning, when the sun peeked through the blinds, she awoke. Igor, on the other hand, was still asleep. She snuck off back into her room before she was made to endure another horrible episode.

Her own bed was cold, at first, but it warmed quickly and soon she was fast asleep.

The sound of someone screaming at her brought her back to stark reality hours later. He was small but he had a loud and intimidating voice and when he was angry, it was even louder.

It took her a few seconds to understand what he was going on about, not because of his accent, she had become used to that, but because she was half-asleep. It wasn't until she saw her nightie in his hand that she caught on.

"It's wet. You were trying to escape! Have you forgotten what I do to those who want to leave?" Then he said to Alexi who was standing behind him, "Send her to the cellar!"

Chloe put her hands out. "Nooo! Wait, please. I wasn't trying to escape."

Alexi had manoeuvred around Igor and grasped her by the hand.

"Make sure you beat her a little for the lie," Igor added.

"No! Please, I'm not lying," Chloe insisted. She dug her feet into the carpet, but against the brute strength of Alexi her resistance was futile.

"You lie! The nightgown is wet. When you were in my room you were standing by the door, except you were not just standing there, you were ready to run, weren't you?" Igor approached, slapping her face without warning. He slapped her so hard, it made a cracking sound and left a large red mark across her cheek.

Tears streamed down her face, but she didn't let out her normal blubbering cry. She held it in. Tried to remain strong.

"My gown was wet because when I went to the toilet I wiped my hands on it after I washed them. Nothing else."

Igor stood looking at the gown as she was talking. He was trying to remember if in fact she had gone to the toilet, as she said. Maybe she had, he thought. He was still half-asleep, and thought a little more. He did remember her saying something when he had found her staring outside.

"Take her to the cellar!" He couldn't afford to show her any kindness. Kindness was often taken as weakness.

Chapter 89

We arrived at Beau's home without a warrant, hoping they wouldn't make a fuss about another search.

Jake did his usual police knock on their front door and I stood a metre behind him, staring down the drive at the shed I was so desperate to search.

Mrs Delacroix answered. "You again! What do you think, that I'm running an illegal brothel this time?" she asked sarcastically.

"We would like your permission to search the shed again," Jake replied.

"Ok, sure, as soon as I see your warrant I'll open it up for you," she replied, blowing smoke into Jake's face on purpose as if to say, fuck you.

"Sorry to shock you, but we don't need a warrant, we believe your son is in the process of committing an indictable offence and as such, we have grounds to search the premises," Jake replied, smiling.

"Oh bullshit. You need a warrant if you want to search. I know my rights. This is police harassment! I'm ringing your boss!" she shouted, running back inside to get her phone.

"I take it you are refusing to cooperate with a police investigation?" Jake called after her.

"Bet your fucking ass I'm refusing. This isn't an investigation; this is a witch hunt. If you have your way, you'll soon have him hanging from the gallows," she replied.

Annabelle's thumbs and fingers were busy on the phone. Within seconds, it was at her ear.

Jake removed himself from the stoop and headed for his car boot. He returned with bolt cutters in his hand.

"Mrs Delacroix, this is your last opportunity to let us in."

She replied by holding up her middle finger. "I would like to speak with Mr Roosevelt," she said to whoever answered the phone. "Well it can't wait till Monday. Can I have his mobile number?"

She disappeared inside the house again and when she reappeared, her fingers were busily punching digits into her mobile. "Mr Roosevelt, it's Annabelle Delacroix. I have police officers here wanting to search the premises again and this time they don't have a warrant. They said they don't need one because they believe a crime is being committed." She paused. "Hold on, I'll ask," she said.

"Detective, what offence is my son supposedly committing?" she called out to me.

"Kidnapping," I replied, as I followed Jake to the shed.

"Kidnapping," she repeated into her phone. "What do you mean they can search without a warrant!" she argued.

Jake had made light work of the bolts on the side door and before I reached him, he was inside the shed.

When I walked through the door, even though I had flicked on the light switch, the light was still flickering as it warmed up.

Jake had removed the ladder off the wall and was inspecting the dirt that remained on the bottom stoppers.

Annabelle had made her way down to the shed. She was off the phone and screaming at us, "Get out of here, immediately!"

"Mrs Delacroix, you have to step out of the way or you will be arrested for interfering in a police investigation," Jake said calmly.

"Well, you better arrest me then, because I'm not going to stop interfering!" she retorted.

I didn't need anything else. I took her by the arm, placed a cuff on her wrist and took the other wrist behind her back to meet it, locking them in place.

I took the chair from inside the shed and placed it outside, then sat Annabelle on the chair and told her not to move. She was no danger to us. We just wanted her out of the way.

I stepped back inside the shed, where Jake was now inspecting the blue train that Beau had been holding in the photo I had shown him.

"Ok, so Scott said he saw these items when the Joker went down to them. We've checked the back yard; there's nothing there. How do we know he doesn't have them somewhere else and he just takes the ladder with him?" Jake asked.

"It's possible I suppose, but how would that account for the train he showed them?"

"Maybe he bought it when he was out visiting them and he just happened to have it with him," Jake replied.

"Maybe," I said, unconvinced. "Wherever he's holding them, one thing we do know is that he was always going down to them, correct?"

"Correct," Jake replied.

"So it must be underground somewhere. We couldn't see anything in the back yard, what about in here under the old van?"

The van was rusted, with bald tyres, no hood and no motor. What he was using it for was anyone's guess. Jake opened the door, moved the gear stick to neutral and pushed. I stood at the back and also pushed, but Jake was doing most of the work. It rolled to a stop just outside the shed. Jake put it back in park position.

I stood there looking at the solid floor. There was nothing under the van. Jake looked at the empty space with a look of pure perplexity. I was sure he was trying to comprehend how it wasn't there. Beau's mother only smiled, the cigarette hanging in the crooked corner of her mouth.

She smiled only briefly but Jake saw the look in her eyes, a look that said, 'I have beaten you.' He had seen the same look many times from guilty people who thought they'd got away with murder.

It was Jake's turn to smile. "You know," he said to her, "I should have guessed you were involved in this. Your son's not smart enough to be doing this on his own."

"I have nothing to do with nothing, don't try pinning it on me because you can't find anything on him. I won't put up with that shit," she replied.

"Brodie, get a divvy van here to take her back to the station. We'll question her later."

I walked to the car to make the call while Jake stayed in the shed and surveyed the empty space. However, before I walked up the drive, I gestured to Jake to walk with me, out of earshot of the prying old woman.

"There's nothing there. It's a concrete floor. There's only an empty space and a train set. He must have them hidden somewhere else," I said.

"The train set. The forest for the trees, Brucey!" Jake replied, his eyes lighting up.

He turned and ran back to the shed.

I followed him back inside the shed and he was already down on his knees, head under the wooden table.

"Help me look," he said.

"What are we looking for?" I asked.

"An unlocking device," Jake replied as he continued to feel around.

"What are you thinking? That it'll unlock a secret passage?"

"Just look," Jake replied.

"This isn't *Scooby Doo*," I said.

Jake just looked at me.

I grabbed what I thought was a handle to lift the table, except when I pulled up, it moved towards me, not up. The whole train town moved. I pulled more. The table fitted perfectly, sideways as well as lengthwise. When it was sideways, it revealed a mat.

Jake flung the mat across the garage. He looked up at me, all smiles.

"We have him now!" he said.

He ran across the shed to the door where he had left his bolt cutters and 20 seconds later, the wooden hatch had been ripped from its hinges and thrown across the other side of the shed to join the mat.

I turned to grab the ladder but before I could pass it to Jake, he had jumped down.

"Fuck!" was the cry that rose from below.

For fear of snapping my fragile ankles, I used the red ladder and headed down after Jake. I landed on a soft bed of gravel. Goosebumps rose up on my arms and all the hairs stood up at the back of my neck. It seemed as if shadow men were lurking in the corners. The path was like the yellow brick road, except it didn't lead to Oz. It led to a red door, the red door of hell, I thought.

On each side of the path were concreted cells only separated by bars. There were food trays, old mattresses, old ratty blankets. There was everything to suggest kidnapped kids, except the kidnapped kids themselves.

The lighting down here was flickering. Before I could refocus, Jake had gone from two feet in front of me to the other end of the path where he was now kicking in the red door.

He let out another cry of profanity. This time it had 'mother' in front of it.

I didn't know I could have goosebumps on goosebumps until I walked into the room with the red door. The endless, horrific possibilities of what Beau had done to these kids flooded through my mind and my rage grew.

Jake was pounding his fist into the wall. He had already flipped the mattress and accompanying spring mattress. He was a giant ape, going crazy.

I began rifling through the drawers opposite the now overturned bed. It wasn't until I opened the second drawer that I found the phone. It was taped to the top of the first drawer. This was something Jake had taught me to look for when searching a house.

"Got a phone!" I called out to him.

Jake had stopped hitting the wall and his head was now buried in his elbow. He was leaning against the wall.

"Awesome," was his muttered response.

Surprisingly, the phone was unlocked, no pin required. I scrolled through the contact numbers. There was only one.

Priest.

Chapter 90

The dead girl who had hung in the cell with Chloe a few days before had now become a rotting corpse. The odour was horrific and the skin was falling from her bones. Chloe no longer had to fear the stare of the dead girl, as her eyes had fallen out.

There was nothing she could do to prevent the pungent smell from wafting up her nose. It made her feel sick. She hoped she could hold in the nausea, but doubted she would be able to.

"Enjoying the smell?" Alexi taunted.

"No, and I didn't try to escape," Chloe replied, as she swung slowly alongside the dead girl.

"This is your last chance. He likes you, yet you keep trying his patience. No more chances for you. Next time this will be you. No threats, it will be you for real."

Alexi paused. "You understand?" he asked.

"Yes, I understand," Chloe said.

Chloe was wearing her pink singlet and pyjama pants. Her left slipper had fallen off in the scuffle or soon after. It now lay on the ground just behind her head.

"We are having another guest joining us tomorrow night. She is your age. I want you to make the room next to yours for her. You will find more clothes in your room. Some for you, some for her. For now, Igor said you have to think about what you have done for a while longer. Then I will come back for you," Alexi said.

"No, no, please, don't leave me here with her and that smell!"

Her cries went unanswered. Alexi left and she was left in darkness. She could hear the flies buzzing around her, and on occasion she would bump against the swinging corpse and the sticky, decomposing flesh.

The smell was even stronger and this time, there was no keeping the contents in her stomach and she vomited.

She guessed most of it was matted in her hair.

Chapter 91

Austin had been sitting at the gravesite for a good half hour, his back resting against the trunk of a large oak near Sarah's grave. She would have loved this spot for sure; she'd loved nature.

When they first started dating, they would often go on picnics, find a large shady tree, set out their blanket and just talk the afternoon away. They would sometimes even spend it doing the crossword from the daily paper. Occasionally they would fool around, if the mood was right, but most of all, they just loved being together.

He distractedly picked apart an acorn that he had found on the ground and talked to himself. The sun was full on his face, but he didn't try to shade his face or block the sun. He just sat there enjoying the warmth, with his head rested against the trunk, basking in the most brilliant sun he had seen in weeks. Even today, the sun had been missing all day until now. He rested his eyes for only a few seconds, or so he thought. It was time enough for him to find himself on the beach again. The wind, the sun, the smell of the sea air were all strongly present. He could see Sarah. She was waiting further up the foreshore, her curly hair blowing in the soft breeze. There was no Mikayla, and no headstones, no boys standing further up the beach, only Sarah and him.

She smiled at him, kissed him on the lips, a lingering kiss. He could feel her love and feel her breathing as he held her in his arms.

"I love you," Austin said.

"I know, I will always love you too," Sarah replied. He nestled her head under his chin.

"Mikayla's gone now. You were too late, you were too late for her. You were too late for us both."

Austin held her by the shoulders and stepped back to answer her, but before he could reply, she turned to dust in front of him. He awoke with a start. The cemetery caretaker was poking at his shoe with the end of his shovel.

"Didn't mean to startle ya, the rains are coming back, ya might want to take some cover."

"I have to go now," Austin replied.

"Didn't mean to bother ya," the older man said.

"You were no bother. Thank you for waking me."

All the other mourners had moved on to the wake, Marcus included. Austin had promised to meet him later so Marcus had loaned him his car.

He walked back through the cemetery and out the front gate to the car park. He had left his phone in the console of Marcus' vehicle.

The words "too late for Mikayla" rang through his head. Austin tapped on the tracking device app.

The last thing he had expected was to see its location register as Hume Highway, Northern Victoria. He held his finger over the triangle that represented Beau's van. The icon showed Beau had been stationary for three minutes.

Beau was stationary but he was at least an hour and a half away.

Where they hell was he going?

Chapter 92

“Put out an APB on Beau's van. We need to find this guy now and get him to tell us what he's done with the kids,” Jake said to me.

“Will do,” I replied.

I moved out of the room and back up the ladder, passing the officer who was now standing on guard duty at the shed door. I headed towards the divisional van and opened the back door, directing myself to Beau's mother.

“We found the underground cells, Annabelle. Your boy's in big trouble now. If you have an ounce of decency in your body, tell us where the kids are. Tell us where he is.”

“Fuck you!” she replied angrily.

I shut the door, leaving her in the darkness of the van.

The day was drawing to a close and we'd had several brief afternoon showers. The officer in the divisional van processed the APB for Beau's van through to head office. All units state-wide would now be looking at every van and for those plates. If Beau was driving around, we had a good chance of finding him. If he had gone underground, then we had little.

“I'll call Forensics,” I called down to Jake, who was still in the cellar, “get them out here as soon as possible.”

“Get put through to Communications. After that give them the Priest's number listed in that phone. We need to find out who and where that person is," Jake replied.

"Will do," I replied.

The sergeant in Communications asked me for the sim followed by the 10-digit number. I gave him both.

"I'm afraid it's untraceable. It was bought off the internet. The only way I can trace it is if you keep him on the line for two minutes, or if he answers I can triangulate the nearest cell tower to the receiver," the sergeant said. "Give me a minute to set everything up and then make the call," he added.

I selected the only contact in the phone and prepared myself to make the call.

"All set," came the sergeant's voice over the phone.

I called the Priest.

"Beau, is the delivery ready?"

"Yes, where do I need to drop them?" I replied.

He hung up without saying anything.

When I redialled, it no longer rang.

I tried four times with the same result.

"I rang the number in the phone, the Priest," I said to Jake, "and he was expecting Beau and a delivery."

"You think Beau's delivering them somewhere?" Jake asked.

"Yes, Communications are trying to triangulate the signal for us."

"Couldn't they trace the call or the other number?" Jake asked.

"No, apparently they're untraceable and they can only trace the call," I replied.

"The call you made, how long did it last?"

"Only seconds," I replied.

My phone buzzed. It was Communications.

"It was answered in Learmonth," I relayed to Jake. "The closest cell tower to the phone is the one near the Saint Alexius home for children."

"Learmonth, home for children?" I confirmed with Communications.

"Yes, that's correct Detective, it's north of Ballarat. I can send you the location of the tower it was sent to."

Before I had time to thank the sergeant, he had sent the message to my phone.

"Thank you!"

I ended the call and asked Jake, "Did you get all that?"

He nodded. "Yes, and we need to go!"

"I think Beau's kidnapping the kids and somehow they're moving or selling the children through this home," I said.

Jake stood, trying to take in all the information.

"When I called the number, whoever answered asked if the delivery was ready. Then when I asked where I needed to take them, the person hung up. I assume it was the Priest, seeing as it was the only contact in the phone."

"Let's go and find out who and what's in Learmonth." Jake said.

Chapter 93

Hayley was standing beside Ryan's bed.

"We're going to have to turn off his life support, his vitals are not improving," Professor Wise said. "The readings on the Glasgow coma scale have stayed at four, but his brain waves haven't changed."

"What are you going to tell his parents?" Hayley asked.

"I think it's time they understand that turning off life support may be the best option. He will only continue to deteriorate for some time until his eventual death," Professor Wise replied. "It's the hardest part of the job, especially when it involves a child."

"I imagine it would be." Hayley smiled, but she was quietly disgruntled at the lack of understanding that she too had similar problems in her job.

"When are the parents in next?" the professor asked.

"Usually, they come and stay for dinner until the end of visiting hours," Hayley replied.

"Could you page me when they come in tonight?" Professor Wise asked.

"Of course, no problem."

After the professor left, Hayley read through Ryan's chart, as she did every morning. She listened as the professor's heels clicked slowly down the hall.

Hayley touched Ryan's hand, "I know I tell you this every day, but honey, you need to come back to your family before it's too late. If you wait much longer you won't be able to come back."

She rubbed his arm on her way to check the IV, and then ran her fingers through his hair as she left him.

Visitors came to all the other patients, but none came for Ryan. Other kids who were well enough played cards or did colouring, drew pictures, but Ryan just lay there with no sign of life. Hayley did her rounds, noticing with one child after another the parents there talking, waiting, helping their children recover. Every time she checked on Ryan, she thought how sad it was that there was no one there for him.

Her shift was one hour off finishing when the parents walked in. She did as she was asked and paged Professor Wise, who arrived soon after.

Ryan's sister sat next to him eating a bucket of chips from the canteen. Her headphones were on, her head was bopping, and her mouth was chewing. Hayley walked over to her. She touched her hand to get her attention. The girl removed her headphones, but continued to eat. "Maybe you could tell your brother what's been happening at school. He would like that," Hayley said.

"Can he hear me? Mum says he can't hear."

"He might be able to hear you. It's like magic. Some people have it but we never know until they wake up," Hayley explained.

The girl sat there for a few seconds contemplating what Hayley had said. Then she leaned forward and began talking to her brother as if he had been away on camp and they had a lot of catching up to do.

That's it, just talk to him, Hayley thought.

Meanwhile, Professor Wise was saying to their parents, "Mr and Mrs Davey, we are concerned that there has been no improvement in Ryan's condition over the past few months. If anything, all the treatment we are giving him is only keeping him alive, but it's not improving him. I am afraid we have to consider the possibility that

Ryan won't come out of the coma. In fact, I would suggest that there is a 99% chance that he will die within the next 12 months. As hard as that is to hear and for me to say, I have no medical reason to keep the machines going."

Mr and Mrs Davey didn't burst into tears, didn't fall screaming to the floor, in fact, they were completely calm and accepting of the information.

"We suspected this day was coming. We haven't been preparing for his funeral or anything, but we have been preparing ourselves for this day," Mrs Davey replied.

"Let me be clear," Professor Wise continued, "we are not saying you have to turn the machines off or that you have to do it soon, but over the next little while, if nothing changes, we will need to start making some formal decisions around Ryan's future."

The couple sadly agreed.

Chapter 94

"Mike, we have a problem," the Priest said into his phone.

"Another one. What now?" Mike asked.

"I just had a call from Beau's phone, but it wasn't Beau. The man asked me when to deliver the goods."

There was a silence followed by tapping on a keyboard. "He has an APB out on Beau," Mike replied.

"Beau is due to deliver the boy within two hours," the Priest told Mike.

"Then what? He's on to the Monster's?" Mike asked.

"If the cops don't get him first," the Priest replied. "The fat fuck will take us both down with him. Maybe we should cancel him while we can?" he suggested.

No response.

"Mike, do we cancel him?" the Priest repeated.

"I was thinking," Mike replied. "Here's what we'll do. If he turns up in two hours, we take the delivery and if all looks clear of cops, I'll give him some new plates and send him on his way to the Monster. That way, the Monster gets his cargo and we know he won't be leaving the Monster's place."

"And if it goes bad?" the Priest asked.

"I will take him down myself," Mike replied.

"We can't have him exposing us," the Priest said.

"He won't get to talk, don't worry. Either way, he won't be a problem for us any longer. By the way, when the cops come, you better have a good reason made up as to who accepted that call from Beau's phone," Mike said.

"But it's a ghost phone, it can't be traced!" the Priest said, panicking.

"You answered a call, old man, the phone can't be traced but the call can be," Mike replied. "Be ready." He hung up.

Chapter 95

I hated flying, but especially by helicopter. They looked as if they didn't belong in the sky and then once they were airborne, I always wondered what would happen if the engine blew.

Jake had organised for the helicopter to take us direct to Ballarat. It was the closest big town to Learmonth. The Ballarat sergeant said he would meet us at the helipad and take us to the tower in Learmonth.

As we stepped off the chopper, the promised cruiser was waiting and set to go.

"I thought we were meeting Superintendent McLeod?" Jake asked.

"I'm Constable Evans. Mike had a domestic violence issue he had to take care of, a repeat offender he had to see to. He sends his apologies; he directed me to take you wherever you need to go."

Evans began to tell us about the town, acting more like a tour guide than a police officer.

"Constable?" I asked, interrupting his guided tour.

"You can call me Dale," he said.

"I wouldn't think you would get many domestic violence issues out here?" I chirped from the back seat of the cruiser.

Dale took his eyes off the road so that he could look at me. I would have felt much better had he just used the rear-vision mirror.

"You would be surprised. A lot of men out this way still think it's the way of life. Dinner not on the table when you come in off the farm, beat the wife."

Cars passed us regularly, at high speed. Maybe it just seemed fast because Dale was also speeding.

"We also get a lot of people from the Ararat Prison. Being the closest biggest town, a lot of people relocate up here once their sentence is finished," Dale explained.

The car pulled up outside the children's home in Learmonth and I was amazed by its size. It was a large bluestone property, vast in width and length. I couldn't see the end of it. We walked towards reception, passing offices on both sides of the long hallway. The building had very high ceilings. Rows of leadlight windows depicted religious scenes. The lights were replica heritage candle fittings. Our shoes clicked along the stone floor. I felt like a school kid again on his way to the principal's office.

This time, however, it could be the principal who might be in trouble, I thought.

Dale approached the desk and told reception we were there to see Father O'Riley. There was no objection.

The door to his office was large and wooden, the carpet was red and the office had a warm welcoming feeling. His desk was a dark wood, mahogany or blackbutt, I wasn't sure.

The man on the other side of the desk stood as we entered. He was older than I had expected. For some reason, I had expected a young priest, but he was probably 20 years older than Jake or me. He was dressed in a long black gown with some sort of red jacket over his shoulders, pinned at the front.

"Nice to meet you," he said in a softly spoken voice. He offered us his hand.

We shook his hand and then he gestured us to some chairs. We sat down, not at his desk, but at a small table to the side of the room with matching club chairs.

"What brings you here, gentlemen?" he asked softly.

"We want to know if you know a Beau Delacroix."

"I can't say I do. It's not a name that I am familiar with. I'm sorry, should I?"

"He's a convicted felon," Jake replied.

"Not all of God's children are perfect, some stray too far from the flock unfortunately," the father replied.

"Could you explain why the cell phone tower you have on the roof here received a call I made from Beau's phone?"

Father O'Riley gave me a confused look. "No, I can't. I'm very confused by these questions," he said.

"We found a number with the name 'Priest' in this phone." Jake produced the phone from his jacket pocket. "We want to know why your name is in this phone?"

"There are a lot of priests in this world," Father O'Riley replied.

"Yes, there are, but they don't all work here. Whoever answered the phone answered it here, and you're the only priest here, correct?"

"Correct," Father O'Riley answered.

"So again, we are back to you."

"I can't offer an explanation, I'm afraid. I have had very few calls today. Please check for yourselves."

"May I look at your phone?" I asked, holding out my hand.

"Of course, I have nothing to hide," he said. Immediately, my ears pricked up. It was usually one of the first things guilty people said.

He handed over his phone. I scrolled through it.

"What is this outgoing call just before six? Who did you call?" I asked.

He placed his glasses on and looked at the phone. "That was to Mike, the superintendent."

"The police superintendent? The one who was supposed to pick us up?"

"Yes, the same one."

"Why did you call him?" Jake asked.

"To confirm his wife was handling the supper for the Sunday service."

Jake looked at me in a way I had seen before. It said, something's not right.

"Father, don't you find it strange that only a few minutes after this mysterious person answered the phone, you called the superintendent?" I asked.

"Detective." His voice was stronger now. "I don't know who answered your phone call, but I can assure you, it wasn't me. Feel free to ask my staff and check their phones, for I am as concerned about this as you are."

"Apart from staff, do you have other people here during the day who would be making calls within the building?"

"We are a church as well as a youth home. We have staff and other people coming and going. Many people come to the church to pray, others to confess. I really am sorry I can't be of more help."

"Thank you for your time. We will be in touch if we have any further questions," Jake said.

"I hope you have luck in solving your case. Paedophiles belong behind bars," Father O'Riley said.

Both Jake and I picked up the stumble the Priest had made, but now was not the time to call him on it.

Chapter 96

Austin had caught up to Beau. He had stopped for dinner, not the standard drive-through but a dine-in restaurant. He needed to refresh and recharge. By the time he was on the move again, Austin was only 20 minutes behind him.

Over the next hour, Austin caught up to him. He wasn't close enough to see him but he was only about 30 seconds behind. He could see Beau was turning into the main entrance of a local cemetery, according to the map. Austin took the street that ran alongside the cemetery. According to the tracking device app, Beau had parked close to the top of the cemetery. Austin needed to be a little higher. He drove up the hill a little and took Marcus' car off-road into the undergrowth. It wasn't entirely hidden but it was out of sight, enough. Along the ridge of the cemetery ran a windbreak of trees. They provided Austin with perfect cover.

By the time Austin actually gained a visual on Beau's van, Beau was out of it. He was wearing a mask, standing opposite another man who was also wearing a mask.

Daylight was fading and the shadows were at their longest, so Austin could barely make out the other mask. His best guess was that it was a Batman's mask. The man wearing it stood in front of a black Chrysler as if it was his Batmobile.

Austin was too far away to see with any great detail. But he couldn't risk trying to get any closer, not until he could be sure where Mikayla was.

* * *

The Batman had been waiting for 15 minutes and was about to call the Joker but before he could remove the phone from his pocket, a van turned into the entrance. This was his man. Deal time. Mike was always nervous around deal time. Mike's crime scenes were usually full of deals that had gone south, mainly because he had caused them.

"You're late," the Batman said.

"Sorry, got held up," the Joker replied.

"You realise the police have an APB out on you?"

"No," the Joker said.

"Well, you better not have led anyone here. You won't leave the cemetery if you have," the Batman said, pulling out his Glock.

"Don't threaten me. No one is here. No one has followed me. I have the goods. Let's just do the deal and we can both be on our way."

"The Priest wanted me to check that you're on your way to the Monster's?"

"Yep, and you can tell him it will be my last delivery."

"Get the cargo. I'm already late for the Judge," the Batman replied.

* * *

The light was fading fast as Austin watched the shadowy figures. He could pick out some words, Judge, Priest, Monster, but what did they mean? It sounded like some bizarre comic book. He could just make out the Joker go to the back of the van and return to the Batman with a hooded captive. It could be Mikayla. In this light, it could be anyone.

Austin was ready to pounce, end them then and there, both of them, but one thing worried him; what if it wasn't Mikayla? What if she was somewhere else? He could kill one of them, and torture the other. But what if he killed the wrong one, the one who knew where Mikayla was? In a gun battle, two against one, he might not have the opportunity to let one live. The risks were too high.

He watched. The Batman handed over a package and in return, the Joker handed him the captive's lead.

The Batman placed the child in the back of the Chrysler and the Joker returned to his van. The deal was done.

The question now was, which one should Austin follow?

Chapter 97

Justice James Aaron had served on the bench at the local magistrate's court for the last seven and a half years. He was a well-respected member of the community, yet he had a secret, and it was a secret only two people new. The police superintendent and the Priest.

He liked boys, and from time to time he would rent them, just for the night, then they would be shipped off again.

Shipped off to whoever had bought them.

The superintendent delivered them and he assumed the Priest organised them. The Judge paid well for this service and extra well for his privacy.

He had lit the fire at his lake house in preparation for his young companion. The room was warming up, there was a soft drink in the fridge chilling and pizza was in the oven.

A fox sat atop the mantelpiece and a bearskin lay on the floor in front of the fire. The lights were low.

All he could do was wait. He would be here soon, he kept telling himself.

The Judge never needed a mask, after all, the kids would never see him again.

Headlights flickered through the window as a car approached.

My guest, the Judge thought.

He walked out to the porch to meet his guest. It was the man he was expecting, the superintendent, the man who always brought his guests. He watched from the porch as Mike opened the rear of the car and removed the guest.

The boy was taller than the others he'd had previously. Mike led the boy past the Judge and into the home. The judge handed him an envelope containing $8,000.

"I'll pick him up at 6," Mike said, and then left the two of them standing inside the entrance.

Mike headed out the door and back into the Chrysler. The Judge watched the taillights disappear as the car left the property.

Once he could no longer see them, he removed the boy's hood.

Scott took a deep breath.

* * *

Austin had watched the exchange from the side of the drive, hidden behind the trees lining the drive. He could finally make out the plate and had committed it to memory.

He had now seen the delivery man without his mask. He would find him in good time. His only concern now was the child. It wasn't Mikayla. He regretted not following the van but now that he was here, he had to save the boy.

The windows were open and he could see the man hand the boy a towel and point him into a room, presumably the bathroom. The Judge sat by the fire waiting for his guest to shower.

It was Austin's opportunity to strike. He sneaked further up the drive, past the living room, around the back of the house. The door off the kitchen was open. He stepped inside onto a slate floor. His boots echoed upon it. He had only moved two steps before he noticed a shotgun hanging on the wall above the table. It was probably for the snakes. They would be rife in the fields up here, Austin thought.

He removed the gun from the wall, and stepped out into the living room.

"I take it you're the Judge?" Austin said. Gun sighted.

The Judge, startled, spilled his wine over his crotch. "Get the hell out of my house!" he demanded.

"Give me the boy," Austin said.

"Who are you?" the Judge replied.

Austin ignored his question. "Do you know who the Monster is or where I can find him?"

"Never heard of him," the Judge replied.

Austin moved closer, towering over the Judge, the barrel of the gun only inches from his face.

"Who is the Monster?" Austin asked again.

"I don't know," replied the Judge.

Austin cracked the gun across the Judge's nose.

"Last chance: who is the Monster?" Austin asked, barrel pressed against his cheek.

"I don't know," the Judge replied.

"Then you can't help me." He lowered the barrel and pressed it against his chest, pulling back the trigger.

"I would normally offer you a chance of redemption but you crossed that line long ago, I'm afraid," Austin said.

Seconds later, the gun exploded and the Judge was sent flying backwards, landing askew in the chair in which he had been sitting moments earlier.

Austin rummaged through the dead man's jacket and found his phone. If he did know the Monster, the number would be here.

Austin entered the bathroom and found the boy cowering in the corner.

"Don't panic, don't be afraid, I'm here to help you. The man is dead, let's get out of here. When we leave, just concentrate on the front door. Don't look at him no matter how much you want to."

They left the bathroom hand in hand, Austin leading the way. The boy looked at the man, he couldn't help it. He had a huge hole in him. The room was covered in blood and it looked as if he had pissed his pants.

The crisp night air hit them after the warmth of the fire in the house. Scott had to run to keep up with Austin. They made their way through the bushes, to the side of the drive where an SUV waited.

"Get in," Austin said, opening the door. Scott got in the driver's side and climbed over to the passenger seat.

Austin got in, throwing the gun over into the back seat. There were no neighbours to worry about. No one would have heard the shot out here. He figured he had until 6 am before anyone would find the Judge's body.

Austin headed back towards the cemetery. He needed a little distance between himself and the house before he worked out what to do next. Everything depended on where Beau was now.

He pulled the car to a halt.

"What's your name?" he asked.

"Scott," the boy replied.

"Ok, Scott, when you were in the van, was there a girl with you?" He nodded.

"Was her name Mikayla?" Austin asked, holding his breath.

"Yes, she looked after me," Scott replied.

"I'm her dad," Austin said, choking out the words. "I need to find her."

He looked at his phone. The tracking icon still showed the van was in the cemetery.

Waiting for the Monster, are you? Austin thought. Maybe I'll show up instead.

Chapter 98

Beau had waited at the cemetery for the Batman to leave. He had never liked him and he felt better after he was gone.

He decided he had better take note of the Batman's warning about the APB and make some changes to his van.

He removed two large magnets from the rear of his van. One for each side. They were for a non-existent dog grooming business. They covered his handyman logo well.

He removed the set of spare plates he kept in the back, along with a screwdriver, and began to unscrew the old plates and screw on the spare ones. He was finishing off the rear plate when the screwdriver slipped from his hand and rolled under the van.

He knelt down on all fours and ducked his head under. Then he saw it. The flashing green light.

It was a tracking device.

He was being tracked, but by whom?

Those two detectives?

Most likely.

The nosey dad?

Possibly.

Either way, the trace ended here.

He removed the magnetised tracking device and gathered his screwdriver. He finished fastening the plate, then took his screwdriver to the device. He scratched two letters into each side of the tracking box.

FU.

Chapter 99

Austin drove back to where the GPS indicated, except there was no van. Nothing. Was this a setup? Was someone in the tree line waiting for him to exit his car, before picking him off with a rifle? Not likely, but a possibility. He scanned the trees but saw no one.

His phone said 30 metres away but there was no van. He decided to track it on foot. He needed to know what was going on. Where was the van and where was his daughter?

The boy sat in the front, peering over the dashboard, like a puppy watching his owner. Austin's shadow lurked large across the road. A gust of wind blew and his eyes scanned the tree line. His eyes darted between locations he would have chosen if he was up there himself lying in wait. All the possible sniper nests looked empty. He hoped that was the case.

He moved forward slowly, always scanning, always listening. Nothing moved; there was no sound. He continued towards the flashing triangle on his phone.

There it was. On the ground. His tracker had been removed and left in the dirt. He picked it up. It had a message for its owner. FU.

Austin returned to the warmth of his vehicle. "Scott, do you know anything about a man named the Monster?" Austin asked.

"No, I never heard of him," Scott replied.

"Did you hear where he was taking Mikayla?"

"No. He bought us burgers, told us to eat up because it was going to be a long trip. Then a few hours later, we stopped for a while. I don't know how long it was but it was a long time. We ate another burger he brought back for us."

"There was nothing said to Mikayla?" Austin asked.

"No," Scott replied, "I was just told to get out, and you know the rest."

"What about when you were in the other car, did he say anything to you?"

"Not a word," Scott replied.

Austin got out the phone Marcus had given him and held it to his ear. No point scaring Scott with any gruesome details he might hear on speaker phone.

Without exchanging pleasantries, he reeled off the number plate of the Chrysler. "Can you get me address? This is the only lead I have," Austin said.

"I have it. It's registered to the church," Marcus replied.

"Send me the address," Austin said. "Thanks," he added, but before he could hang up, Marcus spoke.

"Wait, six months ago there was an insurance claim. The insurance company had a Mike McLeod listed as the driver."

"A lot of companies have multiple drivers," Austin replied.

"He's the police superintendent," Marcus said.

Austin was speechless while his brain processed this information.

"Send me his photo and his address."

The person who had delivered Scott to the Judge was none other than the police superintendent. This was big. It involved a judge, a high-ranking police officer and a priest. Austin wondered how high this went. He would do whatever it took. He had already killed a judge and he was prepared to burn the world if that was what it took to get Mikayla back. He would deal with the consequences. Consequences didn't matter as long as she was safe.

Nothing outweighed her safety.

He needed to find out where Mikayla had been taken and there were only two people who might have that information. Time was running out but he was closing in.

"I'm going to give you this phone," he said to Scott, "and you are going to call this number and ask to be put through to Detective Jake Miller. If they won't put you through, tell them your name. They will protect you."

"Where will you be?" Scott asked.

"I have to find Mikayla," Austin replied. "I will leave you somewhere safe until Detective Miller can get to you. When he asks you about the Judge, just tell the truth. That you were in the bathroom and you heard a gunshot. That's all you need to say. I will tell them everything later. Are you ok doing that?" he asked.

"I am ok. You need to find her," Scott replied.

Austin stopped outside the 24-hour McDonald's in Ballarat.

"Ready?" Austin asked.

Scott nodded and Austin pressed dial on the mobile.

"Is Detective Miller there, please?" Scott asked.

He paused, and covered the phone. "They're putting me through."

Austin heard the voice on the other end. It was him all right.

Scott said to him, "My name is Scott Western, I was kidnapped. I escaped. I'm in the McDonald's at Ballarat. Can you please come and get me? I don't want to speak to anyone else, just you," Scott said.

He pressed the speaker button so Austin could hear the reply.

"We're in Ballarat. We will be there soon. Don't go anywhere," Jake replied.

"I'll be waiting for you," Scott said. Then he said to Austin, "They're coming here, you'd better get going."

"Go inside and wait," Austin replied.

"Good luck finding her," Scott said.

He exited and headed into McDonald's.

Chapter 100

Jake and I were finishing dinner, which consisted of a cold hamburger and a can of drink in the cold night air at the back of the children's home. We didn't have time to have a proper break but we had to eat. Constable Evans was kind enough to have some food brought to us.

We knew the Priest was lying; we just couldn't prove it yet. We suspected he was a key figure in the kidnappings and needed to find out how he fitted in. We had come to a standstill. The only contact from Beau's dungeon phone could no longer be tracked.

There was nothing else to follow, until Jake's phone rang.

The phone call was brief and although I was standing near him, I was too busy finishing my food to pay much attention to what he was saying.

"You're not going to believe this!" Jake said when he hung up.

"Believe what?" I asked.

"That was Scott Western. He wants us to pick him up. Come on, let's go!"

"The missing boy?" I asked.

"Yes, come on, he's waiting for us at McDonald's in town."

I automatically thought he meant Melbourne and that we were in for another chopper ride, and started to head for the car.

"No Brucey, he's just over there," Jake said, pointing across the road to the golden arches.

"If you weren't so vague all the time…" I mumbled.

We both ran. All I could think of was, was he ok, how had he escaped, where were the others. By the time I reached McDonald's, my lungs, thighs and calves were burning. "You all right, Brucey?" Jake asked. He had only jogged and wasn't even breathing heavily.

"I'm fine," I gasped.

We spotted Scott instantly, sitting by himself staring out the window. As we approached him, Jake said, "Scott, I'm Detective Miller, and this is Detective Foxx. Are you ok? Are you hurt in any way?"

"No, I'm fine," Scott replied bravely.

"Are you hungry?" I asked him.

"A little, I didn't get fed much," Scott replied.

Even though he had already had two hamburgers today, he had a long way to go to make up for all the meals he had missed.

"I'll get you a burger," I said.

As Scott ate his cheeseburger meal, we both questioned him about his capture. His story was very similar to Stevie's. He had no idea who had taken him, or why. He had stayed underground somewhere, which we now knew was Beau's shed, and then he was transferred several times, until he ended up in an old man's home. An old man whose first request had been to take a shower. "He said he wanted me clean!"

Then he continued, "When I was in the bathroom, I heard what sounded like a big crash, but the water was running so I couldn't hear it properly. When I opened the bathroom door, the old man was dead, flipped over in his chair with a big hole in his chest. I saw his phone on the table, picked it up and left. I just ran."

"Ok, first thing we do is find out who he is. Can I have the phone you picked up?" Jake asked.

Scott handed the phone over. It had specks of dried blood covering the silver case.

Jake searched the menu, while ringing the office on his own

phone. "Need a record check on 0418... He rattled off the rest of the digits and then waited. "Can you text them through to me, please?" Jake asked.

Then he stood up. "Give us a sec, ok, Scott?"

Scott nodded, a mouthful of cheeseburger making it impossible for him to reply.

We stood three booths back, "This is big. The phone belongs to the magistrate."

I frowned. "Are you saying we have a paedophile magistrate?" I asked.

"A dead one, possibly," Jake responded.

"Where did the magistrate live?" I asked.

Jake looked at the addresses sent via the text. "One address was here in Ballarat, the other just outside of Learmonth."

"How did the boy get here?" I asked.

"Walked?" Jake surmised.

"If he was held here in Ballarat, maybe, but if you're a paedophile judge then you wouldn't have a child at your house. Especially when you have a secluded home out in Learmonth. And he couldn't have walked from there, that's about 50 ks."

"Are you saying the boy is lying?" Jake asked.

"Lying is harsh, omitting most likely," I replied.

Jake strolled back over to Scott's booth.

"Hey Scott, how did you get from there to here?" he asked.

"Hitched. When I found the road, I ran along it until someone passed. A farmer picked me up. He was on his way to pick up his daughter from the train," Scott replied.

Every day he had sat in that cell, Scott had believed he was going to die. There was no way he was going to hinder the man who had saved him from saving his own daughter, Mikayla.

We walked away. "That's a lie," I said to Jake. "There's no way a kid who's been abducted and probably abused is going to jump in a car with a stranger. I just can't imagine it. Look at him, he's still shaking."

"The kids in Ohio ran to the neighbour's house and grabbed the first person they saw. People react differently in hostile situations," Jake replied.

"I still don't buy it, but let's go and look at the crime scene."

"We'll call in the superintendent and ask him to put the boy under guard in hospital. He'll need to be checked out anyway," Jake said.

I grabbed his arm. "Wait! We don't know who's involved, we don't know how deep or high this paedophile ring goes. This is a small town; we need to be really careful."

"You might be right," Jake replied, "but we don't have a choice. We need to admit him and place him under guard."

By the time we did the paperwork and had Scott under guard in the hospital, it was past 12 and we hadn't reached the second home of the judge yet. The judge's residence in Ballarat township was undisturbed.

Dale was back as our driver. "Seems like you guys came to town on the right day. Lot of action today," he said, smiling.

Both of us ignored his comments and Dale mumbled something under his breath and returned to driving.

Chapter 101

Austin was surprised when Mike left his house at 11.52 pm. He had been hunkered down in his car waiting for Mike to leave. There must be a problem, maybe Scott's call to Miller.

His old drill sergeant used to say, if the enemy makes a mistake, then make him pay for it.

Austin's opportunity had now come early.

He crossed the street and jumped the side fence and in less than 15 seconds, he had gone from the passenger seat of his car to being a balaclava-clad man inside the superintendent's home. His military training had once more served him well. He crept down the hall. The household appeared to be asleep. There were twin boys in their cots in one room and his wife asleep in the main bedroom.

Austin placed his hand over her mouth. She woke with a start. "I want you to call your husband and tell him to come home. If you do as I say, I won't hurt you or your children. Do you understand? If you promise not to scream, I will remove my hand. Will you be quiet?" he asked.

She nodded. Austin passed her the phone from her bedside table.

"Hi babe," he answered, "it's early, is everything ok?" he heard Mike ask her.

Austin ripped the phone away from her ear.

"Depends on what you do next, Chief," Austin said.

"Who is this!" Mike screamed.

"Who I am is not important, what I want is," Austin replied.

"What do you want?" Mike asked.

"In return for your family's lives, I want you to come home. We need to have a private discussion. You will come around the back, take your clothes off and enter through the back door. Once you're clean, we will talk in private. Let me warn you: plan anything or call any of your staff, it won't be pretty."

"You have my word."

"Do as I ask and I will leave your family safe."

"Ok, I'm almost back home." He hadn't wasted any time. As he was speaking, Austin heard him running and then the sound of his car starting up. "I'll do as you ask. Just don't hurt anyone," Mike begged.

"That's up to you," Austin replied.

Austin heard the Chrysler pull into the garage as he finished tying the last knot to secure Mike's wife. Then he sat on the inside of the rear door, shotgun pointed at Mike. "Gun belt first." Mike threw the belt, complete with the cuffs and the Smith & Wesson M&P .40 Calibre. It was fastened in the newly designed thigh holster.

Austin removed the mag as well as the spare cartridge. He tucked the gun into the back of his waistband and pocketed the ammo. Next came the vest, then the clothes.

Mike stood there in the freezing midnight air in nothing but his boxers. "Turn around," Austin demanded. He wasn't hiding anything; there was nowhere to hide it.

Austin threw Mike the grey robe he had taken from his bathroom. Then he flung his cuffs back at him. "Put these on," he demanded. "Behind your back. Now back up to the door."

Austin grabbed Mike by the cuffs and tightened them further. Then he pulled him back inside the home and sat him down on a dining room chair.

"I'll show you your family before we leave, so you know they're safe."

Austin led Mike to the rooms, showed him his twins and then his wife. She made a muffled cry as Austin closed the door and led Mike back into the dining room.

"I know you've been dealing children to paedophiles all over the state. All I want is the Monster's address. I won't lie to you, you can't save yourself, but give it to me and it will save your family," Austin said, calmly and matter-of-factly.

"This is the way it will work. I will ask you once for the address. If you don't give it to me, I will kill your wife. Then I will ask you again. If you refuse, I will kill one of your boys. Then I will ask you one more time. If you don't tell me what I need to know, then I will kill your other son. Do you understand?" Austin said.

Mike began to talk.

"Don't say anything unless it's the address," Austin interrupted him.

"I don't have it," Mike said. Austin rose from the table. Then he begged, "Wait, please wait. I can get it. I'm the only one who knows who has it."

Austin stopped a few metres away from the table.

"Please, I'll get it for you now. Just grab my phone and I'll get it."

Austin picked the phone up from the floor.

"Is the number saved under Priest or Father?" Austin asked.

"Father," Mike replied.

"How long does it take to get to the church from here?"

"About 20 minutes," Mike answered reluctantly.

"When you talk to him, tell him you need to pick him up in 25 minutes," Austin said.

He placed the phone on the table, engaged the speaker and levelled the gun at Mike's head.

"Don't do anything stupid."

The phone rang out, and there was no message bank.

"Dial it again," Mike suggested.

Austin pressed the button again followed by the speaker button.

It almost rang out the second time, before a tired, sleepy voice answered. "Everything ok with the Judge?" the Priest asked.

"I need to come and see you, it's important," Mike said.

"What is it?"

"It's best we don't discuss it over the phone," Mike said.

"Whatever you think is best."

Austin hung up the call.

"I told you the consequences of not getting the address," Austin said.

"He won't give it over the phone. You'll have to persuade him. You can kill me and my family but you still won't have the address," Mike replied.

"All right, but if I don't get it, God won't save anyone. It's time I had a chat with the father anyhow," Austin replied. "Where's the Chrysler?"

"In the garage," Mike replied.

"We'll take that. I'll drive." Austin pulled Mike up from the table, collecting the phone on the way.

"Remember: you want your family to stay safe, you get me that address. I don't want to come back here."

Mike had achieved his aim. He had led the man out of his home and away from his family. Now he had to work out how to take him down.

He would make him pay for threatening his family. Who the fuck did this guy think he was?

Chapter 102

Deputy Doofus, as I had come to think of Dale, kept his mouth shut. He hadn't said a word to either Jake or me since we had ignored his last comment.

When we arrived at the Judge's lake house, the light from the living area was shining through the open front door like a lighthouse beacon leading the way.

Apart from the open door, there were no signs of a disturbance from the outside.

It was a beautiful home, built largely from stone and slate. It had large, expansive rooms, and floor-to-ceiling windows to take in the views.

We stepped inside, where the scene was exactly as Scott had described; a man tossed into his armchair with a huge hole in his chest. The blood splatter was significant. The shooting had been performed at close range.

"Constable, call your office. We're going to need Forensics and officers here to help secure the scene," Jake said.

Deputy Doofus was turning green at the sight of blood. He seemed glad of a reason to get out of the house.

"Check the bathroom for me, Brucey," Jake said.

I knew that Jake was trying to verify Scott's version of events and from the evidence, it was looking good. The towel was wet and on the floor, there was still water in the bottom of the shower; it added up.

When I returned to the living room, I noticed Deputy Doofus outside hurling his guts up in the garden bed. Jake was down on his knees looking at the coffee table. I assumed he was checking for blood splatter.

"Doesn't look like there's any trace evidence there?" I said to Jake.

"No, the kid said he took the phone from the coffee table, correct?"

"That's what he said. He's a kid, maybe he picked it up off the floor. He'd have been shit scared and wouldn't have had a clue what he was doing," I replied.

We began our search of the home. The kitchen door wasn't open but it was unlocked. There was a gun rack, but no gun. Based on the half-empty box of shells I found in the bureau next to the rack, it was a shotgun. We also found a spent shotgun casing on the floor near the fire. Our jigsaw pieces were fitting together. The intruder had entered via the kitchen, taken the gun off the wall, loaded it, and killed the Judge. Probably never knew the boy was there.

Maybe this is about the boy, I thought, but how? It didn't seem to be connected to the other murders, or maybe there was a link? In the double murder case, one of them was shot with the other's gun. Maybe that was just a coincidence.

"Who would come in to kill someone without a weapon?" I asked.

"Maybe they knew the Judge had a gun," Jake replied.

"I was just wondering if it could have been someone known to him."

I went into the bedroom. This room didn't look disturbed at all, but I wanted to try and find out what sort of man this judge had been. What sort of man becomes a magistrate and keeps such a dark secret? Jake came into the room and began rummaging through the walk-in robe while I went through the bedside table.

"Looks like he was into something big," Jake said from the closet.

"What have you found?" I asked.

He dumped a black leather shoulder bag on the floor. It was full of bundled cash. Hundreds of thousands by the look of the overflowing bag.

The bottom drawer of the side table contained mainly cufflinks and tie-pins, but I came across a jewellery box. Why would a jewellery box be in a man's drawer? I opened it. It was a jewellery box all right but it was full of cocaine.

"Jake, there's a box full of coke."

I received no response.

"Jake?" I called out again.

Still no response and so I turned towards him and saw him standing there, holding something.

"Jake, what have you got?" I asked.

"Get the constable."

I called Deputy Doofus, who meandered in like he was circulating at a dinner party with cocktail in hand.

Jake showed us both a newspaper clipping. The article was about how pillars of the community were helping the prisoners of Ararat rehabilitate. In the attached photo were four men: Justice Aaron, Father O'Riley, the prisoner Ian Welling, and the fourth man was a uniformed officer.

"It says Palanok Pty donated a million dollars to get the inmates' rehabilitation program 'Restart' off the ground. I bet they'd be pissed if they found out they'd donated to paedophiles," Jake said.

"We know four of these men. Who's the policeman in the picture with the Judge and the Priest?" Jake asked Constable Evans.

"That's Superintendent Mike McLeod."

"Where is he now? Considering his magistrate has been killed in his own home, I thought he would be here," Jake said to the constable.

"We can't get hold of him. He isn't answering the radio and we rang his home and it just rings out. The station sergeant has sent a cruiser to his house."

"Let me know the outcome," Jake instructed.

Once Evans was out of the room, Jake turned to me. "Well, at least now we know they all knew one another."

"What do you think was going on here?" I asked him.

"I think they were organising drugs, weapons and kids and they were sending them wherever they needed to go. This might just be the tip of the iceberg."

"Maybe we're getting too close and someone is erasing any leads before we uncover them," I said.

"I agree, but with syndicates like this, there's usually a head, a rich drug lord. Someone has to be bringing the drugs into the country," Jake said.

"Maybe our Judge here was the boss? Look at all the cash," I said.

"He's rich but he's not in the drug lord. There's someone else."

"Maybe the Priest," I said.

"Maybe he's putting the cash into the church," Jake suggested. "I think we need to pay him another visit when we're done here."

"Detectives!" Evans called, running down the hall towards us. "The unit arrived at the superintendent's house. When they knocked, they heard a cry for help so they broke in to find his wife tied up and the superintendent missing."

"Did she see who took him?" I asked.

"No, she said he was wearing a balaclava, apparently he was a big guy."

"Maybe we should go see the Priest now?" Jake said.

"Constable, can you contact the Priest?" I asked.

"I can ring the children's home, he lives in the monastery at the rear of the chapel," Evans replied.

"Take us there now. He may be in danger."

Chapter 103

Austin drove the Chrysler while Mike directed from the passenger seat next to him.

"When we get to the church, you call him, tell him to get into the back of the car."

As they turned into the church, Austin pressed redial on Mike's phone.

"Yes, I'm ready," the Priest replied.

Mike said, "I'll be there in a minute. When I do, get in the back, we need to talk in private."

Austin stopped the Chrysler and seconds later, the Priest in his black robe with red trim came out from around the back.

He got in as Mike had asked him to. The partition between driver and the back seat was up.

"Mike, what did you want?"

No answer.

"What did you need to talk to me about?"

Still no answer.

The Priest tried the door handles. The childproof lock was on. He couldn't get out.

He banged on the Perspex. No response.

Was there someone in the passenger seat? He thought he could see a silhouette, but it was very hard to tell as the partition was tinted.

Mike's voice came through the speaker. "Not long now, Father."

Austin didn't drive to the cemetery where Beau and Mike had met earlier or where he had parked Marcus' car. He drove past the entrance to the end of the road.

"Get in the back," Austin ordered Mike.

It was now or never for Mike; he had to strike. He got out and instead of heading to the passenger side back seat, he headed around to the driver's side back door.

"I can't open the door," he said, holding up his cuffs behind his back.

Austin reached for the handle and Mike attacked.

He head-butted Austin. It wasn't his first option but it was probably the best of his remaining options.

The head-butt collected Austin on the side of the nose rather than flush on the bridge. It dazed him and sent him staggering backwards and with blurry vision, but Mike still didn't have the advantage.

He charged Austin with his shoulder down, hoping to send him flying, but Austin quickly recovered. He regained his balance and although his vision was still affected, he could see Mike rushing him and knew what his intention was.

Austin stepped aside like a matador at a bullfight. Because Mike had built up such a huge head of steam, and he had his hands cuffed behind his back, he missed his target and crashed face first into the ground.

Austin turned him over with his boot.

"As I said at the house, I won't kill your family if I get the address. As for you, you can't save yourself. Do you have any last words for your family?"

"You said you wouldn't kill me or my family if I got you the address."

"I said I wouldn't kill your family, they're innocent. You're not innocent, you're a money-grabbing child killer. You might not have killed them yourself but you knew what the outcome would be.

There's no way out of this for you.

"Now, the lives of your family are in the Priest's hands. Let's hope he gives me the address."

He pulled out his pistol.

Fearing his own imminent death, and the loss of all hope, Mike did the only thing he could do. He rolled over, gathered himself and ran past the car towards the graveyard entrance. He was fast, considering he was in a night robe with his hands cuffed behind his back. But the bullets were faster and with Austin at the other end of the gun, they were accurate.

Austin fired twice and the second bullet hit within an inch of the first just under Mike's shoulder blade.

Mike fell and became still.

Austin opened the rear door of the Chrysler.

"What in God's name is going on here?" the Priest asked.

"Mike is dead," Austin replied. "Now I want my daughter, and apparently a man called the Monster has ordered her? I want his address and I want it now."

"If I refuse..." the Priest began.

"Then two things will happen. I will kill Mike's wife and twin boys, and their deaths will be on you. Secondly, your death will be excruciating. I have tortured many people when I was in the army and I was very good at it," Austin replied.

"Why kill Mike's family?" the Priest asked.

"He promised me the address in exchange for their lives. You're the only person alive who has it. I live up to my promises. You give it to me, they live; you don't, they die. Simple."

"What happens to me?" the Priest asked.

"It's too late for you, you're no better than the Judge or Mike," Austin replied. "You're even worse."

"You killed the Judge too?" the Priest asked. "Not much incentive for me to give you the address."

"Mike's twins are the best incentive of all. I'm sure you don't want two more children's deaths on your soul as you make your way to answer to Jesus?" Austin said.

"If I give it to you, he won't let you in, he won't see you. You're out of your league, you don't know what you're dealing with. He isn't called the Monster for no reason, you know," the Priest replied.

"Then I will get what's coming to me, won't I. Why don't you let God decide?" Austin replied.

The Priest bowed his head.

"So what's your decision?" Austin asked.

"If you're going to kill me, I'd like to pray on God's soil and with his gracious air flowing through my lungs, if you don't mind."

Austin slid out of the car and waited for the Priest to move.

Then he shut the door.

"I don't fear death, sir, so kill me if it is your will. I have made my peace with God, I have admitted my sins to God and he has forgiven me, as he will do for you." The Priest's voice was shaking.

He was on his knees, head bowed, rosary beads and cross clasped tightly between his fingers. He looked up and gave a smile, a smile he had given at most Sunday services.

"Tell me, Father, how many kids were there? How many years?"

"Hundreds, over decades," he replied.

"Why did you do it, Father?" Austin asked.

"The Monster pays well, too well."

"Give me the address."

The Priest hesitated.

"Don't make me go back to see Mike's twins."

Austin repeated the address into his phone. He was going to check it with Marcus.

Marcus confirmed that the property was registered to Igor Pavlychko. His police record listed his alias variously as the Ukrainian Monster or just the Monster, and showed he had been raided by police in January last year for suspicion of human trafficking. Officers thought he must have been moving the cargo around, because they'd searched both houses and his boat and had come up empty. He hadn't even been there; he must have been tipped off.

"This guy is bad," Marcus said. "We had two of his ex-employees who said they'd testify about what they'd seen in return for protection. But while they were in witness protection, they were killed. Even the officers protecting them were executed. If you're going there, be careful," Marcus warned. "Call me if you need help."

Austin hung up the call.

"Well, Father, have you made your peace?" Austin asked.

"I know where I'm going. Really, you're giving me a gift," the Priest replied.

"You're mistaken, Father, you're under what many call the security illusion," Austin said.

The Priest frowned, confused.

"You believe in your faith so much and think that because you've been a leader in the church, you cannot be lost and you'll be granted immunity from the consequences of your evil deeds." Austin pressed the barrel of Mike's gun against the Priest's head.

"But you've overlooked something very important. 'But if a righteous person turns from their righteousness and commits sin and does the same detestable things the wicked person does, will they live? None of the righteous things that person has done will be remembered,'" Austin said, quoting from Ezekiel.

"You know your scriptures," the Priest said.

"Then you know what comes next," Austin said.

"As you must," the Priest said, and began in his loud sermon voice, "'Because of the unfaithfulness they are guilty of and because of the sins they have committed, they will die.'"

Austin fired a single shot, ending the sermon and the Priest. His body slumped back. Austin dragged him and placed him onto the back seat of the Chrysler. He would need him later.

Jumping into the driver's side, he headed for the address the Priest had given him.

Chapter 104

It was like *déjà vu* walking on the echoing floor of the children's home. We had been there only hours earlier. I felt as if I was in a loop.

The lady at the reception desk was considerably older than the one who had been on duty earlier. She did as Jake asked, and tried calling the Priest at his home. "He's not answering, I'm afraid. He was in earlier when Mike called. Maybe he went out."

"How long ago did the superintendent call?" I asked.

"About an hour, maybe an hour and a half," she replied. "Feel free to knock on his door. His residence is at the back of the chapel. Just go around the side," she said, pointing to show us the way.

The door to his residence was closed but not locked. His bed was unmade as if he had been in it not long ago. There was no sign of him or of a struggle. He had just vanished.

"Let's think about this. We have a dead paedophile judge, a police superintendent who was taken at gunpoint, and now a priest who knows them both. A priest who received a call from Beau. What are we missing, Jake?"

"A second phone," Jake replied.

Jake began pacing. All he needed was a hat and a pipe and he would look like Sherlock Holmes. "The call was traced here. The Priest handed us his phone but he said his phone wasn't the number that Beau called. But what if he has more than one phone?"

"A ghost phone, just like Beau had," I replied. "What do you think is going on?"

"Could be someone is trying to take over the Priest's territory?"

"Either that or the Priest might be afraid we're getting too close and he's now trying to keep his contacts quiet, if you know what I mean."

"You search his office, I'll search here." Jake began rummaging through drawers while I headed to the office.

His office was open, so I helped myself. I searched his desk. There were some keys, pens, pencils. Normal stuff, nothing out of the ordinary. Maybe we were barking up the wrong tree. Maybe he was innocent. Maybe he wasn't like the Judge.

I moved to the glass cabinet behind the desk. It was locked, so I took the keys from a drawer and tried each of them in turn. Finally, one turned. I opened the box sitting in the middle. It was a black carry case made of hardwood with blue velvet lining and black Rexene exterior.

Inside the communion set were:

The gold cross he wore on Sundays and in confessional.

The gold chalice he used at Sunday services.

Two candle holders.

Two glass cruets.

One paten.

One pix.

One purificator.

"Should you be in here?" a deep male voice called from behind me. Half stunned, I spun towards the voice and in doing so, my grip slipped and the box fell to the floor. The contents bounced and flew in different directions.

"We have concerns for the father's welfare. Do you know where he might be?" I asked, showing him my badge.

"At this time of night, he would be asleep, I would suggest," the male security guard replied.

"We've checked there; he's missing," I replied.

"That's terrible," the guard said.

"Why does a children's home have a security guard?" I asked.

"It's for the security of the staff. Some of the kids don't want to be here, and they can get quite violent."

"I suppose," I replied.

We stared at each other briefly and then the security guard said, "I better get back to work."

I looked down at the damage I had done to the box. The contents were all over the floor, and the box itself was broken. The lid was twisted and one of its hinges had snapped.

Among the contents on the carpet was a silver iPhone. I switched it on. There were only two numbers in the contacts list; one 'UM', and the other was digits only, no name or initials beside it. The only messages in the inbox were from UM. In the sent box were dozens of coded messages, the last one 'F11-x2-50ea'.

I thought about calling UM's number, then stopped myself. Maybe if we sent a message, we could get a trace on the phone.

I began looking for more evidence, in books, under shelves, under the desk, but it wasn't until I picked up the Old Testament and flicked through it that I found a second phone. It had one stored number, which coincided with the unnamed number on the silver iPhone.

Why send messages from one phone to another; what was the point? I wondered.

Jake appeared in the office doorway. "I found a journal, it's more like an inventory, actually," he said, placing it on the desk. There were hundreds of entries. The last few matched exactly those in the silver iPhone.

I told Jake about the phone and he took it from me and checked the messages. "I think this guy is ordering kids! Look. 'F11' must be female aged 11, then here 'M12' would be male 12 years old. The figure next to them is the amount he's prepared to pay," he suggested.

"Why do they buy so many kids? What can they do with that many?" I asked.

"Most of them would be sold overseas. The boys probably work in the fields, picking opium usually. They pay $50,000 to $100,000 for a kid and get 10 to 15 years' worth of work out of him. The girls they put into the overseas prostitution market. They get a mint for overseas girls, especially under-age ones," Jake replied, grimacing. Then he added, "This guy, UM, I'd say he's our kingpin. Our rich drug lord."

"Why did the Judge and the other two paedophiles that were holding Stevie have kids if they were meant to be sent overseas to this UM guy?" I asked.

"Maybe the Priest is renting them out before delivering them, like a double dip at profits. He'd get paid twice for the same kid!"

"Maybe they found out these kids were being defiled before being sent. Maybe they weren't getting what they were paying for," I said.

"It's possible this UM person found out and he's sending a message."

Chapter 105

Mikayla had sat in silence since Scott was removed from the van. She knew she was being taken to her death, or something worse. Her father had always told her to believe in herself and that she could do anything, so she had decided wherever she was being taken, she would take her first opportunity to escape. She would get out or die trying.

Beau had been driving the van very fast, taking corners sharply, and she had been tossed from side to side for what felt like hours.

"You lied about us going home, didn't you?" Mikayla said.

"Yes, but you knew I was lying, you're a smart girl," Beau replied.

"Yes, I did. So where am I going?"

"You'll be at your new home in a little while. You should be happy. There's another girl there," Beau said.

"What other girl?" Mikayla asked.

"Hard to remember; all you kids, so many deliveries."

There have been so many he doesn't even remember us, Mikayla thought.

"The people who bought me, what do they want with me?" Mikayla asked.

Beau went to look at her in the mirror, but the view was blocked by the plastic he had installed years ago. He saw only his own reflection. His eyes threw back a look of disgust at himself.

"I don't know," he replied. He did know; he just couldn't tell her.

It was easier when they didn't speak to him, he thought. He lowered his window. He had started to feel sick. He needed some fresh air.

"Are they going to rape me?" she asked.

Beau ignored the question and turned the music up, loud. He would hear no more questions.

Beau hadn't come up with any better plan to get out of the Monster's house alive than by simply delivering the girl early, hoping to get into his good books. Then he would vanish. The Priest would come looking for him when he didn't return with his cut of the money. The Priest had a bad reputation when it came to clients who reneged on deals or cheated him. The result was usually death.

While the Priest was a concern, he was the lesser of two evils right now. He knew the Monster would kill him if given the order.

He doubted the Priest could physically do it himself.

He would find out soon enough.

Chapter 106

By the time Jake and I had rummaged through the Priest's private residence as well as his office and chapel, we had found 13 phones and dozens of buyers. All had had young children placed with them. We had managed to reconcile one of the phone numbers to Ian Welling and now knew that the Priest had supplied Stevie to him.

However, all the other orders paled into insignificance when we compared them to the number of orders to 'UM'.

Jake had requested tech support to trace the phone, however they hadn't yet got back to him.

"I think it's safe to say the Priest is the middle man. He organises the orders and I would imagine the delivery of them too," Jake said.

"I agree," I said.

Apart from Jake rummaging through the rooms at the chapel, the church was eerily quiet. How did a person who devoted his life to love not see the evil living inside himself? A place of hope, love and faith should not know such evil.

When Jake was quiet and all was still, I could hear rain falling on the church roof. It was the most peaceful sound I had heard all day.

Unfortunately, it was broken by the stomping feet of Deputy Doofus.

"I've just received a call from the groundskeeper at the cemetery. We've found the superintendent."

His sombre expression told us what we'd expect to find. "Take us there," Jake said.

"Organise some tarps and tents. We'll need to secure what evidence hasn't been washed away with this rain," I added.

"Already done, Detective," Evans replied.

"Good job," I said.

As much as I thought he was a doofus, good work deserved praise and he had made a smart decision and deserved to know he had done the right thing.

The drive out was quiet and sombre. The heavy rain combined with the darkness reduced visibility and made the country road feel even more isolated. Constable Evans was very shaken at the discovery of a colleague's body. Jake and I had been lucky enough not to experience that with anyone we had directly worked with.

We had been driving for about 15 minutes before we saw blue and red flashing lights off in the distance.

When we arrived on the scene, most of Ballarat's available officers were there, as well as a few from neighbouring areas. Jake had already contacted Monique and requested control. Like him, she believed the recent deaths we were investigating were all related and so she gave her approval.

We produced our badges and strolled through the police line without any issues.

As usual, Jake and I worked from the outside in. As always, we started by getting information from any witnesses, the first respondents, forensics, or pathologists. Then we would move onto the body itself.

The groundskeeper was an elderly guy who had lived on the property since 1999. He received cheap rent and a weekly cheque in return for taking care of the grounds. When he had first started, he had 187 gravestones to take care of and four bare acres of lawn to mow, while now, there were 369 gravestones and two and a quarter bare acres.

"Can you tell us what you heard?" Jake asked.

"I was woken by a loud bang, followed closely by another. I was asleep and I mean, man! I sat straight up in bed; scared the crap out of me. Loudest bang I ever heard. I grabbed my gun and went out onto the porch. By the time I got to the end, I heard one more loud bang. I still couldn't see anything, so I got in my truck to drive to the entrance of the cemetery but before I could, a car passed me. It looked like a black car. It was really travelling. Then when I drove to the entrance and was about to turn in, I saw a lump on the ground about 10 metres away. I got out, realised it was a person and called you guys."

"I take it you didn't get a plate on the vehicle, or the make and model?" I asked.

"It was really dark. I'm pretty sure it was black, and it was a bulky, square shape," he replied, clearly annoyed at himself that he couldn't offer more.

"It's ok, the officer here will take your formal statement and we'll be back in touch with you shortly. Thanks for your help," Jake said.

"Could you do it?" I asked Jake.

"Do what?" he quizzed.

"Live on a cemetery," I replied.

"Fuck, hell no, that's scary shit. I have nightmares about dead people as it is, you?"

"No way, if I wanted ghosts I'd go to Picton Town," I said, referring to one of Australia's most haunted towns.

The first units had done a great job securing the scene and protecting the evidence against the elements.

The ambulance officers reported on initial examination that the deceased had died from two bullets to the heart. However, they wouldn't be able to confirm it until the autopsy had been completed and the toxicology report came back.

Because we'd arrived so soon after the murder, the body hadn't begun to decompose. The superintendent only smelt of stale urine.

Jake went to the left-hand side of the body while I went to the right. The victim's face was planted in the mud. He was only wearing a bathrobe. His black hair was knotted and covered in mud. His hands were cuffed behind his back and his feet were bare. Whatever he had done, it must have been something pretty bad to be left like this, at a place like this.

I noted the two bullet wounds.

"Have you found a third wound?" I asked Jake, referring to the fact the groundskeeper had mentioned three gunshots.

"No, maybe the third bullet missed him," he replied.

"Maybe, but these two are grouped pretty close together. Within about two and a half centimetres, would you say?" I asked.

"Yeah," Jake replied. "Maybe he fired a warning shot, who knows. Let's save the questions for when we have all the evidence, otherwise we'll be out in this shit for the whole night."

"I'm going to see if I can find the casings," I said. "Based on how he's lying, the shots came from up there." I pointed with my torch into the darkness beyond the entrance.

I had walked about 15 metres before I found a partial tyre print, then what appeared to be a shoe print, then a casing, then a second casing, and a few metres over, a third.

I looked at one of the spent casings. It looked like a .40-calibre; standard police issue, I thought. Second person killed tonight most likely with his own weapon.

By the time Jake strode up the track, I was almost soaked through.

"What you got?" he asked.

"Three spent .40-calibre casings, tyre tracks, and one big fucking question," I replied.

"What's the question?" Jake asked.

"Who does this belong to?" I pointed my torch to the ground.

There was a pool of blood next to the tyre cast. It had begun to wash away with the rain, but it was clear that it was recent.

"There's no trail of blood, just a pool, so I doubt it belongs to the victim," I suggested to Jake.

"Interesting," Jake replied.

"Another victim, perhaps?" I probed.

Jake's phone buzzed.

"Miller," he answered, "what you got? Palanok?" he repeated into his phone. "Text me the addresses."

He hung up and shone his torch away from the pool of blood and then bent down and picked something up.

"What is it?" I asked.

"Looks like it's from rosary beads. There are heaps of them, look." Jake shone his torch over them.

"Do you think that the Priest killed the superintendent?" I asked.

"We need to see Scott. I have more questions for him," Jake said urgently.

Chapter 107

The rain had turned into hail and visibility went from limited to near impossible in the car. Yet Constable Evans drove us without hesitation. When we finally arrived at the hospital to visit Scott, Jake directed Evans to wait in the Cruiser.

Jake hadn't spoken on the way over. I could tell he was working on a theory, I just had no idea what it was.

Scott had been placed on a drip to replace lost fluids. He was all skin and bone.

Jake sat on the edge of the bed at Scott's feet. I stood, notepad open, pen poised.

"Scott, the man who saved you is in danger. We need to help him."

"What man?" Scott replied.

Yeah, what man? What the hell are you talking about? I thought.

"The man who saved you from the Judge. Was it Mikayla's dad, was Mikayla in the van? Do you know where they were taking her? We need to find them, Scott, they could be in danger!"

"The Joker said our ransom had been paid and he was dropping us off at different places. We knew he was lying. He always lied."

"We? Is that you and Mikayla?" Jake asked.

"Yes," Scott replied.

"Did he say where he was taking her?" Jake asked.

"No," Scott replied. "Only that this was his last delivery," he remembered.

"Jake, you got a sec?" I asked.

We stepped into the hallway outside Scott's room. "Where are we going with this? Do you think Austin is involved?"

"The phone the Priest used to place his orders was registered to a company called Palanok. Palanok donated the money to get the prisoner 'Restart' program going. But they weren't donating money; they were funding their own paedophile ring. It was their plan from the start. They had the Judge, the police chief and the Priest running the program. They must have all been in Palanok's pocket in some form or another."

"That's like a pub funding AA programs," I replied.

"Yep," Jake said.

"But I don't understand what that has to do with Austin."

"Austin saved Scott, and Stevie said he killed them with their own gun. Why, you ask?" Jake said. "Less evidence. When I saw the Judge had been killed with his own gun, that made two in one day. Big coincidence. Then the policeman; he was killed with his service pistol. That's three. Someone's hunting them. May I suggest a person straight out of the army with a classified army file might be behind this?" Jake said.

"You were right," Jake continued, "a kidnapped kid wouldn't have hitched a ride, but I couldn't work out why he was lying. Now I know; Scott is not trying to protect Austin, he's trying to save Mikayla."

I was dumbfounded.

"What else do we need from Scott?" I asked.

"I want to know if he ever heard the name Igor or Monster. If he heard Beau say it, then it probably confirms where Beau is heading."

Scott had almost dozed off when we entered his room again.

"One more quick question," Jake said as he woke him. "Did the Joker say what he would do once he had made the delivery?"

Half-asleep, Scott answered, "He said he would take the Monster's money and go fishing."

"Go to sleep now, Scott. Your parents will be here soon. We'll see you again in a few days."

Chapter 108

Chloe wasn't sure when she had blacked out, but she had dreamt the eyeless girl hanging next to her was talking to her. "Get out," she said, "this will be you." With every word spoken, a sliver of skin fell from her face onto the blood-soaked, dusty floor. When Chloe woke, she could hear the sound of flies buzzing around her head. She was worried they would go up her nose or mouth. She could feel one crawling across her eyelid.

"Ooww!" she screamed, as Alexi removed her from the chains and carried her over his shoulder. He weaved his way through a labyrinth of connecting tunnels, knowing when to turn right, when to turn left and when to stay the course. At one point, Chloe saw a flash of daylight and swore she heard the sound of barking. She could see the flicker of lights as she bounced around. He then hit the stairs, taking two at a time, and she could see all the upside-down books placed neatly on the shelves in the library, although she could make none of them out.

He sat her down on the bed. "Get cleaned up. We have a visitor arriving tonight, you need to look your best."

Despite the fact that she was now away from the dead girl, she could still smell her. The smell of death at its worst was a thick fatty smell, and it stuck with her. She could smell death even deep in her hair.

Even after her shower, she could still smell it, in waves.

She put on fresh clothes and felt much better about herself, but it was all a façade. She was beginning to think if she remained here, she would be the next girl hanging in the tunnels, or maybe, that was just the dream talking.

It would have only been 8, maybe 8.30 in the morning, as she studied her reflection in the mirror, and she couldn't help but notice how gaunt and sickly she was looking. Her cheekbones were drawn, her eyes were sunken and she looked neglected, she thought.

Then she realised that was her now.

Plain and simple, she was abused and neglected.

Chloe heard the slightly muffled sound of the intercom buzz in the other room.

"The Joker's here," the voice over the intercom said.

"He's early, let me check," Alexi replied.

Chloe then heard his heavy footsteps walk away down the hall and while she could still hear voices, she couldn't decipher what was being said. She heard the footsteps return.

"Let him in but we won't be letting him out," Alexi said. "The boss wants to feed him to the dogs."

"Show him in!" Igor himself ordered.

* * *

After passing the guard at the gate with relative ease, Beau was feeling positive about his chances of coming out the other side. The drive along the winding road up to the country house seemed longer today.

By the time Beau set foot inside the property, he had his excitement in check and was able to give the impression of a calm, disinterested delivery man. He had Mikayla behind him, with a hood over her head.

"I apologise for being early. I didn't want you to have to wait any longer, because you have waited long enough already," Beau said.

"It's fine," Alexi said, dismissing Beau's apology with a careless wave of his hand. "Show us the goods," he demanded.

"Sure…Monster…I mean…Mr Pavlychko," Beau replied.

Alexi stood there laughing.

"I am not the Monster, and I would be very careful using that word around here."

"I wouldn't use that word at all unless you were interested in finding out its origin," a small man at the back of the room said.

Beau knew he had made a mistake, one he was hoping he would escape from.

"Sorry," Beau apologised immediately.

"So, you're the Priest's bagman," the small man said. He stood and walked over in front of Alexi. "Show me what I have bought."

It was only then that Beau realised the small man in front of him was in fact the Monster. It also provided a lesson between myth and reality. Beau thought he would be able to grab him by the neck with one hand and hammer him to the ground with the other. The only thing that scared him about the Monster was the big guy standing next to him, and for that reason he was cautious and apologetic.

He removed the hood, revealing Mikayla as he had promised. "Same as in the photo," he said.

"You have a fantastic eye for quality," the Monster replied, as if he was looking at a painting or an antique.

"Always aim to please," Beau replied. He hoped he appeared genuine and not some slimy scum-bag who couldn't wait to get the fuck out of there. "The Priest said you would have the payment?"

Igor nodded, and clicked his fingers. Andrei, who had been standing in the corner of the room, observing, waiting and ready to act if his boss called, stepped forward and handed a yellow envelope to Beau.

"You will find it's 10,000 short. I took the 10,000 as compensation for the inconvenience, Igor said.

"I shall let the Priest know. If he has an issue he can speak with you," Beau said. He had no intention of speaking to the Priest. Any money collected he intended to keep and use to start his new life. He waited anxiously, wanting to leave but not wanting them to smell the deception.

"Get the new girl cleaned up," Igor said.

Alexi took Mikayla by the arm and led her away.

Beau watched the girl being escorted to the rear of the home and out of sight.

"Is there anything else you need?" Igor asked.

"No, I'll get going now. It's been a long drive and I have a long drive ahead of me," Beau replied.

Igor nodded to the security guard standing behind Beau, giving him the approval to open the door and send him on his way.

Back in his van, Beau was driving down the drive towards the gate, just shy of half a million dollars in his bag and with a new life on the horizon. He hadn't lied to Igor, he did have a long drive except he was heading north, not south. The Gold Coast would be his new destination.

Igor turned to Shevd. "Take out his tyres. Andrei, hunt him down, and make sure you hide the van."

Andrei was about to head off when Igor spoke. "Don't kill him. He needs to see what a true Monster is."

"Yes, boss," Andrei replied.

Shevd took up his position in the attic. He saw the van turn right off the tar-sealed drive and out of the gate, headed down the dirt road and away from the house. He aimed at the rear tyre of the van, calmed his breathing, paused and fired. The shot cracked loud throughout the house and across the land. The van swerved and swayed.

Shevd could see the fat man disembark the cabin and inspect the rear tyre. Shevd fired again; this time, the bullet hit the front tyre. Beau's immediate reaction was to head back to the cabin but the third bullet to the driver's door put that thought out of his mind. He was darting around looking like a trapped animal.

With no idea where the shots were coming from, Beau didn't know where he could go for cover. His immediate thought was to run for the woods. The trees would provide some cover.

He sprinted down the dirt road, going left across the front of his van, when a shot rang out and a bullet landed in the dirt just centimetres from his left foot.

The bullet made him turn right, which kept him closer to the house than he would have liked. Beau decided it would be best to enter the woods at the closest point and then weave away from this place. Otherwise they would be firing pot shots at him all day long.

He ran in a zigzag pattern as fast as he could towards the edge of the woods. The woods began 500 metres from Beau's current position. Then something sent him sprawling onto his belly in the dirt. In the split second it took him to gather himself, he heard a shot ring out.

A sharp pain pierced his calf.

Shevd watched through his scope as the fat man gathered himself and hobbled into the woods at the end of the street beyond Palanok. He could have killed him if he wanted to but the boss had ordered he be brought back alive.

Shevd scanned the area. One of the guards was already on his way to remove the van, and as he scanned back to where Beau had entered the woods, he could see Andrei about 150 metres behind him.

Chapter 109

We were in the hospital café, and Jake was confident that Austin had killed both the Judge and Mike. While I thought it was a possibility, I couldn't rule out that the hits on them both had been performed by a rival cartel, or even the Priest himself.

"So, if it is Austin, we need to arrest him," I said.

"Do we have a case?" Jake asked.

"You said he killed five people. Three paedophiles, the Judge and Mike."

"I'm not sure about one of the paedophiles. The two that died where Stevie was found yes, Judge yes, and Mike yes, but Brodie, what evidence do we have?"

I sat back and thought about it. What evidence did we have? Ballistics? Killed with their own weapons, so there was no murder weapon to speak of. Fingerprints on the guns? Forensics hadn't come back yet so it was possible. Trace evidence? Nil. Witnesses? Neither Stevie nor Scott had seen the murders committed.

Hell, we didn't have a lot. Our only hope was prints.

"You're right, we don't have a lot," I replied. "Where do you think Austin has taken the Priest?"

"I'd say he took the Priest to find out where they shipped his daughter," Jake said.

"Igor," I said.

"Based on the orders, it's a likely destination."

"Let's go then," I said.

"Hold your horses, Brucey. We can't just go into New South Wales and storm the home of some suspected crime boss. Monique would have a fit. I'll call her to organise a raid, but she'll want her New South Wales counterparts in on it."

Jake paced the hospital café as he talked on the phone. Each time he passed, I caught a snippet of his conversation with Monique. As the call grew longer, I became increasingly concerned with what appeared to be our boss's reluctance.

Jake hung up the call and sat down, staring at his half-drunk cup of coffee, which had now gone cold.

"What's the verdict?" I asked.

"She said New South Wales police have been investigating Palanok Investments for years now. They suspect he's involved in trafficking drugs and prostitution. They had some witnesses, ex-employees that had turned State witness, but they were murdered before the trial so the State had to drop the case."

"What the hell are we dealing with here?" I asked.

"It's big. Everyone who's tried to bring him down is dead!" Jake exclaimed. "Monique's trying to get approval for us to search the residences and question him about the phone and the orders. She advised against a raid. She seems to think he has someone in his pocket, high up in the New South Wales Police Force. She believes he would get tipped off over any potential raid by them."

"Well he obviously has more than one informant, not just Mike," I said. "Will they get tipped off if we go?"

"For our sake, let's hope not," Jake replied.

I kept the possibility of the Priest being our shooter to myself. The more I thought about it the less probable it seemed.

When Jake's phone did finally ring, it was Hayley, not Monique. She was checking in to make sure Jake was all right. He had been slack in reporting to her. She always worried about him when he was away.

"Honey, I have to go, I promise I'll call you soon," Jake said, taking the phone away from his ear and looking at the screen. "Babe, I have another call I need to take." He hung up and accepted the new call. This time, it was Monique.

"What's the plan?" he asked.

When the conversation ended and he had he hung up, he was all smiles.

"Ok! She's got us a permit to search the residence and suggests that we interview him about the phone. New South Wales police are picking us up at Jenolan and taking us there."

"Tactical?" I asked. After the last time I'd gone into a property looking for a hostage, I really wanted Tactical on the scene.

"No, just detectives. It'll go smoothly, don't panic," Jake said.

I must have looked worried. Jake hugged me, which he hadn't done in a long while.

I was dreading the answer before I asked the question. "How are we getting there?"

Jake smiled, "You're not going to like the answer. Helicopter."

The helicopter looked in good condition, not as if it was going to fall apart mid-flight.

At least that's something, I thought. "How long is this flight?" I asked.

"About four and a half hours. We have to stop in Albury to refuel, then we land at Jenolan," Jake replied. "Igor's place is about 20 minutes' drive from there."

The flight was a lot smoother than I'd expected and before I knew it, we were refuelling.

"Forensics have cleared both scenes, so now we wait to see if they come up with any evidence that will help us link Austin or anyone else to these crimes," Jake said.

He had obviously received an update from one of Grace's crew.

"Let's hope they find something," I replied.

We were only on the ground 15 or 20 minutes before we were

back in the air heading towards the Blue Mountains.

As the helicopter flew inland over forests and old farming home-steads, my heart started to flutter a little. My memories, smells and fears about the cabin from 10 years previously came flooding back, despite the effort I put into keeping them under control. Anxiety combined with a heart condition was not a good combination. It only lasted for a few seconds, but it reminded me of how vulnerable I really was.

Chapter 110

Austin drove north to NSW with the dead Priest slumped and bleeding in the back seat.

He had set the navigation system for the Palanok residence in the Blue Mountains, the address where the Priest had organised Beau to make the delivery. His daughter.

It was nearing 9 am and Austin had been driving for over eight hours. He had hardly slept. His eyes were heavy and despite his sleep deprivation training, there were only so many days he could go without sleep. He needed a quick nap, just half an hour.

He pulled off the main highway and drove about 500 metres up a side road. It was a secluded spot, remote enough for a nap. Austin stared into the brush at the side of the road, seeing only his daughter's face. Then he fell asleep.

The beach came to him, as it always seemed to lately. Sarah was there, as beautiful as ever, hair blowing in the light wind; the smell of the ocean, the waves crashing, the water gently flowing over his bare feet, seeping between his toes. Sarah was staring out to sea. Austin placed his hand on her shoulder, where her skin was soft and smooth.

She turned and smiled as soon as he touched her. Her smile was wide and comforting. "You need to go and get our daughter, before it's too late."

Austin looked up the beach. Mikayla was playing in the sand.

Drawing a heart shape with a stick.

"She needs to be with you, not here with me," Sarah said.

"I don't want to leave, why can't we all stay here together?"

"It's not your time," Sarah replied.

Austin woke in his usual cold sweat. The image of Sarah had been so vivid again; he could smell her, feel her.

He felt he had been asleep for hours. When he looked at the clock he realised he had been asleep for two hours! He was angry with himself. His daughter had been sold to some crime lord and here he was sleeping. He pounded his hands on the dash and yanked the steering wheel back and forth out of sheer frustration.

He had to forget his mistake and move on, before it was too late.

Chapter 111

Igor liked what he saw when he looked at the new girl. She was much prettier than Chloe. He wasn't completely sure what would become of Chloe. At this stage, he thought he would ship her out to the Ukraine. One of his pimps had been requesting a younger girl for the crew he was running. The one thing Igor was confident about was that he would keep the new girl for a long time. Unless she decided to fight him. If she did that, well she would end up in the tunnels with the other bitch, the one who had taken a piece of his ear one night.

Once Alexi had taken her off to clean her up and give her some fresh clothes, he was on his way to 'introduce' himself when he was interrupted by a call on his cell phone. The caller ID read 'Hutch'. The cop's nickname was taken from the 70's TV show *Starsky & Hutch*.

"Yes," Igor answered. He never used his name when he answered his phone.

"You have visitors coming. They'll be there soon and they'll be looking through both properties," the voice said.

"What the hell am I paying you for?" Igor replied.

"They're from Victoria so I have no control. Apparently someone's taken out a few of the Priest's crew," the voice explained.

"How long we got?"

"Half an hour, maybe less. I only found out when they landed. We were kept totally out of the loop on this one."

Igor angrily hung up without another word and turned to Alexi and Shevd. "We need to clean up. Cops are coming. Everything into the tunnels and get Andrei back with the Joker to hide him down there. Make sure he covers the exit so they can't see it from the outside."

"Yes, boss," they replied and immediately got moving to do as they were asked.

"Alexi, put the girls down there too. Make sure everyone down there is tied and gagged. I don't want some scream giving us away.

One moment Mikayla was getting changed into fresh clothes and the next she was being yanked by the arm and thrown over the big guy's shoulders. The other girl, who Mikayla didn't yet know by name, was grabbed by the neck in a lot more vicious and hostile way.

Mikayla couldn't understand what was happening. Chloe began screaming the moment they started to descend the stairs and Mikayla realised why when they came to the room with the table and the hanging corpse. Then Mikayla let out a scream that would have woken the corpse had it not been stifled by Alexi's big hand, squeezing her cheeks together and her mouth shut.

The men hung both girls upside down. Mikayla had never felt terror like this. Her heart was racing and the tears flowed uncontrollably down her cheeks. The thing hanging beside her barely resembled a human being, let alone a girl.

The other girl was hanging on the other side of the corpse. If Mikayla hadn't had a gag in her mouth, she was certain she would have vomited. The smell was disgusting, the worst smell she had ever experienced, and the flies were in their hundreds. Maybe thousands, swarms of them.

* * *

The blood trail led deep into the woods, further than Andrei thought the Joker would have reached with his injury. As he went deeper, the blood was fresher, brighter. Andrei was getting close.

Then it stopped altogether.

Andrei had killed many people in many different wars. But this was the first person he had lost track of. It was also the first time an injured man had climbed a tree to ambush him.

He felt like an idiot. He was standing there looking at a pool of blood on a log trying to locate the next trace, when out of nowhere the fat man landed on him.

Andrei was sent flying and his gun soared out of his hand into the foliage.

Beau hammered both hands down on the Monster's henchman who had been tracking him and then took the man's head and rammed it into the tree trunk, repeatedly. The man stumbled backwards, dazed.

Beau took advantage of his opponent's momentary daze, and unleashed a flurry of body and facial punches.

There was far more fight in the fat Joker than Andrei had anticipated. He clearly wasn't a trained fighter; he just fought with brute force.

It took Andrei a few seconds to gather his arms in a position that would adequately protect his head. Then he could begin to feel the punches two from the left, then one big punch from the right. This series continued several times. Two and one. Two and one.

Andrei timed his strike.

Two and one, and as the one recoiled, he struck hard and fast, palm out, hitting him flush in the nose. Beau wasn't just dazed, he was nearly out of it. His vision came and went and when he could see, his eyes were teared up. Blood streamed down his face and down the back of his throat. He had lost sight of his attacker. He resorted to swinging haymakers, hoping one would connect. All they did was use up what little energy Beau had left.

Andrei calmly headed over to search for his gun in the scrub where it had fallen. He climbed over a downed trunk and landed on a pile of sticks and twigs, which cracked under his weight.

Beau heard the sound and turned and without thinking, rushed in the general direction. With his vision still severely affected, he could not see the fallen tree and hit it at full speed, sending him semi-cartwheeling over the fallen log and on to the other side, crashing into another tree.

Andrei immediately heard the crack of the fat Joker's neck as his body wrapped itself around the tree but the head stayed in position. It was the first time Andrei had seen a man kill himself by running into a tree.

Igor would not be happy with him, he thought. He'd wanted him alive.

Chapter 112

Jake and I were picked up by two NSW vice detectives. One was called Deakins and the other Hutchinson. "You can call me Deak and we call him Hutch, you know, that TV cop show from back in the 70s? Never thought I'd be working with a star," Deak joked.

Deak was the senior of the two by about 10 years, I guessed. He was a lot less fit than Hutchinson, and going bald, but to his credit he was going graciously, making no attempt to cover his bare head with a comb-over.

Hutchinson had a bit of swag about him; nice new suit, perfect blonde hair, every bit of him resembling a successful businessman rather than a seasoned detective.

"Is this it? Is this all the help we get when we go to sweep a crime lord's property?" I asked, exasperated.

"We've been down this path ourselves and we came up dry; there was nothing there," Hutchinson answered.

"What my partner is trying to say," said Deak, "is that finding the evidence is really tough. We did a search ourselves. We even had witnesses who said he was trafficking drugs and weapons, but the place was clean."

"We have information he might be trafficking children. Ever had information on that?" I asked.

"That's a new one, it's always been drugs or weapons," Hutchinson replied quickly.

"How far is it to the homestead?" Jake asked.

"About 15 minutes," Deak replied.

The road was bumpy and it wound around the mountain. Maybe it was the ride, or maybe it was the fact that I was six foot four and stuffed into the back of a midsize, either way, it was not the best car ride after a five-hour helicopter flight. My stomach was feeling the effects. For a second, I thought I was going to bring up my last meal.

"We'll need a vehicle," Jake said.

"What for? I thought you were just asking a few questions and searching the two houses. That's what we were told. Right, Deak?" Hutchinson said.

"That's what we were told," Deak confirmed.

"You seem a little defensive there, Detective." Jake deliberately didn't use the nickname we'd been given. "We're not stepping on your toes, are we?"

"Hell no, I was just worried I hadn't done something I should have," Hutchinson replied. "Believe me, we want this scumbag as bad as the next guy. Just not sure why you'll need a car, that's all," he added.

"We might need to stay in town a couple of days. Can you organise one for us or not?" Jake replied bluntly.

"Yeah, we have another detective meeting us there. He can come back with us after the search and you can have his vehicle."

"Perfect," Jake said.

I had always imagined a crime lord's home as being one of sheer opulence. While this one was massive, it was not opulent from the outside. It was a graceful heritage home. The security guard waved us through and the gates opened to admit us. The driveway wound up to the homestead, which sat high on the crest.

What looked like two private security guards met us at the door.

"Can we please see the warrant?" one of the guards asked.

"We would just like to ask Mr Pavlychko a few questions," Jake said.

"Mr Pavlychko is a very busy man. Any questions for him can be sent to his legal counsel." The man handed him a card.

"I'll raise you," Jake replied.

He handed across a copy of the warrant Monique had organised before we boarded the helicopter. Then he reached for the front door handle, but the guard stepped across, blocking Jake's access. "I suggest you move, before I move you," Jake said. He stood a good 10 centimetres taller and when he was eye to eye with someone, Jake was a menacing figure.

The guard thought about standing his ground, but then reconsidered.

Jake walked in as if he owned the place, and I followed.

When we stepped inside the house, it was as if they were all waiting for us. There was a room full of businessmen, yet little to no business was taking place.

"My name is Igor, why do you wish to search my home?" he asked.

"It's in the warrant, but the highlights are: kidnapping, human trafficking, drug trafficking, and the sale of prohibited firearms," Jake answered.

"It's absurd, my business is legitimate," Igor replied.

"What exactly is your business?" Jake questioned.

"We import and export products all around the world but they are legitimate businesses. Mainly computer equipment," Igor detailed.

"How many employees do you have?" Jake asked.

"A hundred and seventy-two, why?" Igor asked.

"Do they all get company phones?" Jake returned.

"Some do, but not all, it depends on how long they've been working for us. Is this leading somewhere, Detective?" Igor asked.

"Do you know a priest by the name of Peter O'Riley in Ballarat?"

"Yes, we supported his outreach program for reforming offenders. Is he ok?" Igor pretended to be concerned.

"Can you provide me a list of your company mobile phone numbers?" Jake asked.

"I don't have any of them on me but I could get them to you. I really don't know why you're asking me these questions," Igor said.

"We have reason to believe one of your company phones has been used to place orders for children, from the Priest in Ballarat."

"That's disturbing. I have never really trusted priests. They always seem to be up to no good. We will provide you with any support you need," Igor replied, knowing as long as they didn't find the girls, the phone would lead nowhere. It was the other evidence that would seal their conviction. "Where would you like to start your search?" he asked.

"We will go room by room," Jake said. "You're welcome to watch, but get in the way or prevent us from going somewhere, and you will be detained," Jake warned them all.

Igor allocated one of his security guys to show us around, not that we needed him to guide us. We were going to look anywhere and everywhere. Any piece of the puzzle would do.

We searched the house room by room, all 570 square metres of it, and all of it was clean. Not even a joint, let alone kids in chains.

We searched the grounds, wire fence to wire fence, all 25 acres. There were hay bales and a tractor, and one huge compound that housed what seemed like hundreds of dogs and one large machinery shed. After Beau's house, we were looking for secret rooms everywhere, but there were none to be found.

After finding the hidden treasures at the Priest's, we even searched inside books, looking for photos or the like. We took their computers to be analysed.

The roof cavity only had spiders and more spiders.

There seemed to be nothing of use.

We were about to go inside and talk to Igor and tell him we had found nothing, when Jake pulled me aside.

"What do you think?" he asked me.

"They seemed to be expecting us, don't you think?" I asked.

"Yes, my thought exactly, as if they were tipped off." Jake pulled out his mobile and dialled the number that we had found at the Priest's. The phone from which all the orders were placed. Jake dialled. I heard the recorded message, 'the number you have called could not be reached at this time'.

"You realise we could be looking at the next victim? Whoever killed the Judge and the superintendent, this is his likely next stop," Jake said.

"Unless we're at the killer's," I replied.

"Unlikely, he wouldn't have made it back in time," Jake said.

"He could have sent someone."

"Let's rattle his cage. You keep an eye on his body language," Jake said.

We stepped back inside and met Igor in the library. He was sitting there pretending to work.

"You're all clear. If you could please follow up those phone numbers for us, it would be of great assistance," Jake said.

"My pleasure, I will assure it's done as soon as possible," Igor replied.

"Oh, and one other thing," Jake said, as if it was an afterthought, "we think it's important that you are made aware that your safety could be compromised."

Igor frowned, unsure how that could be.

"Why would I be in danger?" he asked.

"Well, someone has killed the Ballarat superintendent as well as the chief magistrate. Both were involved in the outreach program you sponsor."

"Why do you think that affects me?" Igor asked.

"We haven't been able to locate Father O'Riley either. As you were all involved in the outreach program, we believe you may be next."

"Any ideas who it is?" Igor asked.

"Not yet, but if you have any concerns you should call us immediately," Jake replied.

"Will do," Igor said.

"You have a lot of dogs, what do you use them for?" I asked.

"Hunting wild pigs," Igor replied in a cold and threatening manner.

We left the residence. Hutchinson and Deak looked pleased, as if to say, told you so.

"You still want to stay?" Deak asked.

"Yes, at least for 24 hours," Jake replied.

After Deak and Hutchinson's colleague arrived and the car was handed over to us, Jake and I sat waiting in the car opposite the front gate. I wasn't sure what Jake was expecting to happen or why we were still there.

"What are we doing here, buddy? There's nothing here."

"Something isn't right. Everything was too neat, like they were expecting guests. You thought the same."

"Yeah, but there was nothing there. If they had any kids hidden, they must have moved them off-site. They're not going to go there now, with us out the front, they're not that stupid."

"Call Deak. Tell him we're leaving, that we're going for dinner and then back to the airfield. They can pick the car up from there in the morning. Say we'll leave the car key with the duty manager."

I made the call and passed on the information, just as Jake had asked. He waved at the gate security, thanking them for their assistance, started the vehicle and headed off.

I was thinking about what I would have for dinner, desperate for a nice steak, when Jake turned the vehicle in a totally different direction from what I expected.

"Where are we going?" I asked.

"It's called foxing. We both think they were tipped off and I'm hoping they'll get the call that we've left," Jake replied.

"How does this help us?" I asked.

"If they do have the girls, I'm hoping they'll move them. If they don't, I'll show up again at 6 am unannounced and have another look."

We had driven around to the west side of the property. We could see the side of the home sitting up on the crest. There were four square paddocks between us and the house. The two paddocks closest to the homestead sloped down from the peak of the home and then levelled out to two horse paddocks. Sitting in the far left paddock was their own helicopter. We could have landed here, I thought to myself.

Everything looked the same as when Jake and I had inspected the property, everything except the tractor. It had been moved back into the shed. Probably because of the thunderstorm that was on its way.

Even though dusk was still a few hours off, the sky was darkening with gathering storm clouds.

* * *

Igor had been pacing the library waiting for the phone to ring to give him the all-clear, but no call had come. The library had been swept for bugs; it was all clear. His staff continued to sweep the rest of the house, but it was a slow process and Igor didn't want to be confined to his library for much longer.

He had a new toy downstairs and he wasn't allowed to play with it. It reminded him of when he was a boy; they would celebrate Christmas on Christmas Eve, yet he would never get to play with his presents until the next day.

Alexi and Shevd were sitting in the library opposite Igor's desk.

"What are we going to do with the phone?" Alexi asked.

"Do you know who ordered the phone and put it in the company name?" Igor asked.

Alexi stood up, all six foot eight of him. "It's my fault, boss. I asked Rostov to pick up a ghost phone. I don't know what he did, I thought it was a clean phone."

"You gave the order; it wasn't followed. That was his choice. Tomorrow we will meet with Rostov and fix the situation," Igor replied.

"I will ensure that the phone doesn't lead to you in any way. Perhaps it would be best if Rostov wasn't around to give his version of events," Alexi said.

"Make sure he's found with evidence other than the phone, in fact, use Chloe. I'm sick of her anyway. Kill her, and leave no evidence," Igor ordered.

"I will fix it, boss," Alexi said.

"What happened to Andrei? Did he bring the Joker back?" Igor asked.

"Andrei is in the tunnels. The Joker tried to kill him. During the scuffle, the Joker tripped over, hit a tree trunk and broke his neck."

"What is done is done. Make sure he is buried deep. Send Andrei to clean it up, after all, it is his mess."

"Yes boss," Alexi replied.

Igor's phone vibrated on his desk. It was a message from Hutch.

All clear, the trouble from the south have left with their tails between their legs

"They're gone, Shevd. When the sweep is complete bring the girls back up and check the motion sensor is still active on the south tunnel exit."

Shevd nodded. "When will they be finished with the bug sweeping?" he asked.

"Go ask them, 'quietly'," Igor emphasised.

Shevd slid the study door open and slipped through, closing it behind him.

"Who do you think killed the Judge and Mike?" Alexi asked Igor.

"My bet is on the Priest. He was probably getting heat and he cashed in his own insurance policy. He wouldn't let them turn him in. I'd say he's disappeared because he doesn't want to be found. You know what they do to paedophile priests on the inside," Igor said.

"We will need a new supplier," Alexi said.

"Don't panic, business will continue. There will be plenty of rock spiders to supply us and there will be plenty of cops who won't be able to refuse the money."

Alexi laughed. "I'm sure you're right."

"Until we find the replacements, we will just have to use our connections in other states a little more," Igor said. "Now I want you to do me a favour. Find the Priest. Ensure he can't do our company any harm. We need to silence him."

"I will ensure it is done. I will put the feelers out for him."

Shevd opened the door. "We are all clear, they didn't bug us."

"I will go tell Andrei to bury the Joker and get the girls while I'm down there," Alexi said.

"Good," Igor replied.

Chapter 113

Austin pulled the car over onto another remote road near the village of Edith. He was waiting for nightfall. Marcus had rung to tell him the police had found the superintendent and the Judge. He also informed him that a warrant had been executed on Igor's properties by Victorian Police. Significantly, the police had found nothing.

"Maybe she's not there?" Marcus said.

"She's there somewhere, surely, and if she isn't, they'll tell me where she is whether they want to or not," Austin replied.

"I can't keep feeding you this information. Someone will find out eventually and there's only so much I can erase," Marcus said.

"I understand. Jump out when you need to," Austin replied.

"Let's see where Igor leads and then we'll reassess," Marcus said. "But don't go storming the place now! There's police still floating about."

"Don't worry, I was waiting until tonight. If they do have the children and they want to move them, they'll probably do it then." My guess is they'll head straight for the helicopter."

Austin suspected the police would be following his trail. He had left too many dead people behind for them not to start putting some of the pieces together.

He had Googled Igor's address and noted on street view that the house was big, and surrounded by several acres. The only way he'd be able to get in undetected was through the forest at the rear. It would provide him with the cover to gain entry into the home. He had already saved two of the missing kids and he was confident Mikayla would be in there, somewhere. If not, the predators would tell him where she was.

Austin was approaching the night knowing there was a very real possibility that he could be arrested or killed without discovering Mikayla's wellbeing or location. But he had no choice; he would do whatever it took. His personal safety was of little consequence. Mikayla's safety was his only thought.

He set his watch alarm for 10 pm, released the boot lock and removed his duffel bag. He laid his weapons out. He had decided he would only take the two pistols and the sniper rifle. Even though they were all silenced, they would still make a slight noise.

The rifle had a night-vision scope, top of the line. He attached it, loaded the rifle and placed it back in the boot. Better to be safe than sorry, he thought, as he slipped the bulletproof vest over his head and slid his first pistol into the holster. He placed the second pistol into his belt holster. Finally, he removed his night-vision goggles and fitted them on his head. When he needed them, he would just flick them down.

For now, he could do nothing but wait and soon enough, he dozed off.

Everything was the same; the smell, the wind, the sea, the water over his feet, his wife's bright smile, and of course the warning, except this time it was more urgent. "Hurry or you will lose her for good. This is it, wake up and go."

Austin woke. He was in more than just a cold sweat; he was soaked. His watch alarm was screaming at him, over and over. He looked out into the darkness and then drove the seven kilometres to the area where the property met the forest on the west side. There were four large paddocks between the forest and the homestead.

He managed to manoeuvre the car about 50 metres into the forest.

Weaving through the trees was harder than he imagined, especially with the headlights off and only the moonlight to guide him. But now, the car was well camouflaged amongst the trees.

He removed the Priest from the back seat and laid him on the ground next to the tyre. He was now more than 10 hours dead and smelling, but it was nothing new to Austin.

He opened the boot, removed his rifle and slung it over his right shoulder. Then he removed the jerry can he had filled at his last petrol stop and tied it over his shoulder with one of the Priest's shoelaces.

He was set to go.

Chapter 114

Chloe had almost become used to the smell of rotting flesh, but she would never get used to the swarms of buzzing flies crawling all over her face.

When the big guy finally came for them, Chloe was forced to walk while he carried Mikayla over his shoulder. She struggled to keep up. When he took the steps to the library two at a time, she stumbled and was dragged up the last few steps, scraping her knees.

Arriving back in the main house there were two things she noticed; one, it was dark outside, two, it was raining. Most importantly, it was heavy rain and it sounded like it was going to storm.

Chloe had realised the second Mikayla entered the room that Igor's use for her was over and soon she too would be the rotting corpse in the tunnels. They had to escape. The impending storm could be their only chance.

Alexi threw them in the room, saying, "Get cleaned up."

"We need to get out of here. We need to escape, before we end up like that girl in the tunnels," Chloe whispered as soon as they were alone. "Let's just make a run for it."

"They have guards everywhere," Mikayla replied.

"During the storms, they come inside and stand by the fire, it's our best chance. They can't know we're gone or they'll set the dogs onto us, and they have a lot of them."

"How long have you been here?" Mikayla asked.

"About two weeks," Chloe said.

"Did you ever meet the girl in the tunnels?" Mikayla asked.

"Not while she was alive," Chloe said.

"If either of us gets a chance, we'll make a run for it then. We can't die here," Mikayla said.

"Ok, but let's try to escape together," Chloe said. "If he tries to do stuff to you, let him. If you fight him, he'll get the big guy to take you to the tunnels and he'll beat you bad."

Mikayla didn't need to ask her if she had been raped; she knew that Chloe was speaking from experience.

Thunder cracked overhead.

* * *

The heavy rain was going to affect his plan; nonetheless, Austin had to proceed.

He carried the Priest's body through the woods. It was only about 500 metres but the terrain was tough going, even with his night-vision goggles. He rested the body next to a tree while he took a look at the house though his scope. He noticed there were people on the balcony. They looked like personal security guards. He shifted the scope and saw a dull glow appear between the spaces in the stacks of hay. He could just make out a gate behind the hay. Where did it lead? he wondered.

By the time he had finished sweeping the property through the scope, he had seen six men outside and at least four more inside. He was going to be outnumbered ten to one.

Austin negotiated the electrified fence surrounding the paddock and dragged the Priest through after him. He had sighted the dog house through the scope, and while he didn't have time to kill them all, he needed to delay the guards' access to them. He placed simple cable ties in between all the doors. That would slow them down a great deal.

When he reached the bottom of the paddock, he sprinted to the hay, took a large armful and returned to where he had left the Priest. He rolled the Priest onto the hay, removed his silver cross and began to pour petrol all over the body.

Then he hung the cross around a stick and dug it into the ground. He poured a trail of petrol away from the body towards the gate.

He lit the petrol.

The flames instantly lit up the night sky, even in the rain. Then they took hold and the Priest's body began to burn.

Austin couldn't just stay there; he needed them to come looking for him so he could search the house. He sprinted from the fire past the helicopter back to the hay.

He lay patiently camouflaged within the hay.

Now he had to wait.

* * *

Igor was about to take Mikayla to his room when he saw a large bonfire burning in his back paddock. Was this the Priest coming for them as the police had warned him? he wondered. He would deal with whoever it was.

His men came rushing in from the balcony.

"Alexi! Take three of the security team and go see who is there. Bring them to me dead or alive. Shevd, go to your nest in the attic. If you see anything running around in the woods, kill it," he ordered.

"Alexi, lock the girls in their room, find who is out there and kill them."

As Alexi left, four more members of his private security came rushing inside.

"Stay with the boss!" Alexi ordered.

Another three guards came running in. "You three, one at each door, stay inside, stay low, turn off the lights," Alexei said as he left.

Igor sat on his bed surrounded by his three guards. The house was in darkness. He waited, listening for any sound of conflict. He would have felt better if he had heard some gunfire. Then at least he would have known they had located someone. A rattlesnake loose on the property was very unnerving.

It seemed like an eternity, but in reality it was only a couple of minutes before Alexi returned. When he came through the door, Igor's heart skipped a beat. His mind had told him that the next person through that door would be the Priest, and when the door opened for a split second, that was who he saw. It was Alexi holding a silver cross out in front of him.

"I found the Priest," Alexi said.

"Did you take him to the tunnels?" Igor asked.

"He's burning in the back paddock. Someone set him on fire and left this for us." He handed Igor the cross.

"A message," Igor said.

A large bang cracked overhead. Gunfire? Igor asked himself. No, it was thunder. Normally Igor was fearless, yet tonight he was unusually skittish. He reminded himself that he had killed rivals before and he would again.

When you throw down the gauntlet, be prepared for the fight, Igor thought.

* * *

When the grass burst into flames, Jake and I were taken by surprise. We suspected whoever was killing the Priest's crew had arrived, or that or it was the Priest himself.

"Did you see anyone?" Jake asked.

"No, just flames," I replied.

Jake jumped out of the car and took cover behind the passenger rear guard. I went behind the passenger front wheel.

"Tell me if you see anyone," Jake said.

All the lights in the house went off, and we were in total darkness.

"They've gone into lockdown. There are two sides here now and we'll be in the middle, so be careful," Jake said.

"Why? Are we going in?" I asked.

"We're police. It's what we do," Jake said. "Why don't I go to the back door and you go to the front, that way..." Jake was interrupted by four men who appeared in the paddock seemingly out of nowhere.

"Where the hell did they come from?" Jake whispered.

"I think they came from behind the haystack," I said. "There were no downstairs rooms, were there?" I asked.

"No, maybe they have a secret room somewhere just like Beau," Jake replied.

"I'm so sick of hidden passages and this Scooby Doo shit," I replied.

"Let's go," Jake replied, laughing at my Scooby Doo comment. "Stay close to me," he added.

We were a good 500 metres away from the fire. We couldn't see who the individuals were, but we could see that they were armed, guns pointing in all different directions.

They studied the fire for about 30 seconds before making their way back to the house. The big man was in the lead.

Jake passed me a vest from the boot.

"Where's yours?" I asked.

"The car only has one," Jake replied.

I handed it back. "Jake, you take it."

He refused, as I knew he would.

"Jake, it's not for me, it's not for you, it's not even for Hayley. It's for Indiana." My arm was still extended holding the vest out to him. After a slight pause, he reluctantly took it.

"You stay behind me and do everything I say," Jake said as he put the vest on.

"Of course," I replied. "Just remember, Jake, watch out for snakes." I smiled.

"Don't go there," he growled.

"Still too soon?" I asked.

"Yep."

"After 10 years, if not now, when?" I asked.

"Give it another 10 years," Jake replied, still traumatised at the thought.

* * *

Austin waited for the four men to pass. Not one of them had even looked in the hay. He stepped into the tunnel, drew his pistol and moved forward. He hadn't been inside a tunnel since Afghanistan and it wasn't something that he wanted to be exploring again. He needed to be quick and clinical about this. When he reached a T-intersection, he wasn't sure whether to go forward, left or right. He stepped left and waited in the shadows. He could hear the men coming back. He had to start picking them off one by one, to even up the numbers.

Three men came running past, all in quick succession. The fourth, who had the duty of closing the gate, came lagging behind. Austin waited for the feet to pass before stepping out and taking him. He put his arm around his throat and before he even had the chance to react, the knife slid straight into his back. Austin quickly withdrew his knife from the man's back and slid it across his throat, holding his hand over the man's mouth to prevent any gurgling cry from escaping. He then dragged him into the depths of the tunnel out of sight.

He saw the other three men continue straight ahead and thought it best to follow. He reached three stone arches. Behind each arch was a large room, big enough to park a bus. It was the middle arch that attracted Austin's immediate attention. He had smelt this smell many times before; it was death, the smell of lingering death.

He looked at the hanging corpse in the middle of the arch, like a decomposing wind chime swinging in the draught that blew up the tunnel from the entrance.

Austin walked up to the hanging girl to check that it wasn't Mikayla. He knew immediately that she had been there for some weeks, if not months. He stepped past her to what appeared to be a torture area. There was a large wooden table laden with knives, meat cleavers, steel rods, pliers, and chains.

Many had died here, probably all children, Austin thought. He moved to the end arch and stepped in. Almost empty, except for a few yellow plastic waste barrels in the corner, with the words 'dog food' painted on them. Austin unclipped the bracket holding the lid on, and lifted it. The smell hit him. It was beyond disgusting; it was so bad he vomited instantly. When he regained his composure, he took another look because he simply couldn't believe his eyes. Dismembered body parts apparently for the dogs to eat.

Austin heard voices, yet with the echoes in the tunnels, he had trouble distinguishing where they were coming from. He ducked down behind the barrels. The men were in the arch where the dead girl was, too close for comfort.

He strained to hear them. It was the police, Foxx and Miller. They were half-smart; after all, they had followed him here.

Austin knew what he was about to do would definitely mean jail but it also meant he had triple the chances of getting Mikayla back. That was his only objective.

He stood up and went to the arch. "Officers, I need your help."

Jake spun away from the hanging girl, his gun pointed directly at Austin.

"Don't shoot me," Austin said.

"Put your gun down," Jake demanded.

"Shhh," Austin gestured, "Remember where we are. It's nine against three."

"It's ten against three," Jake corrected him.

"Not any more," Austin replied.

"Drop your gun," Jake again demanded.

"I just want my daughter. Then you can take me in, but I'm not giving up until she's safe," Austin said.

Jake stood firm.

I stepped between them. Austin could have killed me if he'd wanted to, but I knew he wouldn't. He just wanted his daughter. I imagined if I had kids I'd be in the same desperate position.

"You agree to turn yourself in once it's over?" I asked him.

"Agreed," Austin replied without hesitation.

"He's ok, Jake. He wants what we want. Lower the gun, Jake."

Jake obliged.

"Do you know where they went?" Jake asked.

"No, only that they ran that way," Austin said, pointing down past the third arch.

We took two steps towards the third tunnel. Both Jake and I looked at the barrels in the corner. "Do you know what's in the barrels?" Jake asked.

"Body parts," Austin replied. Then he said, "Let me go first. I'll distract them. Buy you some time to search the residence. In about five minutes you follow, just find Mikayla and anyone else who may be up there."

Jake and I looked at each other and Jake said, "Sounds like a plan. Yell out if you need help."

Chapter 115

Igor was shocked. Who would be waging war on his business if it wasn't the Priest? Maybe a rival, but he couldn't think of anyone who would be so bold and direct.

"Make sure the house is secure," he ordered.

Shevd buzzed Alexi on the intercom. "The police are here. Only the two from Victoria from what I can see. They just crossed the back paddock and headed into the tunnel."

Alexi looked at Igor for a reaction.

"Kill them," Igor said. "Maybe they're in on it with Mike. Maybe the police want to take over the operation." It wouldn't be the first time the police have run a crime syndicate, Igor thought.

Alexi buzzed back. "Igor said shoot them all!"

"Yes, boss," came the reply through the intercom.

Igor asked Alexi, "Where's Andrei? Is he back from burying the fat Joker yet?"

"No, boss," Alexi answered.

"Get him back here now!" Igor demanded.

Alexi nodded. "Will do, boss."

He went to leave but Igor stopped him. "Alexi, wait." Alexei turned to face Igor. "Bring the new girl to me," Igor said.

"Yes, boss."

When Alexi returned, he had Mikayla by the hair. Igor could still hear Chloe screaming in the other room.

He was about to tell Alexi to go and shut her up, but then he thought better of it.

"Why don't you use that noisy bitch as bait?" he suggested. "When the cops come to get her, they'll come face to face with you."

"Good idea," Alexi replied, "I'll tie her to the bed and wait in the bathroom for them."

Alexi left Igor with Mikayla sitting in his room. As he left, he said, "I'll be back when it's over."

He headed in the darkness towards Chloe's room.

Chloe and Mikayla had been sitting together in the room, trying to understand what the commotion was down the hall, but with the thunderstorm raging, they could only catch bits and pieces. When Alexi barged in and took Mikayla, it was totally unexpected. Chloe had seized her opportunity and sprinted for the door, only to get yanked back into the room by her ankles. Alexi then grabbed her by the foot so she was hanging by one leg and then flung her across the bed where she landed in the far corner of the room, collecting the lamp and cutting her leg on the bedside table as she hit the floor.

She watched as Alexi took Mikayla from the room. She was being sent to Igor; there was no doubt about it.

She was still sprawled in the corner when Alexi returned a few minutes later. He had a length of rope in one hand. With the other, he dragged her out of the corner by the hair and slammed her down onto the floor. He quickly tied her hands and feet together using the rope. He left Chloe's mouth untaped.

Send them to me, he thought as he left the room. He entered the bathroom from the adjoining room, Mikayla's, and waited.

Send them to me, he repeated.

Chapter 116

Austin followed their flashlights to the arches and after leaving the detectives, he came to a second T-intersection where one tunnel veered off to the left and one to the right. Or he could go straight ahead.

This was a labyrinth, he thought, and he felt like a little mouse being tested.

He decided to go straight ahead but eventually, after passing a tunnel to his right, he came to a dead end. He turned around and returned to the tunnel leading right. Within 20 metres, he came to a flight of steps heading up to a door.

He stood at the bottom of the steps, thinking. They would be waiting on the other side of the door. He inspected it. The door swung left to right, so he expected whoever was waiting for him would most likely be waiting in the corner. He thought about trying to draw them out, but didn't think they would be stupid enough to make the same mistake twice.

He had wasted enough time. He had stormed many houses. This was no different. He removed his SIG p228s, one in each hand, and fired four shots in quick succession. The door shattered and the hinges flew off and landed somewhere on the stairs above him.

No one returned his fire, so he slowly ascended the steps. About halfway up, he knelt down. Now he would see if they were lying in wait. Austin re-holstered his handguns and removed the rifle from his shoulder. He aimed the sight of the rifle to the bullet hole in the door, hoping to get a glimpse of the other side, using every centimetre of voyeuristic vision available into the library. He caught sight of a man down on one knee, gun pointed at the door. The man looked prepared and calm. Waiting.

He was about to pull the trigger when the man caught a glint of light on the scope and hit the floor. Austin guessed he had moved to the other corner.

He moved up the stairs, drew both his guns again and kicked hard at the door. As soon as his boot left the door, he opened fire.

Vonkov was a loyal member of Igor's private security team. He had been sitting in the library waiting for whoever was on the other side of the door to show themselves. Then he would quickly erase the problem. He almost shat his pants when four shots were fired through the door, the last missing his neck by centimetres. He had expected someone to walk through the door, not shoot through it. He was the one who was supposed to be doing the shooting.

After the shots, he steadied himself; now they would step through. But they didn't. He looked at the hole in the bottom of the door. He couldn't see anyone, but thought he caught a glimmer of reflecting light, from a rifle scope he thought. Dropping down, he crawled to the other side of the library.

And waited.

No one came.

He waited a bit longer.

Where the fuck is this guy? Vonkov wondered.

Without warning, the library door was blasted open and it crashed to the floor. In the darkness, he didn't realise that the hinges had gone.

Vonkov fired several shots from his nine-mil Beretta.

Austin fired twice and dived against the stone wall at the top of the stairs. A bullet skimmed his leg; another flew over his head and ricocheted down into the dark labyrinth of tunnels.

He took a breath, his back as far up against the wall as possible. In the library, he could see parts of the shattered door on the floor, but no waiting gunman. He stuck his head out a little further; no fire came.

He peeked even further and saw a man dragging himself across the floor, leaving a trail of blood behind him. The shooter. Austin had hit him twice. He stepped into the library, approached the crawling gunman and fired once more. It was direct hit at close range and it shattered the man's skull.

Austin stepped over the body in the library doorway and headed down the hall. He had only taken a few steps towards the back of the house when the front door opened and another security guy charged in, firing as he entered.

* * *

We'd only been waiting three minutes when we heard the exchange of gunfire. Jake reacted instantly. By the light of his torch, he located the steps at the end of the right tunnel. I stayed a few metres behind him.

Jake crept forward up the steps, pistol drawn standard style, in a thumbs over thumbs, fingers over fingers grip. As he entered the library, he swept the room with his arms out, finger on the trigger ready to shoot. There was a body on the floor in the doorway.

Jake saw a man run through the front door and fire at someone he couldn't see. Before he could pull the trigger, the man flew backwards through the door. Jake continued to creep forwards towards the entrance hall, poking his head to see beyond the library doorway to look down the hall. Austin was crouched in the alcove under the stairs reloading his gun.

"Seven to go," Austin said.

Jake nodded.

"You go upstairs; I'll clear down here," Austin said.

Jake nodded again and waved me over to him. I had planted

myself at the top of the cellar stairs into the library.

"We're going upstairs. If we find any kids, I want you to take them to the forest. Then just lay low, you got that?"

"Yes," I replied.

As we headed upstairs, more gunfire rang out as Austin made his way through the home. I kept checking behind us. None of Austin's combatants came running up the stairs after us.

We came upon three doors, two on the left, the other at the far end of the hall. The first door on the left was about three metres before the second door and four and a bit metres to the door at the end of the hall.

Jake opened the door. A girl was lying on the floor with her hands and feet bound and tied together. Jake picked her up and passed her to me. "What's you name?" he asked gently.

"Chloe," she said.

"Go," Jake said to me.

I took her and ran. Past the body at the library entrance, back down the stairs to the tunnel, my torch bobbing around. A cold wind swept up the tunnels. The girl clung to me tightly. Even though it was dark outside, as we neared the end of the pitch-black tunnels, the entrance became visible under the night sky.

* * *

Jake didn't realise he was in danger when he handed the child to Brodie. Out of nowhere, a wire came from behind him and pulled tight on his throat. He managed to slip his free hand under the wire to prevent it from choking him. Not many people were as solid as Jake, and very few were bigger, but without even seeing his attacker, he knew he was in trouble when he was lifted off the ground.

The only advantage Jake had was his attacker was using both hands. Jake still had his gun in his right. He reached around and fired the gun under his left armpit, hoping to hit him in the body.

His assailant only choked him tighter. Jake threw himself backwards against him, hoping to get some relief from the strangulation, but this only angered his attacker.

Jake fired again. This time, the big guy cried out in anguish. I hit him! Jake thought.

He fired again, and again, and the big guy groaned in pain and dropped the wire to the floor. Jake stepped away, turned, and aimed at the big guy who was several centimetres taller than he was. Even with three bullet holes in his left side, the big guy made a run at him. Jake only managed to fire one more shot before he was picked up off the floor and slammed into the wall next to the open door. His gun went flying as his hand clipped the door on the way through, the plaster from the wall crumbling around him. He felt blood trickle down the side of his head.

How's this guy still going? Jake thought. I've shot him four times! The man slammed him into the wall again and he couldn't help but think he reminded him of the Hulk.

The big guy's hands were around Jake's throat again, lifting him off the ground. Jake kicked, but because both his feet were off the ground, he couldn't get any traction.

Using what he had with the odds against him, he fought dirty, reaching out and plunging his thumbs into his eyes. The big guy released his hold and as soon as Jake's feet hit the floor, he ran at him with his shoulder and sent him crashing to the floor. He was down for the count, Jake thought. He turned to retrieve his gun from the doorway floor when Austin came into view. Jake smiled at him but Austin yelled, "Down!" Jake hit the floor and Austin fired his own pistol three times before Austin himself was hurled backwards onto the hall floor.

Jake turned. All three shots had hit their mark and the big guy was finally silenced.

Jake checked on Austin. There was no blood; the bullets had hit his vest.

"Fuck, that hurt," Austin said.

"Stay down for a few seconds, regain your breath," Jake advised.

"I think I might have a couple of broken ribs," Austin replied.

"You killed the big guy, if it's any consolation," Jake replied. "We found a girl. Chloe. Brodie's taken her to safety."

"Fantastic. Now let's go find Mikayla and the fucker behind all this," Austin said.

Chapter 117

Shevd had watched the cop run from the tunnel, carrying one of the girls, all hero-like.

Soon he would want to return to the thick of the action. Soon he would want to go back in. Soon he would hear the sound of the gun, and before he could react he would be dead.

Shevd hadn't taken his eye from his scope in minutes. He wanted to see the cop's face when he killed him. All he had to do was wait for him to reappear.

His breathing was steady, his eye focused on the target, his finger relaxed and ready. Even in the heavy rain, he found him. The cop's shoe was sticking out from the base of the tree. He had placed the girl out of danger. Now, Shevd just needed to wait for him to run.

It reminded him of when he was shooting deer as a kid in the Ukraine. "Be quiet and patient," his father would say, "the deer will hear the slightest noise." The deer never knew it was about to be killed. It would be at a stream drinking and then the shot would echo through the forest, but before the deer could react to the sound, it would fall to the ground.

The cop was as helpless as the deer.

I'll get you, Shevd thought.

* * *

The storm had ramped up and it was raining so hard, it felt like hail. I was struggling to see more than a few metres in front of me. The girl bounced in my arms as I ran. We made it to the forest edge and I was hit by the smell of forest freshness and rain. The air was fragrant with the smell of pine trees. Christmas would be here soon, I thought.

The large pine provided Chloe with plenty of cover from the storm. I untied her and covered her with my jacket. "You will be safe here," I said.

She sat silently, curled up into a ball.

In the distance I could hear not only gunfire, but voices, loud voices, yelling. There were more children here somewhere, but how many perpetrators were left? The only thing we knew for sure was that we had found the spider's nest. I looked at the base of the tree. They were hell-bent on getting out of here. They were not planning on giving up. There was no jail for them. They knew it was death for them if they couldn't escape.

"Mikayla, you need to go back for Mikayla," Chloe said, quivering with the cold.

I knew there were more kids and I had to go back. I couldn't leave Jake. I had to go back. I had to do my job. I had to help. I would never forgive myself if something happened to Mikayla or Jake.

The thought of the tunnels terrified me, the smell of death; it was the cabin all over again, the fear of the unknown and the darkness, the fear of death. I pushed the fear aside and took a deep breath to steady myself. The smell of the pines once again made its presence felt. It was a beautiful smell and I took in as much oxygen as possible ready for the sprint to the tunnels.

I darted out from the tree. I had taken three steps before an ear-piercing crack echoed through the night.

Chapter 118

As Austin and Jake stood in the hall staring at the door at the end, an ear-piercing crack echoed above them.

"That was a sniper rifle," Austin said immediately. "There's a shooter in the attic."

Jake's thoughts immediately turned to Brodie and a chill ran down his spine. He had to push the thought out of his head and focus on what he had to do now.

"How can I get up into the roof?" he asked Austin.

"There might be alternative access from the laundry room downstairs," Austin suggested, "rather than the stairs the shooter will have taken to get up there."

"You read my mind," Jake replied.

He rushed downstairs towards the laundry room, seeing two bodies sprawled one on top of each other. By his calculation, there were four criminals left.

As he entered the laundry, he revised his count to three. There was another body, gun still in hand, his torch on. A single gunshot wound to the head had ended his resistance. Jake reached up, pulled the cord for the ladder and brought it down as quietly as possible. Whoever's up there will be expecting me, he thought.

He climbed the ladder slowly and quietly and peeked through the opening. Seeing no one, he shone his torch into the darkness. A blanket and a rifle lay in front of the lever window. The room seemed empty and there was no sign of the shooter.

Jake moved further into the roof cavity to get a better look. He had his gun just in front of his face ready to discharge at the slightest movement. Before he had moved another step, the shooter rushed out of the darkness. The silver glint of the gun caught Jake's immediate attention. His reflexes lightning fast, faster than he or his attacker could possibly imagine, Jake managed to knock the attacker's arm down and when the gun discharged, the bullet only grazed his already injured thigh. Before his attacker could get a second shot off, Jake slammed the attacker's arm hard against the timber beam, sending the weapon flying into the darkness. His attacker quickly resorted to equalling the odds by kicking Jake's hand hard and sending the pistol flying into a corner. Jake was yanked up by his throat. "I just killed your mate. You're next." The man was big, although not as big as the brute who had almost killed him in the girl's room. He was about Jake's size. Jake didn't know if he had the fitness to go toe to toe again. It didn't seem he had much choice.

The man was punching him hard in the kidneys.

"Your partner didn't even know what was coming. The look of surprise on his face, it was so exciting, but so short. He died quickly." He sounded disappointed that Brodie hadn't suffered more.

* * *

Andrei had just finished burying the fat Joker when he heard gunfire coming from the homestead. He headed back immediately, stumbling across a black Chrysler dumped in the woods and noticing a bonfire in one of the paddocks. Unwelcome guests.

He saw Shevd nail one of them as he was running for the homestead.

Andrei had survived four wars and had killed a great many people, but one thing he never did was put himself in a position where he might get caught in the crossfire. He wasn't about to start now.

He waited patiently in the dark forest. He was going to see how this played out before he went in guns blazing. Shevd was a nutcase with an itchy trigger finger. He wasn't going to test his loyalty by running across the open paddock too.

* * *

Austin was standing outside the door at the end of the hall.

He knew his daughter was on the other side. He didn't know how he knew, he just did. Parental instinct. He approached the door handle, taking it lightly in his fingertips. His arm was outstretched to protect his body from attack through the door.

He turned the handle and swung the door inwards. His daughter was standing there, in nothing but a t-shirt and undies. She was crying.

Igor was sitting on the bed behind her with a knife to her throat.

"Daddy," Mikayla sniffled.

"Well, didn't I pick the right hostage! Looks like I have the advantage," Igor said.

"Alexi! I have him!" Igor called.

"If you're looking for the big guy, he's busy trying to put his brains back inside his skull," Austin said calmly.

"How about you drop your weapon, or I'll cut her open from ear to ear," Igor said menacingly.

The knife was pressing against her soft delicate skin. The slightest movement from the little man behind her would cut her throat. Austin couldn't risk shooting him. He knew he would hit him, but the chance he might slit her throat as he fell backwards was too great.

"Why don't you be a man and face me without using a child as a shield," Austin said quietly.

"I don't think that would be very good strategically for me right now," Igor replied.

"Should have expected it, all you Russians are cowards," Austin said.

"I am Ukrainian," Igor replied proudly.

"Even worse. At least the Russians have pride. You guys don't know the meaning of the word." Austin was trying to get him riled up.

"No, we are just not stupid. I do not need to fight you. I have your daughter. Why waste my energy? Why give up my advantage? I think it's time you put the gun down or I kill her, now," Igor growled. "I was just leaving."

He stood up. He was only about five foot five and of slight build.

"I'm not going to let you leave with my daughter," Austin said calmly.

"I don't think you really have a choice," Igor said.

"You know, if you flee, I will find you."

"Maybe, but will she still be alive when you do?" Igor taunted.

He manoeuvred Mikayla towards the door, the knife still pressed tight against her throat. Then he exited the room and backed up the hall.

The fight upstairs continued and then a loud bang was followed by a crash and Jake and Shevd came crashing through the celling and bouncing off the kitchen bench to land on the tiles below. Austin spun around and saw that neither man seemed to be winning.

"Looks like your cop friend is in trouble," Igor said, "what are you going to do, help him, or save your daughter?" he mocked.

Austin owed Jake no favours, but he had done the math; if Jake died, the man he was fighting would set his sights on him, and then it would be two against one. He could kill the guy easily but then it would provide the little man with the opportunity to slip away. Where would he go? To the helicopter? The woods? The tunnels? Probably the helicopter, with his daughter as insurance.

Whichever option he chose, Igor would still have Mikayla. He would still have the advantage.

He had to decide quickly.

"It'll be ok, sweetie, I'll see you again soon," he called to the retreating figure of his daughter.

He turned his back on her then, the hardest thing he had ever had to do, and jumped the railing, landing just outside the kitchen. Out of the corner of his eye, he saw Igor lead his daughter through the library and into the tunnel. What Austin had decided to do was the only way to get her out alive, he persuaded himself. He would save Jake and then he would save his daughter.

He heard Mikayla scream, "No Daddy! Don't leave, don't let him take me!"

The words hurt more than any wound he had ever suffered, but it was the only way out.

He entered the kitchen to see Jake backed up against the oven, his attacker about to run him through with a knife.

He rushed up behind him. No hesitation, no time to waste. He took the hand holding the knife and twisted it back on itself, at the same time grabbing the attacker's head with his other hand and ramming it into the glass range hood. Shards of glass pierced the man's forehead and smashed to the floor. Jake grasped a large fragment and rammed it into his opponent's inner thigh. Blood sprayed from the gash.

The man didn't stand a chance.

Austin rammed his elbow down hard on his extended arm, breaking it. The man screamed in pain.

Jake took advantage of his freedom and scrambled towards his service pistol, which was lying several metres away on the floor. He was about to issue his standard call, "Freeze!" But he was too late. Austin had taken the kitchen knife from the man's hand and slammed it into his neck. The shooter fell to the floor. Blood flowed onto the floor as if from a leaking tap.

"I'm going after Mikayla!" Austin panted. "Take my rifle and go up to the attic. If you get a clear shot, take it. He'll be focusing on me, not you. Whatever happens, don't let him board that helicopter!" He moved quickly through the library and into the tunnels.

Jake moved a lot slower, having sustained two beatings, a cracked rib and damage to his leg. He collected the rifle, headed to the laundry and climbed the ladder back into the attic. There was a huge hole where he and the shooter had fallen through. He had to make sure that when he jumped, he landed on a beam so that he didn't fall through the celling again.

He jumped and for a split second, thought he had overshot it. But he landed on the beam like an Olympic gymnast.

He removed the gun from his shoulder holster and laid it on the window ledge. He looked through the scope of Austin's rifle and saw Igor running towards the woods away from the homestead. The helicopter was in Jake's line of sight and because he couldn't tell which option of escape Igor had chosen, he decided to eliminate one for him.

He fired several shots into the windscreen of the helicopter and then three more into the motor. It was a good choice. Igor veered away from the helicopter and the incoming bullets and headed into the forest instead, dragging Mikayla closer to him to prevent any chance of being picked off.

Jake aligned the sight, hoping for a clear shot. But he couldn't risk it. Mikayla was too close; he might hit her.

He watched as Igor continued running with Mikayla.

Then he saw Austin appear from the tunnel and run after them.

Unable to get a clear shot, he knew his best course of action was to go and help Austin. He gathered Austin's rifle and by the time he had exited the tunnels, the three of them had disappeared into the woods.

Jake was struggling to run. He reached the spot where Brodie was lying, then paused and checked his pulse. It was weak but it was still present.

He raced over to the helicopter as fast as his gimpy leg would carry him and called for backup and an ambulance. He chanced another look over at Brodie but he had to hurry. He had to catch up with Igor and Mikayla.

Scrambling through the fence, he headed into the woods in pursuit. The terrain was tough going on his injured leg but he pushed on regardless. He couldn't see them. It was too dark. Then he saw what looked like the outline of a rocky ridge away on the horizon. Maybe they were headed there?

He sat on a nearby log to gather himself, placing Austin's rifle at his side. How could he have forgotten the scope? He picked it up again and placed the scope against his eye, scanning the ridge. Austin was manoeuvring between the trees. Jake scanned ahead of Austin. There they were! Igor was holding a gun in his right hand – he must have collected it on his escape – and with his left, he was still holding tightly onto Mikayla.

It looked like Igor was running out of ground to retreat to. Soon, the woods hit the water catchment. Surely he wasn't planning on swimming across it? A stand-off was imminent.

Jake lay down on the ground, checked his mag; two rounds left. Good, he thought, I only need one shot. He rested his check against the butt and kept his eye focused against the scope.

He was waiting for the prime shot. He couldn't risk Mikayla getting injured.

* * *

Austin was within striking distance.

"There's nowhere else to run, little man. It's over," Austin said.

Igor spun around and faced Austin, his gun against Mikayla's temple.

"I guess you're right. Neither of us wins," Igor said.

"You win this time, boss," said a strange voice out of the darkness.

Austin twisted to his right.

A tall man stood in the shadows, his gun pointed at Austin's head. "Andrei, kill him."

Where had this guy come from? Austin wondered. He thought he had killed them all.

No time for debate.

Austin reacted by aiming his gun at Andrei rather than at Igor. Andrei hesitated.

"Just shoot him!" Igor ordered.

"Shoot!"

* * *

Jake didn't see the other man until Austin spun around and pointed his gun at him.

Without missing a beat, Jake squeezed the trigger.

A loud crack broke through the night air. He watched through the scope as Igor's head whiplashed backwards. Then he adjusted the scope over to the other man. Before Jake could set his sight on the mystery man, three more shots rang out.

Jake lost sight of Austin.

When he finally saw the mystery man, he was coming straight towards him and he had to duck for cover. The man was firing continually.

Jake had only one shot left.

He took cover behind a tree. Three more shots rang out. One passed his nose. One just missed his back. He stole a look around the tree. The man was now about seven metres away and gaining.

The mystery man continued his movement towards Jake, continually firing.

Bullets kept thudding into the tree at Jake's back. Others flew near his face.

Jake was pinned down.

Between shots, Jake stole another look. The man was closer; too close to use the scope now.

Then he heard footsteps.

He risked another glance.

The man was out in the open. He had to act now.

He could hear the man pause in his advance, planning his next move.

Jake aimed quickly with his naked eye and fired.

His aim was true and the bullet pierced the man's chest just left of centre. He dropped to the forest floor instantly.

Jake looked through the scope again. He could see both Austin and Mikayla on the ground. Austin was still but Mikayla looked as if she was moving.

He headed up the hill. He didn't know how much longer he could stand up.

Reaching them, he saw that Mikayla was pinned under her father. He knelt down beside them.

"He shot my dad," Mikayla cried.

Jake rolled him off his daughter and felt for a pulse. There was a strong one.

"Austin!" Jake called.

Jake rolled him back over and lifted up his shirt. Three bullets were buried in the back of his bulletproof vest. He had dived in front of his daughter to prevent her from getting hit.

Without his vest he'd be dead.

Austin came to with a deep breath and a sigh of anguish.

"You better get out of here," Jake said.

"I thought you were going to arrest me," Austin replied.

"I never saw you take the car. Dump it. Find a hotel. I'll look after Mikayla until tomorrow. I have your number. I'll call you to come and collect her. You were never here."

"Thank you," Austin said.

"Are the guns registered?" Jake asked.

"No, they're ghosts."

"Then leave them," Jake said.

Austin whispered into Mikayla's ear, gave her a hug and a kiss and then disappeared into the dense brush.

Jake took Mikayla by the hand and headed back towards Brodie. Chloe was still under the tree where Brodie had left her and as Mikayla approached her, she ran to Chloe and they hugged and cried. Then they all sat next to Brodie and waited for help to arrive.

Chapter 119

They say you can smell your death before it happens. It's true. From the moment I stepped out from behind that tree, the smell of the pine forest and Christmas had disappeared, replaced by an impending sense of doom. I ignored the fear and just kept on going towards the tunnels. But the fear came on stronger than before, like a warning.

When I took my next step, I heard an earth-shattering crack.

I felt the burning sensation in my chest immediately, and even though my heart hadn't stopped, I could feel my slow demise and my body beginning to go cold.

I died there that Sunday morning in the pouring rain, staring face-up at the thunderous sky. For the last few minutes of my life, the feeling of doom was replaced by an overwhelming sense of calm.

Once your body dies, your soul disconnects and for the first few minutes, you watch over your body and see the events around you. I saw the gun battle play out in the woods between the four men. I saw Austin dive in front of three bullets to protect Mikayla. I saw Jake come perilously close to joining me in the heavens.

Then I saw something unexpected.

Jake letting Austin go.

Maybe Jake realised Austin would have done the same thing for him.

I watched Jake return to my side and kneel down, crying. He was angry, sad and guilt-ridden all at the same time. I just wanted to tell him I was ok, and not to worry.

But I would never be able to tell him anything ever again.

By the time the paramedics arrived, I could see their efforts were futile, yet they didn't give up.

Jake rode with me to the hospital.

The paramedics continued working on me all the way to the Sydney Royal Prince Alfred Hospital.

They revived me once in emergency before sending me to the operating theatre, where they put me on by-pass while they tried to work their magic. It didn't seem to help. I died again in ICU. Again, they revived me. I doubted it would last.

Then a voice called to me from…well, I don't know exactly where from, but wherever they were calling from it was all white. It wasn't heaven, it was the in-between. A place you go when you're stuck. Although I didn't think I was stuck; I thought it was pretty clear that I was dead but for some reason, I had to stay in the white.

"They need you," a voice called out to me.

It was the voice of a young boy. I did not recognise it.

* * *

Jake sat in the waiting room, waiting to speak with the doctors. He had seen gunshot victims before. He knew the likely outcome. Brodie was cold when he finally got back to him and he had no pulse.

"Detective Miller, we've managed to repair the damage done by the bullet," the surgeon told him. "Your friend was lucky. Had the bullet been a couple of centimetres lower, we wouldn't have been able to repair the injury. I won't lie to you; his chances are slim and his heart has undergone incredible trauma. Since the operation, he's flat-lined and we've revived him. His brain was without oxygen for a long time, so even if he does survive I doubt he'll ever be the same." He paused and looked at Jake. "Right now, he's under heavy sedation and the next 48 hours are critical."

Hayley arrived at Sydney airport. Jake had checked them into the Hilton Hotel, knowing they would be there for several days, possibly weeks. Monique needed Jake to go over the crime scene with her. He was the only adult survivor.

The only one who had made it out.

Monique had asked him some questions over the phone. "Internal Affairs are going to want to know why you were still there. Why were you staking out the house, when the search turned up nothing? What made you go in and who started the shooting? How did the Priest end up there?"

All tough questions, when he was trying not to involve Austin in any of the answers.

Given the circumstances, Monique was agreeable to him writing out his statements of events over the next 24 hours and going through it with her initially, and then later with Internal Affairs when they did their review.

When Monique arrived at the hospital the next day, and once she had read Jake's statement, they commenced the official interview. Internal Affairs would come after Homicide had completed their enquiries. Monique had other officers with her although she was the only one who asked the questions. Jake thought it was out of consideration for him. He was sure she was cutting him a little slack.

"I have a few concerns over some inconsistencies," Monique began. "You say while you were staking out the home, the first you knew of any unusual activity was when the Priest was set alight?"

"Correct," Jake replied.

"I take it you assumed he was delivered by one of Igor's men. Do you have any way of confirming this assumption?"

"No," Jake replied.

"You say you believe this employee of Igor's killed the Judge and the superintendent. That's another assumption, I take it?" Monique asked.

"Yes," Jake said. "It was one of them."

"And now they're all dead," Monique stated.

Jake was answering her questions in a semi-comatose state with only one real concern: Brodie.

"We also found a man in the tunnels with his throat cut. Do you know anything about this?"

For the first time, Jake didn't know, and that was the best answer he could give. "I never knew about him. Maybe they thought he had tipped us off?"

"There was a SIG p228 used, which is a really unusual gun, used only in the military. Any idea where this came from?" Monique asked.

"I don't know, there were a lot of weapons lying around. I think I picked it up off the floor after I was thrown through the ceiling. Monique, I know it's a mess, but we just busted the biggest crime gang in Australia! They kidnapped children, lending them out to paedophiles and then selling them overseas. And you're asking me about a pistol?"

He stood up and took a deep breath. "I was going to leave this until everything had settled down, but I'm leaving the force. I already told Brodie. He asked me to stay on until we'd solved the kidnappings. I gave him until the end of the year."

"Jake, don't overreact, we're just finalising the statement." She frowned. "We've done this many times before."

Jake placed his badge and his pistol on the table. "It's not about the questions. I've made my decision. You have my statement; I can't offer you any answers other than what I've already told you. I did what I had to do to save those girls. So did Brodie."

"I can't get you to change your mind?" Monique asked.

"No." He began to walk away when Monique called after him.

"I thought you might like to know that we found Igor's number in Hutchinson's phone. That crooked detective contacted him twice that day, a phone call before you arrived and a text just minutes after you called him to say you were going home. So for the record, you were right." Monique was smiling.

Jake paused. It mattered little now.

"Internal Affairs will want to question you as part of their investigation so expect to answer more questions when you return to Melbourne," she reminded him.

He left the interview room and headed back to Brodie's bedside in ICU. Hayley was there waiting for him with a fresh coffee.

Jake told her he had quit the force. She knew it had been coming, but they'd only had one discussion about it. Now was not the time to discuss it further.

Jake just sat there staring at Brodie. One thought ran through his mind.

I should have given him the vest.

Chapter 120

I was still in the in-between. The boy who had called me stood before me fully clothed but soaking wet. I looked at him and he smiled at me.

"I was told I had to wait for you," he said.

"Why?"

"The girl asked me to tell you they need your help."

"What girl?" I asked.

"The dead one. The one from Picton Town. He's still out there, you know."

"Who's still out there?" I asked.

"The Hat Man," he said.

"How can I do anything about it? I'm dead."

"You need to wake up. You need to go to her" he repeated. He pointed to the white door behind me. "She is waiting for you in there."

"Why are you here?"

"I drowned." He pointed to a hospital bed below mine. The floor had disappeared and it was like looking through glass.

"They think I fell in but I was pushed. Josh pushed me."

I looked through the floor again and could see the accident happen, as if someone was showing me a live replay. The boy was trapped under the pool cover and he couldn't get out.

I watched as he was rushed to hospital. I could see his parents' bedside vigil. I could see the doctors and nurses. I could hear the conversations. I could see Hayley. I had heard about this boy; this was Ryan. Jake had told me all about him.

"You need to go back. Your parents are waiting; your room is waiting for you back home."

He looked at me. "Help the girl, she is waiting," he repeated.

"I will, if you go back."

He hugged me. Then he vanished.

Chapter 121

2 Weeks Later

I had been transferred from Sydney to The Alfred Hospital in Melbourne. I was still trapped in the in-between. I watched Jake from above. He was having trouble coping with everything that had happened but he had done the one thing I least expected, covered for Austin.

I watched as Austin took Mikayla to visit her mother's grave for the first time since they were reunited. They walked hand in hand, down the stone path towards the large oak that overhung her plot.

Mikayla started to cry as soon as she read her mother's name on the headstone.

She drew closer to her father.

"It's ok honey, this is a good place full of Mummy's love. Why don't you go and replace the flowers, she would like that," Austin said.

"Will you come with me?" Mikayla asked, still a little scared.

"Yes of course, we will do it together," Austin replied

Mikayla removed the old flowers and handed them to her dad. They weren't dead but they were starting to wilt.

"Do you think Mummy knows we're here?" Mikayla asked.

"Yes, I think she watches us from above and if you talk to her she can hear you," Austin replied.

"Can she answer us back?" Mikayla asked, looking up at Austin.

"Not by talking, but sometimes if you look carefully she will send you a sign to say she has heard you." Austin rubbed her back and put his arm around her shoulder.

Austin looked back up the path to see a face he didn't expect to see, not here anyway. Jake stood atop the hill waiting.

"Honey, I need to go talk to Jake. You remember Jake, from the house?"

"Of course Daddy. He helped save me."

"Why don't you stay here and talk to Mummy for a minute. Would you be ok to do that?"

Mikayla nodded.

Austin walked towards Jake.

"I didn't mean to interrupt," Jake apologised.

"It's ok, what can I do for you?" Austin replied.

"Just wanted to let you know, Homicide have come to the conclusion that the Judge and Mike were killed as part of a turf war between the Priest and the Monster and Beau, all ending at the Monster's residence.

"Homicide believe Beau may have been the mystery man that set the Priest alight and began a one-man war against the Monster. They have located his van dumped in nearby bushland but are yet to locate him," Jake finished.

"Why didn't you arrest me? You don't owe me anything. I wouldn't have resisted once Mikayla was safe," Austin said.

"She needs you. She's been through so much; she can't lose you as well as her mum. Sometimes the good guys need to win." Jake smiled.

"Thank you," Austin replied. "So they won't be looking for me anymore?"

"They never were. Homicide has closed the case," Jake replied. "Even Internal Affairs have closed their case on me," he added.

"I heard that you quit the force? What you going to do with yourself now?" Austin asked.

"Private detective, no politics, better pay. There's plenty of work if you want to join me. You'll need to pay the bills somehow," Jake replied.

"Thanks for the offer but I need to be with Mikayla right now. She's very traumatised," Austin said.

"I understand. You have my number if you ever need anything," Jake replied. He turned to leave.

"Jake, how are the other kids?" Austin asked.

Jake turned back, "They're doing ok, going through counselling, but the main thing is they are home with their parents and they're alive because of you." Then he turned and left.

Austin stood and watched Mikayla who was still deep in conversation with her mother. She had taken up a seat on the lawn next to her mother's resting place. Austin had no idea what she would be talking about, but he was glad she was talking to her. It must be doing her good, he thought.

"I'm sorry Mummy, I wish I could have stopped him. I hope you can hear me. I want you to know how much I love you and how much I will miss you. I will get Daddy to bring me here as much as possible, so I can talk to you."

* * *

From the in-between, I watched Mikayla continue her conversation with her mother.

It was a heart-warming one-way conversation. Then out of the darkness, a beautiful lady appeared at my side. A lady I had only met once before, when I'd inspected her dead body in her house.

"Sarah?" I asked.

"Yes, Detective."

"But you're dead?"

"Yes, but you can always come back to the in-between to watch over people. It's once you cross over you can't go back to the land of the living."

"So am I dead?" I asked.

"No, you haven't crossed yet," Sarah replied. "You have more people to help. You need to go back, but first you need to talk to the girl you promised you would help. Remember?" She pointed to the white door behind me.

It looked ominous.

"I will," I replied.

"Thank you for saving Mikayla," she said.

"Anytime," I replied.

Sarah clasped her thumbs together to form her hands into wings. I watched as a red, blue and green Rosella appeared next to Mikalya. It landed right at her feet. It wasn't frightened, it didn't fly off, it hopped up onto her leg and just sat there.

It didn't chirp or flutter around, it was very still and quiet, perched on Mikayla's leg staring at her as if it didn't have a care in the world.

"How did you do that?" I asked.

"You can do a lot of things from the in-between," Sarah replied.

"You need to save some others," Sarah repeated, "you need to go back."

Then as quickly as she appeared, she was gone.

* * *

For the first time since Sarah's death, Austin stepped foot inside his home.

Sarah's parents had made sure the property no longer had any traces of the tragedy that had occurred there.

"We don't have to live here anymore if you don't want to," Austin said, as they opened the front door together.

"I don't know if I will be able to, Daddy," Mikayla replied.

"How about you go to your room, pack your favourite things and we'll go to Grandma and Pops?"

Mikayla agreed and headed to her room.

She sat on her bed and looked at her photos, her posters, some of bands, some of friends, some of her mum and dad. She thought of Chloe and hoped she was ok. She opened the curtains to let some afternoon sun into her room. Sitting on the brick windowsill was the Rosella from the cemetery. Instantly, Mikalya ran to the doorway and called her dad.

Fearing she was in shock of some kind, he bounded the stairs two at a time.

"Honey, what's wrong?"

"It's the Rosella from the cemetery, it's here. Do you think Mummy sent it?"

It did look remarkably similar to the one they'd seen at the cemetery. "How do you know it's the same one?" Austin asked.

"Its eye has yellow around it, see?" She pointed to the left eye.

"So it does," Austin said. "Maybe Mummy sent it to tell you she is ok."

"I think I will be ok to stay here, Daddy. Mummy is here with us."

"Ok, let me know if you change your mind." Austin left her to settle in.

* * *

I turned away from the room below me and focused on the mystery door. The door itself was solid white, but the glow from underneath was a bright red and it filled me with an immense fear.

Epilogue

James Mitchell had only been released for two days. He couldn't believe his cousin Ian had died. He'd been shot, apparently in a bad drug deal along with his lover Bill. But James didn't believe it. He believed the cops had killed them both.

Ian had warned him that if anything happened to him, the police would be involved. It looked as if he was right.

James sat on the couch at home alone, watching the idiot box, flicking from channel to channel. He paused on the special report of the Pavlychko crime operation. It had all come crashing down due to the investigative skills of Detectives Brodie Foxx and Jake Miller. The scroll across the bottom read that Detective Foxx was in a critical condition in hospital after Australia's largest paedophile ring had been busted. Ten had died in the police shootout. The scroll continued. The Restart program funded by Palanok and overseen by Justice Aaron had been a front for the Pavlychko crime operation.

As the news report continued, it became apparent to James that it was biased in favour of the police.

Arrogant bastards.

The news detailed how suburban paedophiles had been buying children from the ring run by the Pavlychko company. Photos of the three dead paedophiles were shown, including his recently deceased cousin Ian.

James shook his head in disgust. He hadn't had any kids with him, he was being used to make the police look better. James decided the police needed to be taken down a peg or two, they needed to be held accountable for the error of their ways. They were a deceitful organisation, and he would bring them to their knees.

Starting with Miller. Miller would find out what it was like to lose his family.

He would soon feel his pain.

He watched the next news item.

A young boy who had drowned in a friend's pool had miraculously awakened from his coma.

Like Jake Miller?
Check out the first thriller about him:

HUNTED

Melbourne is a city living in fear.

A sadistic killer is on the loose.

Policewomen are being targeted and the count stands at seven.

Detective Jake Miller and Criminal Psychologist Brodie Foxx head the task force.

As they race to find the killer, the body count continues to rise, leading them deep into a world of pure evil.

Will they succeed where all others have failed?

Or will the hunters become the hunted?

Will they pay the ultimate price?

A spine-chilling thriller that takes you deep into the mind of a killer.

www.jasperwolfauthor.com

Miller is back in:

PICTON TOWN

Due out late 2017

For more, go to: www.jasperwolfauthor.com